"Set in 1987 and 1988... some of the characters are plainly recognizable."
—*The Wall Street Journal*

"Well-placed plot twists and sharp, believable dialogue..." —*Booklist*

ZHDANOV'S VOICE CUT THE GLOOM LIKE A KNIFE.

"Spare me your diplomatic evasions, Ambassador! I am a simple man, and I simply want to know whose side you are on. The time is upon us to separate the conciliators from the patriots. We have struggled along too long with one foot on both rocks. The Americans want an all-out arms race. Let's give them one! We will bury the capitalists under the weight of their own nuclear arsenal."

Zhdanov's eyes had widened and his shallow breathing came faster. "You must decide and decide quickly, Comrade Ambassador. There is no middle course."

Makarov remained silent. He knew his response would determine his future. And, perhaps, the future of humanity.

"Hart joins the suspense ranks as an impressive contender."—*Library Journal*

"The book... does a nice job of holding the reader." —*The Baltimore Sun*

GARY HART

The Strategies of ZEUS

WORLDWIDE®

TORONTO • NEW YORK • LONDON • PARIS
AMSTERDAM • STOCKHOLM • HAMBURG
ATHENS • MILAN • TOKYO • SYDNEY

THE STRATEGIES OF ZEUS

A Worldwide Library Book/March 1988

ISBN 0-373-97060-9

Agamemnon, in the *Oresteia*, by Aeschylus,
translated by Robert Fagles.
Copyright © 1966, 1967, 1975 by Robert Fagles.
Reprinted by permission of Viking Penguin, Inc.

First published by William Morrow and Company, Inc.,
January 1987

To all the men and women who have given portions of their lives to negotiate limits on nuclear weapons out of love for their countries and a desire for a safer world for their children

And now if one of them still has the breath
he's saying *we* are lost. Why not?
We say the same of him. Well,
here's to the best.

         And Menelaus?
Look to it, he's come back, and yet . . .
if a shaft of the sun can track him down,
alive, and his eyes full of the old fire—
thanks to the strategies of Zeus, Zeus
would never tear the house out by the roots—
then there's hope our man will make it home.

You've heard it all. Now you have the truth.

    —AESCHYLUS, *The Oresteia, Agamemnon*
      Translated by Robert Fagles

part

ONE

NOVEMBER 26, 1987
THANKSGIVING DAY

1

THE EARTH SHOOK like the gods' fury. And the boiling, curling flames could have been taken for the wrath of hell.

A thousand yards away, eyes widened and fists clenched as if by the collective will of the watchers the tall silver Titan column could be lifted free of gravity's grasp.

Poised for painful moments, then inching upward, then faster and faster the roaring, trembling column rose and broke free. And its many creators and launchers grinned and shook hands all around.

Amid the cigar smoke and effervescent champagne of celebration, few at Vandenberg Air Force Base actually knew what cargo the Titan bore. For that was one of the more closely held secrets in the National Reconnaissance Office, an intentionally obscure unit within the United States Air Force that coordinated the launching, operation and maintenance of clandestine surveillance satellites. Very few people, certainly no members of the press, knew when the NRO launched a satellite. Fewer still knew that this launch had taken place on Thanksgiving Day, November 26, 1987.

No more than ten people in the world could accurately identify the singular instrument borne aloft by the Titan monster. The President of the United States was not one of these people.

The Titan curved and arched away, now lost to sight. But not to mind. Dozens of sensitive computers listened carefully to the millions of bits of information sent back by tiny sensors. They reported back, and the computers dutifully recorded, that the Titan followed its intended course as if drawn by a celestial magnet. Burn, Titan, burn. The National Reconnaissance Office has a place in heaven for you. Or at least for your payload.

Once the computers confirmed the Titan's incredibly precise trajectory, the Director of the NRO, a four-star Air Force general named Kohlhaus, retired to his highly secure office. He picked up a blue telephone, which immediately rang a similar phone hundreds of miles away. The Chief of Staff of the Air Force, General Omar King, answered.

"Omar, it's a 'go,'" Kohlhaus said.

"Call me when you have confirmation of deployment," King replied and hung up. He lit a large cigar and waited, thumbing through the current *Playboy*.

Fifteen minutes later the blue telephone rang again. "Omar, we have deployment. Perfect."

General King dumped his cigar into the half-cup of cold coffee on his desk and said simply, "Thanks, Mike. Good job." King hung up the blue telephone, picked up the white telephone next to it, and violently punched five numbers with a blunt forefinger. The connection made, he said, "Joe, we're in business. Vandenberg called. It's a perfect shot. Right. You bet. Talk to you tomorrow."

At the other end of the line, the Secretary of Defense broke the connection and looked at the digital clock on the desk in his study. It was almost 1 A.M.. He hesitated, then lifted the receiver and dialed a six-digit number. The dial tone changed as he was automatically connected to a secure line available only to very senior administration officials.

A sleepy voice answered after three rings. "Harold, this is Joe Sternberg. The first phase of the operation has been successfully completed. Very successfully. I'm sorry to wake you, but you asked me to call. OK? I'll see you at lunch. Good night."

The Vice-President of the United States, Harold Burgoon, lay awake just long enough to remember the project and then was instantly asleep again.

At Vandenberg the launch team held a debrief meeting in the launch director's office, took a last look at the giant wall plotter showing the satellite's orbit, then individually began to drift toward the parking lot. To monitor the early hours of the newest of more than two hundred U.S. and Soviet satellites there remained behind a small number of expert technicians. General Kohlhaus wrote intensely in a logbook. He was interrupted by his second-in-command. "General, that sure went well. But I still don't understand why the NRO thought it was so all-fired urgent to get up another geosynchronous high-altitude bird. I have to say, this is my tenth launch and I've never seen the kind of secrecy we've had on this one. Was there something special here that I missed?"

"No, Colonel," Kohlhaus responded with only partially concealed irritation. "We're just running some highly experimental tests with this bird that could improve our ability to monitor the Soviets through cloud cover. Just what the briefings said. We don't want them, or anyone else, to know how far along we are, or even that we're going for a breakthrough here. Nothing more mysterious than that, so I wouldn't worry about it. OK?"

The colonel still looked puzzled, or, more specifically, left out. "It just seemed strange to me that the normal NASA types weren't included and that we even had so few of our own people around if it's that important."

"Colonel, you don't seem to understand." Kohlhaus was now clearly unhappy. "This is experimental. We're trying out some new things with this bird. If they work, we don't want the Russkies to know. If they don't work, we don't want the press and the goddam Congress to know. They'll be out here asking questions about why we're wasting launchers and taxpayers' dollars. All the usual rhetoric and horseshit. Now do you get the message? Just get on the plane back to Washington tomorrow and forget about this launch until you hear otherwise. Which may be never! Got it?''

"Yes, sir, General. I got it.'' The colonel walked back to the quarters at Vandenberg, unhappy that he was being kept in the dark and treated like a child in the bargain.

This colonel was not alone in the dark. With very few exceptions the launch crew at Vandenberg, accustomed to highly classified documents and top-secret missile and satellite operations, were briefed to believe they had just launched the third in a series of top-secret all-weather reconnaissance satellites.

The exceptions to this general understanding included only three individuals present at the Vandenberg launch. Besides General Kohlhaus, they were Ernest Pytell, a young astrophysicist responsible for designing this special payload, and Arlette Gwynn, chief engineer for Datasync, the highly specialized military contractor that had produced it. Each had every possible security clearance and each presumed the personal surveillance that went with such clearances.

Now their respective missions were complete. The unique and complex constellation of circuits, sensors, computers, and relays that they had taken from engineering drawing to workbench to maneuverable space orbit was their finished product. Their careers depended on absolute amnesia about the project thereafter.

For the product of their two-year effort was now under the control of the National Reconnaissance Office in Washington. The links and computers that controlled its performance were located in the NRO's supersecret command facilities. And only the direct orders of the Secretary of Defense or the Chief of Staff of the Air Force could command its performance.

Its name was Cyclops.

2

CONNAUGHTON TOOK HIS customary place at the conference table within the Soviet Mission in Geneva. As representative of the U.S. Arms Control and Disarmament Agency, he was two places to the right of the American Ambassador, with the Ambassador's deputy negotiator, Charlie Curtis, between them. He withdrew his files from the antique leather briefcase tanned and sewn from the hide of one of his father's Hereford cows when Connaughton had gone off to the university. Connaughton amused himself by wondering whether the cow or his father would be more surprised that this particular hunk of tough Montana cowhide ended up carrying nuclear secrets into meetings with Bolsheviks. According to well-established routine, like a batter pursuing his ritual on entering the box, Connaughton sorted the quarter-inch stack of papers before looking up and across the table at his Soviet counterpart.

Vronsky winked. Connaughton winked back. What was first merely cute had become a routine, then a habit, then a conspiratorial signal. This wordless communication meant: God, here we go again; this process is unbelievably boring; no progress again today; why don't we get out of here and have a drink; how did we get into this line of work in the first place? The wink always seemed to amuse Vronsky immensely. But underneath the placid surface, reservoirs of frustration were deep and full.

Soon Soviet Ambassador Makarov spoke. "Mr. Ambassador, this plenary session of our discussions is most special and solemn. It is special because we all leave soon for our homelands to celebrate the year-end holidays. Solemn it is, if you permit me to say, because this is our last formal meeting of 1987 and, in spite of the heavy burden of our task, we have made so little progress. We have such little good news to give our fellow countrymen and the world to bring in the new year—so little to show for our hard labors this year.''

Makarov's basically a decent sort, Connaughton thought. One thing he had learned as a negotiator was to avoid quick judgments about character—particularly the Russian character. He had been wrong too often. Some who seemed to be good guys at first turned out to be bad guys, and vice versa. But Makarov was a good one when his bosses in the Kremlin let him alone, Connaughton had learned.

"Mr. Ambassador." Now Barrett Arkwright, the chief American negotiator, took his turn. "Sadly, I couldn't agree with you more. Our government is extremely distressed that more progress has not been made. And, as I have expressed many times, we are more than willing to consider any reasonable proposal our Soviet friends have to offer to break this stalemate. As for ourselves, I am prepared to lead off this morning, as is our normal custom, with a statement on behalf of the American side. If that is agreeable to our hosts.''

"May I say to my friend, the American Ambassador, we wish to hear his statement and offer our response." Makarov sounded suddenly weary even though the negotiators had just taken their seats.

Arkwright nodded unenthusiastically and lifted his five-page prepared statement. It seemed for a fleeting second that he was considering throwing it away and spontaneously pouring out a stored-up lake of anger and frustration. But the moment escaped and Arkwright began.

"My government instructs me to urge you to consider seriously in the coming days the United States' offer—which is our final position. We once again state our willingness to undertake mutual and verifiable limits on the number and range of all cruise missiles, land, sea, and air... establish agreed conditions for deployment of space-based defensive systems...develop on-sight inspection measures as a means of achieving and verifying an overall nuclear test ban... reduce the total number of Soviet missile systems in Eastern Europe...''

Connaughton could see the Russian team exchanging contemptuous glances. Damn those bone-headed ideologues in Washington, he thought. They didn't have to suffer the embarrassment of seeing their best negotiator walking the plank with yet another restatement of a position that he'd known was untenable and doomed to rejection when offered a year ago, and that had become even more futile since then. Now, coming to the last plenary session of 1987, with both teams headed home for holiday consultations, commanding a dreary restatement of a lifeless proposal was unfair to Arkwright and bound to send the Russians into orbit.

There was stirring on the other side of the table as the American's statement wound down to its predictable conclusion, hoping that mutual goodwill would produce a breakthrough when the negotiations resumed after the holidays.

Makarov leaned forward in his chair as Arkwright settled back in his. All the elements of chess were here, Connaughton thought. Move, response. Countermove, counterresponse. Suddenly, Makarov did a strange and uncharacteristic thing. He tossed his prepared statement across the table to Ambassador Arkwright like a man flicking a match at tinder. His momentary expression of anxiety, even fear, gave way to genuine anger.

"Mr. Ambassador." The tone was harsh, almost belligerent. "Why are we wasting our time? The performance of the United States government at this time is ridiculous and each of us knows it. The delicate dance of diplomacy is important—but only up to a point. That point was passed long ago. Your government is simply not serious about this negotiating effort. I am a Russian and being a Russian I know, above all men, the value of patience. But as a Russian I also value life, and I believe I have now totally wasted almost a year of mine at this bargaining table."

Makarov was working himself up, growing intoxicated with his own voice. "My government has made it clear time and time again that we cannot and will not accept the premises of the American proposal. I say with all respect and much personal friendship to my fellow negotiator that the net effect of this one-sided approach is to leave the Soviet Union in a vastly inferior position, and to place the United States in a position of mammoth nuclear superiority.

"Now maybe it is"—Makarov glanced first along his own side of the table and then down the American side past Connaughton—"maybe it is a naïve notion of my American friends that the Soviet people are thin in the head—how do you say it, air-brained—and will finally accept a policy simply because it is repeated over and over until finally our brains are washed. And then we will so accommodate the American government by treading upon our own national interest. Well, it is not so easy, I say to my good friends. We poor simple Russians may be soft in the head, but we are hard in the butt. History has well proved we have the hardest butts of any people on earth."

Makarov eased back in his chair slightly and smiled. His Soviet colleagues chuckled approvingly and the earthy, slightly deaf General Polyakov guffawed loudly.

The tension suspended temporarily, Arkwright intervened smoothly. "I think the hardness of all of our butts has been pretty well demonstrated over the past twelve months. But in the holiday spirit, and in the interest of international goodwill, my government is willing to concede to our Soviet friends the world championship hard-butt prize.''

As the American translator completed Arkwright's remark, Polyakov barked again like a great hound.

"So our understanding will be clear and the record we take home to our governments complete," Arkwright continued, "I wonder if my Soviet friend would be willing one additional time to summarize his government's response to the American proposal tabled here this morning."

Smile gone and stern countenance restored, Makarov came forward in his chair again. "Very well. The American Ambassador is a patient man and I am a patient man, so I will restate once more the Soviet response. First, on the question of the cruise missiles. This is a weapon system we confess the Americans have a certain temporary leadership in. But it will not last. Because the Soviet government and our scientists are committed to closing the gap on cruise— both in numbers and capability. The real question, as we know, is not numbers of cruise missiles, but how to count these systems. Really how to verify their numbers and their capabilities, such as their range. You have offered limitations on numbers and range. But you have not proposed how to verify those important limits.

"Now, on the question of weapons in space or 'Star Wars' or whatever the American government is now calling this new competition, my government maintains its willingness to negotiate a total ban—a total prohibition—on such weapons." Makarov managed to sound firm, tired, and frustrated all at once. In tone he approximated an elementary catechism teacher. "Your government claims publicly it wants to stop the arms race, yet you insist on continuing your research and development of both offensive and defensive space weapons in order to seize some permanent advantage over our country. But this is a simple proposition. Either we prohibit these weapons or we don't. As with the cruise missiles, *there will not be American superiority in space*. If you choose to continue in this provocative and hostile way, my government will take whatever steps are necessary to respond."

Calmly but forcefully, Arkwright broke into the Russian's controlled tirade. "Mr. Ambassador, history requires an *accurate* record. And as you well recall it was the *Soviet* government which *pioneered* in antisatellite weapons, and the American government which had to respond. We seek no long-term supremacy in space. We continue to believe in the possibility of peace through development of purely defensive capabilities. But, as my friend the Ambassador knows, we stand ready to respond to any thoughtful proposal the Soviet negotiators have to offer—"

"I find it difficult," Makarov interrupted sarcastically, "to believe my American friend is serious when he says now that his government is interested in limitations on weapons in space. The American policy on this issue has been one of constant delay, of prevarication . . ."

The chief Soviet translator sitting directly behind Makarov leaned forward. Connaughton watched as she whispered quietly in Makarov's ear. His eyebrows raised, he whispered back. She insistently whispered again.

Makarov smiled and continued in Russian: "I apologize to my friend the American Ambassador. Madame Davydova points out that I might have been heard to say 'prevaricate' when clearly my meaning was 'procrastinate.' Delay, that is my meaning for the American policy on space weapons."

Connaughton watched Davydova. He always enjoyed the firm but diplomatic way she straightened out Makarov's syntax with a minimum of embarrassment to the Ambassador's substantial ego. Besides, Davydova wasn't bad to watch, Connaughton reflected to himself as he had often in the past.

Arkwright smiled. "My Soviet friend has committed what we sometimes call a Freudian slip, I believe. But there is no offense taken. The main issue is limiting strategic weapons in space. And I can only say that the government of the United States unconditionally rejects the suggestion that we are manipulating this question to our benefit or"—here his voice became stern, almost harsh—"that we are somehow involved in a massive deception of some kind. The stakes are far too high for that."

"Well," Makarov resumed sardonically, "I hope the American Ambassador speaks not only for his President but also all who make nuclear policy in his government. Because it appears to us that the Americans are seeking the same kind of superiority in space that eluded them first in ICBMs, then in multiple-warhead land-based missiles, then in the accuracy of those land-based missiles, and now in cruise missiles. There is a pattern here, and it is a dangerous pattern. Some new technology occurs to the American scientists. The policy makers grasp this technology as a miraculous solution to the arms race, handing the United States an advantage and forcing the Soviet Union to accept a truce that guarantees the U.S. permanent superiority. In a simple word, *we will not accept this!*"

Makarov threw his hands in the air in his most characteristic gesture, which the American negotiators knew signified the triumph of his logic and the end of the discussion on this subject.

Connaughton had found it impossible to negotiate limits on the nuclear arms balance between the two superpowers—and perhaps the fate of the earth—without a sense of awesome responsibility.

Yet after a time, particularly when there was little progress, even these momentous discussions tended to become routine, even mundane. Numbers of missiles became abstractions; destructive yields of warheads became everyday calculations. The job itself threatened to become simply another way station on a long career résumé.

But even within the mind-numbing abstractions and frustrations of fruitless bargaining, Connaughton had occasionally seen the sense of historic consequence reassert itself and insistently prevail. Like a thunderclap, some chemistry would arise to jerk the negotiators back to the unreality of the reality with which they were burdened. In the sudden silence in the spartan conference room in the Soviet Mission in Geneva, brought on by Makarov's outburst, that chemistry worked its awful magic.

For the first time in a year of casual observation, Connaughton thought Mme. Davydova was about to cry. Vronsky, usually so like his literary namesake, looked uncharacteristically sober, even frightened. General Polyakov was suddenly alert, and obviously angry. Down the table on the American side, Admiral Quainton, the representative of the Joint Chiefs of Staff, glared at the Soviets and might have drawn his saber had he been in parade dress. Arkwright's deputy, Charles Curtis, stared down at his papers in dismay. And it remained for Arkwright himself to break the desperate silence.

"Mr. Ambassador, I must say, you leave me somewhat at a loss for words. Throughout these proceedings we have both operated, or so it seemed, as if no obstacle were insurmountable. Indeed, the attitude of mutual hope and perseverance against great odds has kept us at this table for more than a year. I plead with my Soviet counterpart not to lose that hope, nor to prepare to return to his home country with a sense that all is lost. I know I speak for my government when I say that men of goodwill...people of goodwill"—glancing at Eileen Malmstrom, Connaughton's feminist deputy from the Arms Control and Disarmament Agency—"can surely find areas of agreement, if we are sufficiently patient and persistent, and if we are determined enough not to let our personal fatigue overcome us."

Arkwright's gentle, even pleading tones became stern. "On the other hand, if the Soviet delegation, and its government, believe the cause is lost, that there is no hope of finding a common ground, that our only course is the terrible danger of an unlimited nuclear arms race, then we should hear about it right now. So that we can then all pack our bags, abandon the hope this conference table has represented, and return to our home countries for good—to arm ourselves as we each see fit and prepare for the consequences.

"For I can assure the representatives from the Soviet government," Arkwright continued in a tone rising almost to defiance, "I can assure the Soviet negotiators, and their principals in Moscow, that the United States will take whatever actions are necessary to protect itself against Soviet global ambitions. We will, as our beloved President Kennedy once said, 'pay any price, bear any burden'—and if necessary build any nuclear weapon—'to assure the success of liberty.' "

Arkwright and Makarov, both now flushed and on the edge of their chairs, had delivered their final statements full into each other's faces. And neither side blinked.

God, thought Connaughton. What have we both done to ourselves now? This wasn't the way the last session of the year was supposed to end. They were supposed to have, at least, given themselves maneuvering room to return home and make the pragmatic case to keep the talks alive, to return to Geneva in January of 1988, and see if one side or the other might have come up with some magic formula to break the intractable logjam.

Now what? he thought, as he held his breath waiting for one ambassador or the other to fracture the lead-crystal tension.

Makarov moved first. He carefully slid his chair back a foot and very slowly stood up. Arkwright did the same. The room was absolutely silent. Transfixed, Connaughton could only think of the wild stories his old grandfather had told him of desperate cowboys whose wounded pride had caused them to reenact in dusty saloons in frontier Montana of the 1890s the ancient draw-down rituals of the American West.

The second hand ticked five times, then Arkwright, the guest, inclined his head in a slight, stiff bow, turned, and left the room. All the American negotiating team stood and followed. The entire Soviet delegation stood to join Makarov and watch the Americans depart.

The drivers of the Americans' cars were caught off-guard by the abrupt, unanticipated appearance of the negotiators at the entrance to the Soviet Mission. They scrambled for the cars as Arkwright and his team waited silently on the steps.

The snowstorm he'd seen building as they drove to the Soviet Mission had arrived, Connaughton reflected absently, as the four-car caravan made its way to the American headquarters at the U.S. Mission off the Avenue de la Paix. The dense lead-gray clouds had, in the past hour, rolled over Geneva to hover ominously low overhead.

Most startling to Connaughton were the huge snowflakes. They seemed the size of silver dollars. Or perhaps, he thought, as round as old Swiss pocket watches. He could remember only once when, as a small boy in Montana, he'd seen snowflakes of such extraordinary dimensions. Perhaps this remarkable phenomenon coming against a backdrop of such gloom was a symbol of slim hope.

BACK AT THE AMERICAN headquarters, each of the principal members of the negotiating team was summoned for a meeting in the "bubble." The only truly secure facility available in the building, the bubble was designed to resist every conceivable effort to eavesdrop electronically. Actually a conference room constructed of several layers of thick Plexiglas, the bubble was in turn surrounded by specially treated heavy curtains that further hindered surveillance and prevented anyone from seeing into the room. This curtain-clad plastic chamber was in turn sealed within a steel-reinforced, concrete-block outer room. The heavy steel door providing entrance to this outer room could be opened only by tapping a coded number into its special lock. This number was known only by the Ambassador and delegation security officer, who alone could authorize admittance to the bubble. The code number was constantly changed. And the outer door was guarded around the clock by a uniformed Marine.

In various states of shock and confusion, the eight members of the United States negotiating delegation gathered in the bubble. Barrett Arkwright entered last. "I've just spoken with the Secretary on the scrambler phone," he started without formality as he took his customary head-of-the-table position. "I gave him my candid reaction to the events of this morning. I told him that, from the standpoint of arms control, we have just experienced a catastrophe, and that the resumption of talks in January is doubtful. At the very best this morning's session means that we've wasted the last year. At the worst . . . I hate to think.

"Before filing a complete cable report this afternoon, I'd like to go around the room and hear your individual reactions. Charlie?"

Charlie Curtis, the delegation's number two, looking morose, waved a hand absently. "I think we all are somewhat stunned by the way what should have been a routine end-of-the-year wrap-up session got out of hand and left us with our guns drawn. The chemistry just suddenly went sour. You could feel it. It was a disaster. I'll tell you for sure, I don't think it was calculated on Makarov's part. If it was, he should get an Oscar. It was just too genuine to be an act and as slick as he is, he isn't good enough to pretend that well."

"I agree with you, Charlie." Arkwright frowned. "I know now I overreacted. But I couldn't very well let Makarov get away with that one-sided diatribe. I had to respond, but I'm afraid I merely escalated the confrontation. What do you think, Walt?''

Admiral Walt Quainton, the oldest member of the team at fifty-five, considered himself the anchor of the delegation. Not only did he speak for the Joint Chiefs, but he had also been involved in the design, testing and command of nuclear missiles. Hands-on experience, he called it. ''You did exactly right, Barrett. You can't let them get away with that bullyboy rhetoric. If you do, they think it's weakness. But I'd be less than honest if I didn't agree with you on the implications of this morning's exchange. It's serious. There's no way around it. It seems to me we've got a very short period of time to figure out whether we want to come back here in January and, if we do, how to patch things up. It seems to me that's the Boss's call.''

''You're right, Walt,'' Arkwright responded, ''but our principals back in Washington are going to have to advise him, and they, in turn, are going to want our recommendation. It seems to me that we have to start the damage limitation before we—and Makarov—leave town. And that could be only a few days, if not hours. Sid, what do you and your people make of the politics of this right now? Was Makarov reflecting a new dominant hard-line view in the Kremlin?''

All turned to Sidney Murray, the CIA representative on the delegation, who was, as always, listening rather than talking. It was widely conceded throughout the delegation that Murray was far and away the most intelligent of them all, on issues of nuclear arms and everything else. He had been a musical and mathematical prodigy in his youth and today carried more specifications of nuclear weapons—Soviet and American—in his head than most experts could carry in a packed briefcase.

''The Agency has a somewhat different view of recent developments in the Soviet Union.'' Murray's voice was dry, almost remote. ''We've believed for some time that the continuing struggle between the pragmatic and ideological factions in the Politburo has been tilting toward the rigid ideologues. Makarov's performance this morning may be taken as a strong signal of this new ideological hard line, or at the very least as an effort by Makarov himself to prove his credentials with the hard-line faction. In any case the most significant aspect of the performance was what Makarov didn't do. If his initial outburst was the product merely of fatigue and frustration, he had plenty of time during your response to compose himself and come back with a moderate tone at the end to take the edge off the rhetoric. But"—here Murray jabbed his finger at the conference table—"he did not. He let his statements stand and we witnessed the extraordinary scene of the American and Soviet ambassadors about to poke each other in the nose. It was positively... Wagnerian."

Everyone, including Arkwright, laughed—except Murray, who had not intended the remark to be particularly humorous. "In any case," he continued, "the intelligence community is going to have to get to the bottom of this power struggle, and apparently pretty fast."

After half an hour in the bubble, Connaughton always got claustrophobic. He figured it was his Montana upbringing.

According to the custom, Arkwright's nod meant it was his turn to talk. "I have very little to add, Barrett. I think Sid has it about right. We've known for a while that the Russians are having trouble getting their line straight. My own view is that Makarov's caught in the middle. It seems to me what we saw this morning was an ambassador in a vise. I think he knew what he was doing this morning—may have even calculated it—he's too good, too professional to pop his cork by accident. But I don't believe he meant to go as far as he did, to jeopardize continuation of the talks altogether." Connaughton hesitated, then went forward. "I watched the Russian delegation very closely during the exchange. Makarov's statement sobered them up—even woke up old Polyakov. But your response really scared them, Barrett. I saw some worried people across the table. They seemed to realize things had gotten out of hand.''

The silence in the isolated conference room gave tacit consensus to Connaughton's assessment. The implications of the morning's events were now beginning to sink in. "Well, what do you think, Barrett," Connaughton queried, "should we pack up for good, cancel our leases?"

Arkwright knew it was a serious question, only slightly humorously asked, and one on everyone's mind. "File your reports, send your cables, and take the rest of the day off to do some Christmas shopping. I'm going to try to put all of this together. Your thoughts and observations have been very helpful. I'm going to get them back to the secretary on a priority basis and wait for his instructions. I think he will want to talk to President Lawkard before giving us our orders. And depending on where the President is and how long it takes them to get together, this may take some time. Maybe even a day or two. In the meantime I have to decide whether to contact Makarov on my own and try to patch things up a little. At least to keep our options open."

The door to the bubble cracked open to reveal the Marine guard. He handed Arkwright a slip of paper without comment and closed the door. The Ambassador read the typed note, then slipped it into his coat pocket.

"We just received part of our answer, Frank. The Soviet plane is preparing for departure to Moscow this afternoon—they must have been recalled as soon as they reported to the Kremlin—and Ambassador Makarov has just issued the following statement: 'The Soviet Union regrets to announce that the current round of SALT III arms control talks is suspended . . . indefinitely.'"

THE EAGLE AND THE BEAR. And the Eagle was on its way home aboard a TWA flight from Geneva to Washington through Frankfurt. Frank Connaughton and most of the other members of the American arms control delegation were on board. Arkwright had remained behind at the request of the Secretary of State to tour the NATO capitals and brief the appropriate foreign ministers. Explaining to the increasingly nervous European allies that the principal hope for the avoidance of nuclear confrontation was on the brink of collapse, was not going to be an amusing assignment. Arkwright would earn his salary that week.

For all across Europe, protests under way for months had mushroomed overnight. In every European capital, major and minor, demonstrations were occurring daily. In the past week the number of demonstrators had increased tenfold. And most ominously, these were not ordinary peaceful demonstrations. They were increasingly violent.

In Stockholm the normally tolerant police had been forced to jail dozens of demonstration leaders. In Paris hundreds of demonstrators out of a parade of thousands had broken windows and damaged property along a two-mile section of the Champs Élysées. Antiwar and particularly anti-American protestors in London had stopped traffic at rush hour every night for two weeks and were chaining themselves to security fences at American military bases throughout the British Isles. In Rome and Milan a total of seven "peace" demonstrators had been shot by the police for endangering public safety in the past three days.

And things would only get worse, Connaughton thought. If we don't get back together with the Russians in Geneva soon, then we've only seen the tip of the iceberg. If Makarov's icy statement a week ago was capable of unleashing this furor, think of the chaos a full-fledged nuclear arms race would bring.

Makarov was lucky. The Russians had it easy. No demonstrations in Moscow, or Leningrad, or Kiev. And except for an occasional right-wing group outside a Soviet embassy in a Western capital, they didn't feel any of the impact of the protests and demonstrations in the democracies. Sweet deal for them, thought Connaughton. Their guys help instigate the protests against us, and our guys can't even mount a comparable response against them. Life—at least life in politics—wasn't fair. But, of course, he had given up on that some time ago.

He was glad to be going home. As the 747 lifted off from Frankfurt for the seven-and-a-half-hour flight to Washington, he recollected, as he had every day recently, that, by the time he saw Francesca that night, it would be the first time in four months. He had left Washington for the fall round of negotiations and she had returned for her second year at Madeira.

He wondered repeatedly at the irony that he did what he did for Francesca, and what he did took him away from her. He had spent a precious year of his life away from the one he loved at a critical period in her life, holed up in a strange European city dividing his time between the Soviet Mission and a thick plastic bubble—trying to do what little he could against imponderable odds to prevent her from being blown up by a nuclear warhead sent along by some ignorant general under the mistaken impression he was doing what was called for at the time.

Something was desperately wrong with the circumstances that produced that logic, he thought as he sipped his whiskey. Desperately wrong.

But, of course, there was something unorthodox about Frank Connaughton himself. A third-generation Montana rancher who cherished the land, adrift in a small boat on the sea of international diplomacy. A private man in a public job. A Westerner with an Eastern education. A family man trying to create a family without its basic ingredients. A patriot in the service of a president he considered little better than a fool, or perhaps a dunce. He wasn't sure which was worse.

Connaughton was a singular man who enjoyed the company of others but who used his privacy—his aloneness—as a bird uses the air. His aura of separateness made him seem, to those around him, strong but elusive.

He yearned for the day—it would come soon, he hoped—when he could walk away from warheads, missiles, megatons, Russians, and death. He thought he could convince Frankie, probably after she finished school, to come back to Montana. On the other hand, she would probably develop some interests on her own that would make Montana seem pretty tame. He had seen a lot of the world and wasn't too keen on it. She would have to find that out for herself. I just hope, he thought, that she doesn't let her idealism, her basic nobility, tempt her into some quixotic existence like mine. This ridiculous need to save the world from itself, this never-ending search for sanity, always against impossible odds and without any sense of final satisfaction. Maybe she would do something sane, something that could be completed in one lifetime. Well, in any case, he would see her tonight and they would have this Christmas together.

In the meantime, he could imagine the hellish infighting consuming Washington. Defense against State. Connaughton's Arms Control and Disarmament Agency after Defense. The CIA maneuvering behind it all, preparing itself for the long bureaucratic wars. The hawks and doves circling the only thing that mattered in the whole game, the soul of the President. Did this President have a soul? Maybe that was the real question in the total drama. If he did, there was hope.

What if he didn't? What if he really was a fraud or a dupe? Then what? We will soon find out, Connaughton thought. We will soon find out. He probably doesn't even know himself. But we must find out; because as Grandfather used to say, he's goin' to have to fish or cut bait. He would either side with the tough guys—the ones who had been pushing for a showdown all along. Or he was going to give the old hard-butt approach one more chance—try one more time for the sake of sanity, and possibly even survival, to find a rational answer. It really was the President's call, Connaughton concluded, as he drained the whiskey and dropped his head in sleep.

3

THE SPECIAL AEROFLOT PLANE eased up to a gate reserved for government officials at Sheremetyevo Airport. Outside the temperature was below freezing and there were three layers of snow, accumulating to almost a foot, from the first deposits of the winter. It would be at least April before the frozen skin of Mother Russia would be exposed for its spring thaw.

The negotiating party, led by Ambassador Makarov, made its way down the modern, enclosed deplaning ramp to the new airport terminal, the most recent pride of the Soviet government. Suddenly, Makarov hesitated a beat, stunned. Instead of middle-level bureaucrats sent from the Foreign Ministry to escort them to their cars, there stood Vladimir Zhdanov.

Cadaverous and elderly, Zhdanov was among the most powerful men in the Politburo. There were nervous jokes that every train leaving for the Gulag had a car reserved for Zhdanov's enemies. He knew about the jokes, and let them circulate. In Zhdanov's world, no one was ever pure enough, no one was ever committed enough, no one appreciated the capitalist-imperialist threat enough—perhaps not even Vladimir Zhdanov himself. The most dedicated true believer since Lenin, he was tormented that the socialist revolution had not swept capitalistic democracy from the face of the earth. And he did not hesitate to take his own personal torment out on all those around him, up to and including the General Secretary of the USSR. He held the unassailable position of the Party's chief theoretician, and from that post he had made himself, over the course of decades, the Soviet Union's Grand Inquisitor. Thus, Makarov's fear.

With a gesture, but without a handshake, Zhdanov led Makarov out a private exit of the terminal to the waiting Zil limousine. Still shocked, the remainder of the negotiating team followed their drivers and security escorts to the half-dozen smaller Foreign Ministry cars waiting with motors running. The motorcade, with a white and blue police car in front, sped out of the airport complex onto Leningradsky Prospekt and past heavily cloaked, fur-hatted crossing guards at the major intersections into central Moscow. Leningradsky Prospekt became Gorkovo at the Belorussia train station, then at the Tchaikovsky Concert Hall the large limousine containing Zhdanov and Makarov shot forward while the trailing cars, minus the police escort, wheeled right onto Sadovaya heading south. The driver was silent, but the negotiators sharing the lead car, Yurovov, Metrinko, and Davydova, knew by custom they would be taken to the Foreign Ministry, where they would sign an official registry evidencing their return and then would be given transportation to their homes for the night. No one spoke during the twenty-five-minute ride. The driver, like Metrinko, was KGB and would report any speculation on the dramatic kidnapping of the Ambassador. Metrinko seemed as nonplussed as the others by the stunning events of the last half-hour, and between the crisp, cold night air and Zhdanov's materialization, all had quickly lost the euphoria produced by the airplane cocktails and their return home.

After waiting her turn by rank to complete the official return forms at the ministry, Ekaterina Davydova hurried outside just as the clock showed midnight. She decided, as she often did in better weather and almost never during the worst winter months, to walk the half mile down Arbat Street to her apartment. She thought as she hurried along the empty street that tomorrow could turn out to be monumentally important. She pondered Makarov's fate and was surprised that she cared whether he was now in trouble, and how seriously. If he was in trouble, perhaps they were all in trouble. Something clearly was up. Her last thoughts that night were of her two sons whom she would joyously greet in Leningrad in three short days. Or perhaps in three long days.

JUST AS EKATERINA DAVYDOVA was falling asleep, Mikhail Makarov was trying just as desperately as he ever had in his life to wake up. As he had conquered his liquor drowsiness within seconds of seeing Zhdanov at the airport, now he was concentrating every effort into shaking off days of negotiating fatigue.

Across from him at his clean desk in his small, spartan office sat Vladimir Zhdanov, head down, scanning a paper as if committing it to memory. They were in a remote third-floor room in the Council of Ministers Building in the Kremlin. Begun during the American Revolution, to the design of the Russian architect Kazakov, and completed twelve years later, this great building was the original home of the Soviet government when it came from Leningrad to Moscow in 1918, and now housed offices of the Central Committee and the highest executive and administrative officials of the USSR. Not far away, Makarov knew, was Lenin's apartment and study, the holy of holies in the Kremlin.

"I commend you, Comrade Ambassador," Zhdanov's hollow voice intoned. "I was beginning to think you didn't have it in you." Looking up from the cable Makarov had filed before leaving Geneva, in the dim lamplight Zhdanov seemed terribly old, but his eyes were burning with a fierce inner light. "So you finally got up courage to put the Americans in their place. I've been waiting for that for quite a while, and, if I may say so, had just about given up."

Beneath Makarov's diplomatic veneer of calm, he went weak with sudden relief: The blowup in Geneva might have saved his job, if not his neck. He'd known he was in trouble with the hard-liners like Zhdanov, and his outburst—though sincerely felt—had been intended to placate them and restore him to equilibrium among the Kremlin factions, none of which he dared offend.

"I ask you to come down with me this evening, Comrade Ambassador, to see if we could not reach a meeting of the minds on our future negotiating course before your debriefing sessions at the ministry tomorrow," Zhdanov continued. "There will be great pressure on the part of some in our midst who do not clearly understand the nature of the American threat to rush back to the bargaining table and try to patch things up—to seek some quick accommodations on these nuclear questions with our adversaries. In my mind"—Zhdanov's dark eyes glittered—"that would be a most serious mistake, perhaps almost a treasonous mistake. I know there are the professional diplomats, the 'peacemakers,'"—he spat the words out as if they were poison—"who can only see the rosy world of a phony 'détente.' I only seek to reassure myself, comrade, in the interest of the security of the great Soviet system, that you are not one of them. You see, in the next few days, we must decide who among us truly believe in strength, who are the real patriots, who will stand up to the capitalist interests that threaten our revolution. And for the sake of all of us, Comrade Ambassador, I want you to be with us."

Zhdanov sat back and in the seconds that passed in the dim silence, Makarov knew his response would determine his future.

"Comrade Zhdanov, first I must confess to being taken off-guard by your appearance in greeting me tonight," Makarov began, circling to establish his footing and buy time. "Needless to say I was surprised... but very honored... to see you at the airport. I knew of your deep personal concerns about the progress, or lack thereof, in our negotiations. But I was not aware you were following them so closely in a personal way.'' Makarov felt himself being drawn into a titanic ideological struggle and sought desperately to avoid a trap that held no escape for him. "I would be more than happy to provide you a detailed briefing on events in Geneva...."

"Please, Ambassador!" Zhdanov's voice cut the gloom and Makarov's nervous equivocating like a knife. "Spare me your diplomatic evasions. I am a simple man, and I simply want to know whose side you are on. The time is upon us to separate the conciliators from the patriots. It is impossible to be both. There are many of us who believe we have struggled along too long with one foot on both rocks. Now the stream is rising. The Americans want an all-out arms race. Let's give them one! Let's turn loose the determination and will of the mighty Soviet people—last seen so powerfully in the war against Fascist aggression—and we will bury the capitalists under the weight of their own nuclear arsenal." Zhdanov's eyes had widened and his shallow breathing came faster. He lit a coarse Russian cigarette and inhaled the rank smoke as if his life depended on it. "You must decide and decide quickly, Comrade Ambassador. There is no middle course. The Soviet government is not going to send a spineless détentist back to Geneva if I have anything to do with it. And we just might decide not to send anyone back at all—depending on which path furthers our new interests."

New interests? thought Makarov. What's this? I have returned to a real political mess, some viper's nest, some gigantic vise that is going to squeeze me like a lemon. "I have always been a patriot, comrade. I have always put my country's interests before my own. I only wish to be of service and do what is best for the Soviet people. I understand arms control policy and have thus achieved my present place of honor in the glorious people's revolution." Makarov's voice sounded to him too whining, and he wondered whether he was laying on the patriotic rhetoric too heavily to be convincing to a doctrinaire ideologue like Zhdanov who used such language as second nature. "But, Comrade Zhdanov, I am not a politician and I never have been able to participate in what the Americans call the back-room power struggles." He gripped the chair's arm and hoped, for God's sake, he had said it right.

The look on the old man's face as he retreated into his chair and out of the fringe of light from the outdated desk lamp told him he had not. Breath hissed from Zhdanov's devastated lungs. "Ambassador, I fear you are the worst kind of politician—one who takes the soft life that high position in government offers without the guts to take a stand when your nation's life is on the line."

Zhdanov suddenly stood. "Good night. I have no further use for you."

4

AMBASSADOR MAKAROV sank gratefully into his chair at the long table. Zhdanov had murdered his sleep. Makarov's wife, angry at his endless trips to Geneva and a dozen other countries over the past two decades, had sat up all night more angry than usual, convinced his late arrival was irrefutable evidence he had stopped off to see his girlfriend on Kalinina Prospekt. This morning, the familiar surroundings of the secured conference room in the Foreign Ministry restored some confidence. But the frightening confrontation with Zhdanov ten hours before had left him rattled. As he cleared his throat, he mentally contemplated the trade of his left arm for a tall glass of scotch.

"We are prepared to summarize the situation in Geneva for you, comrades, answer your questions, and await your instructions," he began. Across the table sat Foreign Minister Pyotr Zoshchenko; Vladimir Ulyanov, the Central Committee's foreign policy and arms control expert; Deputy Defense Minister and Chief of the General Staff Viktor Rusakov, representing his boss, Minister of Defense Georgi Kozlovsky; and representatives of the Supreme Soviet and middle-level note-takers from the ministries, committees, and the KGB. The KGB would get its own briefing later, with special emphasis on the American personalities involved and shadings and nuances of less interest to the others.

Makarov had never seen this high-powered array at any previous briefing on the arms control negotiations during the past year. He had seldom been in the same room with this much horsepower except at state occasions when he was very much a secondary figure. With him he had the other five senior members of the negotiating team. Their deputies and support staff had been specifically excluded, with the exception of Comrade Davydova.

"Please begin, Ambassador Makarov," said Pyotr Zoshchenko. "We have all read your cables, including the most recent one of yesterday before your return. Start from there and give us, if you please, your most cogent summary of the present state of affairs." At sixty-two, the Foreign Minister was the most Westernized Russian in the Soviet hierarchy. He spoke excellent English with a trace of a British accent. His career as a junior Foreign Ministry officer had begun at the United Nations in 1955, eventually followed by ambassadorial posts in London, Bonn, and Washington. His political instincts, though laden with ambition, had been flawless. He had been on the right side of every leadership succession struggle since Stalin. After four years in the Washington embassy, he had moved surely and swiftly through the executive echelons of the ministry to his present position on top. Though Zoshchenko was a lifelong Party member, Vladimir Zhdanov thought him soft on the Americans. General Secretary Kamenev's patronage was his unassailable shield and source of power.

Makarov began. "Very well, Comrade Minister. My colleagues and I agree that the year-end holiday break in negotiations came about with a rupture. The Americans—Barrett Arkwright—took a tough, unrelenting line. I believe on purpose and under explicit instructions. He did not appear to me to behave comfortably, either in his dreary restatement of the position the Americans opened with almost a year ago or in his insistence that his government intended to go forward with development and deployment of new systems in space, cruise missiles—particularly sea-based—or a new generation of highly accurate ICBMs. But he took that line nevertheless. And I can only conclude, regrettably, that his government has instructed him to stall. Each of us tested American resolve and attitudes in the working-group discussions over the past two or three months since we were last home. And to a person, I believe my colleagues would agree, we found no indication that this was other than the official position." He looked right and left and all heads nodded.

"For our part, comrades," he continued, "as instructed, we persistently maintained our agreed policy that there would be no progress in the negotiations so long as the Americans continued their so-called modernization programs and refused to present any concessions in response to our more than generous bargaining proposals."

Deputy Defense Minister Rusakov, a cantankerous old man awaiting retirement with honors as a war hero, intervened: "Comrade Ambassador, if the Americans are so anxious to show us their new systems, why don't they just go ahead and do it and quit wasting our time in Geneva? Why do we need to keep wasting the state's valuable rubles on the cost of maintaining a bunch of diplomats—no offense—in Switzerland when we know the Americans don't want a treaty?" Rusakov knew the answer was political, but false naïveté was one of his games.

Makarov shrugged. "The question is for my superiors, Comrade Deputy Minister. When the Politburo decides to quit negotiating, I will quit going to Geneva."

"Mikhail Ivanovich"—the unctuous voice belonged to Ulyanov—"we welcome you and our other superb negotiators back. We know and appreciate all that you have gone through the past year, and the Soviet people are in your debt. But I know within the Central Committee the same feelings expressed by Comrade General Rusakov are being discussed. Why negotiate at all when the Americans are so adamant about going forward with their massive effort to prepare a first-strike war-fighting capability against us? Those who formerly favored negotiations are now being heard to say we are wasting our time, that the Americans are merely luring us into a trap and lulling us to sleep with all this diplomacy. Surely the time as come, Mikhail Ivanovich, to settle this thing one way or the other. Arms or talks, which should it be?''

Makarov's experience on the edges of the Byzantine world of Kremlin politics—reinforced by the eerie midnight seance with Zhdanov—had already alerted him that sides were forming in a vicious struggle over Soviet arms control policy. Unlike similar skirmishes in the past, this one was clearly a watershed. Zhdanov had put it bluntly: Will we parley or will we prepare to fight? The traditional middle ground—let's continue a moderate improvement in our nuclear forces, but go to the conference table with the hope of avoiding confrontation and possible war—either was disappearing, or in the past three months already had. And a lot of people's careers might disappear along with it.

This made life interesting, to say the least, for the Makarovs of the world. The Ambassador had spent the better part of the previous night sleeplessly rearranging the political chessboard, always with the ominous Zhdanov and the Gulag just over his shoulder. Some pieces were obvious. If Zhdanov was leading a palace coup against the policy of negotiations, he would have close to half of the Politburo, much of the Defense Ministry, the hard-liners in the Foreign Ministry, and a representative group from the Supreme Soviet behind him. Zoshchenko, the Foreign Minister, was a gray fox whose ambition would undoubtedly lead him to jump to the side about to checkmate. Nikolai Kamenev, the nation's leader as General Secretary of the Communist Party, was sadly old, more in mind than in body. He would have been a restraining force against the hard-liners, freshly reliving every day the horrors of war, the twenty million Soviet casualties in World War II, and the mounds of mass graves of those who had starved in Leningrad, which he had helped liberate after nine hundred days of siege. But that was more days than he had left in his regime or his life, and he was becoming dreamy. No, if there was a balance of power in this struggle, it would have to be Kozlovsky, the Defense Minister. Strong, genuinely strong, almost morally strong. His strength came from his steadfast refusal to play politics. He was more intelligent than most of his peers, unwavering in his commitment to the Party, and most of all dedicated to the security of the Soviet Union.

Zoshchenko would have to lead the fight for continued negotiations, because that was his policy and still the official policy of the Central Committee. He would have the support of the bureaucracy in the Foreign Ministry and a substantial faction in the Politburo, including the Secretariat. Kamenev was his anchor, but a slipping one. The negotiating faction was safe so long as Kamenev was alive and in office. But he was a weak reed, and so, in fact, was Zoshchenko. He would be one of the first to jump if, as captain, he saw his ship going down.

The key was Kozlovsky. If the Defense Minister joined one side or the other, he might be able to bring enough senior military commanders and the swing votes in the Politburo with him to make the difference.

This potentially fatal chess game had played itself out in Makarov's mind all night. Since these were forces beyond his control, he had no choice but to try to buy time while the heavy battalions deployed and a winner began to emerge. "Comrade Ulyanov, the Central Committee, the Politburo, the Secretariat, the Defense Committee, all of you, including my superior, Comrade Minister Zoshchenko, who make policy for the Republics of the Soviet Union must decide these questions. My excellent negotiating team and I merely wish to implement that policy at the bargaining table. That is, if bargaining is determined to be our course," he hastened to add.

"I can only hope to enlighten that decision by giving you my informed impressions of American attitudes and actions in Geneva."

"That is exactly what we are seeking, Comrade Ambassador." Ulyanov's ingratiating smile seemed threatening.

"I believe—and I invite my colleagues here to speak up if they have a different point of view—I believe there is a struggle going on in the United States government. I believe the President and his administration are being torn between two factions. A faction on the one hand that genuinely wants to reduce the risk of nuclear war by reducing nuclear weapons. And a faction on the other hand that dislikes negotiations—and us; that tolerates the Geneva talks, but is basically committed to achieving nuclear superiority through an arms race. Right now, Arkwright cautiously comes down slightly on the latter side because neither faction has yet prevailed and he has no clear marching orders. He is a sincere and genuine character who personally probably belongs in the first faction. But, with all due respect, comrades, like me he does not determine policy."

Makarov shot nervous glances around the table. So far the bigwigs were buying it; no one was attacking him. Thank God. Now he looked to his right for support. Oleg Yurovov, his deputy, took the cue. "I think I speak for the rest of our negotiators, comrades, when I say Ambassador Makarov has accurately summarized our impressions of the American situation in Geneva."

Sergei Metrinko, the senior KGB member of the negotiating team, spoke up. "You all, of course, have access to our intelligence cables and briefings. And they tend to support the summary presented by Ambassador Makarov. Our sources lead us to believe the upcoming elections in the United States next year could well be the deciding factor in this factional dispute. President Lawkard's party will probably be represented by Harold Burgoon, his Vice-President. Given their desperation to stay in power, they will be closely monitoring public opinion to determine their course on negotiations. But, of course, we must never underestimate the role of the CIA in this struggle. They hold themselves out as neutral, or as favoring negotiations. But we know behind the scenes they have great impact on American policy.''

Cool character, Makarov thought. He wondered if the big shots across the table understood how clever Metrinko really was. He had just held a mirror up to the Soviet government itself in a way that made Makarov envy both his guts and his agility.

''Well, if I may speak for all of us, Comrade Ambassador,'' Zoshchenko hurriedly intervened, ''we thank you and your fine team for an excellent job on our behalf in Geneva and for a most enlightening briefing here this morning. After drafting your comprehensive memos and reports on the past three months, we urge you to take time with your families or''—he essayed a roguish smile—''other loved ones, and enjoy the New Year's holiday. The Foreign Ministry sends each of you a bottle of the finest scotch to help you celebrate and to show our appreciation.'' Delighted smiles now all around the table. ''And we particularly appreciate the presence here this morning of the ministry's finest and, if I may say so, most attractive and charming interpreter, Comrade Davydova. Perhaps the real solution to this conundrum is to send Comrade Davydova to Geneva alone, and she would have the Americans eating out of her hand in days.''

Despite her self-control, Ekaterina's cheeks glowed, making her black hair seem even blacker. The men in the room guffawed as they eyed her approvingly.

5

AT 11:30 P.M. on the night of December 20, Ekaterina Davydova arrived at the Leningrad Station for the midnight departure of the overnight train for Moscow to Leningrad. Rather than carry on guerrilla warfare with the impenetrable bureaucracy of the ministry to get a car and driver, she carried her luggage on and off the Metro for her ride across town. In spite of the stoic remoteness of her fellow Russians on the subway, she always enjoyed the cleanliness and efficiency of the Metro ride and particularly the mosaics and statuary in the older, prewar stations. She struggled with her luggage—heavy with clothes for the two-week visit and gifts for her parents and sons—from the Metro station to the railway station. She located her coach and the sour train matron pointed her to her compartment. Struggling with the heavy bags and parcels, she pushed her way in to find her compartment-mate already there. A studious-looking young woman peering dimly at a heavy book through thick glasses, she merely nodded.

Ekaterina distributed her load in the spaces beneath the bunk and sat down with relief. No words passed, but in a few minutes the train began to roll and the girl reached into a new imitation-leather bag, withdrew a small bottle of brandy, and, as she held it up for Ekaterina to see, winked. After the train matron brought two small glasses, the girl filled them with brandy and pushed one across the small table by the window. Ekaterina picked it up and said, *"Spasebo."* The girl took a tiny sip, smiled, then downed the whole glass with a gulp. Ekaterina was amazed. Her former husband, a brash, not particularly couth engineer now living in Minsk with his mousy second wife, was the only person she had ever seen drink brandy in that fashion.

Gathering speed, the train followed the arrow-straight track through the northern outposts of Moscow, abandoning the train yards, passing industrial plants dormant in the frozen night air, small ill-shaped prewar houses with single lights in corner rooms, irregular belts of ten- and twelve-story apartment buildings curling smoke from rooftop heating plants, and finally entering the still, white, barren fields beyond the city. Ekaterina felt relief for the first time in four months. Now she was free—free of the alternating tedium and pressure of Geneva and free of the oppressive politics of Moscow. She longed for sleep and swift passage of the eight-and-a-half-hour ride to the city of her birth, where Ivan and little Anton would be waiting on the station platform.

She sipped the brandy, looked from the window to the watching girl, and again said, *"Spasebo."* Her training, not only culturally but also personally, was nineteenth century. Unlike the upbringing of most her age, raised in the proletarian cultural wasteland, it called for politeness. She felt obliged to ask, "Do you live in Leningrad?"

The girl shrugged, seemingly taken aback at first by Ekaterina's low, refined voice. "Not at all. I'm going to meet my boyfriend's family." She giggled, halfway through the second brandy. "He thinks we're going to be married."

"I gather you don't necessarily share that ambition." Ekaterina was always game for an interesting real-life story having nothing to do with nuclear weapons.

"Oh, he's nice enough, I guess. But who wants a military life? Who wants to go from isolated outpost to dreary barracks year after year waiting for your husband to fight his way—tooth and nail—up the military ladder? Besides. All those missiles and rockets and atomic bombs scare me to death. That's all Eduard, my boyfriend, thinks about. He counts warheads to get to sleep. Sometimes I think he'd rather sleep with one of those bombs than he would with me." She yawned and stretched, then leered at Ekaterina out of the corner of her eye. "Maybe he thinks I'm not explosive enough in bed."

Ekaterina smiled and looked at the floor, as much as anything to conceal her amazement at the casual vulgarity of the next generation. Her very proper aristocratic mother would have given the girl a swat and brushed her teeth with harsh soap. "What service is your gentleman friend in?"

"The almighty, best-on-earth, superpowerful Strategic Rocket Forces." The girl's tipsy-mocking voice ricocheted around the tiny compartment. "The guys who protect us from the warmongering, capitalist-dog Americans. The boys with the *big* missiles." She laughed contemptuously, like a whore offered too little money. "Except old Eduard isn't one of them, believe me."

Shifting uncomfortably, Ekaterina tried to avoid relative rocket sizes. "Where is he based?"

"First one place, then another. Here today, gone tomorrow. Sary Shagan—one of those places." The girl suddenly tested the compartment door, inspected the compartment suspiciously, and leaned forward into Ekaterina's face. "But they're up to something, those guys. Eduard has only three days at home. The rest was canceled. Some big test or something. Very secret. I teased him a little to tell me. You know..." She did a little sitdown bump and grind, to Ekaterina's horror. The brandy-soaked whispers were almost too much by themselves. "Couldn't get a thing from the big shot. Except old Eduard was showing off that night last week. Sort of demonstrating his missile, if you know what I mean. And he did say it was something brand-new. Not just another test shot. Some totally new one. He was so proud of himself to be one of the chosen few that he couldn't keep it from me, hot as I was." She preened.

Ekaterina settled back on the stiff bunk. The brandy had brought sleep at last. But before awakening on the outskirts of Leningrad seven hours later she searched her memory unsuccessfully for any recollection of Makarov talking about a new missile system.

6

A FULL TWO HOURS before Ekaterina Davydova's 8:30 A.M. arrival in Leningrad, there was serious activity in the Kremlin. In two straight-backed chairs at the end of his long, narrow office sat Vladimir Zhdanov sipping a glass of black volcanically hot tea with the Soviet Defense Minister, Georgi Kozlovsky. They hunched forward over a round table conversing in the low urgent tones used by conspirators throughout the ages. Each believed the conversation was being recorded, Kozlovsky by Zhdanov and Zhdanov by God knows whom, certainly the KGB.

"Georgi, believe me, the time has come. The Americans are stalling and you know it. Dzerzhinsky Street confirms they can now deploy enough space-based defenses to protect at least a third of their very accurate ICBMs and they have a ninety percent chance of protecting Washington, the Strategic Air Command, and NORAD."

Kozlovsky looked into the burning eyes of the old ascetic then down into the steaming blackness of the tea.

Zhdanov's hollow voice was barely audible. "They are setting us up, Georgi. You must see it. Our future may well rest on your seeing it. They never have intended to reach any agreement with us on nuclear arms. They have just bought themselves a year—a crucial year to achieve a breakout on the defensive side. We are on the verge of the most gigantic blackmail in history. Another round of negotiations and they will have their radars and interceptors in place. Then what happens? I will tell you what happens. President

Lawkard calls up old Kamenev...calls up our Comrade General Secretary..."

What's he talking about? Kozlovsky thought. He and Kamenev are the same age.

"...and says, 'Secretary Kamenev, we have placed our strategic conventional forces on full alert. We invite you to begin a withdrawal from Eastern Europe, forthwith. If you refuse, we must consider that an act of war.' When Kamenev found out the Americans were virtually insulated from attack, we would have another state funeral on our hands. Not just Kamenev from his heart attack, but a literal state funeral—for the state."

"Vladimir, I clearly understand the logic of what you are saying and, of course, we've gone over this in the Defense Committee many times. We haven't been exactly standing still during this year's negotiations, as you are well aware. In fact, the test scheduled in two weeks is our best answer to the American 'defense initiative.'" He sipped from his tea glass. "We in the Defense Ministry are about to bankrupt the nation to match the American buildup. I would be glad to go over all our production and deployment schedules for the next twenty-four months again if you would like." He paused. "I'm not sure exactly what else you had in mind for this unusual little meeting. It certainly wasn't a hearty breakfast."

Zhdanov refused to match his chuckle. Kozlovsky turned serious once again, leaning into Zhdanov's old, wolfish face. "What did you have in mind, comrade, a little palace coup, a little shake-up at the top, a little government overthrow?" Leaning back and raising his voice for hidden auditors: "Because if you did, put this little chess piece off the board. I don't do business in dark alleys. Consider me a conventional, bureaucratic lackey if you wish, but I play by the rules. Right now the policy is negotiate in good faith and keep our powder dry. And while that's official policy, it's my policy."

Zhdanov stood, his cavernous breathing echoing. "Comrade Minister," becoming pointedly more formal, "none of us who share my concerns would have it otherwise. We intend, by force of argument, nòt force of arms, to change that policy. Let Makarov and his ineffective 'diplomats' go back to Geneva. Let all be sweetness and light, all compromise and conciliation. But"—he came to hover specterlike over Kozlovsky—"let us, the Politburo and the Defense Ministry, take immediate and urgent steps to prepare for the inevitable confrontation. It is quite simply unavoidable."

Kozlovsky emerged heavily from the stiff chair and walked around the small table to the single window. Zhdanov's dark-shrouded figure pursued. "This confrontation you seem so eager for... does it include launching our missiles if the Americans call our bluff? Where will it occur? In Central Europe? Germany? The Middle East? Iran? The Sea of Japan? How about Central America? Nicaragua. That's it. We did so well in Cuba in '62, why not send some intermediate-range missiles to the Sandinistas...presuming they are crazy enough to accept them. I can assure you, that will guarantee your 'confrontation.'"

Zhdanov stared at him a long moment. Kozlovsky saw an emotion very close to hatred in the feverish black eyes. "Comrade, you still do not understand, do you? The confrontation is coming. It is simply unavoidable, regardless of what you want. For all our sakes, I simply thought you should get ready."

7

THE VIOLIN MUSIC soared. As it had all her life, it caused tears to slip from her eyes. She thought nothing so moving as her father playing Tchaikovsky. With a son close to each side of her, her mother rocking nearby, contentedly leading an imaginary orchestra, and the white-haired old man lifting almost-sightless eyes toward the early sunset out the high window as he played, Ekaterina thought she had never known such peace. What if she were to take him back with her to Geneva, have him put on a private concert just for the negotiators? How could they not then take steps to halt the mad nuclear dash? That rivaled her other idea. Why not ask every member of both negotiating teams to bring their children with them? What if they all had to debate the fate of the world not in the abstract, but before the audience that mattered the most, their own children? What if, at the end of every day, they had to look into the eyes of their own children and explain the abstractions of megatonnage, why national prestige was more important than safety, why the meaningless nitpicking and babbling continued on so fruitlessly?

The music stopped. Anna Nikolayevna smiled at her husband. Ekaterina rushed to embrace her father. He had, for many years, been first violinist in the Kirov opera and ballet orchestra and a soloist with the Leningrad Philharmonic as well. Next to his family, music was his life. Because of his advanced years and his distinguished position in the artistic community in Leningrad, Anton and Anna

Davydov had been granted a relatively large apartment on Maklina Prospekt between the Griboyedov Canal and the Turgenev Place park. In good weather the old couple could walk the few blocks both to the Kirov Theater as well as the Rimsky-Korsakov Conservatory studio where Anton Davydov could weekly join some contemporaries in a string quartet. The apartment, situated in a nineteenth-century building almost completely restored after the terrible bombings of 1942–43 during the Siege, was large enough for the elder Davydovs and the two boys, as well as Ekaterina when she was able to visit. This time, as always, she went through the ritual of insisting on staying at the Astoriya Hotel on St. Isaac's Square across from the cathedral, but, as always, they would not hear of it.

Their only child, the old couple wanted her with them as much as possible in their waning years. She seemed in recent years, with her senior interpreting position in the Foreign Ministry, to be gone all the time. And when she was in Moscow, she could come up to Leningrad only on weekends. She had been raised in the old style. Anna Nikolayevna had been raised the daughter of a prominent doctor who attended most of the important figures in Czar Nicholas's court. She herself was an accomplished linguist having, with her father's wide travels, mastered a half-dozen languages while in her teens. Ekaterina had acquired her skills as much by her mother's insistence as by natural talent. But the languages had come easily. She had always favored English, primarily because of the literature. From her late elementary school years she had read widely, from Shakespeare to modern Americans like Faulkner. She often spoke English with her parents and had taught Ivan and Anton even before sending them off to school. Anton senior, her father, was the fourth son of a czarist admiral killed in the early years of World War I, before the Revolution. Being essentially apolitical, neither of the Davydovs had joined the Communist Party. But, in spite of Anna Nikolayevna's upbringing, their loyalty had never been seriously questioned by the state, even during the intense investigation and interrogations involved in Ekaterina's security checks upon entering the Foreign Service. Anton merely played his beautiful music for the people of Leningrad and Anna gave her private lessons in six different languages.

Ekaterina had graduated from Leningrad University before her twentieth birthday, majoring in English language and literature. She had received the equivalent of a master's degree in comparative literature and was studying for her doctorate at Moscow University when she encountered Boris Orlovsky, a brilliant and, she thought, dashing graduate engineer five years her senior. He seemed worldly, a skeptic, and, for an engineer, almost poetic. He appealed, according to that age-old contradiction, to her needs both for an authority figure and for an adolescent she could mother and protect. In her one important rebellion against parental advice, she quickly married Orlovsky, under the strong impression she was in love. Ivan, then Anton were soon born and fatherhood turned out not to be Orlovsky's strong suit. His worldliness soon became lassitude, skepticism gave way to cynicism, and what Ekaterina romantically took for poetry turned out to be nothing but old-fashioned decadence. The state granted a routine divorce after less than five years of marriage.

Ekaterina left her two small sons with their grandparents and sought employment in the most apparent field, interpreting and translating. After a year of teaching at the Foreign Language Institute in Moscow, her application to the Foreign Ministry was quickly accepted. She hoped to be transferred quickly to a post in Leningrad, but five years went by with no success. She tried having her sons with her in Moscow, but after a year that proved futile. Her extraordinary skills with languages, particularly English, took her on a whirlwind of international travel. The boys were happier in Leningrad with the Davydovs. Now that they were nine and seven, she knew that soon she must leave the ministry and return to Leningrad to teach so that she could raise them to manhood herself.

Like her mother, Ekaterina was remarkable for a Russian woman. Tall and slender, she showed no signs of giving way, at the age of thirty-five, to the affliction of most around her—spreading out like a peasant earth mother. Her mother's striking example, and the Western women she saw on her travels, convinced her it was not a necessary aspect of aging. What distinguished her further—made her striking in fact—was her coloring. Her hair was very black and her skin very pale. She was often thought, in her travels, to be Irish. Among her colleagues at the ministry she socialized and was considered sociable. But she resisted the advances of men, particularly her superiors. Most of them were already married, and she thought relationships among co-workers unprofessional. Mostly, she found the men she met boring. What social life she had was largely confined to concertgoing with a few female friends in Moscow. Occasionally, alone at night in her small apartment, she longed for male companionship and dreaded the thought of living by herself after her sons were grown.

"Now, Ivan, you and Anton jump up and help Grandmama clear the table while I talk with your grandfather. Then we will take turns pulling each other on your new sled down to the Bronze Horseman." Ekaterina pushed the boys toward the dining room.

They were chattering excitedly, happy to have their mother back with them for two weeks and anxious to undertake the adventure of sledding at night to their favorite spot, Decembrist Square on the Neva River with its dramatic equestrian statue of Peter the Great. Her father leaned over to kiss her cheek as Ekaterina sat next to him. "How is all this nuclear business going, Katya? I cannot tell you how perverse it all seems to a humble fiddler like myself.

What in God's name are we doing—what are the Americans doing—with all this destruction? I cannot believe they seriously want to blow us up. They may be ambitious, they may even be imperialists, but can they really be insane enough to risk annihilation? It makes no sense to me. None of it makes any sense. Why can't we and the Americans simply be friends as we were during the war?''

Ekaterina knew what was next, but it was important for the old man to talk about it. "Katya, you know what happened in our city in the war. Worse than Dresden, worse than Hiroshima. The longest siege since the times of the Bible. They say more than six hundred thousand people starved here, mostly in the terrible winter of 1941 and 1942. But it was more than that, many more. Stalin covered it up. Eight hundred thousand, maybe a million or more people died here. It is only God's will that I am alive today. I saw that your mother was evacuated early because I didn't trust the politicians or the generals who told us it would be all right. Hitler vowed that he would make this great city a wasteland and he was insane enough to try. So, during each day I ducked the bombs and picked up and buried the dead, and at night . . . at night I played my violin to retain my sanity. No one who has seen what I have seen could possibly understand all these nuclear bombs. Each one can kill as many people as died in three years of siege here. Katya, it is nothing but the greatest folly.''

Anton Davydova had been her age when the war ended, Ekaterina thought. He had lived with these memories for over four decades. They would haunt him to his grave. "Dear Papa, I wish I knew the answer. I cannot tell you what goes on during the negotiations, because it is secret, as you know. Besides, the answer is not in the details. It is in the minds of those at the top in both governments. There is such pressure to 'keep up' with the other side. The military people do not dare fall behind. All they can think of are numbers. For the politicians it is prestige and the power these weapons bring. They think no other nation will cross them with all that destructive power. The scientists have a stake: They come up with new inventions. They think they can make these weapons 'better,' so then it must be done. If we don't do it, the other side surely will. But mostly, Papa, it is the ideologues, the 'true believers,' that are the danger. The ones out to force their ideas on others. Those who insist we believe the way they do. They are the most dangerous. More than the generals, more than the politicians, more than the scientists. If we get blown up, it will be because of the true believers.''

In the apartment entryway they could hear Anna Nikolayevna helping the boys put on their coats and new heavy gloves. They were laughing, excited about the late-night sled ride.

"Katya, in many ways my world has already been blown up by those ideologues. The boys, Ivan and Anton, they are the ones we must save." The nearly sightless old eyes that had seen so much suffering and destruction sought her face in the dimly lit parlor. "You must do everything you can to save them."

8

CONNAUGHTON HAD ALMOST forgotten the sense-stunning beauty of a clear December day in Montana. He started out early that morning riding the fences on the place his grandfather had homesteaded in 1885 and called Careless Ranch after the creek and gulch of the same name that bisected the original 160 acres. Over the next decade and a half, old John Connaughton had acquired close to 5,000 acres from neighbors victimized by nature, uncertain cattle markets, and wanderlust. The original Frank Connaughton, John's father, had lost his life at Shiloh as a captain of Massachusetts irregulars when John was five. Most of John Connaughton's first neighbors had been young men like him who walked West on the ties of E. H. Harriman's railroad, beating spikes into those ties fourteen hours a day with ten-pound mauls. Soon most of those other young men came to despise the quiet of the low mountain valleys, the cattle, their plain frontier wives, or all three, and headed for the glamour of San Francisco. John picked up their land for a few cents an acre, always making sure the abandoned families were looked after in the trading post that came to be Great Falls.

Then came the crash before Roosevelt—the one in '93, before Teddy. John junior was born that year and old John lost much of his land. He managed to hold on to eighteen hundred acres, enough to run a respectable herd of white-faces on, even during the crash in '29. By that time the old man was in his seventies and losing his sight. But John junior had taken over management of the property and augmented his income for his wife and children by becoming an engineer on Harriman's railroad, taking long freight trains over the mountains to Vancouver and back. His son Frank's earliest memory was of old Grandfather John, totally blind, storming out of the house with his original Winchester and his ancient sheepdog after some wolves he was sure he had heard among the cattle in the near pasture. Old John died later that year, straight as his walking stick and white hair flying to the end.

Frank's three sisters took their mother to the city with them when John junior died the year Frank graduated from Dartmouth. So the land was his by default, and he never intended to give it up. The only question was whether his daughter, Francesca, would want it after him.

He was sure she would. He had ridden three quarters of the fence line when he saw her coming across the meadow on the small chestnut mare he had given her for her thirteenth birthday. He rode toward her through the eighteen-inch blanket of snow on the meadow and slowly followed the hundred-odd head of cattle as they plodded toward the barn and pasture near the house.

Chilled to the bone, Connaughton shook the late-afternoon snow from his battered stetson and kicked his boots against the rock steps leading into the low ranch house. He playfully brushed his daughter's parka off, managing as he usually did to tickle her ribs through the thick down. "Daddy! Stop that! Stop that!" She squealed as she ran into the warm kitchen, throwing gloves, parka, and fur hat behind her. He stopped in mid-laughter in the doorway, thinking, I'm not going back. Not to Washington, not to Geneva, not to the arms race, not to the rat race. They don't need me. Let them make their own peace—or their own war. Whatever they decide, they can do it without me.

He looked back at the Herefords settling in for the night against the barn that old John and his father had built before he was born. Then he closed the door. He crossed the kitchen and poured himself half a water glass of straight Jameson. He began to heat water for a toddy, the strongest drink he permitted his daughter, when she ran to answer the insistent telephone ring in the den. "Who in the world is it, Frankie?"

"Dad, it's Uncle Harry. He sounds nearby. He says he has to talk to you."

Taking his Jameson with him, Connaughton ducked below the low door frame into the den. "Harry, where in the world are you? Here? You told me when I saw you three days ago you were going to spend the holidays in Washington. What's going on? Tonight? Sure, Frankie and I are thawing some venison steaks and there's plenty for three. Come on over. You sure? Well, come on over later, then, for a nightcap. Okay, see you then."

"Oh, great. Do I get to see Uncle Harry?" Frankie pirouetted gleefully, just as she had when delighted at the age of three. "Harry's my favorite, Dad. Can I propose to him tonight?"

"I'm sure Bonnie won't mind, Sis. Lord knows there's plenty of Harry to go around." Connaughton sipped the whiskey wondering what brought his friend Harry Rafferty all the way out from Washington during the holidays. Maybe a speech or some constituent work. He wasn't up for election for another three years, so it must be an important event for him to leave his family back East.

He spun Frankie around and smacked the rear of her Levi's. "Let's go, Sis. My night to cook and yours to do dishes." She uttered her best fifteen-year-old groan. "Besides, you're never going to catch a husband if you don't learn the secrets of venison a la Connaughton."

As he lit the broiler and checked the baking potatoes, she said, "I'm liberated, Dad, remember? I don't have to know how to cook. Besides''—her voice became suddenly serious—''I don't intend to get married.''

Connaughton looked at her from the corner of his eye. ''Sure, sure. I know. You can't ever hope to find anyone as great as good old Dad. Right?''

She slowly placed the old silver and battered china, his mother's trousseau legacy, on the kitchen table. ''That's true. But it's something else.'' She turned to him and he was startled to see how much she looked like her mother. ''I don't want to have children...ever. I don't want to get married. It doesn't make any sense anymore.'' She turned back to the table.

He pushed the steaks under the broiler, closed the oven door, and studied her long, dark-red hair. ''What do you mean, Sis? What do you mean, it doesn't make any sense anymore?'' He crossed the kitchen slowly, expecting her to break into laughter with one of her schoolgirl jokes. Instead, she turned and tears ran from her eyes. He closed his arms around her and held her, something he had wanted to do so many nights in Geneva. ''Frankie, tell me what's wrong. What is it? Did I do something? Is it because I've been gone so much?''

She shook her head and closed her arms around him. ''No. I hate it when you're gone. But you're the best father there is. It isn't that, it's what you're doing. It just isn't going to work. Even you can't stop what's going on, as hard as you may try. We took a vote at school and just about everybody in my class said they thought there was going to be a nuclear war. It's just going to happen. So why get married? Why think about a family or having children, when you know sooner or later they're all going to be blown up?''

Connaughton dried the still-streaming tears, sat her in the straight wooden kitchen chair, and brought her the steaming toddy. ''Sis,'' he said, lifting her chin, ''look at me. It's not true. There is not going to be a nuclear war. There cannot be. It simply will not happen. There are too many sane people on both sides who will simply not let it happen.''

He took her hand and led her across the kitchen. She sipped the toddy as he finished broiling the venison and put it on their plates with the vegetables and baked potatoes. By the time they returned to the table with the steaming plates, the warm toddy had helped somewhat restore her sense of well-being.

They bowed their heads in a traditional silent grace; Frank kissed her hand, then swallowed a shot of Jameson as he dug into the dinner. ''Please do not accept the fashionable notion among your peers that the so-called adults in the world are hell-bent on blowing it up or too ignorant to prevent it from happening. Sis, it's like these cattle out here''— gesturing at the barn—''they're pretty stupid but they aren't going to race off a cliff. We just need to find a formula. This nuclear stuff is still pretty new, believe it or not. These genius scientists have been at it over forty years. But it's only in the past few years that some of the rest of us have begun to figure out how to tame this tornado. It's like a stampede. If it began to lightning out there, those Herefords would be up and gone. Then we would have to go out, saddle up, and try to catch them. That gives them a head start. The first job is to catch them and then you have to turn them. And once you've turned them and got them to circle and mill, then you can begin to herd them back to the barn.''

Frankie sat chewing the venison and watching her father. She loved to hear him talk. She wished there was even one boy half as smart as he was. But she wasn't so easily persuaded. ''But Dad, how can you catch the cattle, let alone turn them, when the lightning is still flashing? That's what's wrong with the stupid arms race. It just keeps going. No one will just quit...stop. Why don't we quit building more bombs and warheads? We have enough to blow every Russian up ten times. I can't understand it. I know all that about being strong and not letting them get ahead of us. But enough is enough. We learned in political science class the numbers of warheads and missiles on both sides and they keep getting larger. Every time there's been an arms race in history it's ended in war. Except this time it'll be the last war."

Connaughton leaned across the table and smoothed her hair. "Sis, this time we don't have a choice. That's why I decided to get into this area when you were born. I felt I had some understanding of it, some aptitude for it, and I had to try to do some little part to change it...to stop it. That's why I'm spending so much time in these negotiations and away from you when I'd rather be with you. My conscience tells me I have to. Besides, it's an unbelievable chance to be on the inside in changing history or preventing the future or however you say it." He was feeling the Jameson. "I know I can't make you feel better by just saying 'Trust me,' but that's what you must do. I won't lie to you, I never have. It *is* possible to stop. We have no alternative but to stop, and the way to do it is through these negotiations—as unproductive as they seem to be."

Frankie had picked up the plates, emptied as they talked, and taken them to the sink. Connaughton followed and once more enclosed her in his arms. "Think about your future, Francesca. You have a wonderful future. You'll marry a wonderful man, who may almost be worthy of you. And if you want to, you'll have children. And if you're a grateful and obedient daughter, you and your family will let me live out my days like old John and be buried next to him and Dad up on the mountain. So forget about nuclear weapons, at least for a while, and get on with your life. Trust me on that."

The auburn-haired girl reached up and kissed him on the cheek. There were tears in her eyes once more. "If you live as long as old John and Grandfather, you won't be going up on the mountain for a long, long time."

They heard a vehicle heading up the long road to the front gate. At that hour it had to be Harry Rafferty. She started for the front door, then turned and said, "I have to trust you, Dad. I have no other choice."

9

IN WASHINGTON, at the same hour as Senator Harry Rafferty's Bronco was bouncing up Connaughton's road, Andrea Cass of *The New York Times* was pouring her third cup of coffee and looking at her watch. Except for a couple of clerks from the White House Press Office and the omnipresent wire service reporters dozing and reading paperbacks, she had the press office to herself. She twirled a lock of golden hair around a finger and calculated that the National Security Council meeting was now in its third hour. The chances of catching anyone on the way out were slim. But it was worth a try, particularly since she was the only serious reporter on the story. Her best source inside the State Department, actually inside the Secretary of State's office, had tipped her to the meeting. And, given the circumstances, it had to be important. The President and Mrs. Lawkard, together with the normal traveling press corps, were spending the holidays at the winter White House at Padre Island on the Texas Gulf Coast. Official Washington was quiet, except for the usual holiday dinners at embassies and private Georgetown homes.

She knew it could only be one thing—arms control. The abrupt and bitter suspension of talks for the holidays in Geneva had left American policy up in the air. Even worse, it had reopened partisan and ideological warfare in the administration and in Congress over whether to negotiate at all. Cass knew that a decision had to be made soon whether to send the negotiators back to Geneva in mid-January, and whether they should seriously conduct negotiations once they got there. She looked at the calendar over her desk. December 29, 1987. For better or worse these decisions were being overwhelmed by politics. In three days the bridge would be crossed into an election year and there was no separating arms control policy from the whirlwind of presidential politics.

Cass looked at her watch again: 10:50 P.M. She sighed, put on her coat, and walked down the hallway of the West Wing, out onto the drive leading to the north front of the White House. She lit a cigarette and studied the lights in the National Security Adviser's corner office. They were going out. She dashed down the drive to the north gate. The guards, used to her mad rushes for the gate, opened it as she approached and waved her out. She broke to the left just outside the gate and covered the thirty yards to Executive Drive, running between the West Wing of the White House and the Executive Office Building and leading out onto Pennsylvania Avenue. Just as she reached the pedestrian crossing, a dark-blue chauffeured Chrysler squealed to a stop to avoid hitting her. She was right. She approached the car with its wide-eyed driver and saw Arnold Danzig, the National Security Adviser, peering at her over a copy of her newspaper. She knocked on his window and he waved her away. She shook her head and leaned against the car. They couldn't move without throwing her down. She tapped on the window again and Danzig finally rolled it down.

"What do you want, Andrea?" His disgust was leavened with fatigue and resignation.

She leaned against the car. "You know what I want, Arnie. Give me five minutes or I'll have to go with speculation. And I can get some high-level sources to speculate."

The bluff worked. "You are an extortionist, Andrea, do you know that?" He instructed the driver to back the car behind the gate and opened the back door. She got in wondering how many times she could get by with stunts like this, or cared to. She reached into her purse for her notepad, saying, "What's up?"

"The usual stuff," he said, "year-end wrap-ups, long-term projections for '88, routine assessments." His thin, accented voice sounded weary and unconvincing. "Norton is off to Padre Island tomorrow to brief the Boss and we are all making sure we are singing out of the same hymnbook, as the Boss says."

"What else, Arnie? Any discussion of Geneva... arms control...negotiations...things like that? I've been around too long to believe you had the security council in late for three hours practically on New Year's Eve for routine business. I'll be glad to put this on background or use the standard rule." The standard rule with Danzig was "a high-level administration official."

"All right, Andrea, here it is—but no names. You know... half this town knows... we are split on the negotiations. Some in the administration—call them hard-liners if you must—want to wash our hands of the talks. We have not made any progress and the Russians won't give on their heavy missiles. And, frankly, these same people on our side won't give on the space systems or the cruise missiles, which bother the Russians the most. So the President is being urged to tell them to go to hell. Don't print that."

Cass was writing furiously with only a distant streetlight for help. Her notes were going to be indecipherable. "Who are the hard-liners, Arnie? That matters a lot."

"Don't ask." He rubbed his eyes. "There are an equal number, or at least a number with equal weight, who say, 'Hang on and tough it out.' We need the negotiations, some say for political reasons and others to prevent a serious confrontation. I genuinely do not know which side will prevail."

"Jesus, Arnie, what's the problem? You haven't said anything. My Uncle Fred in Cleveland knows everything you just told me." She shook her notepad. "This is news?

The Kremlin knows more about what's going on inside the administration than I do. Come on, who are the swing votes on this... what do the Joint Chiefs say... which way does Lawkard lean?''

"Stop it, Andrea. The Boss has not decided. And he will not decide until there is some consensus among the top advisers." He leaned forward and tapped the driver. "I have to go home. Two divorces is too many, even for this job."

She opened the car door, stepped out, then put her head back inside. "What about Congress, Arnie? Is Lawkard going to pay any attention to those guys at all? For a change," she added gratuitously.

"Good night, Andrea. Do not get me started on Congress, particularly the Senate. We have a better chance of negotiating an agreement with the Russians than we do with senators like Harry Rafferty." He pulled the door shut, then rolled the window halfway down. The last thing she heard as the car pulled away was Danzig's voice shouting, "Don't print that!"

10

"I ACCEPT, FRANCESCA. I'll go home tonight and break the news to Bonnie and we'll run away tomorrow. You can have your choice of honeymoons, a month in Acapulco or a weekend in Great Falls. Which will it be?"

"Oh, Uncle Harry, you're awesome." Francesca jumped up from the arm of Rafferty's leather chair before the fireplace and said, "I have to run upstairs and pack my trousseau and my wedding gown. You've made me so happy. I think I'll cry." She and her father along with Rafferty broke into laughter. Her romance with her godfather had started twelve years ago when she was three. Her earliest memories were of the bearlike man she called uncle throwing her in the air, taking her riding on his tall horse, and teaching her to spot a jackrabbit sitting motionless in a hedgerow. She kissed Rafferty, then her father, and said from the stairs, "Tell Bonnie I look forward to dinner at your house before I go back to school. Good night, you handsome men."

"She breaks my heart, Frank," Rafferty said as they watched her run up the stairs, long hair flying. "God, what an extraordinary human being." Connaughton nodded, momentarily too moved to respond. He sipped on his second glass of Jameson, while Rafferty stretched his long legs, thick as fence posts.

"How are things in the Senate, Harry?" Connaughton asked after staring a long moment into the blazing fireplace. His father had built the ranch house in the late 1930s before Connaughton was born. Harry's father had helped

him and together they had carried and set the huge rocks
that framed the massive fireplace. He and Harry had been
born in the same year, 1943, and had grown up together as
neighbors, attending the same rural school and hunting
game birds from the time they could safely handle long
guns. They had both gone East to school, Harry on a football scholarship, and had courted the same girls. Connaughton had gone on to graduate school and then the
Foreign Service. Harry had come back to Montana to practice law and ranch and dabble in politics. After a term in the
state legislature, he'd won an upset victory for a United
States Senate seat and then, three years ago, handily won
reelection. Distance and time had only strengthened their
friendship and they could still spend a silent day working a
glistening, swift trout stream and feel as if they had communicated volumes. Connaughton's will made Harry and
his wife, Bonnie, legal guardians of his only love, Francesca.

"God, Frank, this is great." He poured another shot of
Jameson into his glass. "Washington drives me nuts. Those
people back there think it's the hub of the universe and that
nothing that happens anywhere else matters worth a damn.
I only stay sane by reminding myself that it's exactly the
other way around. If bullshit were a river, the Potomac
would be a crick."

Connaughton and Francesca had had dinner with the
Raffertys the night a week earlier they'd come West for the
holidays. So Connaughton knew his friend's call earlier in
the evening had not been purely social. He waited for Rafferty to open up what was on both their minds, the Geneva
negotiations.

"Frank, there is some heavy-duty stuff going on back
there." Connaughton knew "back there" was always
Washington. "For the past few weeks, even before the
farcical break-off of the talks, the antinegotiation forces
here have been mustering. I think they've about persuaded

Lawkard to break off all talks with the Russians, go to the American people with a huge, big Red scare, and give the Pentagon the keys to the Treasury Department. I'm talking about the biggest goddam arms race since the Trojan War.''

"Hell, Harry, they can't do much more than we're already doing. We're going all out on MX, the B-1 bomber, cruise missiles, the Trident submarine, the D-5 missile. What else is there?''

"You know what else there is, Frank. Space. The other stuff is just more of the same—'modernization.' These guys are talking about an all-out effort in the next two or three years to guarantee American superiority in space—offensively and defensively. Then when we get the Russians' backs to the wall, we dictate terms—get out of Afghanistan, get out of Poland, abandon Castro, dismantle the Warsaw Pact and withdraw Russian troops from Eastern Europe. The whole agenda.''

Connaughton gave a harsh laugh. "Sounds good to me, Rafferty. What else are nuclear weapons good for if you can't throw your weight around and threaten the shit out of the other guy? I'll vote for that program. Isn't that what this whole game is about?''

"Damn straight, Frank. Don't laugh. That *is* what it's about. The smart guys in Lawkard's party, Lawkard's brains, know he's a lame duck and that Burgoon is a wimp and a fool." Connaughton's laugh this time was genuine and hearty. After months of delicate diplomatic language, he loved Rafferty's blunt style. "They know Burgoon is going to get his party's nomination next summer and their polls show the public knows he's got a spine made out of oatmeal. So this way they show the administration is 'strong' and that we can't change horses when the stream is ass deep and rising.''

"But, Harry, the same polls show the American people want an arms agreement and strongly support the negotiation approach as the only way out of an arms race that's bleeding both of us white. If Lawkard comes out with this kind of a policy in a couple of weeks, it will just scare the shit out of everybody, at least everybody with half a brain. Not to mention the allies. Look what's going on in Europe today—even in Mexico and Canada and Australia. Huge demonstrations, protests, real violence some places. It's at least as bad as the worst days of Vietnam. Just about every Western government is calling publicly, or privately, for us and the Russians to get on with it, to do something, to stop the buildup. If the administration takes this course, it'll be Katy-bar-the-door, in every major capital this side of Warsaw."

Rafferty leaned forward in his chair and set his drink on the floor. "That's the point, Frank. They aren't going to announce it." His voice dropped almost to a whisper even though, except for Francesca, there were only Hereford cattle for five miles in any direction. "Back in November I began to sniff around, because I was picking up some stuff I didn't like."

Connaughton now leaned forward also. "What kind of 'stuff'?"

"This kind of stuff. The last three 'civilian' Space Shuttles took up some Air Force satellites that are so 'black' even the Intelligence Committees didn't know about them. Livermore and Los Alamos laboratories may have jointly come up with some kind of breakthrough on lasers on size reduction through miniaturization and some exotic new power sources. Also, it doesn't take much, as you know, to convert the Midgetman to an interceptor missile. It's in full-scale production and the line can be altered in a matter of weeks, if not days, to make the conversion. It's mobile, which means it could be deployed around command centers and missile fields very quickly."

"That I did know," Connaughton said, "but not about the shuttle payloads. Do you have any idea what they are?"

"If, as I have heard from a source in the CIA, they represent a brand-new, highly accurate early-warning capability, then you put that together with the lasers and the interceptors and you have about ninety to ninety-five percent of an effective missile-defense system and a hell of an imbalance that tilts the nuclear equation in our favor. Now you and I know the Russians can and will catch up in time. But in the meantime that situation represents an incredible temptation for the muscle-flexers on our side to take advantage of it in one or more of the ways I've already mentioned. All they have to do is scare the hell out of the American people—you know, 'The Russians are coming, the Russians are coming, and they're thirty feet tall'—and now is the time to punch the Bear in the nose and put him back in his cage."

"What do you think can be done, Harry?"

"I'll tell you what I can do, Frank. I intend to continue trying to find out what's going on with all this space stuff. If the administration is actually deploying some elaborate space systems without public debate or even classified notification of the congressional Intelligence Committees, then there will be all hell to pay. It worries me because later, when all this comes out, they can always claim national security, the need for secrecy, some new threat. If they do precipitate a crisis and the Russians respond, not too many people are going to worry about the niceties of the constitutional process or the checks-and-balances system. The other thing I've begun to do is organize on both sides of the aisle in the Senate. There is a solid one third or more of the Senate, including some members of Lawkard's party, who think it's folly to expand the arms race into space or break off negotiations. I've organized an informal luncheon group to keep track of developments in Geneva and new weapons production. We'll form the base for getting a treaty ratified in the Senate—if in fact a satisfactory treaty can ever be negotiated."

Rafferty lumbered awkwardly out of the big chair and paced back and forth before the fireplace. "The Senate will be back in session the second week in January. Why don't I get the group together, about a dozen sympathetic colleagues, and have you talk to us before you go back to Geneva—*if* you go back to Geneva. Actually, that's a great idea! You can get a sense of the kind of guys we've got on our side already. And it will give them a good chance to meet you and have you fill them in on the negotiations. What do you think?"

Connaughton stood and joined his friend before the fireplace. "I'd enjoy it. But there's a protocol problem. We're under instructions from the White House not to talk to any members of Congress. Paranoia is rampant in the White House, particularly on arms control, and they insist on total control of the flow of information. I think they're scared to death a few of you in the Senate are actually going to find out what's going on, or what's *not* going on."

"What if I called Secretary Norton and specifically asked his blessing for you to do this?"

Connaughton sighed. "That would help, Harry. If he said OK, it would definitely be all right to do. I would be protected. But the White House would still be unhappy. The President's staff, to the degree they even know who I am, do not consider me a Lawkard loyalist, a true believer. I don't particularly care, except I would hate to lose my job right at this critical moment. I've been able to counter some of the hard-line philosophy being pushed by some of the administration."

"We'll do this, Frank. After New Year's, I'll track Norton down and ask if you can give us a briefing. He knows we're friends and he's not unsympathetic to what we're trying to do."

Rafferty picked up his heavy shearling coat, put on his well-worn stetson, and headed for the door. "Bonnie and I want you and Frankie to come to dinner again back in

Washington. She'll call you about it. Tell my sweetheart to give me a whistle when she's ready to elope." He hesitated momentarily with his hand on the door latch, trying to collect a thought at the back of his mind. "Frank, have you heard anything about the launching of any new antisatellite capability?"

Connaughton thought. "No, Harry, I don't believe so. I know most of the stuff that goes on, because I have to, but from what you say it sounds like we have a small government inside our own that may in fact be running things. I hope it's not true. Antisatellite is dangerous stuff. Nothing would bring us closer to real confrontation with the Soviets than to put something like that in place. You and I both know that if we knock out their reconnaissance satellites, and they're blind—they wouldn't be able to see an attack coming. Just put up a killer satellite, and they'd assume we were getting ready to attack—it would be a terrific provocation."

With a wave over his broad shoulder the big man was out the door and headed for his Bronco. Connaughton stood on the low porch for several minutes watching the headlights disappear down the road thinking, What the hell is going on?

11

"I'LL TELL YOU what's going on, gentlemen." The speaker was the Vice-President of the United States, Harold Burgoon. It was 3 P.M. on the last day of 1987. Around the table in the Situation Room of the White House were Philip Warrenton, Director of Central Intelligence, Secretary of Defense Joe Sternberg, and Arnold Danzig. "In two hours I am getting on Air Force Two at Andrews and flying to Padre Island. And I fully intend to tell the Boss that the four of us unanimously agree that we have no choice but to go forward with Operation Blue Thunder. Now, there is a time for talk and there is a time for decision. Contrary to what the sonsofbitches in the press say, I *can* make a decision and I—we—just have."

Burgoon was a man who operated consistently so far beyond his limitations he had forgotten where they were.

He looked at the other three. Every one of them was desperate to keep his job in the next administration. And, by God, he *was* the next administration. "If Willie—the President—knows he has Defense, the Agency, and the National Security Council behind him, that's it. He'll know we're right."

"Wait a minute, Harold." Warrenton looked vaguely ill at ease. "You cannot say the Agency agrees. We do not make policy, and you know it. Don't sandbag me on this. What you are proposing is a monumental policy step for this country. It could radically alter the balance of power—at least for the time being. I personally agree, with considerable reluctance, that this is probably the course to take. But to say the Agency recommends or supports this is an overstatement." Warrenton was laconic, sedentary, and elliptical. He was occasionally so cryptic (his critics said) that even he did not understand the secret of his utterances.

Danzig, eternally worried looking, chimed in, "Also, Harold, it is not right to say the National Security Council agrees. I am only the National Security Adviser and, like Philip, I have no authority to commit the whole council. You know that. Besides, I'm afraid I have a lot of the same reservations Philip does. This is a major step, to say the least."

"Goddammit, what's wrong with you guys?" Sternberg was on his feet, pacing around the table. "We've been talking about this for months. I haven't talked to every last clerk and sergeant in the Pentagon, but by God I can say that Defense is behind it—all the way! We don't have any other choice. Phil, there comes a time when you run a department that you have to speak for that department. Now the Agency is going to support this operation because you know we have no choice and history is going to make you and the Agency look pretty sick if you don't. What do you think Congress and the American people would do if they found out we could have headed the Russians off at the pass and turned down the chance because we were afraid?"

Normally a reticent man, Warrenton rebelled. "You are not dealing with a schoolboy here, Joe. You won't get me to commit the Agency to a major escalation of the arms race by threats or by concocting some guilt trip."

Burgoon's voice was soft and insinuating. "Philip, I wouldn't think of threatening you or anyone else. Besides, in my mind, and certainly in the President's mind, you are already committed to this operation. You, and every one of us here, signed off on Blue Thunder when we okayed the launch of Cyclops. Now it's up there. It's in a perfect, secure orbit and ready to go. That means we're ready for

Phase Two and I simply want to be able to assure the Boss that his team is still on board, that you still share his deep concern about Soviet intentions and our national security, and that you're ready to go to the well with him during this critical period."

"You can count on me, Harold. The going will get tough, and the tough better get going." Sternberg had financed his M.B.A. studies by coaching high school football and, when pressed, could always be counted on to resort to locker-room parlance. "You tell the Boss that Defense is there for the whole nine yards."

"Does that include the Chiefs, Joe?" Burgoon's voice now held a certain edge.

"Hell, yes. I'll guarantee every one of them. But, goddammit, it's not the Chiefs we have to worry about, it's Norton." Sternberg was obsessed with Emerson Norton, the Secretary of State, considering him a weak sister, indecisive and vacillating. On the surface their relationship was cordial. Underneath, Sternberg had waited almost four years to settle scores, mostly real and imagined social slights, with Norton. All his life Sternberg had fought to achieve status, imagining that would permit him automatic entrance to the same doors as the Warrentons and Nortons of the world in Georgetown, Beverly Hills, and Palm Springs. It hadn't worked out that way. Sternberg was a cauldron of resentments. He struggled to be happy with himself. But his insecurity knew no bounds.

Danzig said wearily, "We will get to Emerson in a minute. But don't be so glib about the Chiefs. They tend to have minds of their own on things—particularly where the possibility of hostilities exists. And every one of us knows if we go forward with this operation, that possibility does exist. Let's review the bidding. The Air Force is all for it. This is their operation and they are absolutely convinced they have all-out technological superiority over the Soviets in space. This is General King's operation and he and the entire Air

Force will be behind it all the way. The Army is less enthusiastic, but on board. General Ellison believes—I think wrongly—that NATO has its reserve problems in Europe licked and that they can mobilize quickly. Again I think wrongly. But the Army will vote aye.

"The problem is the Navy. Admiral Bigby put all that money into a couple of big carriers and now he says he does not have enough ships. Well, for a change, he's right. The Soviets have a huge submarine advantage and now, finally, the Navy is asking itself whether it can resupply Europe in a conflict lasting longer than twenty or thirty days. That is a problem some of us have been urging you to think about, Joe, for a number of years. Nevertheless, now the Navy is scared and I don't think we will get Bigby to support an operation with an immediate risk of conflict. The Marines will go along with the Navy, so that makes the vote two to two."

"Which of course leaves the Chairman," Burgoon intervened. "Perhaps you should leave General Proctor to me."

What a crude man he is, thought Danzig. President Lawkard had appointed Proctor, a decent up-from-the-ranks soldier, to the chairmanship of the Joint Chiefs of Staff less than a year ago. Now Burgoon was bargaining that Proctor liked the position so much he could be influenced to cast the deciding vote on Blue Thunder with the understanding that, once selected, President Burgoon would keep him on as Chairman.

Danzig looked even more morose than usual. "Supposing your considerable powers of persuasion can produce Proctor's support for the operation, that still leaves Emerson. He knows about Blue Thunder in principle. But he does not know we've gone forward with Cyclops, or Phase One or whatever you want to call it. When he finds out, it is safe to say he will not be pleased."

"He'll be super-pissed," Sternberg said, unable to suppress a smile.

Danzig ignored him. "And it is also safe to say he will make his displeasure known to the President of the United States who, by the way, has rather higher regard for his judgment than you do, Joe. Emerson is totally committed to continued negotiations in Geneva. And to the degree preparing for war makes it difficult to negotiate," Danzig concluded sardonically, "you can bet Emerson is not going to support preparing for war, to say the very least."

Burgoon stood. "All right, gentlemen, thank you. I intend to tell the President this evening that, with the support of General Proctor, we have the Joint Chiefs, the Secretary of Defense, the Director of Central Intelligence, and a clear majority of the National Security Council behind Blue Thunder and that we all recommend moving to Phase Two. If Emerson wants to negotiate," he added contemptuously, "let him. For the rest of us, those who believe in strength, we intend to take whatever steps are necessary to defend this country and its long-term security."

Sounds like the beginning of a presidential campaign to me, Danzig thought.

12

AT FIRST Connaughton thought he was still in Geneva. Then his sleep-numbed mind said, No, Montana. Only as he rolled over in the unfamiliar surroundings to look at the clock did he remember, Washington. The ringing stopped just as he picked up the telephone.

Thinking first it might be Frankie in trouble, his standard first reaction to late-night calls, he remembered he had just spoken to her two hours ago as she was going to sleep in her dormitory in Virginia. No one else but the State Department duty officer knew he was at the Jefferson Hotel. Had to be a wrong number or a screw-up at the switchboard.

He started to doze off and the phone rang again. More puzzled than angry he picked it up and answered. There was a silence of some seconds during which he knew someone was on the line. Just as he started to hang up the caller said, "Frank Connaughton?" As he answered "Yes?" he thought how odd the voice was, flat and androgynous, in that range which was either high male or low female.

"You are Frank Connaughton who works for the State Department?"

"More or less. May I ask what you want at this hour and perhaps if you might identify yourself?"

"Identifying myself isn't particularly important right now, but I would like to meet you."

"I'm sorry? You want to meet me. You mean socially?"

"Not really, Mr. Connaughton. More on a business basis."

"Well, since my business, if you want to call it that, is diplomacy, perhaps you should call my office tomorrow through the main switchboard at the Arms Control and Disarmament Agency and we will set up a time—during the day—to discuss whatever you have in mind. All right?"

"I'm afraid that won't work, Mr. Connaughton."

"What other arrangements did you have in mind? And what did you wish to discuss?" Connaughton put a distinct edge in his voice, hoping to discourage whoever this kook was. He was now wide awake and alarm bells were beginning to go off in his brain. He hoped this wasn't some scheme to kidnap Frankie—couldn't be, he had no money— or some wacky blackmail threat—same response. Besides the voice seemed curiously seductive in its weird, sexually ambiguous way.

"Let me suggest something else, Mr. Connaughton," the caller said. "On the edge of Rock Creek Parkway just before you turn off for Massachusetts Avenue there is the Oak Hill Cemetery. Do you know where I mean?"

The hair on the back of Connaughton's neck bristled slightly. That was the spot where Secretary of State Woodrow Harrold's family had been brutally assassinated three years earlier. "Yes—I do."

"On the hillside in that cemetery overlooking the parkway is a small covered resting place, almost a gazebo. Would you be there tomorrow night—I suppose I mean tonight— at eleven P.M. It will be very dark, so you might want to familiarize yourself with the place beforehand."

Connaughton said, "Now wait a minute. Who are you? You want me to meet you, a total stranger, in a dark cemetery at eleven o'clock at night? This is a joke." He thought of Rafferty and started laughing. Harry had put someone up to a practical joke. "OK, OK, I get it. When I get there you and Harry Rafferty will jump out from behind a tree and say boo. His idea of fun. Next time, friend. Tell Harry we're getting pretty old for this kind of prank; he's going to have to do better than this.''

As Connaughton started to hang up, the voice said, "Cyclops."

"What?" Connaughton said, startled.

"I don't know anything about Mr. Rafferty, but I do know something about Cyclops," the caller said, for the first time with a note of intensity.

"I'll be there at eleven." Connaughton slowly hung up the phone.

13

"MR. PRESIDENT, either I am responsible for this administration's foreign policy or Harold Burgoon is." Emerson Norton was furious. "No issue is more important to this nation's security or to world peace than nuclear arms control. And unless I am badly mistaken, the policy of this administration which I am sworn to carry out is to negotiate balanced, enforceable, verifiable agreements with the Soviet Union to limit nuclear weapons. Am I right or wrong, Mr. President?"

Willie Lawkard shifted uncomfortably in his pool-side chair. He wasn't accustomed to being confronted—to being spoken to so directly. His staff was superb at constructing a cocoon of euphoria all about him. Norton was angrily unraveling the cocoon. "Of course you're right, Emerson."

"Well, if that is the case, Mr. President, what in the hell is Harold Burgoon doing slipping around behind my back, and I presume yours, organizing a cabal to torpedo the negotiations in Geneva?"

"Now, Emerson, I really don't think that's what he's doing. He's merely concerned about the lack of progress and Soviet intransigence. He, and I must say many others, are convinced the Soviets are using these talks as a smokescreen to hide an effort to achieve some breakthrough, possibly in space. Besides, Emerson"—here the President leaned forward as if taking Norton into his confidence—"Harold is going to be our candidate for President this year and he just wants to be seen as a leader on this issue."

"Soviet policy is a legitimate concern, Mr. President. As to Harold's political ambitions, that's really up to the two of you and the party."

"Well, then, we see eye to eye, don't we?" Lawkard said pleasantly. Over the years he had made amiability into an art form. He had traded God ten IQ points for his grin—and won, at least politically, in the bargain.

Norton thought there was no end to the man's simplicity. "I am afraid it is not so easy, Mr. President. I am reliably told that Harold has some scheme to circumvent the negotiations and implement the Blue Thunder operation. That approach is extremely dangerous and should, at best, represent a contingency plan only if all efforts at peaceful resolution fail. As difficult as negotiations are, they haven't totally failed yet. We still have hope." Norton rose to pace up and down between the President's chair and the pool at the Padre Island White House. "Harold of course will have Joe Sternberg with him. And Arnie Danzig will sign up if it's what he thinks you want. But Phil Warrenton is very uneasy, to say the least. He had a visit yesterday from Admiral Bigby, who said that Harold is busily organizing the Chiefs and making very pointed promises of benefits and retribution in the next administration depending on the individual Chief's responses—it's virtual blackmail."

"Oh, Emerson," Lawkard sighed, clearly anxious for the year, and these power struggles, to end so that he could move to the golf course permanently. "I really don't believe Harold would do that. He and Martha did come down for New Year's Eve and after considerable discussion he did convince me we should go forward with this Blue Thunder business. I agree with him that we have to be ready to counter any Russian moves in space. But he assured me this was supported by just about everybody in the administration."

"Goddammit, Wil...Mr. President, I'm sick and tired of Harold pulling these end runs on me. He knows I was shut out of this from the beginning. And the reason I was shut out was because he knows I don't approve. Your Secretary of State does not approve of high-risk military operations that sharply increase the arms race, destabilize the strategic balance, and jeopardize any chance at successful negotiations."

Norton stopped in front of Lawkard's chair. "Mr. President, if you accept this recommendation to seek an offensive capability in space and thereby destroy our ability to negotiate, I have no choice but to offer you my resignation."

Lawkard stood up, putting his hand on Norton's shoulder, and said with his patented grin, "Now, Em, don't be going off half-cocked. If you think we ought to send Arkwright and the others back to Geneva, and the Russians agree, then go ahead. I don't think it's going to produce much, but go ahead. Contact the Soviet Foreign Minister, and give that speech at Georgetown that says we're willing to return to the bargaining table, and let's see what happens."

"Well, that makes me feel a little better, Mr. President. It's the right course to follow and I believe history will prove it so. But, if I may presume"—Norton leaned forward slightly—"watch Harold and Sternberg. Don't let them convince you to let this Blue Thunder cat out of the bag."

They shook hands. And as the Secretary of State took his leave to catch his plane back to Washington, the President wondered whether and how to tell him he was too late.

The President decided it could wait.

14

As ANDREA CASS cradled the phone to her left ear, her fingers flew across the keyboard of the word processor in her office. As she listened and typed she kept saying, "Yeah, yeah, yeah, go ahead." Then: "Let me read this back to you to see if I have it right." She punched two keys on the machine and the screen brought up the beginning of the text she had entered:

Highly placed sources in the administration today confirmed that President Lawkard has authorized Secretary of State Emerson Norton to contact Soviet Foreign Minister Zoshchenko with a firm offer to resume nuclear arms control negotiations within two weeks in Geneva. Since there has been serious doubt whether such negotiations would be resumed after their harsh preholiday conclusion three weeks ago, this decision was seen in Washington as a victory for the pro-negotiation forces led by Secretary Norton. But informed sources who insisted their names not be used said that hard-line elements in the administration, including Vice-President Burgoon and Defense Secretary Sternberg, have convinced the President to consider certain highly classified space initiatives. These initiatives are apparently designed to anticipate the failure of negotiations and place the United States in an advantageous position in any subsequent race to control the high ground of space.

Cass was excited. "Are you sure that's what they're up to? Yeah? Why can't you give me more details? Yeah, yeah, yeah, security...I understand all that, but I need to know more. Can we get together? No, you're not going to lose your job. I'll protect you. I promise. I just need to get more facts." The reporter listened a moment, then said, "I tell you what. Let me get this in print. Then call me tomorrow about this time and I'll arrange a place where we can talk privately. OK?"

15

CONNAUGHTON STOPPED to catch his breath. He had only a small flashlight because he wanted to avoid alerting any police cruiser patroling the parkway. And with four inches of crusted old snow in the cemetery, he had to struggle down the slippery hillside toward the gazebo. After a minute's rest, he covered the remaining twenty-five yards in the dark, stumbling over only one low headstone. He looked at his watch. Its luminous dial showed 11:10.

He had thought about the *New York Times* story all day. There it was at his hotel door that morning, as if to confirm the mysterious call seven hours before. He could not see within the small shelter, but he sensed someone's presence.

"Please do not use your flashlight, Mr. Connaughton." It was clearly the same voice, with its curious sexual ambiguity. Nevertheless, he jumped when he first heard it. "Please sit down, I've brushed the snow from the bench." The iciness of the stone bench penetrated his heavy coat and trousers, and he quickly jumped to his feet. To his annoyance, he heard a chuckle. At least he—or she—had a sense of humor.

"Don't worry," his companion said. "We won't be here long. It's too cold and what I have to say will only take a moment."

Connaughton said, "First of all, why don't you tell me who you are? Wouldn't that be the normal way to proceed?"

"It doesn't matter who I am. I'm a career employee of an organization involved in the production of advanced space systems."

"So that's how you know about Cyclops," Connaughton muttered. He knew the project to have the highest classification in government. There wouldn't be three dozen people who knew about it in any detail.

"Mr. Connaughton, I'm told you're a good man, that you're committed to negotiating controls on nuclear weapons. Therefore, I think it's important that you know something about Cyclops." The speaker hesitated.

"I know about Cyclops. At least I know its capabilities," Connaughton said by way of encouragement.

After a pause the other spoke. His eyes somewhat adjusted, Connaughton could make out a slender figure, about medium height, in a dark coat. "What you do not know, Mr. Connaughton, is that Cyclops was launched exactly seven weeks ago very secretly and is now ready for action."

16

POLICE ESTIMATED the crowd that surged past The Hague at two hundred thousand. It was, by and large, peaceful. But an eerier sight was scarcely conceivable, most of the marchers having painted their faces corpse-white to create a silent, torch-lit parade of the doomed and damned.

The only violence to occur involved a young Belgian policeman, of the marchers' generation, who lost his nerve or hallucinated in the apocalyptic air and charged a rank of marchers on the edge of the main body. He'd inflicted concussions on three teen-age students from a nearby Catholic girls' school when the marchers erupted, trampling the rookie almost to death before a patrol of his mounted colleagues pulled him free.

Five young people, all in their teens, died in rioting in Bonn. The organizers of the antinuclear demonstrations either did not know how to control the participants or did not care to. As tens of thousands of marchers plunged past the government buildings, roving bands of chain-swinging, leather-covered youths split off to smash windows or intimidate shoppers. Hostages were pulled from shops and forced to join the protest. If they refused, they were often clubbed or beaten. Mounted police who tried to rescue the victims were themselves pulled from the horses, stripped, and forced to join the marchers. At least twenty rapes were reported, mostly occurring in side streets and back alleys. Only after militia from nearby barracks were brought in was order restored in the early hours of the morning.

Equally chaotic was the situation in Italy. Whereas the major demonstrations in Rome were largely without casualties—except for two undercover agents who were trying to infiltrate the headquarters of the protest groups and accidentally suffocated in the trunks of small cars before being discovered—terrible violence had erupted in Naples and Milan. The antinuclear, anti-American protesters in Naples had taken to blocking traffic during rush hours by sitting down on major bridges and highways. They were then challenged and charged by angry commuters. Forty-one people died in individual clashes and shootings in a three-day period. At the NATO naval headquarters in Naples, Marine guards in desperate, last-ditch efforts to stop an assault group of protesters fired their automatic pistols above, then into, the mob. Seven people, two of whom were fourteen years old, lost their lives. One Marine was permanently paralyzed when his back was broken in retaliation before reinforcements arrived.

In Milan, two leading members of the city council who opposed the demonstrations were fatally shot by a colleague who supported them. The American Consulate instructed all Americans, whether residents or tourists, to stay off the streets, particularly at night. The warning came too late for four American students at the University of Milan. A local gang of hooligans, for whom the antinuclear movement was incidental, took the Americans from their roominghouse, raped the two girls and shaved the heads of all four, then marched them naked through the streets throwing freezing water on them all the while. They were all treated for pneumonia and sent home, lucky to be alive.

By far the worst situation arose in Great Britain during the early days of January. There resentment had grown over deployment of land-based cruise missiles since 1984. Then came the fruitless talks in 1987 and, more important, their breach at the close of that year. Reports from Geneva in

December suggesting that the breakdown might be permanent acted like a match in a refinery.

In Britain, as in the rest of Europe, memories were also still fresh concerning the Chernobyl disaster. The melted Soviet reactor was now an international symbol of renegade nuclear technology and reports were leaking through the Iron Curtain now, two years later, that radiation damage to the current generation would run into the tens of thousands and genetic damage to future generations would run into the hundreds of thousands of victims.

Suddenly, chemically, everyone with a complaint against the Thatcher government was in the streets. Striking miners, students whose financial aid had been cut, unemployed youths, idealistic mothers, ardent unilateral disarmers from the age of Bertrand Russell, Anglican and Roman Catholic clerics, trade-union shop stewards, schoolchildren.

For a few days, activities were peaceful. Local police departments cooperated in scheduling marches and issuing permits. And, except for grumbling about traffic slowdowns, the British muddled along, as always.

Then came Tuesday, January 12. At high noon in large urban areas throughout the land, demonstrators dropped to their knees in silent prayers for peace. Leaders with large placards were located at each corner as focal points. But by now extreme right-wing neofascist groups, long dormant, were aroused and forewarned. After elaborate preparation they descended on the supplicants at preselected corners in London and other major centers. Surprised demonstrators were clubbed and kicked. Skulls were cracked with heavy boards. Arms and legs were snapped. In panic schoolchildren and senior citizens were trampled as peace demonstrators fled the rampaging gangs. Nineteen dead were left behind.

Then the furies broke their chains. Angry, violent elements took control of the "peace" movement. The counsel of the peacemakers was abandoned and a vast lake of frustration and anxiety about nuclear weapons breached its dam. Some in the movement were closet or even avowed Communists, in direct communication with Moscow. Others were economically motivated, fed up with a system that had denied them jobs. Others saw this as a bright chance to overturn a government they disliked, or perhaps to sever what they considered an unhealthy umbilical cord connecting Great Britain's security to the United States.

But it was later concluded that the vast majority of those who took to the streets of Britain were ordinary men and women with no affiliation or organizational ax to grind, simply people whose cup of anxiety had run over after forty years of a frightening cold war. They couldn't take it anymore. They couldn't take the loss of control over their own safety and their own destiny. They couldn't take having someone else's finger on the trigger of doom. They had no answers. But they were fed up with the problem.

It was estimated that within seventy-two hours three to four million people filled the streets. Factories and shops closed spontaneously. Schools could not operate because there were neither students nor teachers. For the frivolous it was a unique holiday. For most it was a brewing storm of protest. Once again, clashes broke out. Whenever members of right-wing gangs emerged to taunt or threaten, they were attacked and beatings were exchanged. Gradually, the violent extremes began to prevail. Massive property damage began to mount. And more lives were threatened and lost. Eleven more in London. Thirteen in Liverpool. Five in Manchester. Two elderly people were trampled by teenagers in the resort area of Brighton.

Curfews were invoked. On the fifteenth of January, the Prime Minister summoned her Cabinet and martial law was declared. That had not occurred even during two world wars. Still the unrest grew, as it did throughout Europe. On the edge of panic, the Prime Minister called President Lawkard, pleading for action by the United States. The

President had just returned from his holiday stay at the Padre Island White House. Convinced finally of the seriousness of the situation, he summoned Secretary of State Norton and instructed him to move up his Georgetown University speech by three days, and also contact the Soviet Ambassador to the United States.

Norton moved his speech up and, on the morning before it was to be given, he asked the Soviet Ambassador to come to the State Department. He told the Ambassador to inform his government that later that day, on instructions from the President, he would give a major policy speech calling for the resumption of talks and committing the United States to at least one more round of negotiations designed to break the deadlock.

The Soviet Ambassador thanked the Secretary of State for the notice and congratulated him on his statesmanship, then departed to communicate with his government. That afternoon Norton spoke at Georgetown to an enthusiastic young audience that welcomed his speech as an overdue return to the rule of reason.

The speech was timed to dominate the evening network news and it did. It also led the morning newspapers, including *The New York Times*. Andrea Cass, the principal reporter assigned to the story, wrote the first four paragraphs straight, quoting Norton: "As President Kennedy once said. 'Let us never negotiate out of fear, but let us never fear to negotiate.'"

But there followed this ominous paragraph: "There are highly placed sources in the administration, however, who are willing to say on a background basis that they believe that is exactly what the Lawkard administration is doing—negotiating out of fear. They believe returning to the bargaining table in the present atmosphere of turmoil is a mistake and a sign of weakness."

17

"COLLEAGUES, LET ME thank you all for being here." Harry Rafferty stood at the end of the table in a small conference room in the Senate wing of the Capitol. He was addressing eleven of his fellow senators, four from the President's party and seven, like himself, from the opposition. "First, let me tell you a little about my friend, Frank Connaughton."

The two waiters quietly removed luncheon plates and replaced them with coffee and sherbet, then seemed to vanish from the room as Rafferty began speaking. "Frank and I, as some of you know, grew up together in Montana and have been lifelong friends. But unlike me, Frank chose to stay out of politics and go straight." The predictable chuckle rippled down the table. "After graduating from Dartmouth, Frank got a master's degree from the Fletcher School of Law and Diplomacy in Soviet studies and got his Ph.D. from Georgetown in strategic studies. He wrote his dissertation on modern arms control negotiations. After a couple of years of teaching—which he was awful at—he joined the Foreign Service—which he was happily better at." Another chuckle. Connaughton, embarrassed, looked at his shoes. "Frank helped staff the SALT II and START negotiating teams in the nineteen-seventies and early eighties. For the past two years he has served as Deputy Director of the Arms Control and Disarmament Agency and is its representative on the current SALT III negotiating team in Geneva."

Rafferty continued. "Along with the rest of the negotiating team, Frank has been back in the States since mid-December and now, with Secretary Norton's speech and the decision of both sides to continue negotiations, he will be returning to Geneva in a few days. Since all of you here have been concerned about the talks and interested in arms control generally, I thought this lunch would be a good chance to get a firsthand account of what is, and is not, going on." He turned to Connaughton: "Frank?"

Connaughton had testified before congressional committees and on many more occasions had accompanied senior officials who were witnesses. But he never ceased to be slightly nervous, even in informal surroundings, among a group of politicians. "Thanks, Harry—Senator Rafferty. I guess I have to call you that out of respect. But given some of the things I happen to know about you, it's pretty hard." He got a laugh and that loosened up the atmosphere.

"I greatly appreciate the opportunity to meet with you, but I must establish the ground rules. Although I'm here with the approval of Secretary Norton, since the White House has discouraged these kinds of contacts between our negotiators and the Congress, I'm afraid all my comments must be off the record."

Connaughton looked at Rafferty, who waved his cigar over the table as if to bless it. "Right, Frank. I told all the senators here to leave their staff people out of it and keep our conversation to themselves." Heads nodded around the table. "Of course, getting politicians—especially senators—to keep quiet," Rafferty said with a grin, "is like whistling into the wind."

"That's not all you people in Montana try to do into the wind," growled old Orville Sandstrom of North Dakota. The table erupted in laughter. Estelle Parker of Maine wore an expression that said, Boys will be boys.

"Mr. Connaughton, what are the principal conflicts in the negotiations right now?" It was Arthur Milbank, the aristocratic Senator from New York.

Connaughton was ready for that question. "Senator, right now the issues are these: The Soviets object to our full-scale deployment of cruise missiles, particularly at sea. They want an agreement to limit the number each side can have. But we don't believe such an agreement can be verified— that is, that we can count all their cruise missiles. Besides, right now we're ahead in cruise missile technology and don't want to surrender our advantage."

"That sounds like what happened with multiple warheads in the seventies, doesn't it, Mr. Connaughton?" This was Senator Parker.

"That's essentially correct, Senator," Connaughton responded. "We were ahead then and didn't want to negotiate limits. Now they're ahead of us. Which leads to the second issue—land-based missiles, ICBMs. Improved accuracy on both sides, particularly the Russians', has now made the backbone of the strategic forces—our ICBMs— the most vulnerable, therefore the most dangerous weapons we both possess. The issue in Geneva is how to reduce the numbers of these weapons on both sides. They're going forward with three or four new land-based missiles while we continue to deploy the MX in our silos."

"These missiles almost invite the other side to strike first and destroy them, don't they? Nuclear weapons used to be called deterrents, not invitations to war," said Estelle Parker sharply. "Why keep on building them?"

Connaughton sighed. "Well, the Soviets continue to build them because they don't have the bomber fleet we have and are farther behind in submarines. We put our missiles in silos because no one seems to want the things on trucks or tracks in their states, even though it would make them hard for the Soviets to target.

"Basically," Connaughton continued, "I must tell you it is momentum on both sides that continues these, and perhaps other, weapons. Assembly lines get started which are hard to close down and constituencies, both military and civilian, get created which continue to press for more. Even when the purpose of a weapon disappears, the thing continues to go forward." He knew that two or three in the room had voted for missiles they didn't believe in because of home-state economic and political pressure.

Orville Sandstrom rasped, "Well, Mr. Connaughton, I understand the problems with the ICBMs. But isn't the real concern these newfangled gadgets in outer space? I mean, haven't we just about taken this whole arms race up into the heavens?"

"Yes, sir, Senator, I was about to come to that area. The real roadblock in Geneva is the question of space. Basically, the Soviets say they want to prohibit all activities, defensive and offensive, in space. We say we want to continue to explore the possibilities of space-based defenses. But as you all know, it's not quite that simple. The Soviets for some time have been investing heavily in research on antisatellite weapons, which are far from defensive, as well as exotic new technologies such as lasers and particle-beam weapons. In our case, we're trying to catch up in antisatellite capabilities and get ahead in these other new weapons."

Rafferty spoke up. "Yeah, but Frank, isn't that good? I mean, can't you argue that this Buck Rogers stuff makes nuclear war obsolete? At least that's the pitch Lawkard and the space wienies over at the Pentagon make, that someday they'll be able to intercept ICBMs in flight and save us all from Armageddon."

"If I could be converted to that religion, Harry, I'd sure sleep better at night. But it's not quite that simple. First, it will be tens of billions of dollars and many years before we know whether most of it works, at least works well enough to bet our nation's life on. Then it will cost hundreds of billions of dollars to produce and deploy. In the meantime, we're not building fewer offensive nuclear weapons—both sides are building more. And those increasingly dangerous and unstable weapons will be around for decades. In fact, for a long, long time, it'll be cheaper to build these attack warheads than it will be to build the exotic space weapons to knock them down. Finally, these new weapons are not just defensive. They can be used to fight a war, to visit massive destruction on military and nonmilitary targets on either side."

Arthur Milbank said, "Well, Mr. Connaughton, thank you for coming by today. It's most helpful to have a first-hand account of the negotiations. But to return to that, where do the talks go from here? You're going back to Geneva within the week. What will our side offer and what will be the Russian response?"

"That, Senator Milbank, is the sixty-four-dollar question. I'm afraid I am under instructions not to reveal the United States bargaining stance at this point." Connaughton was cut off by a buzz from offended senators, and ransacked his memory for tidbits he could throw out.

"I believe I can tell you this, Senator," Connaughton resumed. "We intend to make an offer to reduce the number of ICBMs, and the number of warheads they contain, to equal levels on both sides. We're willing to limit overall numbers of cruise missiles, but the Soviets are going to have to let us carry out some on-site inspection of production facilities. And, most important, I believe—I guess I should say, I hope, since I don't know for sure—that we'll propose some comprehensive rules to control deployment of anti-satellite weapons and ballistic missile defense systems."

Connaughton looked around the table. "Ultimately, I can only say this. If we let the genie out of the bottle in space, I don't think we'll ever get it back in. We are right on the brink of letting nuclear technology outrun our ability to master it."

18

HARRY RAFFERTY sat in his office that night trying to sort things out. He called Bonnie to tell her to delay dinner another hour. He smiled to himself when she told him about the date she had arranged that evening for Connaughton with Cynthia. Good old Frank, he thought, that was just what he needed. A little diversion, female companionship. He had never heard his old friend even suggest a social life in Geneva. He must be lonely as hell. Rafferty would give him a call in the morning...not too early...to find out how it went. That old dog, he thought. A little fleeting romance with Cynthia wouldn't be half-bad. She was a great girl, and terrific to look at besides. Poor bastard. What a tough time he'd had with that marriage. Rafferty briefly congratulated himself on his own luck in being married to Bonnie. Couldn't do better, he thought.

He needed to talk to Frank anyway about this Cyclops business. Stranger than hell. Connaughton would be leaving in a day or two and be gone for a couple of months. They surely needed to compare notes.

Rafferty thought a moment, then decided to keep his appointment with the mystery caller who had contacted him earlier. He took the elevator to the basement of the Dirksen Senate Office Building, entered his car, and drove out the basement exit. He followed the Potomac River around to the edge of Georgetown, then drove up Twenty-ninth Street and parked between Q and R streets. He walked one block north and turned left on R Street.

He waited for traffic to pass, then started to cross the street to the dark trees surrounding the tennis courts at Montrose Park adjacent to Dumbarton Oaks. Less than fifty yards away, a van without headlights heading west on R Street accelerated swiftly. The Senator neither saw it nor heard it.

Rafferty had almost reached the park when the right front fender of the van slammed into his right side and hurled him into a clump of bushes. And then it was gone, speeding away through the night.

19

THE MINUTE HE WALKED in the door he knew he had made a mistake. In the first place, the music was too loud. But even worse, the people were louder than the music. And it was crowded. Crowds made him claustrophobic. It had something to do with being raised in expansive surroundings. Connaughton rued his decision.

It had seemed like a good idea at the time. He was leaving for Europe in three days. He hadn't really socialized, wasted an evening, or gone out on the town in almost a month in the States. And Bonnie Rafferty had introduced him to this gorgeous younger woman who worked in Bonnie's small public-relations firm.

But now he felt uneasy and awkward. This exclusive, noisy bar in Georgetown was not his kind of place. Aside from all the obvious drawbacks, after his eyes adjusted to the smoky dimness he realized almost everyone there was younger than he was and younger even than his date. They threaded their way past the crowded bar and into the fern-clad room in the back, where the din was at least less overwhelming. On the way to their table the young professional males in the place followed his companion Cynthia's lithe form with blatant glances. These guys have a lot to learn about subtlety, let alone manners, Connaughton grumbled to himself. I must be getting old. He felt like a mountain man returning to "civilization" after many years.

"Now tell me again exactly what you do," Cynthia said, managing to sound slightly breathless in the din. "Bonnie explained it to me, but it sounds so complicated. Something to do with nuclear weapons. Isn't that right?''

Connaughton shouted into her face three feet away, "Yes and no. I'm part of a team of Americans trying to reach an agreement with the Soviet government to limit nuclear weapons.''

Although Connaughton thought everyone in the place could have heard him and Cynthia nodded knowingly, he was sure she hadn't understood a word he had said. She was damned attractive though, he thought. He moved his chair partway around the table to get closer. Their elbows were almost touching. It helped. He didn't have to shout and he began to feel less intimidated by his surroundings.

"Actually," he continued, "Geneva is a pleasant place to be and I get back to the States pretty often." A drunk wove past, ogling her low-cut silk blouse. "I also happen to believe what we're doing is pretty important." God, I refuse to talk about this tonight, he thought. "Tell me about your work . . . how you and Bonnie got acquainted."

She leaned even closer. Perfume. "We met at a management seminar three years ago. I graduated from the University of Virginia with a degree in business administration and was getting ready to open my own firm. I wanted to advise new companies coming to the Washington area on how to locate themselves here. It turned out that Bonnie had pretty much the same idea, so we got together."

Connaughton signaled the waiter for more drinks. Despite the din, he was beginning to relax and enjoy himself. He began to see the appreciative glances of the unattached men toward his date as a compliment, not a threat. He thought ruefully about how little time he had spent socializing, and particularly in the dating ritual, over the past few years as he had pursued, single-mindedly, his crusade against the nuclear demon. Increasingly, he had come to wonder whether he was becoming a crank or fanatic on the subject. Perhaps oddly twisted so that he didn't fit in the company of more normal people who worried about more practical things like checkbooks, diets, or vacations.

"Bonnie says you have a daughter?" Her question brought him back to the moment. The masked lanterns on the walls made her look especially soft and beautiful.

He smiled. "Yes, Francesca. She's a sophomore at Madeira. She's fifteen going on thirty."

Cynthia laughed. "I know what you're talking about. I have a younger sister the same age." She looked pensive a moment, then smiled. "Where is Francesca's mother?" She hesitated. "I don't mean to pry."

Connaughton glanced up, then away for a long moment. It was always the hardest thing to deal with. He took a long swallow from his drink, then smiled to relax them both.

"My wife," he said, "is in the hospital." Cynthia's brow furrowed. "No, she's all right ... I mean physically. She's had a difficult time for a number of years and requires professional ... psychiatric ... help.   Unfortunately"—he smiled again, wanly—"she needs the help pretty much full-time."

Cynthia said, "I'm very sorry for you, and her." Her seriousness seemed to mature her in Connaughton's eyes. "I know it must be a difficult thing for you, and your daughter, to deal with. Particularly with you out of the country so much."

"Well, the place where Katherine is, over in Virginia, is very good and they take excellent care of her," he said. Almost ten years, he thought. Incurable, they said. A hopeless schizophrenic, unable to live in the day-to-day world for more than a few days without lapsing into some romantic or destructive fantasy. Recurringly, she heard the leaders of the world inviting her to a historic and conclusive peace conference that would usher in the millennium. On other days, including yesterday, she greeted Connaughton brightly and soberly, as keen as the idealistic graduate student in art history he had met and married while at Fletcher. About the time Francesca started school, the strange symptoms had begun. Those times came back to him often. He wondered if more prompt attention on his part, more early insistence on counseling and treatment, might have prevented or delayed the progressive decline. The doctors said no. There was still no prevention and no cure. She could only be stabilized and watched. Perhaps, miraculously, the disease would remit, would disappear as mysteriously as it had arrived. But, in the meantime, there was little he could do but express his dedication and concern, as he had that morning. Just before he left, she had wandered away down a forest path and, following behind, he'd heard her begin to appeal to the trees for peace and greater understanding. As always, her quiet voice had been solemn and reasonable. As he walked to his car later, he had, as always, wept so hard he could not drive for several minutes.

"How does Francesca handle all this?" Cynthia asked sympathetically.

"In many ways better than I have," Connaughton said. "That's the thing about kids. They're a lot more adaptable—even to life's griefs and sorrows—than we 'adults' are. She needs a mature woman around, particularly at this stage in her life and with me gone so much, to be I guess what you would call a role model. But she has always been more mature than her years, and Bonnie and Harry have been a great help in my absence." He hesitated a moment, thinking. "Frankie went out to see her mother before she went back to school. It amazes me how well she's able to handle it."

Cynthia looked intently at Connaughton for a moment, then said, "Can we go for a walk? I'd like to get out of here." He eased her chair back and followed her out of the teeming bar.

By the time they exited onto M Street in Georgetown and started walking through the evening crowd toward Wisconsin Avenue, Connaughton concluded Cynthia had heard enough about this wacky nuclear weapons expert and his complicated personal life and was calling it an evening early. They walked in silence for a block. She stopped in a doorway as if to window-shop, then turned to him with glistening eyes. "You know, I suddenly feel as if my life is absolutely useless. I'm not doing anything important—particularly compared to someone like you. I have no family to care for and no one really needs me. All I do is exist. I could disappear and who would care or even notice? Sometimes this kind of existence seems so hollow. I make money. I have a nice home and car. I go out with successful men. But in terms of any real significance…there isn't any."

Connaughton was dumbfounded. She was on the verge of tears. And he had known her less than two hours. He touched her hands clutched tightly in front of her. "Please don't be upset. I'm sorry for talking about my family and my work. It wasn't fair. I didn't mean to upset you at all. It was rude of me to talk about myself and my problems."

"No, you don't understand," she said. "I wanted you to and I still do. It's just that you're living a real life—even with all of your trouble—and I'm not. You're doing something worthwhile and important—trying to change things—for Francesca and for all of us."

Couples passing a few feet away glanced over as they passed, assuming a lovers' quarrel. "Cynthia, you're the one who doesn't understand. Everyone can't get involved in arms negotiations. It's something I've been training for all my life. No person's life is more important than anyone else's." He took her arm and they started walking again, talking quietly. "You're doing what you want to do and what you're good at. Bonnie tells me how much your clients rely on your judgment and how much you're respected. Besides," he said with a grin, "anyone as attractive as you could have a husband and family about any time you wanted to. I saw those Romeos back in that hangout."

She took the hint. "Right. Why don't we go back and you can help me pick one out. They all seemed so serious and thoughtful—and available." Now she chuckled as they turned up Wisconsin Avenue. "Mostly available." She looked at him, feigning excitement. "I know. We'll pick one out and I'll propose. In fact, we can probably get a justice of the peace out of bed and have the wedding and reception right there among the ferns. Save on decorations." She held his arm in both of hers. "Be a good fellow and help me pick a place for my honeymoon. How about Gaithersburg, Maryland?" By now they were both laughing loudly enough to draw stares again.

Exasperated by the attention of passersby, Cynthia led Connaughton a block up N Street to her parked car. They drove out of Georgetown around the Watergate and the Kennedy Center and across Memorial Bridge onto the George Washington Parkway. She held his hand as he maneuvered her Triumph Spitfire through the traffic. He kept the mood light by entertaining her with stories of the Russians' behavior in Geneva and the role of vodka in international negotiations. She directed him through the heart of Alexandria to her small two-story townhouse. Luckily they located a parking space just large enough for the tiny car and she briskly invited him in.

He thought how envious the oglers at the bar would be right now. Cynthia's house was as he had expected, tasteful and elegantly simple. "Take your boots off. They're wet from the snow. And take your coat off and get comfortable while you're at it." She was now at home and clearly in command. "It just so happens that I have a fresh bottle of Jameson." She winked over her shoulder as she headed for the kitchen. "If you've guessed that Bonnie tipped me off, you're right." She laughed merrily.

He threw his jacket over a chair and pulled off his Western boots. She returned with his drink and gave a slight wave as she disappeared up the stairs. Connaughton checked out the fireplace, saw that it was in working order, and stuffed a few pages of *The Washington Post* under the grate holding three small logs. Just as he struck a match, he heard a cry from the staircase. He blew out the match and took four strides to the stairs. He heard her say, "Frank!" She came down the steps holding the railing, her face very pale. "On my answering machine. Bonnie called. Harry's in George Washington Hospital. They think he was struck by a car."

20

THE RESPONSE to Secretary Norton's Georgetown University speech had been overwhelmingly positive at home and abroad. Though random demonstrations occurred in foreign capitals, they were small by comparison with those of the previous weeks, and they were orderly and peaceful. Opinion leaders in the United States applauded the administration's patience and farsightedness in reclaiming the diplomatic high ground and reducing the risk of confrontation and possible hostility.

It was widely believed that President Lawkard wished his last year in office to be one in which some dramatic breakthrough in arms control was achieved, thus capping a long, but otherwise undistinguished, public career. Lawkard himself enjoyed the public acclaim of his statesmanship and without subtlety suggested to senior members of his party that he would find a Nobel Peace Prize nomination welcome.

It concerned him somewhat that Norton didn't know preparations for Operation Blue Thunder were under way, or that Cyclops had been launched. But the President wasn't all that certain himself exactly what Cyclops did, and there had been no other way to appease Vice-President Burgoon and Defense Secretary Sternberg, calming the feud within the administration. Lawkard was sure something would prevent Blue Thunder from going into action. He just hoped word of it wouldn't leak out.

Chances of this happening were slim. The subject was not raised in regular National Security Council meetings where Emerson Norton was in attendance. And even the Joint Chiefs left the subject off the agenda with Admiral Bigby present. Instead, Vice-President Burgoon organized a "Special Group," also known as the April Committee (after the month when they believed their plans would become known), which met twice weekly and included Danzig, Sternberg, and Generals Proctor and King. Likewise, the Joint Chiefs formed an ad hoc working group that met three times a week in Proctor's office, without notice to Bigby.

Carrying out Blue Thunder without detection was difficult, but not impossible. The plan was based upon worldwide alert exercises by the United States and its NATO allies as a cover for actual mobilization and preparation for war. Blue Thunder combined a massive reserve call-up, maneuver of active-duty and reserve divisions along the Central Front in Europe, fleet exercises in the North Atlantic and the Mediterranean, an alert of the strategic nuclear command-and-control system worldwide, deployment of the bomber fleet, and an evacuation exercise for the senior civilian and military command.

In a period of crisis, such activities would be highly visible and highly threatening to the Soviet Union. But similar exercises had taken place every three to five years since World War II. And in each case formal and informal notice was given to the Soviets to expect activities along these lines and not to mistake them for the real thing. Besides, with seemingly good-faith efforts under way in Geneva to negotiate nuclear limits, there was little cause for saber-rattling. If both sides were serious about the negotiations, and from Secretary Norton's speech the Americans seemed to be, there would be little gain and much loss from duplicity.

But duplicity abounded. Even as the Air Force plane carrying Ambassador Arkwright and the American negotiating team crossed the Atlantic, Harold Burgoon convened the April Committee in his study at the Vice-President's residence on Observatory Hill that gloomy Sunday afternoon. The only item on the agenda was Blue Thunder.

Burgoon's ambition and self-confidence were blossoming. He made it clear to the others that neither he nor the President expected anything to come from the current round of negotiations. He also told them that the President had given him total authority to prepare for the confrontation that would likely follow a failure and break-off of the talks.

Relishing that authority, he assigned Joe Sternberg and General Proctor to make a swing through the NATO capitals to meet with defense ministers and senior military commanders. Their job would be to seek agreement in principle to convert Blue Thunder military exercises to serious preparedness for conflict if negotiations should fail and the Soviets began to behave belligerently.

Arnold Danzig was given the job of coordinating intelligence and monitoring day-to-day progress of activities in Geneva. All intelligence estimates and reports crossed his desk routinely to be predigested for presidential consumption, so Danzig would be able to keep an eye on A. Philip Warrenton to prevent any double cross of Blue Thunder by the CIA. Danzig could also use his unique position next to the President to alert the Special Group if Lawkard seemed to be waffling on the two-track policy of negotiation while preparing for war, or if the President became too inquisitive about the evolution of Blue Thunder. The group discussed a late-March trip to the Far East to occupy Lawkard's time during the crucial period just before the mobilization exercises.

Burgoon himself undertook to line up political support for the moment when congressional cooperation would be crucial. When the shit hit the fan, as he said several times, it could be critical to have key members of Congress in both parties supporting the President's bold initiative to save the country. Burgoon would make sure that ambitious or weak members of the administration's party were on board as "team players" or to "support the program," regardless of its risk. And he also knew he could pick off some members of Congress in the opposition party who were either more ideologically comfortable with the administration's hard-line, confrontational approach or afraid to be thought "weak" when the President said that national security was at stake.

After an hour-and-a-half discussion over drinks, and after agreeing that Sternberg and Proctor would start their ten-day mission while the press was distracted by the resumed negotiations in Geneva, Burgoon said, "Well, gentlemen, what do you think? Are the pieces in place?"

Sternberg responded, "Damn right, Hal. I think it looks good. We've got a chance to catch those goddam Russians flatfooted. This could be the most important and courageous thing the freedom-loving people of this world have done since VE Day."

Chairman Proctor of the Joint Chiefs agreed doggedly. "Joe's right. The risks are high, but I don't think anything worthwhile is going to happen in Geneva, so we might as well get ready for the inevitable. The scheduled exercises with Blue Thunder give us the cover we need to get a jump on the Soviets and throw them on the defensive for a change." He hesitated. "I'd feel a little better about this thing if Bigby were on board. It's hard as hell to plan a serious scale-up without the Navy knowing what's going on."

"We'll just have to figure a way around that in the next few weeks, Jim. What do you think, Arnie?"

"I think history is going to judge us either as heroes . . . or fools. We are taking a hell of a risk. If we don't get a treaty, I guess we will have to do something. And that something right now seems to be prepare for the worst." Danzig looked out the window a moment, then said, "I worry about the President. I'm pretty sure he does not know exactly what Blue Thunder is or what it is meant to do.''

Burgoon stood up impatiently. ''Arnie, you worry too much. Leave the President to me. I'll make sure he's kept abreast, generally, of what we're doing. He'll be all right. He's on our side.'' Burgoon patted Danzig on the shoulder. ''Let's not bother him with the details.''

Burgoon turned to Proctor. ''Jim, we're going to keep Bigby on the outside up until the last minute. Continue to work with him in planning the exercise part of this operation, but let's not bring him inside. He can get his ships out there, and then when the balloon goes up he'll see he has no choice but to stay the course, whether he likes it or not. The Navy is not going to pull out of an exercise that suddenly becomes a full-scale alert.''

General Proctor shifted in his chair, ribbons rippling. ''Hal, we haven't discussed the real business end of this operation. How are we going to handle command of the strategic systems? Sure, we can tell the Russians we're going to exercise the conventional forces, and even bring the bombers up.'' Proctor leaned forward, his forehead corrugated. ''But we will not get maximum effect from Blue Thunder unless we put the Trident subs to sea and bring the ICBMs up to a higher alert—Defcon 2 at least.''

Proctor looked at General King, who had been uncharacteristically silent. The Air Force commanded the land-based missiles as well as the bomber fleet. King looked uncomfortable. ''Yeah, that's generally true, Jim,'' Omar King said. ''But I think we ought to put the strategic side of this operation off till the next session. As you know, we've got the JCS staff working on this matter . . . laying out options for the handling of the subs and ICBMs for Blue Thunder. They're supposed to be ready in about ten days.'' King turned to Burgoon, who looked equally uncomfortable.

"Omar's right," Burgoon said. "I have to go to a dinner for party leaders, and we've been here almost two hours. Let's get together in a week or ten days and compare notes. In the meantime, let's keep this closely held. No deputies, no wives. No one."

They started for the door as chauffeured cars outside roared to life. General King took his time getting his coat and fumbling in his briefcase. He lingered in the Vice-President's hallway, using the phone to let his wife know he was on his way home. After the others were gone, Burgoon closed the door and waited for King.

"What's up, Omar? You didn't have much to say tonight."

King leaned close to the Vice-President. "Hal, I was hoping the nuclear systems wouldn't come up tonight. If this plan falls apart, it will be over the question of how to handle the MXs and the subs. Any time we go into a major NATO exercise, the Russians watch our nuclear alert status like hawks. That's the way they decide whether we're up to something or not. They don't take our word for it. If we begin Blue Thunder and they see us going to a higher state of alert with the nukes, they'll know they're dealing with something a lot hotter than just another training exercise."

King took Burgoon by the arm and steered him back into the study, as if someone might be outside the door. "Look, Hal, the Russians know when we raise the Defcon. They watch those subs leaving port, and they even know when we warm the missiles up. When they see that, things are going to be tense as all hell."

Burgoon smiled. "Yes, but what if they can't see the subs and missiles, Buddy? What if Cyclops pokes out their eyes, at just the right minute? If this thing works the way our hotshot scientists tell us, it'll knock out every Russian high-altitude spy satellite—the Molyinas and Electrons we call 'em—before they can think. They won't know what the hell is going on."

They walked to the door. King still seemed preoccupied. "I was just thinking, Hal. Suppose the Soviets are doing the same thing we are. Suppose they have their own contingency plan for when the talks fail." He thought momentarily. "It would be interesting to know what they call their Blue Thunder."

As he started down the steps, he turned. "Are we still working on the same timetable as before?"

"Yep," Burgoon said. "The middle of April."

21

KOZLOVSKY WAS WORRIED. And that was against his nature. His wife liked to tell her friends that he was a great family man who kept politics out of his private life. The burly man had been a wrestler in the schools of Kiev and had once tried out in the preliminary rounds of Olympic competition while a student at the Technological Institute. Now fifty-seven, he helped control his weight and temper by early evening workouts in the Defense Ministry gym maintained exclusively for senior officers and the ministry elite. But lately the workouts had failed to control his anxiety. For the first time in his life he was snappish with Eleni, his equally burly wife, and the four of their seven children still at home.

Kozlovsky knew what it was. It was the sense that things were flying out of control. He had waged and won his share of policy battles. Else he wouldn't be Defense Minister. But this goddam struggle with Zhdanov and his cabal was different. This wasn't about whether to sell MiG-25s to the Sandinistas in Nicaragua or even put a sub base in Cuba. It wasn't even a big policy question like giving Admiral Gorshkov that huge Navy he wanted. This struggle was about preparing for World War III—while pretending to negotiate.

What made it worse was that the struggle was being waged so far behind the scenes, much of the Soviet government couldn't even tell it was going on. Most big policy battles were fought out in endless Politburo meetings or in the Secretariat. Sure, there was lobbying by this side or that side. But sooner or later the thing was resolved and everyone got with the program. Only the really nasty fights took place in the private offices and hideaways, the dachas and the men's rooms. Since the break-off of the Geneva negotiations in December, this was shaping up to be the nastiest bloodletting in a long time.

Kozlovsky shook his head and growled to himself. He wished he had never heard of Red Star. What concerned him the most was an unfamiliar emotion—fear. He couldn't remember ever being afraid of anything, basically because he had always been in control. It was that need for control that had propelled him to the top of the Defense Ministry. But now he could not guarantee even to himself that if Operation Red Star took place, he could control it.

Kozlovsky had already lost one crucial battle. The day the Soviet negotiators departed to resume their talks in Geneva, Vladimir Zhdanov had lined up sufficient votes in the Politburo to approve Red Star. He had done so quite simply. He called upon the General Secretary of the USSR.

"Comrade Secretary," Zhdanov began, "the issue is straightforward. Do we or do we not go forward with our annual Warsaw Pact exercises? The negotiations have nothing to do with it. The KGB assures us the Americans and NATO have no intention of standing down their planned maneuvers. Routine military exercises have often been conducted while arms control talks were under way. It is just apples and oranges, as they say." His rasping breath and gaunt long face belied the implacable strength of Zhdanov's will.

The old General Secretary's ailments now made him appear constantly distressed and preoccupied. "Oh, Vladimir, it is not so much the defense exercises. It is all the rest of it. Getting our missiles ready and preparing strikes against American satellites. I know how things can get out of hand if someone makes a mistake or gets the wrong signal." He sighed the sigh of the resigned. "We cannot afford mistakes . . . getting too close to the line . . . with all this new technology. So much is at stake. I don't think it's possible to have a *small* war. But even if we could, think what it would do to our efforts to get more crops from the soil . . . to make our factories work."

"Well, Comrade Secretary," Zhdanov persisted, "I agree of course. But if the West goes forward with its maneuvers and we do not, they will take it as a sign of weakness on our part. More important, the Poles and Czechs and Hungarians are going to start asking questions about our will and resolve. We need to remind them constantly that we are alert . . . to activities on *both* sides of the East-West border."

In the end, Kamenev had capitulated, as much from fatigue as conviction. Zhdanov simply wore him down. Foreign Minister Zoshchenko quickly saw which way the wind was blowing and sided with Zhdanov and the pro-Red Star faction. Vladimir Ulyanov, the unctuous foreign policy expert on the Central Committee, always lining himself up to become Foreign Minister if Zoshchenko was tapped as General Secretary, jumped into line. With his other allies, that gave Zhdanov eight votes out of twelve. Kozlovsky could only get General Rusakov and two others to support delay in Red Star.

Kozlovsky concerned himself most with the consequences of the new space systems. Suppose NATO undertook full-scale exercises—divisions deploying and brigades maneuvering, air cover aloft and artillery positioned, carrier task forces in the Greenland-Iceland-U.K. gap and the eastern Mediterranean. Then suppose the Warsaw Pact began the same activities in the East and put their northern Pacific fleet out to sea from the home port of Vladivostok. That would be a staggering amount of military exercising and muscle flexing going on at the same time. Each side would automatically go to a higher alert simply because the other was charging around in its tanks, planes, and ships. Then came the nuclear systems and the space systems.

If Red Star got under way and the Politburo decided to implement its second stage, bringing the nuclear systems to high alert, and the Americans saw this as provocation, or say negotiations had broken down and there was great tension, then, Kozlovsky thought, somebody could pull the trigger by accident. Zhdanov thought the Americans could be bluffed or blackmailed, that the threat of war would frighten them and shift the balance of power toward the Soviet Union. And he was willing to take the risk, the old bastard. Kozlovsky knew the angry ideologue had nothing to lose. He was a monk. No family. Few years left. Why not?

Kozlovsky briefly pondered whether Zhdanov was mad. He certainly got an extraordinary look in his eye when he talked about the struggle between communism and capitalism. In fact, that was all he ever talked about now. Too bad Politburo members couldn't be given occasional psychiatric tests, Kozlovsky thought.

Command and control was the problem. The Minister of Defense knew—knew painfully well—how fragile were the linkages among satellites and ground stations, computers and humans, Siberian radars and Moscow commissars. He had seen these links collapse pathetically in war games. It was all on a hair trigger. And if you let confrontation occur, genuine hostility with the guns drawn, then you better be able to communicate flawlessly. No mistakes. No misunderstandings. No screw-ups.

Kozlovsky's fear stalked him like a beast of prey because he knew the system couldn't be controlled.

part
TWO

22

OF COURSE, the Politburo had not conveyed its decision to assume the high risks of Red Star to its chief arms control negotiator, Ambassador Makarov. And since Mikhail Makarov knew nothing of this highest-level policy decision, certainly his subordinate, interpreter Ekaterina Davydova, wouldn't know of it either.

She was glad to be arriving in Geneva again. Not that she didn't miss her sons already. In fact, she did so desperately. But she greeted the decision to return for negotiations with a depth of relief that surprised even her. The fact that her government and the Americans were willing to continue to talk meant that all was not lost, that maybe this time the threat of war would spur some dramatic breakthrough.

As the new Ilyushin airliner bearing Ekaterina and her colleagues settled into the landing pattern at the Geneva airport, she also thought—guiltily—to herself that she was glad to be out of Moscow for the remainder of the winter and back in the quiet, but cosmopolitan, Swiss city with its Western shops, stylish clothes, and more edible food. She reflected on how much more she came to value such things the more she lived abroad. She smiled to herself. Maybe what the Party types always said about exposure to the West was true. Maybe she was becoming a capitalist.

But one thing had kept coming back to her throughout the holiday period. That strange, crass girl on the Leningrad train, talking about some secret missile launch. It had been an odd and unsettling experience that refused to recede from her memory. It had to do in part with the girl talking so blithely about something so clearly secret. But it was more than that.

It had something to do in Ekaterina's mind with the fact that she had heard of no such test or launch in any of the many top-secret briefings she had attended in preparation for the coming round of negotiations. Even at the KGB presentation on new satellite programs for treaty verification, there had been no suggestion of a major launch in early January. And the Defense Ministry briefings contained no information on any new missile deployment.

With elaborate discretion Ekaterina had asked Sergei Metrinko, the youngish KGB man on the delegation, whether they should expect any surprises—from either side—as the talks resumed. And he had said no with unfeigned candor. She judged him to be unusually straightforward for a KGB type and she was convinced she could tell when he was dissembling. If anyone would know of some terribly secret operation under way, it would be Sergei Metrinko.

The Soviet Mission staff met them at the special gate reserved for their government plane and shepherded them around the normal customs barriers. The delegation loaded in the mission cars, as usual by rank, and headed into Geneva. Within fifteen minutes they had arrived at the mission and returned to the rooms they had left just over a month ago.

It was like returning to the spartan dormitory rooms at Moscow University, Ekaterina thought. Neat, clean, no frills, no decorations. Her bags were carried in by a glum mission employee who was clearly unhappy about drawing the duty of hauling for the lady with the heaviest and most numerous suitcases. She quickly closed the door behind him and unpacked her decorations before even touching the clothes. She first put up the pictures of her sons on one bedside table and of her parents on the other. Then she hung two colorful posters of the Leningrad Music Festival on the wall across from her bed. She put out three small vases and unwrapped several synthetic but realistic-looking flowers given her by her mother for the new year. They would brighten things up until the real ones bloomed in the spring. She then carefully laid out an antique toiletry set, brushes, combs, and mirror, left her by her grandmother Davydova, which she had treasured even as a young girl.

Finally, she arranged a small, ancient icon passed down through her mother's family for almost 250 years. The Party types dismissed such totems as art, not religion. Only the stern mission staff seemed to find the icon offensive. She didn't care at all what they thought. It was none of their business. It was, besides, her most valuable tangible possession.

Ekaterina, as the only woman on the arms control delegation, was treated deferentially. She was given a corner room in the mission housing complex, near the exit stairs. She had, from the third floor, a view of Mont Blanc over Lake Geneva.

As she carefully unpacked her clothes, she thought how nice it would be to go into the city tomorrow and visit the shops. She spent more of her income than she should on clothes, her single personal extravagance. But she preferred to save for a few well-tailored Western-style suits and dresses of good material rather than have a larger wardrobe of the heavy, square-cut Russian outfits. She was vain enough about her appearance and figure to know she looked good in the clothes she selected. She smiled as she anticipated the looks she always got from the American men involved in the negotiations.

In three days there would be the traditional cocktail party-reception to celebrate another round of talks. And she touched the striking black dress she suddenly decided she would wear. For no reason she thought of Frank Connaughton. The thought surprised her. She kept individual men—at least as members of a gender separate from hers—as far in the back of her mind as possible. And besides, there was nothing that should have made her think of the American. But occasionally the thought of an attractive man crossed her mind despite her systematic repressions.

She realized she had thought of Connaughton in connection with the upcoming reception. She wanted to see him again. There was nothing special to recommend his looks. But unlike most Russian men, he had remained slender into his middle years and he was taller than average. He was from the American West, she knew. And he reminded her of that most romantic of American figures, the cowboy. She was disgusted with herself for suddenly feeling giddy.

23

CONNAUGHTON WAS GLAD to be back in Geneva. But his brief time over the holidays on the Montana ranch had reminded him why that was his home, irrevocably his home, there and nowhere else—why, the older he got, the more he was drawn there. He had cherished the time with Frankie and he marveled at the sense of roots almost literally sinking into the rocky canyon walls of his ancestral home. He had reached a stage in his life where the word "home" immediately, necessarily, conjured up only that one picture—the place, the ranch, the rocky slopes and summer green meadows, the cattle, the house where he'd been born and would probably die, the graves of his father and old John.

His deep concern for Harry Rafferty had abated in the past seventy-two hours. The cold fear that Harry might be badly hurt, even dead, had given way to relief at the diagnosis. As the TWA flight banked into Geneva, he recalled with a sudden chill the breakneck ride in Cynthia's car through Alexandria, up the George Washington Parkway, over the Memorial Bridge, and up to the emergency entrance at Georgetown Hospital on Reservoir Road. Cynthia was barely keeping up as he dashed into the receiving room and pulled Bonnie Rafferty into his arms. One of the hospital's chief surgeons, called in because of Harry's senatorial status, shortly emerged and explained that the X rays showed no serious cranial injuries and that Harry suffered from a concussion, a broken right arm, and considerable bruises. Nothing that wouldn't heal. Bonnie, torn between concern and relief, sobbed on Connaughton's shoulder.

The following noon, after Harry had spent the night under sedation and with the doctor's approval, Connaughton dropped by his private hospital room. Though still groggy, Harry recalled the events of the previous evening. To offer a rational account to the press of his presence at Montrose Park late at night, Harry would instruct his Senate staff to say he had worked late and wanted some fresh air on his way to his home in the Spring Valley area of the District. It wasn't totally plausible, but it would have to do. Bonnie, sensitive to nuance, left the room briefly on a phony errand. Harry told Connaughton about the mysterious contact he had received from an unidentified source offering information on Cyclops. How he'd decided to take a chance on the mysterious informant, which in turn had led him to the rendezvous point at the park.

Connaughton had listened with increasing astonishment, then told Rafferty about the bizarre contact on Cyclops he'd received a few days earlier.

"One other thing," Connaughton had asked his friend: "Did you see who hit you?"

"Sure didn't, Frank; it all happened too fast."

And the driver hadn't stopped, Connaughton thought as the plane touched down in Geneva. And something told him the police would never find the vehicle. Well, thank God tough old Rafferty would be all right and back in the fight in a few days. But Cyclops was turning into a magnet for trouble. Who was this person so desperate to let someone know about Cyclops? From Rafferty's description of the unique voice, it had to be Connaughton's contact from the cemetery. Was Harry Rafferty's phone being tapped? Otherwise how would anyone know about the meeting place and time? But even asking that question presumed someone had tried to wipe Rafferty out on purpose. Could it have been an accident? If so, why hadn't the car stopped?

These thoughts occupied him as the American Mission car briskly covered the distance from the airport to his small one-bedroom apartment in one of the old but well-kept eighteenth-century houses on the Grand' Rue. Just down the hill from the historic Cathédrale de Saint-Pierre, Connaughton's place was a corner of the third floor of one of the original town residences of a royal family. He had been lucky to find the place and was willing to sacrifice a little from his own pocket to supplement the U.S. government's per diem for the advantages of privacy and nonhotel living.

Just what was it about Cyclops? he thought as he unpacked his luggage. No one would dare run down a United States senator simply because he'd asked a few questions. It simply wasn't a rational possibility. On the other hand, coincidence piled upon coincidence. Connaughton knew Cyclops to be a system to disrupt or destroy key Soviet surveillance satellites. Its program mission called for it to be deployed in time of crisis so that U.S. military activities—strategic submarines putting to sea, bombers on alert, troop movements, ship deployments—could be carried out undetected.

There were no plans that Connaughton was aware of to put Cyclops into place, barring a national emergency. Even putting the thing into space could be taken as a preliminary act of aggression. In an age of satellite surveillance and short warning times, interference with another nation's satellites was tantamount to slaying a scouting party in simpler times. Why in the world, Connaughton thought, would the President agree to such a step? Could it be possible the President hadn't authorized the launch of Cyclops? It was more probable that the mysterious caller who had contacted him and Harry Rafferty was a crank. Most likely, it was some bureaucratic malcontent trying to even some score, real or imagined. Connaughton continued to hang up suits and shirts and put away socks and shorts as he pondered. But it wouldn't do any good to tell a lie about something as important as Cyclops. That wouldn't settle any scores. The possibility the informant was crazy had to be dismissed also. There were simply too few people who knew anything about Cyclops.

None of it made any sense—unless there was something very wrong going on. Perhaps Arkwright would know. He would have to, Connaughton thought as he finished unpacking and dropped off his rent check with his ancient Swiss landlord. He returned to the street to reclaim his car and driver, waiting to take him to the American Mission for a late-afternoon meeting with Ambassador Arkwright and other delegation members. The others were already gathered in Arkwright's office when he arrived.

"Good to see you, Frank. Hope you had a good flight." Arkwright seemed relaxed and ready for work. "Secretary Norton has approved our instructions and the National Security Council has authorized the offer we discussed in Washington earlier this week. As you know, we have our opening-round reception with the Russians in two days— this Friday—then we resume formal discussions on Tuesday. It's my plan to table our latest proposal. Now, to refresh everyone's recollection, we have something a little different to offer this time. We'll propose an overall limit on heavy ICBMs—their SS-18s and 19s and our MXs; a limit on the number of cruise missiles on any individual carrier—land, sea, or air; a joint effort to increase verification capabilities—with a view toward separate negotiation of a comprehensive test ban; and, finally and perhaps most importantly, a moratorium on testing and deployment of antisatellite weapons."

Arkwright looked around the room. "We all know this is a substantial change in our bargaining position." Connaughton knew he almost said "improvement." "It will take the Soviets off-guard. They'll immediately call it a propaganda ploy. We know that. And, at the very least, it will give us a certain advantage in the arena of world opinion."

Everyone laughed. It was a standard joke that everything the Russians put forward was for propaganda, and everything the Americans proposed was a legitimate effort to communicate in "the arena of world opinion."

"Before we talk tactics, let's see if we're all straight on these positions. You'll have to defend them in the working groups." Arkwright looked at Admiral Quainton. "Walt?"

Quainton leaned forward and harrumped, appreciating the recognition of his seniority and status. "Barrett, you know the Joint Chiefs have some problems with these proposals, particularly the test ban idea and the ban on anti-satellite technology. We can live with the ICBM limits because Congress is probably going to cap the number of MXs anyway."

"I understand, Walt." Charlie Curtis, Arkwright's deputy from the State Department, spoke up. "But if we're going to negotiate—and we sure as hell better get started at it—then we have to put one or two things we like on the table. At least if we expect to get any movement from the Soviets. We can't expect to get concessions from them unless we're prepared to give a few ourselves."

Connaughton knew this debate had gone on within the American government since the beginning of negotiations in the early sixties. Do we get results by bargaining—I'll give up something if you'll give up something—or by "strength"—you give up something or I'll build more of them than you do? Something like that debate was always going on within the Soviet government as well. Neither would ever be conclusively settled.

Arkwright scanned the ceiling as if for deliverance. "Walt, I think the NSC pretty well resolved these questions as official policy before we left. And I think it would be a pretty serious mistake to start squabbling over the proposals on the eve of tabling them." He paused. "On the other hand, I have always tried to accommodate open discussion within the delegation, if for no other reason than that it helps us all understand our positions better. Why don't you just briefly go over the Chiefs' concerns about the other two issues."

"OK, Barrett, I appreciate it," Quainton nodded. "Now, the Limited Test Ban Treaty has worked out all right, although some folks at the Pentagon think the Russians still cheat when they can. But a total ban on testing just about shuts down all weapons development. Besides, as you know, we still cannot verify very low yield tests on their part."

Connaughton spoke up patiently. "But, Walt, that's what this proposal is all about. It doesn't say, 'Negotiate a treaty.' It says, 'Let's pool our resources to see if we can eliminate technical limits that prevent such a treaty from being negotiated.'"

"Well, I suppose that's all right," Quainton continued. "But it sounds damned idealistic to me, if you want my opinion. Anyway, it's the last item that caused the most uproar in the NSC, as I understand it. The Chiefs only went along with this antisatellite thing because the Boss said so. And he had a helluva time convincing Secretary Sternberg and the Chiefs to approve it. We've done a lot to catch up to the Russians on antisatellite stuff. But we've got a ways to go. All I can say is, we better hope the Russians don't take us up on this notion or it will put a heckuva crimp in programs like Cyclops—"

Arkwright interrupted, "Walt, we're not in the bubble. Hold off on that until we are." He glanced at Sid Murray, who was staring worriedly out the window at the building across the street. "Let's reconvene tomorrow at ten A.M. to go over classified items and let everyone get unpacked and used to the time change in the meantime." He stood up at his desk. "See you all tomorrow."

Arkwright gave Connaughton a look that he knew from practice meant for him to linger behind. Although almost fifteen years younger, Connaughton had become Arkwright's friend and confidant. He stayed behind as the others filed out. "As usual, Walt is behind the power curve," Arkwright sighed, gesturing Connaughton back to the couch. "Frankly, the Chiefs and Sternberg gave up on this antisatellite issue too easily for me, Frank. I talked to Emerson about it and he feels the same way. He thinks"— here Arkwright got up and closed his door—"he thinks something funny may be going on behind the scenes." Arkwright suddenly looked uneasy. He leaned forward and asked, "Do you have dinner plans? If you don't, Evelyn and I would love to have you come over. Perhaps we could have a private chat after dinner at the house." Connaughton quickly thanked him for his hospitality and agreed to see him at the Arkwright house for dinner, glad not to spend the first night in town alone.

24

AMBASSADOR ARKWRIGHT'S rented house on the south shore of Lake Geneva was palatial. Connaughton enjoyed going there at every opportunity. Tonight especially he was glad to escape his more modest cramped quarters and avoid the loneliness he always felt the first few days away from home. Arkwright and his wife were both from well-connected Philadelphia families of considerable wealth, and had attended all the right schools. The U.S. government provided them a comfortable house. But Arkwright's wife, Evelyn, chose the more elegant surroundings that they personally financed. They both enjoyed entertaining and were fond of Connaughton.

The Ambassador's car delivered Connaughton at the residence promptly at eight. Evelyn Arkwright, a patrician lady in her early sixties, met him at the door and took him to the Ambassador's study for cocktails. The Arkwrights asked after Francesca and Connaughton's wife, whose condition they were generally aware of. Dinner was served early since Evelyn Arkwright was aware that the two men had business to conduct.

After an excellent dinner of lake trout a la meunière served by the Arkwrights' French-Swiss chef, Evelyn excused herself and the two men returned to Arkwright's study. The Ambassador poured Cognac and gave Connaughton a Montecristo. He put Mozart's Symphony no. 40 on the expensive compact-disc player and set the volume somewhat high. Connaughton knew this to be standard practice to complicate eavesdropping efforts.

"Frank, do you know anything about Operation Blue Thunder that is extraordinarily sensitive or might in any way complicate our efforts here?" Arkwright asked, dropping into the deep leather chair next to Connaughton's.

The younger man shifted toward his host. "Nothing official, Barrett. But I came away from the visit home with some strange feelings."

"Such as?"

"Such as that Emerson Norton's on the outside and Burgoon's on the inside. That, together with Sternberg, Burgoon has most of the Chiefs together in an effort to convince the President that the talks will fail and that we better get ready for a major confrontation with the Soviets."

Arkwright hmmed to himself. "Who told you all this, if I may ask? Harry Rafferty?"

"Certainly not all of it," Connaughton said. "I did some snooping around State and particularly among the political-military types at Defense. I also have a contact or two out at Langley. They're all talking about Blue Thunder. As you know, it's scheduled for April. The thinking seems to be that it will go forward only if it looks like we're getting nowhere here. And the hawks—Burgoon's cabal—will use it as a club on the Russians to show them what they can expect if they don't cave in on the talks."

"That's Emerson's thought too," Arkwright said. Connaughton knew he was now being taken into the Secretary of State's confidence on a matter of highest government policy and highest-level politics. "He believes we were sent back here as a political concession to the arms control mood prevalent in the country—the fear at home caused by the near break-off of talks in December—as well as the violent reaction around the world." Arkwright waited for an especially beautiful Mozart passage to conclude, then resumed.

"He also thinks we were authorized to put forward this new bargaining position as kind of a trap or setup."

Connaughton leaned forward. "What do you mean?"

"I mean that we will look good proposing a more sweeping agreement and the Soviets can be blamed if they reject any part of it—which they surely will."

"How do we know that?" Connaughton asked.

Arkwright sipped the Cognac. "Simply because they're always reluctant to cooperate on anything, particularly anything as sensitive as verification. Can you imagine them letting American scientists into their laboratories, or near their test sites to plant 'black boxes'? They're also behind us in cruise missiles and not inclined to accept present levels as overall limits. And finally, they're really spooky, as you know, about antisatellite stuff. They think we're way ahead and trying to trick them into an inferior position."

"I understand all that, Barrett. But that sounds like a powerful set of arguments for the Soviets to reject our offer out of hand. Is that what Burgoon and Sternberg and the others want?"

"Exactly, Frank. If the Russians behave as they always have, then we come out looking like the good guys and they're the evil force. Public opinion is quieted down. We've done all we could. So now it's time to conduct our military exercises, flex our muscles, and rattle our sabers." Arkwright got up to change discs and relight his cigar. "That's exactly what Burgoon wants."

"Well, why didn't Emerson...Secretary Norton... confront them with this scheme? Why didn't he take it to the President and have it out?"

"He did in a way, Frank. We went down to Padre Island during the holidays when he thought we were about to call off negotiations altogether. And believe me, that was a close option. And he got the President last week to accept this sweeping agenda we brought back with us. But it's a little difficult, I think you would agree, to convince the President of the United States that his Vice-President, Secretary of Defense, and Joint Chiefs are conniving to bring us to the brink of war."

"Well, Barrett, do you believe the Soviets will flat-out reject this new proposal? If you do, why are we even going through the motions? It seems to me that puts us in a pretty hopeless situation."

"Frank, I pray the Soviets have enough sense to understand the situation and begin to bargain—for a change. As I see it, Makarov is no closer to making policy than I am. He's just here carrying out orders. Now I think he's got ties with a faction in the Politburo—how strong we don't know—that genuinely wants to make a deal. They've got serious economic problems—three straight crop failures, steel production is down, as well as oil export prices—and political problems—Kamenev is old and they'll have to go through a succession struggle once again soon. But, like us, they've got some tough guys who are spoiling for a showdown."

Arkwright leaned forward and motioned Connaughton to do likewise. "Phil Warrenton showed Emerson some very high level intelligence reports that suggest an enormous power struggle inside the Politburo along ideological lines. That's not unusual, but this could be the biggest fight of this sort since Stalin had Trotsky dispatched with the ice pick."

Connaughton gazed into the dying fire. "Barrett, is it possible the same kind of situation is going on in both camps? Is it possible they could be back here in Geneva buying time while their military gets ready for some confrontation?"

"I don't rule it out, Frank. Particularly if the Agency's information from the Politburo is true."

"Jesus," Connaughton breathed. He stared into the fire a long moment, then said, "Do you know about Cyclops, Barrett?"

"I know we have it and know what it does," Arkwright replied. His voice was low. "It's what we'll use as the last step before war. If the goddam thing works the way they say it will, it'll blind every important Soviet surveillance satellite within hours. If we get that far down the road, we might as well declare war." Arkwright studied his face as if to peer behind Connaughton's eyes. "That project is pretty closely held, Frank. Why are you asking about it?"

"Three days after New Year's, just after I came back from Montana, I got a strange call. The caller asked me to meet him under some pretty bizarre circumstances. It had to do with Cyclops. Four days ago, as you know, Harry Rafferty had an accident—smacked into by some kind of vehicle late at night in Washington. He was on his way to the same kind of meeting with someone I think was the same person who contacted me. Whoever contacted Harry said it had to do with Cyclops."

"My God, Frank, are you saying Harry may have been run over by someone on purpose? Who in God's name would want to do a thing like that, let alone take the risk of killing a United States senator?"

Connaughton said, "I have no proof Harry was hit on purpose. But you know how Thoreau defined circumstantial evidence...finding a trout in the milk. Someone is trying to tell us something and thinks it's pretty damn important. And if it has to do with Cyclops and it is important, there might be a lot of people who don't want that information known."

"Do you know who called you?" Arkwright's forehead was wrinkled and his eyes intense.

"No, I don't. I did meet with this person. But it was outdoors, very late at night. And I couldn't honestly tell you if it's a man or woman. Whoever it is, is scared to death, but very much wants the information out to me, Harry, or someone concerned about the arms race whom they can trust."

"Is it someone who knows what they're talking about?"

"I think so, Barrett. I believe this is someone highly placed in one of the intelligence agencies who may be risking loss of job, if not possible prosecution."

"Did you find out what it was about Cyclops that has this person so worried?" Arkwright asked insistently.

"Yes, Barrett. The informant says Cyclops has been launched."

"Holy God, Frank!" Arkwright sank back in his chair, stunned. "You can't be serious. I simply can't believe it. Emerson would have been consulted if we were going to take a step like that. And I am absolutely positive he doesn't have that kind of information."

"What does it mean, Barrett? I mean, if we've put that capability into space, what the hell's going on?"

"What it means," Arkwright said, "if it's true, is, at the very least, that some key people in our government have already decided these negotiations are going nowhere before they start. And, at the worst, it means we've taken a very serious—perhaps giant—step towards war."

Connaughton stood up and walked toward the fireplace. "Is there any chance these talks might work? What if the Soviets saw some benefits to our proposals and became a little more flexible themselves?"

Arkwright walked over to join him. "It's not out of the question. But it's a long shot. It's particularly tough with forces inside both our governments that want to scuttle any kind of concession or accommodation." He puffed furiously on his cigar for a moment. "It would take some kind of miracle. And I don't even know what that would be."

Connaughton thrust his hand out to say good night. "I don't know, Barrett. Maybe it just takes some people on both sides with some common sense." He turned for the door, Arkwright following. "But then, the way things have been going, common sense might seem like a miracle."

25

BY CUSTOM AT the beginning of each round of negotiations the Soviets and the Americans held a cocktail reception either at the Soviet Mission or the residence of the American Ambassador, for the delegations and their staffs. The reception in the evening of January 22 was at the residence of Ambassador and Mrs. Arkwright, scheduled for 7 P.M., and the Soviet delegation arrived promptly, as usual.

The residence was abloom with flowers. The canapés and hors d'oeuvres were avidly sought after by all guests, but particularly the Russians accustomed to less exotic fare. The residence itself had been leased from an old Geneva banking family and was located in the heights of the Cologny district near the spot where Lord Byron watched the sunset over the city and its harbor. It was a favorite of the Russians not merely for Evelyn Arkwright's cuisine, but because it offered one of the most dramatic views of Geneva. This winter night was crisp and clear and the lights of the city were brilliant against the night sky and reflected in the still lake.

Mikhail Makarov was enjoying himself grandly and set the tone for his comrades. His natural ebullience was being oiled by his second Black Label as he moved from group to group slapping Walt Quainton's shoulder, nudging Sidney Murray and whispering the latest Polish joke, embracing the Russian-speaker Charlie Curtis. All three winced imperceptibly. After greeting each American effusively and by name, Makarov made a point of hooking Arkwright's arm and leading him off to the study, where they would trade courtesies and perhaps informal but high-level messages.

Connaughton looked around the crowded room, having arrived a few minutes late from sending his first end-of-week summary cable to Washington. He took a breath, steeled himself, and swung into the diplomatic minuet. He exchanged polite greetings with the near-deaf old General Polyakov, the interpreter shouting to make contact. He shook hands with the deputy negotiator, Oleg Yurovov, and broke away briefly to thank Evelyn Arkwright for her hospitality both on that occasion and two nights previously. He felt a tap on his shoulder and turned to see the slightly inebriated grin of his counterpart, Lev Vronsky. They shook hands vigorously, slapped shoulders, and Vronsky delivered his patented wink. One more drink and he would be in the kitchen laying hands on the Arkwrights' young maids.

"How are you, my American cowboy friend?" Vronsky queried in his thickly accented English. "Did you shoot a lot of Indians on your visit to Moan-tahna? Or was it simply boof-a-loh? Did you stay up late to see old Saint Nik-o-lahs?"

Connaughton sighed. "No, Lev, I was a bad boy. I stayed up late and shot old Saint Nik-o-lahs. You know how it is out in Montana—things get kind of boring. Must be a lot like Siberia."

Connaughton leaned forward to whisper. "Speaking of which, I'm surprised you haven't ended up there if you chase the wives of some high Party officials the way you do these Swiss girls." Vronsky loved to be teased about his sexual prowess, Connaughton knew.

"Oh, my cowboy friend, you should try it zometime. It would do you good. Take your mind off all these horrible missiles and varheads." Vronsky stepped back dramatically. "Look at me. Do I look vorried? Of course not. Ack-too-ahly, I had vondervul vacation in Crimea with Ludmilla. Ah, Ludmilla. Zuch a . . . a plate." His hands traced curves meant to suggest voluptuousness.

"Dish, Lev. Dish."

"No, Frahnk, plate. Ludmilla is much bigger than deesh."

Vronsky's laugh made heads turn. And suddenly Connaughton saw Ekaterina Davydova standing with Evelyn Arkwright near the piano. He was stunned at how lovely she looked. Her black hair had grown longer and framed her ivory face. She wore a simple but stylish black cocktail dress, which set off her slender figure and soft, bare arms. Her gaze slowly swept the room, found his, and stopped still. He didn't breathe. She smiled slightly, looked down, then away.

As Vronsky pursued a canapé tray and its young blond bearer, Connaughton made his way around the edges of the room. He prayed that the ambassadors not reappear because he knew toasts would begin soon and the Soviets would depart shortly thereafter. He maneuvered around the piano until he was behind Ekaterina.

"Good evening, Miss Davydova, welcome back."

She turned, not entirely surprised. "How are you, Mr. Connaughton? I hope you had a pleasant visit home and happy holidays with your family."

Connaughton was always delighted to hear her speak English. Her voice was low and carefully modulated. She had just enough accent to seem mysterious and different. It was a highly cultivated voice that fit with her almost aristocratic bearing. Her eyes were green with light brown and gold flecks and were framed by lashes as dark as her hair.

Connaughton suddenly realized he had never had a real conversation with her in almost a year. "Actually, I spent most of my time in Washington. But I did have a chance to go to my home in Montana with my daughter."

Her eyebrows raised slightly. "Ah, you have a daughter. How lovely. What is her name, if I may ask?"

"Her name is Francesca. She's now fifteen years old."

"What a lovely name. And she must be a lovely young lady to match a name like that."

"Even if I do say so, I believe she is. She's managed to avoid most of her father's bad traits." Connaughton looked toward the study, fearing movement. There was none, yet. He plunged on. "And you. Were you with your family during the New Year's holiday?"

"Yes, thank you. My sons are with my parents in Leningrad, and we had a wonderful time together. But much too brief, I am afraid." A look of faint sadness crossed her face. Clearly, she was feeling the same homesickness for her children as Connaughton.

He suddenly wanted to spend the evening with her. It was an almost desperate longing. "And your sons. How old are they?"

"Ivan is ten and little Anton is eight. Anton is named for his grandfather. And it sounds as if your daughter is named for you?"

Connaughton was somehow surprised that she knew his first name. He smiled. "I'm afraid she has that burden. But her version is much prettier, I agree." He paused, desperate to continue the conversation and fearful someone might interrupt. He gestured toward a small window seat in a quiet corner away from the increasingly noisy cocktail chatter. He knew his time was limited. He wanted to take her into the adjoining room, but knew that would raise eyebrows among the KGB types. "What do your sons think of your position, particularly since it requires you to be away from them so much?"

"Oh, they have come to understand it is part of my work, being away. I must say, it was more difficult leaving them this time. But I promised them I would try to have them come down here after their school is out. If there is another round of talks this spring."

"Do you think there will be talks going on this spring?" Connaughton asked, then wished he hadn't. It sounded like the kind of incidental information each side tried to pick up from the other on such occasions. In fact, the intelligence services of both sides treasured these rare informal gatherings as unique opportunities to probe for tidbits, mood, and feeling.

"Well, I hope so, Mr. Connaughton. That is, unless we are able to reach some agreement before the spring."

He noted that she did not return the question, which he took to mean she did not feel obliged to pursue the vague testing. "Your sons, do they understand what you do—your job?"

"Definitely yes," she said. "They understand quite well I am a linguist and that I interpret for these very important negotiations about nuclear arms. They are also quite fascinated that I deal on a day-to-day basis with Americans like you. They think it is so interesting, one or the other of them may try it himself someday." She turned her steady green gaze on him. What lay behind those eyes? Was she as concerned and sympathetic as she seemed? "And your daughter. Does she have feelings about all this?"

Connaughton said quietly, "Yes, she does. Nuclear weapons frighten her a great deal. She understands the danger sometimes, I believe, almost too much. Certainly too much for someone her age. But that fear helps her understand why I do what I do and why it takes me away. She knows I have a very important job." He looked a long moment across Lake Geneva, then back to Ekaterina. "In olden times it was the job of a father to protect his children against all dangers. When my grandfather went to Montana almost a hundred years ago, that sometimes meant wild animals, bears and wildcats. I feel the same way about nuclear weapons. They're a threat to my daughter. Just as much as my grandfather thought those animals were to his children." He looked out the window again. "And that's why I'm here."

Ekaterina studied him a moment with bright eyes, as if a veil between them had been lifted, then said intensely, "I believe just as you do, Mr. Connaughton, that all of us here—particularly those of us with children—have a deep responsibility, but also a real opportunity. If we succeed, the true beneficiaries will be my sons and your daughter." She looked around the room and convinced herself they were not drawing any special attention. "My father is a veteran of the Leningrad Siege. He remained in our city throughout the terrible nine hundred days. He is a wonderful man who reminded me again during our holiday that I must do all that I can for my sons to see that they never have such a horrible experience or the even more horrible experience of nuclear war. That is also why I am here."

Connaughton longed to ask her more about herself and her family. He wanted to know about the father of her sons, whom she had not mentioned. But he was afraid he might drive her away if he became too personal. He suddenly realized how lonely he was for the closeness of a woman. Not any woman, but one like Ekaterina Davydova. "Do you get away from your work at all?" he asked. "Do you ever find time to tour Geneva or the surrounding areas?"

She replied, more lightheartedly now, "Of course. Some of the ladies from the mission and I occasionally visit the museums or form a group to have lunch or dinner in the beautiful villages of Switzerland. I must confess I usually spend too much money on clothes when we go to the shops, so I try not to do that too often." She laughed in a low, melodious tone. "My other indulgence is presents for my sons. I'm afraid they are very spoiled—is that what you say, spoiled?—by their mother and their grandparents."

Connaughton wanted to see if they looked like her. "I know exactly what you mean. I do the same thing with my daughter. Do you have a picture of your children?" He somehow knew the answer.

She blushed, unsure what to do. "Mr. Connaughton, that would be very self-indulgent on my part—to bore you with my pictures." She smiled, then reached for her purse. "But if you insist."

She withdrew a small wallet with several photographs. She opened it to facing pictures of two dark-haired boys standing next to a large statue. "This is Ivan, and the smaller one is Anton. He looks like his grandfather. So serious. He is also a musician."

"They are very handsome boys. They look a great deal like their mother." She blushed again, acknowledging the compliment. He reached for the wallet and their hands touched as she surrendered it. He looked at the half-dozen other pictures. There was a picture of Ekaterina together with her sons on a troika in winter. There were two pictures of an elderly couple, one before a great palace and the other before a large concert hall.

She smiled again and pointed to them. "This is my mother and father. Here they are at the Catherine Palace in Pushkin and there before the Kirov Theater in Leningrad where my father played for many years."

Connaughton thought he saw movement in the door of the study. "You said your father is a musician?"

"Yes, I am very proud of him. He was for many years first violinist in the Kirov Orchestra. He plays beautifully."

Connaughton said, "I hope I will hear him play sometime."

Her gaze was warm and steady as she took the wallet back. "I hope you have that opportunity as well."

Makarov and Arkwright emerged from the study smiling congenially and Connaughton and Ekaterina stood as everyone looked toward the two men with expectation. What they had to say now would set the mood of the negotiations the following week.

They walked past the couple near the window seat and stood beside the piano. "Ladies and gentlemen, and particularly our Soviet guests," Arkwright began. "Evelyn and I are pleased to welcome you once again to our home—at least our Swiss home. We all know there was a question when we last saw each other whether we would return here and take up our critical negotiations. The fact that we are back in Geneva, having a good time but ready to go to work next week, is a tribute to the goodwill and good intentions of both our great nations." There was enthusiastic applause. "On behalf of the American delegation let me toast the health of our Soviet guests, the success of our efforts, and peace in 1988."

All in the large hall drank then clapped heartily again.

"Mr. Ambassador, Mrs. Arkwright, ladies and gentlemen," Makarov responded. "No less than our American friends, those of us representing the Union of Soviet Socialist Republics in these history-making negotiations are happy to be together with you again." He spoke in Russian; Ekaterina had moved quietly behind the Soviet Ambassador's right shoulder and delivered his words in flawless English. "We come in the spirit of peace and friendship. The eyes of the world are now upon us and the hopes of the world rest with us. We must not fail." Applause once again. "I propose a toast to understanding, cooperation, and—like my friend Barrett—peace now." Glasses were lifted, followed again by enthusiastic applause.

A buzz of conversation broke out immediately as the Russians began to organize their departure. Connaughton could hear their cars coughing to life outside and moving slowly across the gravel drive to the door. Ekaterina moved toward him, hand extended.

"Mr. Connaughton, it was lovely to speak with you. I am sorry we have never had the opportunity before."

He took her hand, slightly awkwardly. "The pleasure was mine, Miss Davydova. I hope we have another opportunity soon." She started to turn and he said, "I hope your weekend is pleasant, I mean before we have to go back to work."

He felt the same way he had when he first asked a girl for a date in the sixth grade.

She smiled as the butler brought her coat. "I am afraid I am headed back into temptation. The temptation of spending money, I mean. I must find a present for my mother's birthday. Please have a pleasant weekend yourself." She smiled serenely over her shoulder as she went through the imposing doorway into the night.

26

IT WAS AN UNUSUALLY warm winter morning that following day, Saturday, as Connaughton strolled into the Place du Bourg-de-Four behind the cathedral and leaned against the stone retaining wall around the slender fountain spire. By midmorning residents of the old town had begun to bustle in pursuit of end-of-week business and weekend shopping, including preparation for sumptuous postworship Sunday brunches and dinners. Connaughton continued to marvel, as he had for the past year, at how the Swiss in general and Genevans in particular seemed to lack the capacity to idle. Temperature in the Place rose into the high forties as the sun appeared well above the roofs of the surrounding four- and five-story buildings housing businesses on the ground floors and residences on the upper floors.

Connaughton knew this very square had been an early wheat and cattle market, an earlier crossroads for routes to southern France, Italy, the Chablais, and throughout central Europe, and an even earlier Roman forum. He tried briefly to conjure up the countless generations of travelers whose steps had traversed this square. It was too much to contemplate. It made far-off Montana seem still untamed by comparison. The few trees in the Place were still winter-bare, unlike the evergreens of Montana.

Connaughton strolled up the winding cobbled streets to the Cathédrale de Saint-Pierre and down the same streets on the other side. He stopped at a small café on the Grand' Rue, the oldest street in the city, and joined a few hardy souls sitting outdoors in their coats at sunlit tables. He had two cups of strong black coffee and a croissant. He felt warmed and slightly more awake. It would be several more days until he adjusted to the six-time-zone difference from the United States.

After a few minutes he walked down a narrow, winding street to the new city and Geneva's main shopping area, bounded by the Rue du Rhône, the Rue du Marché, the Rue de la Croix-d'Or, and the Rue de Rive. Connaughton had nothing particular in mind. He enjoyed the winter air and enjoyed observing the determined Swiss going about their business. Except for some hurried Christmas shopping, he had not visited the shops for some time. His only errands were to pick up toiletry items and replenish his pantry for the coming week. But mixed among the banks and department stores there were always the antique shops and art galleries, which were pleasurable to visit.

There were classified briefing papers in his office across town that had to be read in preparation for the reopening of negotiations on Monday. That would take no more than two hours later that afternoon. Otherwise, he was alone and on his own for the first time in several weeks. As he strolled down the Rue Nueve-Molard, he planned an early dinner in his favorite restaurant and then an early movie. He could be back in his apartment by 10 P.M. and get a long night's sleep. If the weather continued to be pleasant he might even take the touring boat out on the lake for a short Sunday cruise.

Connaughton turned right for a block, then walked left along the Rue du Rhône to the Bon Génie department store. He made his way down the aisles crowded with heavy-coated shoppers carrying large bags of purchases, saying *"Excusez-moi"* as he occasionally bumped into a fellow shopper. He purchased shaving cream and a new razor, toothpaste and a new toothbrush. He then crossed the floor to the elevator and, after it disgorged its passengers, went to the fifth floor to see if the fine Swiss-made men's shirts were on sale.

As the elevator door opened, Connaughton stepped out squarely into the path of a tall distinguished figure in a fur hat. It was Ekaterina Davydova. They both stared, stunned. She spoke first. "Mr. Connaughton—what a surprise! Here you are."

"Ah, Miss Davydova. Ah, what a surprise." Connaughton stopped—confused for the moment. "You just said that, didn't you? How are you? What brings you here?"

Ekaterina smiled. "I have just bought this present for my mother's birthday. But I guess I told you about that last evening, didn't I?" They were blocking the elevator entrance and a small crowd had gathered. No one was muttering, but dark looks glowered.

Connaughton took her elbow and they moved a few steps away from the elevator. "This is a pleasant surprise...to see you so soon again. I enjoyed our discussion last evening very much. It was wonderful to see your sons' and your parents' pictures."

"The pleasure was mine, Mr. Connaughton." Ekaterina smiled again. "And I also enjoyed learning about your lovely daughter. Perhaps she might be able to join you here sometime. Is that possible?"

Connaughton hesitated. "Actually that's a wonderful idea. I frankly hadn't thought seriously about it. She hopes to come study here sometime during her schooling. If we do our work well here in the next few months, perhaps I'll be going back to the United States. If we're not successful in the next few months, I guess we'll all be returning home for good sometime this spring."

"I genuinely hope we will be successful, Mr. Connaughton," Ekaterina said. "It seems to me we have little choice. But, of course, we agreed on that last evening."

Connaughton had recaptured some composure. "Miss Davydova, I wonder if you would care to join me for lunch or at least for a cup of coffee. I would be very pleased if you could."

Now Ekaterina seemed taken aback. "Oh, Mr. Connaughton, how thoughtful. That is a lovely idea." She looked over her shoulder. It was the first time Connaughton thought of her as a Soviet citizen in an official capacity. It brought him back to some sense of reality. "You see, I am here with some other ladies from our mission. And we are preparing to return very shortly," she said. "Otherwise, your invitation would be very welcome. Perhaps sometime in the future that could be arranged." She said "arranged" as if she were referring to preparation for a summit meeting.

Connaughton suddenly was overcome by a sense of urgency, almost of desperation. "Miss Davydova, I would very much like to talk to you. I have a sense that we look upon our duties with much the same, ah, feeling of responsibility. I don't mean to be out of place...." He noticed she was beginning to seem tense. "And I certainly don't want to cause you difficulties. But we really ought to have a chance to continue our conversation sometime soon." He was now very aware that his suggestion—almost appeal—would probably begin to be seen as the opening move in an espionage recruitment. His only salvation was the amateurish way he was handling the seduction.

Ekaterina placed a hand on his arm, then quickly withdrew it, looking toward the elevator once again. "Mr. Connaughton, I must go. The others are waiting downstairs. They may become worried if I do not return soon. The situation is difficult; I know you will understand. Perhaps some way can be found. I will give it some thought. It would be enjoyable." She started away. "Thank you for your invitation."

"Miss Davydova," Connaughton said, stepping toward her. He had a smile on his face so that any observer would conclude these were old acquaintances having a pleasant conversation. "Miss Davydova, tomorrow between eleven o'clock and noon, I intend to visit the Russian Orthodox Church...the one located just off the Boulevard Helvétique. Do you know where it is?"

She nodded, her brow creased with concern.

"Please join me there. See if there is any way you can visit there at the same time. Will you do that?"

She was now headed for the elevator. As the door opened, just before she stepped in, she turned and nodded again. The door closed and the green arrow showed her slow descent to the Russians waiting below.

27

ANDREA CASS KNEW something was wrong. And she always trusted her instincts. Her ability to sense, to "feel" that something was going to happen—usually something unfortunate—had led her parents to think she was psychic and have her tested by psychologists at the local university. They found nothing, of course. What could they "find"?

But those instincts, plus a driving sense of a need to know and to tell, led her straight into a career in journalism. She felt at home. She was licensed to ask questions, to probe, to test, to inquire—but most of all to follow her instincts.

Right now, her instincts said something was wrong here in Geneva. All her colleagues in foreign reporting or diplomatic journalism were writing it straight. Arms control talks had resumed. The pre-Christmas flap had seemed serious but now was erased by resumed negotiations. Things were back on track. The same boring process was under way again, and very little was expected soon. But she didn't follow the group reading. The administration was still bitterly divided, with elections coming on. Whatever had been going on in Washington over the holidays with secret surveillance systems, mysterious launches, and ominous military preparations had not been canceled out by the individual decision by the superpowers to return to Geneva. Somewhere, something was going on.

She had called Ambassador Arkwright for an assessment and gotten predictable diplomatic verbiage. She confronted him with rumors of new Soviet missile systems and perhaps a new U.S. satellite capability. He, of course, denied knowledge of either. But she had thought his tone was too cautious—more cautious even than usual for him. Makarov also seemed increasingly strained and unwilling almost to acknowledge that the water in Lake Geneva was cold in winter. His ebullience seemed more forced than usual.

In the rare moments she took for herself, Cass sometimes wondered if she wasn't obsessive. As she sat in her small office in Geneva's business district, she tried with increasing frustration and without success to trace the source of her deep unease about the arms control story. It just wasn't right. Something else is going on here, she thought. What is it? Why can't I leave this alone? Either I'm going crazy or there's more going on here. But what's the key? What unlocks the mystery? Why does this situation not seem right?

She had to get better sources inside the American delegation. That was the only solution. Plus continue to work her sources back in Washington. Arkwright would only give out the State Department line. Charlie Curtis, his deputy, was occasionally good for a tidbit, but by and large wasn't much better. Quainton would only bluster about the Soviet threat and how large the new Russian missiles were. Sid Murray was a sphinx. Frank Connaughton...there was a possibility. He rarely talked to reporters, and when he did it was about the negotiating process in the abstract—how important it was, how difficult the world would be if there were no system for discussing limits on nuclear weapons. But he seemed a likable sort, and knowledgeable about the issues. He also was rumored to be close to Arkwright and therefore to Norton.

Cass speculated idly about Connaughton's personal life. From what little she had seen of him, he seemed to be an attractive man in a plain sort of way. Yet she knew he had no family with him in Geneva. She had checked. She always got all the details first. That meant he was single, which was unlikely, or that his family chose not to accompany him. Could be small children, she thought. How did someone like him get into a convoluted business like arms negotiations? Suddenly she smiled. That was the angle. She would call Connaughton for a profile. Perfect. Arms control negotiations just resuming. A lot of interest. Here's a toiler in the vineyard. An expert. An unknown professional who did this year in and year out. Could be an interesting fellow. And that would give her the hook, the reason to spend time with him, and she could get behind the scenes on these negotiations.

She then settled back to think. All the information she had gathered in Washington during December and early January—not totally denied by Arnold Danzig and others—underscored a deep division in the administration over arms control. Unlike similar struggles in previous administrations this one was not over personalities or even ideology. It seemed to involve the basic questions of the use of power. It seemed to have resulted with frustration over what President Kennedy called the "long twilight struggle" between the East and the West. Clearly some officials in Washington were losing or had lost patience and wanted to get to a final confrontation. It seemed to Cass, as she sorted through her confusion and vague trepidation, to have an almost apocalyptic quality to it.

She had felt the angry public demonstrations in early January to be symptomatic of a deepening sense of fear. For the first time since the nuclear era had dawned, people around the world had become skeptical about both the will and the intent of civilized governments to agree on limits for weapons of mass destruction. Once that sense of public confidence had eroded, it was difficult to imagine reestablishing it soon. Perhaps political leaders on both sides were merely reflecting this mood of doom. Perhaps for the first time the majority sentiment was to get it over with—to roll the dice and see what came up. Perhaps patience with this convoluted, obscure process that droned on and on in Geneva had simply been stretched to its limit and snapped.

Cass reflected as she looked out at the lake on past negotiations that had failed—and the wars that had inevitably followed.

28

CONNAUGHTON AWOKE SUDDENLY from a dream. His first thought was that he had overslept—that he was late for work or an appointment. Light was streaming into his bedroom through the single window whose drapes he had neglected to pull the night before. He looked at the bedside clock and saw that it was a quarter past nine. He lay back on the pillow and pulled up the bedcovers against the cold in the room. He felt physically exhausted and was perspiring at the nape of his neck, despite the cold. In his dream, still clear in his mind, he had been running—escaping. His pursuers were definitely authorities—responsible pursuers, not evildoers. He had most certainly been in the wrong. He had been running to avoid punishment, not escape attack. Less clear to him was what he had done wrong.

He rubbed his eyes to come awake and wondered if it had been the movie. He had gone to a theater to see one of his favorite films, *The Stunt Man*, where Peter O'Toole played God as a film director. There was a good deal of chasing in that, both in the film and in the film being made within the film. That had to be it. Or perhaps it was the *Torte mit Schlage* followed by brandy that he had enjoyed at L'Armoire restaurant near his apartment after the movie.

No matter, he thought, now awake. He got up, put on the worn robe given to him by Francesca three Christmases ago, and started a pot of coffee. He mixed the orange juice that never tasted quite the same as in the States while he waited for the coffee to drip. He poured some Swiss *Beucher-*

muesli into a bowl and retrieved the newspaper *La Suisse* from outside his door. He slowly chewed the thick cereal as he leafed through the paper. It had a front-page story about the resumption of arms control talks and the arrival of the two negotiating teams. The paper also carried a story about the reception at the Arkwrights' for the American and Russian teams, with a picture of Ambassador Arkwright greeting Ambassador Makarov at the door of the residence. Beaming, they shook hands.

The coffee finished and Connaughton poured a cup, pleased at its blackness and thickness, as he turned to the editorial and opinion page. The respected political columnist Werner Witschi held that the upcoming round of negotiations could be the most important in the three-decade search for arms limitations. He noted the strong ideological clash and the increasing tensions between the two sides, the dangerous unrest and physical violence in the capitals of the West, and the impending national elections in the United States, and concluded that a serious bargain had to be struck soon or "a new and possibly irretrievable escalation of weaponry into space" would occur.

Right you are, Werner, Connaughton thought as the coffee brought him awake with a shock. The rendezvous, he remembered. The impetuous invitation to Ekaterina Davydova to meet him at the Russian Church. He looked at his watch and realized he had an hour to get ready. He could walk to the church in ten minutes. He poured another coffee and sat back. What had he done? She obviously couldn't escape the Soviet Mission alone and without an explanation. He was assuming. But his assumption was based on security briefings that made it clear the members of the Soviet delegation, except for Makarov, had little latitude in their personal lives and scheduling. The Russians were paranoid about their personnel, but not without cause. There were, after all, occasional defections. And the Soviets, of course, knew of many instances where lone Soviet citizens, particularly Soviet officials, were recruited as agents for Western powers. The Soviets did the same thing. It was part of the game. Everyone's employees were fair game. Each side did the best it could. The Soviets went after Westerners and occasionally got one. The United States and its allies went after Communist bloc targets and occasionally got one. The difference was the Soviets had more control over their nationals, especially their government employees and officials, and set down strict rules about when and where and under what circumstances they could go out into what was perceived as the hostile world. They rarely, if ever, went out alone. The larger the group, the better. Itineraries were planned. Unscheduled stops and events were discouraged or even prohibited. Most important, almost all official delegations were composed of those with close family members and loved ones back in the USSR. Those ties were considered very important.

In any case, Connaughton now had to show up, even though the chances of Ekaterina's meeting him were almost non-existent. For her part, she had to believe she was being recruited, Connaughton thought. It was all happening too fast and almost by the book. Connaughton had been home for over a month. At the first reunion of the negotiating teams he sought her out and orchestrated a highly personal—almost intimate—conversation about children and families and the need for peace. Then immediately, the very next day, he arranged—with the help of a tracking CIA bird dog—to put himself in her path at the precise moment she was separated from her companions. Then he brazenly invited her to lunch or some private rendezvous, knowing that to be anathema to an employee of the Soviet government.

You must be out of your mind, Connaughton, he thought as he delivered himself a swift mental kick. She's over at the mission right now laughing it up with Makarov, that KGB lackey Metrinko, and the rest of their security people. Another clumsy American recruitment charade. It was going to be tough facing them all Tuesday at the first plenary session of this negotiating round. He knew they would all be grinning to themselves behind their fists at his amateur espionage theatrics. Worst of all, they would probably assume he was operating on his own to become some kind of hero back home with the big shots. How else to account for the crudeness of the approach? He groaned, rubbed his forehead, and almost felt himself blush at his own stupidity.

As he ran hot water into the ancient tub with its clawed feet, he decided he would skip it. Surely they would send someone from the KGB who would stand off fifty yards or so and take his picture entering the church and slinking out again. The Russians would get another round of laughs out of that. And the pictures would go into his files. Not that it mattered. He eased into the steaming tub and realized he had to go through with it. He was operating on instinct and his instinct told him someone had to begin to take some chances. There were too many people and too many interests—on both sides—who didn't want any kind of controls on nuclear weapons for this effort to succeed without some risks being taken.

Besides, the rumor that Cyclops had been launched had turned Connaughton's frustration into desperation. What had been a serious occupation now became obsession. Where once he had been troubled, now he was besieged and haunted. In seeking out Ekaterina Davydova, he had done what he instinctively felt that he should and there was nothing to be ashamed of. Better to have tried everything and be perceived a fool than to go to your grave, or atomized death, without exhausting all possibilities.

Following his bath Connaughton shaved, and as he dressed he remembered the highly classified briefing materials he had read in the bubble yesterday afternoon. The best intelligence estimates concluded that a power struggle in the Politburo had been won by the hard-liners and that the So-

viets were prepared to follow the collapse of negotiations
with a major military initiative, probably in space. There
had been a significant increase in missile flight tests since
New Year's. Two of the tests were of a new type of missile
not previously seen by the West, and its specifications had
been obscured by total encryption of all flight test data, in
violation of treaty commitments. This was the first time this
had been done and it had set off alarms in the American intelligence community. Secretary of State Norton had pro-
tested in a strong note to his Soviet counterpart. So far no
reply. Additionally, and ominously, the Soviets had
launched several new satellites from the top-secret facility at
Tyuratam. Their orbits and azimuths were identical to those
of killer satellites tested earlier by the Russians.

It was all very serious, Connaughton thought as he threw
his topcoat over his arm and locked the door of his apartment behind him. He wondered for the thousandth time
whether his job was making some kind of antiwar crank or
fear-driven, punchdrunk wacko out of him. He walked
downstairs into the Sunday morning sunlight and quickly
put on his dark glasses against the sudden glare. He looked
at his watch, which showed a few minutes before eleven, as
he started to cover the few blocks to the Russian Church. It
happened to some people in this game. The biggest chess
match in history eventually turned some negotiators into
Jeremiahs calling for repentance before the end of the
world. Or months and years of dealing with cold-eyed, in-
transigent Soviets made them Russophobes, hating everything about their adversaries and bringing them to the brink
of preemptive first-strike advocacy. Difficult to maintain
some balance, Connaughton thought as he turned down the
street. He had decided during his last days on the ranch in
Montana that this would be his last round in Geneva. He
could pursue the cause a while longer in Washington before
leaving government altogether. And he could be a nearer
father as Francesca finished school.

He heard the bells of the Russian Church from a block away, signaling the end of the morning mass. Lingering worshipers and tourists would be welcome for another hour before the great doors were closed for the day at noon. He walked into the small courtyard before the church as the handful of congregants were departing, pulling scarves over heads and buttoning coats against the winter morning breeze. He stopped and waited while the area cleared and looked about. No one, it seemed, had come that morning except those on spiritual business.

Connaughton walked slowly around the imposing structure, the sanctuary for Russian Orthodox faithful in Geneva, their numbers swollen in the aftermath of the Bolshevik Revolution and since dwindling as the devout died off and their heirs found little reason to maintain the faith. Connaughton entered the church and made his way to a chair on the right side in front of one of the imposing interior columns. He saw only a middle-aged priest extinguishing and removing the smoking candles, and what appeared to be an ancient church warden replacing prayer books in their racks.

"You look like a spy," a soft voice said, and he started. As he turned he suddenly remembered the dark glasses and clumsily removed them, only to see the partly hidden face of Ekaterina Davydova just behind him and to the right. She had been hidden by the stone pillar when he had come in. Her head was covered by a thick lace mantilla. Her pale face looked almost ethereal.

"My God, you're here," he whispered.

"I thought you asked me to be, Mr. Connaughton." Her smile was both enigmatic and amused.

"Well I did...but I somehow didn't think you would...you could...be here." He still spoke in a low voice, almost a whisper. "I woke up this morning and suddenly realized what you must have thought."

"I have thought all kinds of things, Mr. Connaughton," she whispered back. "But in the end I thought your motives were probably those of an honorable man—at least a well-intentioned man."

Connaughton stood up and moved around the corner of the pillar to the seat next to her. He shot a glance toward the back of the old church.

"I assure you, I came alone," she said.

"Do you mind if I ask how you did that?" Connaughton's voice was still low. "Yesterday, you seemed highly doubtful, to say the least, that you could accept my invitation. Now you seem to be very much at ease."

"It's quite simple, Mr. Connaughton. I informed the Ambassador of your invitation, as is our customary practice, and he assured me it would be all right if I were to join you." She studied her hands, folded as if in prayer, briefly. "That does not mean I am—what did you say?—at ease. I am not accustomed to meeting relatively strange men in dark places, even dark churches."

"In the States, Miss Davydova, we might even call this a date," Connaughton muttered. He saw her smile. "But since, with or without a chaperon, we're here under more or less official auspices, I guess we're obliged to consider this a business meeting." He studied her momentarily, suddenly irritated by the mantilla half-hiding her face. "Does the Ambassador require that you report back to him concerning this conversation?"

Ekaterina now turned her eyes fully toward his. "Please do not be cross..." She hesitated, and he thought she almost used his first name. "Without the Ambassador's approval, I would not be here at all. We are both in Geneva on official business that happens to be highly secret as well as of enormous importance. You should not be upset that I took the steps necessary to do what it seemed you were eager for me to do."

He dropped his glance. "I'm sorry. I was being unreasonable. Actually, I didn't think you would be able to come here, under any circumstances." He looked up at her again. "But I'm glad you did...however you did it."

"No apology is required," she said. And after a pause, "I am also glad that I came here."

They sat silently for a moment. Then Connaughton, looking at the distant altar, spoke. "Miss Davydova, I am about to break every rule I have been taught. And I do so for one simple reason—and that is that I am becoming a desperate man. They should not let desperate people into the business we're in. But they also shouldn't push reasonable people to the brink where they become desperate."

He was not looking at her, but he imagined she shifted slightly away. "Please don't be frightened. I just want to say what I've been wanting to say since Friday night...or maybe a long time before that. Something has to be done, and it has to be done soon. We're not getting anywhere and time is slipping away. It's not slipping away—it's flying out the window." His hand leaped forward like a launched rocket. She seemed to edge away again.

Finished with the candles, the Russian Orthodox priest glanced toward the couple talking quietly, intensely, at the darkened side of the small sanctuary. He then went to his post near the door, prepared to collect the one-Swiss-franc admission fee asked of any tourist or visitor who might wish to inspect the remarkable interior.

"Miss Davydova," Connaughton whispered, "I am not here representing the CIA."

"Who are you representing, Mr. Connaughton?"

Connaughton looked out the iconographic window a moment. "Myself, I guess. I hadn't really thought about it."

"Perhaps you should...before you go further," she said.

Connaughton leaned very close again and the intensity of his gaze and voice seemed to plead for credibility. "Believe me, no one sent me. This is not a recruitment. It's an

idea . . . probably a crazy idea . . . that's been forming in my
mind since I got back to Geneva. Some way must be found
to prevent these negotiations from failing. You and I both
know that there isn't going to be another chance. All you
have to do is read the newspapers to know there are people
on both sides itching for a chance to freeze the Soviet-
American relationship as solid as the Neva in January and
bring about a showdown once and for all. I can think of
only one way to get a treaty that will prevent that showdown,'' he continued. ''We have to exchange information.''

A long moment of silence ticked away. ''Mr. Connaughton, that is the most outrageous suggestion I have ever
heard. It is totally unacceptable. It is . . . treason.'' She looked
pale and slightly desperate as she gazed straight ahead. She
shifted her feet under her, as if preparing to bolt. ''I refuse
to accept that as a serious suggestion.''

Connaughton heard a chair scrape behind him as the
priest moved from behind his small table. He glanced at his
watch. It was 11:45. The church closed at noon. ''Look,''
he said, ''this is not a trap and it is not a recruitment. But it
is a serious proposal . . . probably the most serious I've ever
made in my life. You have to at least think about it. You
don't have any choice.''

The priest could be heard pacing behind them. Ekaterina
suddenly stood up and started across the intimate sanctuary, avoiding the small platform in the center of the church.
Connaughton, startled, slowly followed her. Her tall form
in its winter cloak seemed stately but tense. He wondered
fleetingly if she might not have been, given a different turn
of history, a countess or even a czarina. She paused before
an ancient icon enclosed in glass and studied it as might a
well-trained student of ecclesiastical history. He stood beside her.

"We all have a choice, Mr. Connaughton." Her whisper could barely be heard. "The choices for some are more limited than for others."

"I'm not talking about political choices," he murmured. "I'm talking about human choices. If people like you and me treat this as just another diplomatic exercise, with little consequence of failure, then we're not doing our duty to our children...and everyone else's children. We simply *can't...let...this...fail*." His voice seemed to hiss in the silence.

The priest carried his small coin box to an office hidden behind the high altar, and Ekaterina turned for the large door at the rear of the sanctuary. Once again, Connaughton followed a step behind.

She stopped just inside the door. "Mr. Connaughton, how could it possibly work? We would both be followed. We would both be suspect. How do I know whether I even have information of use to you? I'm just an interpreter. It is a completely ridiculous notion."

Connaughton spoke softly but quickly. "Miss Davydova, you must have attended most of the planning sessions of your delegation, if nothing else to learn the jargon. You're smart...you would have heard and listened. You know these negotiations have been deadlocked over numbers...how many missiles and warheads and what types we have versus how many you have. Deployment plans for new systems. Locations. Reliability of satellites and other verification systems. I believe this information, once authenticated, would show that neither side has a decisive advantage over the other...if we stop now. But I also believe we're both poised to break out with some new weapons and counter-weapons that will make any controls impossible in the future. And there are those on both sides who want exactly that. You know it and I know it. If my side had an authentic notion of any possible breakthroughs—new weapons coming on—and if your side had the same, then we might have the confidence to negotiate real controls and limits. We could arrange the exchanges—and it would probably take several—with the full knowledge of our superiors and security services. You tell Makarov I've become a total peacenik and want nothing more than for you to have all this information. And I'll do the same with Arkwright. They can't say no. It would be like rejecting a gold mine.''

He paused, almost out of breath, afraid he might have overwhelmed her. She looked at him, then out the open door, then down. "I must think about this—at least a few days." Then after a moment she said, "We will be found out, you know. They will eventually discover the complicated deception... what do you call it, the double cross. They will catch up with us sooner or later."

He wanted desperately to lie, but couldn't. "I hope not. If we're clever enough, they needn't. It isn't inevitable." He paused. "We may get a treaty first. That's what counts."

"Is it, Mr. Connaughton? Is it worth being shot as a traitor? That's what they do in my country, you know."

"It is not treason, Ekat... Miss Davydova. That is unless those in both our governments who want this treaty are traitors also."

She looked suddenly older, in her eyes, he thought. "But now is not the time to debate complex theories of citizenship, duty, and morality, is it, Mr. Connaughton? Perhaps during what you have already called our 'exchanges,'" she said.

They heard the door to the priest's office open and close. She said, "If Ambassador Makarov approves, shall we have lunch on Wednesday at the Restaurant Trois Mousquetaires in Chambesy just off the Lausanne highway? If it is approved, I will be there at one-thirty. And I will give you my answer then. There is a small room upstairs. Do you know the place?"

Connaughton nodded, overtaken by a sudden chill down his spine. The implications of the machinery now set in motion suddenly descended on him and terrified him. He reached out to say something, perhaps to qualify or condition his own preposterous proposal, but she was already out the great door and walking down the few steps leading down from the church. He pondered her choice of meeting places and wondered whether the third musketeer would be visible nearby or simply be a tiny transmitter in her purse.

29

THE OFFICIAL LIMOUSINE, curtains tightly drawn, wheeled through the gates of the monumental Spassky Tower of the Kremlin as the chimes of the Kremlin clock, the Big Ben of Moscow, tolled 6:45 with its "quarter bells." The sun had long since set and the stately honor guards warned winter tourists away from the speeding limousine's path with batons and whistles.

The car bore to the right out of Red Square. The lone occupant was too preoccupied with official papers to take note of the brilliantly illuminated Cathedral of St. Basil the Blessed on the left. Gathering speed the heavy car swung onto the elevated stone arch of the Moskvoretsky bridge over the Moskva River, the southern boundary of the Kremlin. The icy crust along the river's banks reflected a thousand lights from the massive Rossiya Hotel a hundred yards to the east.

The lone figure in the car's backseat, Vladimir Zhdanov, rarely looked up as the car passed factories and housing projects, then swayed onto the Kashira Highway, one of the oldest southbound roads in Moscow. Soon trees were clustering along the snowy roadside, and through them he could see the lights of Kolomenskoye—first a thirteenth-century village, then the "Czar's village" in the sixteenth and seventeenth centuries, and now a gorgeous museum reserve. In previous days, Zhdanov had often come to view the tent-shaped stone spire of the Church of the Ascension, called by the French composer Hector Berlioz "the beauty of perfection." Its striking whiteness was accentuated in the early night by the illuminated structures of the church and bell tower of St. George the Victorious on the left and the Water Tower on the right. Set nearer the broad highway were the Church of the Beheading of John the Baptist, the architectural prototype of the Cathedral of St. Basil on Red Square, and the seventeenth-century wooden cottage of Peter the Great transported from Archangel. Zhdanov visited Kolomenskoye, his favorite retreat, often after ordinary visitors' hours. Seeing his powerful passenger gaze out the window, the driver slowed, thinking perhaps to turn in. But Zhdanov tapped on the glass partition behind the driver's head and waved him on.

The car once again gained speed and passed the All-Union Cancer Research Center, the largest in the world. Zhdanov pulled the curtain again. He had spent too much time in recent months visiting the VIP section of the giant complex to want to see it again. Shortly after the car whisked past the Outer Ring Road surrounding Moscow, Zhdanov, out of custom and reverence, glanced up to see the village near Gorki and the heavily wooded area where Lenin had spent his last days.

If Lenin's revolution was finally to succeed, then the next few weeks would be crucial, and the next few hours could determine the outcome of those weeks. Vladimir Zhdanov felt real excitement for the first time in many years. This mission and the role he was to play might prove to be critical to the future of the Soviet Union. This was the meaning of his life. This was the purpose for his existence. Well beyond Moscow's lights, the night was black. Only an occasional heavy truck competed with the speeding limousine on its course through the countryside.

The car followed the Kashira Highway for almost twenty miles, then slowed and turned left at an otherwise unmarked side road. The driver was now following directions given by his passenger. He had been Zhdanov's driver for many years. If asked later, even by the KGB, he would swear this trip had never occurred. Though there was little chance that anyone in the KGB, except perhaps some ignorant underling, would inquire about the events of this particular evening. The total blackness of the tree-lined country road was pierced by the headlights of the heavy car as it wound its way for three miles through the early February snow, now heavier than in the city. The road had been plowed more recently than others in the area—a sure sign of a prestigious owner at the end of the lane.

The road ran perpendicularly into another, narrower road and, at Zhdanov's instruction, the driver turned right. After a hundred yards the cumbersome vehicle lumbered across a heavy timbered bridge, which rattled under the weight. Lights could be seen as the car then rounded a grove of leafless poplar trees and pulled up at the steps of a large rustic house. An elderly man emerged, crept down the steps, and opened Zhdanov's door, muttering, "Good evening, comrade." Zhdanov followed the old man up the steps, down a long porch, and into the main door, as his driver pulled the limousine out of sight behind the house.

"Well, Vlad, what a welcome sight." A man of medium height and weight turned from throwing a huge log into a rock fireplace. He was about sixty with receding gray hair, and totally unremarkable except for a small irregular birthmark on his left temple. He was the Deputy Director of the KGB and his name was Lev Malenkov.

Characteristically, Zhdanov had no time for sociability. He threw off his thick coat and fur hat with the help of the ancient servant, who disappeared with them. "Lev, the cables from Geneva show amiability and light on all sides. I suppose that has to be done in diplomatic circles. But the key is that that fool Makarov not think he is there for some serious purpose. We mustn't let him think his mission is genuine. Otherwise before we know it he could have come up with some kind of basis for an agreement. I want to make sure we all know what is going on here."

Malenkov smiled grimly. He had known Zhdanov for thirty years and, even while granting the older man's seniority, treated him as an equal. "Vlad, as much as I enjoy your company, you needn't have driven all the way out here on a cold night to fret about something that isn't going to happen. Makarov is not so much of a fool that he will go off on his own. And his boss, Zoshchenko, knows that the power—and the future—are with Red Star." Malenkov smiled again. "And we all know that Zoshchenko has his eye clearly on the future. He will not let the Foreign Ministry stray from our policy on this matter." He paused and gazed at the fire. "Besides, our sources say the Americans are not much more anxious for a treaty than we are. Apparently Burgoon and his hard-liners will not be moved by public opinion, at home or among the NATO allies. Don't worry about Makarov. Young Metrinko is there to watch and he reports directly to me. Makarov just wants to get these negotiations over and retire somewhere other than the Gulag." Malenkov issued a hard chuckle.

The old servant came in with the thick black tea Zhdanov favored, then scuttled out without a word. Zhdanov said, "Makarov is not why I'm here. Red Star is scheduled for the spring—April—and we must clear away all obstacles. If the exercises are delayed, the entire policy could unwind. It could unravel like one of those cheap sweaters GUM is now bringing in from Poland." Malenkov's steely chuckle rattled again, surprising Zhdanov, who was never intentionally humorous. "In all seriousness, Kozlovsky must not be permitted to sabotage these maneuvers. You are the key, Lev, to guaranteeing that the Defense Ministry, bottom to top, carries forward the Politburo's policy."

Malenkov stood nearer the fire as the winter chill deepened around the handsome log dacha. He shrugged elaborately. "Now Vlad, I may be able to, shall we say, monitor

Georgi's actions and remarks, but we would be asking for a monumental fracas if KGB tried to take over the Defense Ministry. You know how long we've struggled with those damned thick-headed generals and their damned independent ways. Let's not start one of those internal revolutionary wars. It'll just end up with a lot of people on both sides getting retired or sent off.''

Zhdanov, who had ''sent off'' his share of dissidents and crucified infighters, wasn't moved by the argument. ''Don't obscure the point, Lev.'' The older man's hollow, emotionless voice made the large room echo like a tomb. ''You don't have to take over the Defense Ministry to let Kozlovsky know his behavior is being observed. He's a tough fellow. But he is not so tough as to ignore the implications of the KGB quietly but surely looking over his shoulder, and perhaps 'safeguarding' his family.'' Zhdanov now shrugged. ''So what if the word gets around the general staff? Most of those old strutters care more about their beloved pensions than they do about Kozlovsky anyway.'' Zhdanov rose with some difficulty and walked nearer Malenkov. ''I want to put the fear of God in Kozlovsky and the military. I don't want one of those bastards to be less than one hundred percent committed to the program. These are not ordinary times and, by God, we are not going to permit ordinary behavior.'' Zhdanov's breath hissed out as if to match the whisper of the arctic wind outside.

Malenkov had seen about all there was to see of the human spirit under physical and mental stress. Very little moved him anymore. But Zhdanov in his role as a wrathful and vindictive prophet raised the small hairs on the back of his neck. Zhdanov was the only person in the world who still frightened him.

Malenkov's attempt at a smile didn't work. His earlier air of comradeship slipped quietly away. ''We can certainly increase our attention to Comrade Kozlovsky, and perhaps his family as well. It will, of course, require some of our most sophisticated people. A number of them are already in place in the Defense Ministry—one or two close to the Minister himself. If attention is drawn, it can be explained as concern for stability of the government in case anything should happen to our beloved General Secretary. His precarious condition is well known to all of us. Additionally, it is legitimate for the KGB to have increased concern over the success of the impending Red Star exercises. No one can quarrel with that."

"Goddammit, Lev, you can sound like the worst kind of bureaucrat sometimes. You don't have to justify this. The only justification you need is the security of the state and the success of the socialist revolution." Zhdanov noticed Malenkov shift almost imperceptibly away. "Why is it," Zhdanov hissed almost in a rage, "even those like you who've done the best under this system suddenly start getting uneasy when anyone mentions the socialist revolution or Lenin himself? Has everyone now gotten so sophisticated they don't like to be reminded what our goal is or the purpose of our undertaking?" Zhdanov threw up his arms in disgust and stalked away from the fire. "There is no fire, no intensity, no sense of urgency anymore. The leadership of this country," he said as he wheeled on Malenkov, "is no better than the corrupt goddam Americans. Everyone has his dacha and his car and his Crimean vacation, and who gives a damn about the struggle with capitalism?"

Zhdanov pointed a spectral finger at Malenkov. "Let me tell you this. You are going to watch Kozlovsky and you are going to let him know you are watching him right up until the troops begin to move under Red Star. And you are going to tell me if he or anyone else in the Defense Ministry so much as lifts a finger to undermine the policy. We'll hang one or two of the bastards who have forgotten what this revolution is about and then we'll see how everyone responds to that."

Malenkov had seen Zhdanov in this mood before and in each case it had resulted in executions, in some cases unjustified but always involving very high level officials. Given a choice between confrontation and cooperation, Malenkov hardly hesitated. "Vlad, of course we'll do as you suggest. Just so we're all prepared for a face-off with Georgi. And for myself, let me assure you I have not given my life to state security without remembering every day the reason for it and the constant desire of the forces of reaction to humiliate and defeat the Soviet Union. The KGB is totally behind Red Star and the necessity to confront imperialistic forces. We will not waver, rest assured."

"Well then," Zhdanov said, less angrily but no less intensely, "there are other tasks that will enable you to demonstrate your obvious conviction. We must have a thorough review of the loyalty of the senior commanders of the Rocket Forces. We must assume that Red Star will lead to confrontation, and confrontation will lead to conflict. If conflict occurs, we must be prepared to use every resource, including our strategic missiles, to gain our objective. Every commander must be prepared to fire when ordered by the central authority without question or hesitation. No humiliating back-down like in '62 in Cuba. I want you to examine thoroughly every commander who must respond to the launch order and give me a complete report on each. I want the KGB's guarantee that they all will launch on command."

"How do you see the Red Star exercises unfolding?" Malenkov asked, seeking to avoid response to Zhdanov's sweeping order.

Zhdanov essayed a thin smile. "Since you raise no objection to the last request, let us assume it will be done forthwith." Arms folded, the older man slowly, stiffly returned to the fire. "The Geneva talks will exhaust themselves sometime in April. Red Star is scheduled to begin on or about April fifteenth. We will issue through diplomatic channels the customary notice of major military maneuvers in Europe and elsewhere and, of course, deliberately understate their scope and purpose. Unlike previous Warsaw Pact exercises of this sort, we will also bring our nuclear forces to higher degrees of alert—again with some minimal notice to the West. The two events will concern them and, after some delay, there will be an expression of concern. Too late. By that time the better part of our fleet will be at sea in four oceans and the bulk of our land forces will be deployed to make a lightning strike into Central Europe. Our strategic forces will by then be in a position to achieve combat status in a matter of minutes. Finally, and this is the key, we will quickly launch three additional high-altitude orbiters to join the two in place and thus possess an ability to destroy the American satellites that monitor our land-based missile launches and track our fleet movements. Those strikes will be made simultaneously with a set of demands by our government that substantially alter the balance of power in Europe and remove the United States as a major world power in that region.''

Malenkov had thought himself completely familiar with the Red Star plan, but was now dumbfounded to learn of the antisatellite strikes and the scope of the planned Soviet demands on the United States. ''Exactly what do we expect the Americans to do in response to these demands?''

Zhdanov's eyes now glistened as they gazed through a window into the distant fir trees outside Malenkov's dacha. ''They will be taken by surprise. They have no idea of the sophistication of our antisatellite program; when we confront them with carefully deployed conventional forces and highly alert nuclear forces, and then we put out their eyes, they will be as helpless as Samson blinded and weakened. There will be bluster and threats on their part and we must be prepared to weather a few days of serious threats of our destruction. But in the end, with no ability to see where we are or what steps we are prepared to take, they will not risk the destruction of Europe, let alone the United States, when there is a much more reasonable alternative. We simply want them out of Europe. We want them to accept that we are the dominant military and political power on the Continent, as destiny always knew must ultimately happen. American politicians will be able to imagine all sorts of arguments as to why this really makes good sense from their point of view. They have been there for over half a century since the last war. It is draining their budget and weakening their position in other parts of the world, and it is finally time for the Western Europeans to look after themselves.'' Zhdanov smiled again, almost to himself. "So you see, my friend, we are really doing them a favor.''

Malenkov was horrified to hear a hacking laugh emanate from the old man's cadaverous frame. It was the first time he could ever remember Zhdanov laughing. To cover his surprise he joined in with his metallic chuckle. But he did not feel amusement. Instead he felt fear, a fear well beyond the normal paranoia rampant in the highest levels of the Politburo and Central Committee. He thought Zhdanov increasingly mad and marveled at the skill and patience with which the monomaniacal ideologue had maneuvered virtually the entire Soviet government around to the policy of converting the routine Red Star exercise into the most serious confrontation between the East and the West in the history of the cold war. He had done it because of mounting frustration with the ineffective arms negotiations. He knew the leadership was looking for a way to unite the Russian people behind a patriotic, nationalistic challenge to justify continuing sacrifice and mask domestic economic shortcomings in the system. Zhdanov had capitalized on Secretary Kamenev's failing health and unsteady leadership, inserting his own stark vision into the national void. He had understood brilliantly how thin had grown the tolerance on both sides of the Atlantic for the stress created by the ambiguity and tension of more than forty years of cold war.

And most of all he used fear—fear that a member of the Politburo might be thought weak if he refused to stare the Americans down, fear that one's position on Red Star would be the standard for judging qualification for national leadership, and fear that he, Zhdanov, would get even.

These were the fears now boring like worms inside Malenkov's soul. And with fear came hope, hope for reward. If he supported Zhdanov on Red Star, he could become head of the KGB after Kamenev died. If he kept Makarov in line, that would be a gold star on his record. If he vetted the strategic commanders, he would know who could and could not be trusted, and therefore would be a powerful person to know. And if he intimidated Kozlovsky, he would have achieved the enormous coup of having controlled the Defense Ministry on an issue of historic significance. If he did *not* do these things, he would face Zhdanov's implacable hatred.

"This has been a most interesting evening, Comrade Vlad. Can I now get you some dinner or perhaps a scotch?" Malenkov sounded solicitous.

Zhdanov read him as obsequious and put the evening down as a total success. "Thank you, no, Lev. I must get back into town. Much to do this evening. Tell me, how is that son of yours doing, the one who's working for the Central Committee?"

Malenkov had spent much political capital getting an incompetent and worthless son a middle-level post in the Party apparatus. He had used the position, Zhdanov and others knew, to become a first-class smuggler and black marketeer. He was constantly on thin ice. One prosecution and he would serve a long sentence in an unpleasant prison.

"How nice of you to ask, Vlad. He's doing quite well. Just married and soon I will be a grandfather." Malenkov's forehead wrinkled involuntarily as his mouth smiled.

"Good. Good. Such a nice young man. I hope, for your sake, he does well. Please say that I asked after him and say that I will continue to keep my eye on him." Zhdanov took his heavy coat and fur hat from the ancient servant and started for his waiting car. "You will do that for me, won't you, Lev?"

30

SENATOR HARRY RAFFERTY felt like a fool. He had gotten flattened, and almost killed, by a truck on his way to an idiotic late-night rendezvous with some ridiculous informant who probably did not even exist. And he had gotten off easy on that one because the reporters chose to believe he was responding to nature's call. Now his colleagues in the Senate were beginning to believe he was some kind of crackpot on the arms control issue. He was constantly offering resolutions on the floor of the Senate urging support for the negotiations in Geneva and trying to put the Senate on record as demanding that the administration not take any steps that would impede successful negotiation of a treaty.

His latest foray into the diplomatic-military thicket had been to offer an amendment to the pending military authorization bill that would prohibit the expenditure of any funds for the testing or deployment of any antisatellite weapons while the Geneva negotiations were under way. That had set off alarm bells all over Washington. He had not notified the Armed Services Committee Chairman, Senator Bart Shorter, or the Majority Leader, Richard Bond, of his intention to offer the amendment. He merely obtained recognition from the chair and introduced the measure. Parliamentary hell broke loose. Shorter objected that this matter jeopardized national security and tied the Defense Department's hands at a crucial period when the Soviets were going forward with such tests. Bond came roaring onto the Senate floor crying foul play, that this was a matter of crucial interest to the administration as Senator Rafferty well knew, and that a sneak attack like this was beneath the dignity of any senator who claimed to care about national security. Rafferty placidly listened as the two raved on, soon joined by other defenders of the administration's position, all of whom suggested one way or the other that the United States Senate had no business inserting itself into anything as exotic and important as anti-satellite weapons.

Rafferty had been in the Senate long enough to know when a nerve had been struck. Bond's appearance and the hue and cry raised by the President's party meant signals had immediately gone out from the White House to defeat the amendment and prevent any serious debate on its merits. The clincher was when Majority Leader Bond announced he would lead a filibuster against the amendment and prevent it from being voted on for as long as it took. Rafferty returned whimsy for outrage, suggesting that all this firepower was not mounted against just every innocent amendment such as his. Something bigger must be at stake here. Reporters began to filter into the gallery when the fireworks started and came in larger numbers to hear the response to Rafferty's speculation.

No explanation was given. Bond and Shorter simply declared that there would be no more votes that day, or any future day, so long as Rafferty's amendment was the pending business and, further, that the merits of the amendment would not be debated in open session. They asserted that too much highly classified information was at stake and that an extremely rare closed session of the Senate would be required to discuss even preliminarily the subject of anti-satellite weaponry. They suggested still further that their distinguished colleague from Montana was grandstanding and headline grabbing, since, as a member of the Senate Intelligence Committee, he knew full well these matters were extremely secret. And he was privileged to debate the merits and timing of any antisatellite research the United States was conducting in the Intelligence Committee if he was serious about protecting the nation's security.

This hubbub was all Rafferty needed to confirm that this was an extremely sensitive issue . . . one that someone very high up wanted buried. Perhaps the strange informant who had lured him to Montrose Park was serious after all. Rafferty concluded there was a direct relationship between his controversial amendment to limit antisatellite capability and Cyclops itself. His strategy of smoking out the opposition seemed to have worked. As he sat in his office later that day putting the pieces together, he pondered his next move. He had to have proof that Cyclops had been launched and that its deployment had something to do with the grander scheme. Who in the administration was in on the deal and why? What could they expect to achieve by risking all-out war?

Rafferty didn't expect to get much out of the CIA. He had managed to alienate Warrenton long ago with his skeptical questioning in the Intelligence Committee. He seriously doubted that any of his Senate colleagues really knew what was going on with Cyclops, especially if it was a closely held operation. How many people might know about it? he pondered. It would be virtually impossible to deploy a major new weapon system without Secretary of Defense Sternberg knowing about it. Besides, Rafferty thought, Cyclops was Joe Sternberg's kind of action. Another player would have to be General King, Chief of Staff of the Air Force. His service had performed the research and designed the weapon, Rafferty knew from the Intelligence Committee. A lot of people knew that much. The Air Force's "black" operation, the National Reconnaissance Office, would have carried out the engineering, testing, and procurement with one or more defense contractors—undoubtedly on the west coast. If Cyclops had indeed been launched, it almost surely was from Vandenberg in California sometime in the past few weeks, under King's direction if not supervision.

All right, then, Sternberg and King were the key players. Rafferty would get nowhere with them. But some handful of people had to be in on the actual launch and had to have known what they were launching. There was no way Rafferty would get that information out of the Pentagon. Why not approach it from the other end? Rafferty reached for the phone and asked his secretary and administrative assistant to come into his office.

Within an hour Rafferty had scheduled a trip to the west coast. The Senate would be out of session for a week for Washington's and Lincoln's birthdays. He had planned to spend most of the week in Montana, but now had his staff schedule speeches over both weekends, leaving him the five days in between to spend at Vandenberg and with two or three of the key satellite contractors in southern California and Silicon Valley.

THE OFFICIALS OF THE Datasync Corporation could not have been more cordial. Senator Harry Rafferty was known throughout the military-industrial complex as a Pentagon critic, but he came from a Western "pro-defense" state and had a reputation for reasonableness and willingness to listen and learn. Because of this reputation and his position on the important Intelligence Committee, his last-minute visit was greeted by the president of Datasync's Western Division and the vice-president for governmental affairs of the giant defense conglomerate. Rafferty's staff had stressed his interest in antisatellite research and development, but he was subjected to an endless briefing on all programs under way at the Western Division before he got to his subject of interest.

From a review of the files and briefing by the Intelligence Committee staff, Rafferty knew Datasync to be the prime contractor on the Cyclops project. And his patience was finally rewarded with a slide briefing on Cyclops by the project manager, Dr. Ernest Pytell. Pytell described how Cyclops was designed to operate at high orbit, roughly twenty-three thousand miles above earth, how it was maneuverable within the range of that orbit, and how for the first time in the antisatellite program it permitted the United States to intercept and destroy at least half a dozen opposing satellites within the space of a few hours. Carefully avoiding the questions of when and why such a capability might be used, Rafferty asked: How many high-orbit surveillance satellites do the Soviets have deployed? Probably no more than six of real importance. Can Cyclops blind them all? With a reasonably high degree of probability? Why not absolutely? Because you do not know absolutely about any new technology until you try it and Cyclops hasn't been tried yet, except in limited low-orbit tests. How would Cyclops disable a satellite? Essentially by means of "tin cans" or "smart rocks"—nonexplosive objects placed in a satellite's orbit on a collision course, or projectiles that seek the energy source of the satellite. Don't you have to blow the satellite up? No. All you have to do to disable it is bang into it sharply. Won't the Soviets know we're the culprits? If only one or two of their satellites go down near the same time, probably not. That would be chalked up to damn bad luck. If all the main ones go down about the same time, that's pretty good evidence the other side is up to something naughty.

Is that an act of war—using Cyclops—Rafferty asked? Oh, Senator, Dr. Pytell said after a long sip of lukewarm coffee, you're asking the wrong man. If I were Kamenev or Kozlovsky I sure would think so. But we don't make policy around here. We just bid on projects, do designs and research, and build what the Defense Department asks us to. You better take that kind of question up with Secretary Sternberg or General King or the President himself. Pytell interrupted this line of questions by quickly suggesting a tour of the plant.

Accompanied by the corporate executives attending solicitously, by Dr. Pytell, and by one of the project engineers, Dr. Arlette Gwynn, Rafferty walked from the plant offices to the giant development complex. The group passed through two security checkpoints. Each time they submitted sensitized badges to a scanning machine and had badge pictures compared with their actual features. Rafferty displayed a high-classification visitor's badge, showed his Senate ID, and was vouched for by his escorts. Once in the engineering facility, the entire group donned sanitized white coveralls, specially treated white shoe covers, and clear protective goggles. Pytell then led them through a third security checkpoint and on to the production floor.

Although Rafferty had been through a similar routine several times before, he was staggered anew. Adjoining buildings housed missile production, radar development, supersophisticated avionics, and cruise-missile development facilities. The immense cavern they were in was solely dedicated to satellite production. Pytell indicated with a wide gesture the area where surveillance satellites were under construction. They walked to the rear of the building, to an area segregated by sheer white material extending from ceiling to floor. Once inside Rafferty saw the center of the area to be occupied by two large cylinders, approximately twenty feet high and eight to ten feet in diameter. Each was surrounded by a delicate scaffold with three levels. On each level were half a dozen workers dressed like heart surgeons. They wore closed coveralls buttoned at the neck, in several pastel colors. Rafferty asked and was told each color represented a different task. Each wore goggles, a respiratory mask, a tight cap matching the coveralls in color, and what appeared to be sheer linen gloves. No one seemed to notice or care about the visiting party.

Pytell explained to Rafferty that these were Cyclops antisatellite satellites. With gestures he pointed out thruster jets at the bottom and on the sides of the cylinders. He indicated internal fuel bottles for the thrusters and "rock" launchers visible where external panels were yet to be placed. Nearby he pointed out collapsed solar-power collectors that would deploy into large screens, and a similar folded apparatus like a large umbrella that would open to receive orders from earth once the entire behemoth was in orbit. These, he said, were two Cyclops weapons.

Rafferty thought them monsters. They were huge. A layman, he marveled at the size and thrust of the rockets necessary to carry them thousands of miles above the earth. He was staggered by their sophistication and complexity. Math and science had never been his strong suit. What he beheld was practically beyond his imagination. After he asked a series of questions meant to explore the technical mysteries of these space phenomena, but whose answers escaped him, the group started back for the corporate office at the front entrance to the complex.

Rafferty instinctively tried to find out about people he met. It was considered a good political trait, since he asked a lot of questions and seemed genuinely interested in the information people offered about themselves in response. He found himself curious about the woman engineer in the group.

"Dr. Gwynn, how long have you been with Datasync?"

She blushed, surprised to be singled out by the distinguished visitor. "Almost eight years now. I joined the company right out of Cal Tech as I was completing my doctorate in astrophysics."

"This is going to sound predictable, I know," Rafferty apologized, "but how did someone like you get into an exotic field like this?"

This time she spoke with slight irritation shading into resignation. "I guess you mean, how did a woman get into astrophysics?'' It was his turn to blush at the implication of male chauvinism. ''It's just something I've always wanted to do. I was always good at the math and science and I guess I'm just a space-age baby.'' She laughed slightly to let him off the hook. He thought she seemed very shy.

''Do you like your work?'' he asked.

''Yes,'' she said, ''very much.''

Although they had fallen a few steps behind their escorts, they were still within earshot, so he could not be totally sure of her candor. ''How did you decide to work for Datasync?''

She looked thoughtful, even preoccupied, as if the question had been anticipated and she wanted to be careful. ''My father worked for the corporation for a number of years. He was able to open some doors when I was finishing my degree, and Datasync does exactly the kind of advanced research, design, and engineering I'm interested in.'' She paused as they approached the offices. ''I hope those of you in government find some way so that we can turn this tremendous capability—these people, this technology and equipment, this talent—to peaceful efforts.'' She suddenly seemed frightened by her own statement and quickly added, ''Please, if you have any questions about what you've seen, I'm sure Dr. Pytell or any of our other people will be glad to help. Thank you. It was very nice to meet you. Goodbye.'' And she was gone in a flash before Rafferty could even respond.

Odd, he thought, as the rest of the party entered the corporate offices. Rafferty collected his briefcase, and drawn-out thanks and good-byes were exchanged. The vice-president for governmental affairs took his visitor's badge and walked him to his car. ''We're glad we could share our pride in the Cyclops program with you,'' he said.

Rafferty thanked him and shook hands. Just as he opened the rental-car door, he turned and said, ''By the way, you're nearing completion of two Cyclops payloads in there. I just remembered the Intelligence Committee authorized three of them two years ago.''

His host suddenly seemed flustered. He said, "Well, ah, yes, that's true. The first has already been delivered to the Air Force. I'm sure General King would be more than happy to take that up with you." He hurriedly thanked Rafferty again and turned quickly for his office.

Rafferty was out of the parking lot and onto the nearby Santa Monica Freeway heading for downtown Los Angeles when the oddest thought popped out of the welter of information and impressions that he had accumulated over the past two and a half hours. He suddenly thought Arlette Gwynn's voice sounded familiar.

AT SIX THE NEXT MORNING an Air Force car picked him up at the carriage entrance of the Beverly Wilshire Hotel and drove him to the military terminal at Los Angeles Airport. Within minutes he was aboard an Air Force T-38 headed up the California coast to Vandenberg Air Force Base. He barely had time to finish a strong black cup of coffee when the plane came in for a high-speed landing at the air base runway. The commanding general, Ben Townsend, saluted as Rafferty hopped from the plane and took him immediately into the briefing room adjoining his office.

After an orderly poured more coffee from a polished aluminum pot—Rafferty guessed they wanted him awake for their PR show—General Townsend, a two-star, began.

"Senator Rafferty, welcome back to Vandenberg. I know you were out here in 1985 when construction was being completed, but as you see we're now fully operational and carrying out a full-scale launch program. I have a brief slide show that will only take a few minutes to run through, then we'll go look at the facilities and the pads, and show you what we've got."

Rafferty noticed Townsend's ring: He was one of those new-generation Air Force Academy generals who seemed so self-assured and capable in a technocratic age. "Thanks for your hospitality, General. I've got a couple of particular questions, but let's see what you have to show first."

After the obligatory slides, they toured the space-age facility and once again Rafferty was dumbfounded by size, dimension, and scope. That his country had the resources and genius to create such a place always made him feel proud and even excited. That so much of it went for military purposes continued to concern him. But he always reminded himself that so much of the entire space effort had begun with President Kennedy as a peaceful exploratory effort . . . pioneering in the best American tradition. Perhaps if the Connaughtons of the world prevailed, this genius could be devoted to elevating mankind to the stars.

"Any questions, Senator?" Townsend asked as they drove back to his office in their chauffeured sedan.

"Not many, General, you've covered a lot of ground as usual." Rafferty paused. "I'd appreciate kind of a rundown on the launches you've been undertaking . . . some notion of the scope of your mission. Maybe you could just go over the launches for the past few months so I could get some idea of the balance, say, between military and civilian, or the kinds of payloads that you have to handle and their purposes."

"Very well, Senator," Townsend said as they entered his office again. "As you know, we handle all launches on the west coast and virtually everything for NASA and the Air Force that doesn't go up from Cape Kennedy. We're also equipped to handle Space Shuttle landings, both military and civilian. Most of our missions have a military purpose. We are the principal launch facility for the NRO and its reconnaissance and surveillance satellites."

"I guess, as a member of the Intelligence Committee, that interests me more than anything else," Rafferty injected. "I was just down at Datasync getting up to date on Cyclops." He thought he saw Townsend shift slightly in his chair. "If and when we decided to launch Cyclops, would that launch take place here, General?''

Townsend poured them both some coffee. Rafferty believed he was watching a careful, clever man think very quickly.

"Yes, Senator, that's right," Townsend said presently. He reached for a cigarette. His first of the morning. Rafferty, the former Montana trial lawyer, was beginning to enjoy this.

"General, do you happen to know whether certain members of Congress, say on the key committees, are routinely notified of important launches—deployment of new weapons like Cyclops that might represent a new departure in defense strategy or policy?"

"No, sir, Senator." Townsend seemed temporarily relieved. "That's a matter above my pay and grade. You would have to take that up with my bosses in Washington."

Rafferty decided to let him have it between the eyes. "General Townsend, have you launched a Cyclops payload from Vandenberg anytime in the past few months?"

"Senator," Townsend said, after studying the ceiling for an eternity, "I'm afraid I'll have to refer you to General King for an answer to that."

Rafferty said very softly, "General Townsend, I will remind you that I am a duly elected United States senator and a member of the Senate Intelligence Committee with access to the most highly classified secrets this nation possesses. May I see your logbook of launches?"

Townsend flushed. "I'm sorry, Senator; with all due respect, I am not authorized to make those records available to anyone except my seniors in command."

"I believe I've gotten what I came for, General," Rafferty said, rising from his chair. "If you would be good enough to take me to my plane. I believe Cyclops is in orbit and that it was launched here at Vandenberg. Now I intend to find out why."

31

CONNAUGHTON EASED THE U.S. Mission sedan out of the underground garage and past the saluting Marine guard. He drove onto the Rue de Lausanne. It was 12:30 and he had half an hour to make the fifteen-minute drive. He could use the extra time to look over the surroundings. He followed the main highway leading along the northern coast of the lake for a few miles, then as the highway broadened and headed slightly inland to become the Geneva-Lausanne Autoroute, he took the cloverleaf turn toward the small village of Chambesy. The skies were gloomy and rain had begun falling steadily that morning. The remarkably bright days of January had given way to the more customary gloom of a wet winter. Following his memory and written instructions, he turned left and then right and soon found himself at an intersection of small streets on the edge of the village where stood the Restaurant Trois Mousquetaires. He drove another block and parked and locked the government sedan around the corner. He buttoned his raincoat and walked around to the restaurant from the opposite direction. He saw no occupied cars as he approached the place, somewhat to his surprise. The KGB photographer would probably get him leaving. He paused briefly under the overhanging eaves of a nearby house. A few patrons were arriving for lunch. He scanned the three houses facing the restaurant and saw no unusual movement.

Connaughton entered the simple but cheery restaurant, checked his coat, bonjoured the maître d', and asked in

French for the private room reserved for a party of two. The maître d' bowed slightly and requested that Connaughton follow him up the nearby stairs. On the second floor he was shown to a small room reserved for private parties. The decor was plain—a small table with four chairs, a serving buffet, simple flowered curtains covering the single window, and half a dozen high-quality Matisse prints on the walls. A waiter appeared just behind the maître d' and Connaughton ordered a glass of wine. Alone, Connaughton walked to the front window and parted the curtains slightly. Just after the wine arrived, Connaughton saw a plain black sedan much like the one he had driven arrive at the door below. Two men, including a driver Connaughton recognized from the Soviet Mission, sat in the front seat. After a minute, which seemed to involve a discussion between the other man in the front and the backseat passenger, Ekaterina Davydova emerged quickly from the car and entered the restaurant. Connaughton watched a few more seconds as the sedan drove slowly away. He heard movement on the stairs and moved away from the window. The maître d' bowed Ekaterina into the room as she brushed raindrops from her forehead.

"Hello, Mr. Connaughton." She extended her hand. She seemed composed but tense. "It is very nice to see you again." A glass of wine, ordered below, arrived for her.

Connaughton thought she was attractively flustered. "It is my pleasure, as always, Miss Davydova. I hope these arrangements did not prove too...complicated for you."

"Not really." She sipped the wine. "I discussed this meeting with Ambassador Makarov, as I did before, and he was perfectly agreeable."

"Perfectly?"

A wry smile. "Perhaps not perfectly. Perhaps cautiously." She moved toward the table and he helped seat her. "And yourself. What do your superiors think about your socializing with a member of the Soviet delegation?"

"Frankly, I'm not sure Arkwright knows what to make of it. I didn't tell him in advance that I invited you to the Russian Church. Because that was an impulsive move and I had no idea what would come of it. When the possibility of this lunch arose, I told him—and only him—about it, including the meeting in the Russian Church. Needless to say, he was surprised...but not shocked. He's been around too long for that. He encouraged me to come today."

Ekaterina started to speak just as the waiter arrived, and she broke off. The menu was described in expressive detail and after consulting with Ekaterina, Connaughton ordered tomato soup seasoned with basil and the tournedos grill with béarnaise sauce for them both.

"Did you also tell Ambassador Arkwright about your notion of exchanging information?" she asked after the waiter departed. Her voice now was lower than before.

"Not exactly. We know and respect each other...we're friends, and I believe he trusts my judgment. He's smart enough to realize this could be extremely helpful to him and our side. But to be more direct, no, I didn't tell him about what you call my notion." He paused. "And in case you're wondering, no one else in our mission or our government knows about our meeting at the Russian Church or this lunch. That includes the CIA."

"That's gratifying to know, Mr. Connaughton." (He wished she would be less formal.) "The situation is somewhat different where I'm concerned, as you might imagine. I am here only because Ambassador Makarov expressly approved it. He approved it, I suspect, because he hopes I can recruit you. He made some suggestion that I might do whatever is necessary to attract you"—she hesitated—"physically, a suggestion I considered crude, quite frankly." Her offense seemed genuine, but she managed a smile. "I am not Mata Hari."

They both laughed spontaneously as the waiter arrived with the soup. He would think this an ordinary couple conducting a private liaison in a room often used for that purpose—if he was only a waiter. They fell silent as he served, each wondering if he worked for the other side or even some third interest.

"Unlike my situation," Connaughton said, "I assume Makarov would not have authorized these meetings without informing higher authorities as well as your security people." He carefully did not say the KGB. "So you are here with the knowledge of a lot of people in your government. Just thinking aloud," he continued, "that would bring considerable pressure to bear on you. Is that correct?"

She nodded as she tasted the soup. "Yes. It certainly means something must come of this...or further contact will be refused."

"What is 'something'?" Connaughton probed.

"Some evidence of your willingness to be helpful to us, or at least the promise...a fairly concrete promise...of such."

"How soon will that evidence be required?"

"Today."

"Well that gets to the point, doesn't it?" he said. She did not respond. "Then let me pick up where our conversation ended Sunday at the church." The waiter returned to remove the soup dishes and serve the entree as the pair watched in silence, and then wished them *bon appétit* as he bowed himself from the room and closed the door.

Connaughton gestured for Ekaterina to begin eating as he talked, but she waited with chin on folded hands, intent on his words yet somehow wary and remote. "We can count your large land-based missiles. And we have an idea of your plans to replace older existing systems with modern types." He spoke quietly, evenly, but in a rush. "If we had assurance about those plans, particularly that you did not intend to increase the overall number of land-based missiles as you deployed the modern types, and if we knew their range and accuracy, that would enormously strengthen the hand of those on our side who want an agreement."

She nodded and asked, "What else?"

"We have to know about your testing program. Are you testing some exotic new weapons? Why do you continue to test more than you need to, to maintain the level of weapons production you have?"

Ekaterina nodded, then picked tentatively at her food. "Are there other areas?"

"Yes," Connaughton said, "people on our side are worried about your antisatellite weapons program. You've been at it longer than we have and, although we may be more technologically sophisticated—begging your pardon—we need to know whether you can today destroy our surveillance satellites or whether you'll be able to do that soon. This is extremely important. If we can't have some assurance of protecting our satellites, our ability to monitor your activities, then it puts everything on a hair trigger. Warning times get reduced and everyone gets very nervous. And we are on the edge of the holocaust."

Connaughton paused to try the steak and found it delicious. But he discovered his ordinarily strong appetite diminished. To his surprise he suddenly realized how nervous he was. He noticed Ekaterina had hardly touched her food.

"Mr. Connaughton, what I don't understand is how you could trust anything I might tell you. What is to prevent my superiors from simply using me as a false agent…someone who passes inaccurate information?"

He thought a moment. "Obviously you could be used, knowingly or unknowingly, to give us false information. But we have some things to go on—satellite pictures, logical extrapolation, other sources. What you might tell us would be squared with everything else we know and it would primarily be used for verification—for confirming what we already believe."

Ekaterina seemed lost in thought. "Would you expect me to collect secrets not readily available to me? Do you expect me to be a spy as well as a traitor? I ask only out of curiosity."

Before Connaughton could respond there was a light tap on the door and the waiter entered. He refilled their glasses with the fine Bordeaux, Château Prince Larquey, he had proposed with the meal, then expressed deep concern that they had not eaten more of the house specialty. Ekaterina assured him that it was indeed exquisite cuisine but that their appetites had fled. A raised eyebrow and nod on his part indicated he was totally sympathetic with the effects of romance on the palate and he quickly removed the dishes.

Once the door had again quietly closed, Ekaterina turned back to Connaughton. "Your notion, I believe, was that this should be a two-way street—that to justify my meetings with you I must be able to demonstrate some benefit to our interests. Is that correct?"

"Essentially yes," he said, still somewhat put off by her cool, detached air. "I doubt your superiors would continue to permit these contacts to continue if you had nothing to show for it. Your government has never shown a great interest in promoting uninhibited socializing, let alone romance, between its officials and Americans, particularly Americans in my line of work."

She looked amused for the first time. "Romance?" He thought briefly of how she had almost seemed to toy with him during their previous contacts. It threw him off-guard.

"You know what I mean. The only way this can possibly work is if you have some justification for continuing to see me. The only justification that's worthwhile is information important to your government."

"You seem almost eager to give away secrets," she said. "Won't people on my side raise the same questions you raised before about me? Why exactly is he doing this? How do I explain that?"

"Strangely enough," he replied, "the truth works here. Tell them I'm deeply troubled by the confrontation and convinced the arms race is out of hand. Tell them we're running out of time and, unless something dramatic isn't done soon, we're going to blow ourselves up. Make me out to be a fanatic or a madman or some well-meaning peacenik . . . anything that fits. You can figure out the line pretty easily. Besides, I'm sure your files on me have me pretty much on the 'soft' side anyway. The profile will fit. They'll believe it." He sounded convincing and rueful at the same time.

The waiter brought coffee for Connaughton and the tea Ekaterina had ordered. They declined the offer of dessert and he departed with a wistful smile once again.

"You will probably not be surprised to know that Ambassador Makarov himself has already indicated the kind of information that it would be most useful for us to obtain. He clearly hopes I might be able to develop these contacts into that kind of relationship," she said.

"I'm not surprised," Connaughton replied wryly. "He's no fool and I'm sure he has already taken this up with the KGB and his superiors in Moscow. What kinds of things does he have in mind for old Frank?"

Ekaterina smiled wanly at his sense of resignation. "It seems we are most interested in the degree of accuracy of both your land-based and sea-based missiles, particularly the degree to which they place our own land-based missiles at risk from a possible first strike." Connaughton nodded. "My government wants to know how many cruise missiles you intend to put aboard mobile carriers—bombers and ships. We can count those in Europe pretty accurately but not those we cannot see. Our military people are willing to consider limits on cruise missiles, but frankly they do not know how to achieve that goal and they've gotten no help from your side." Connaughton nodded again. "Finally," she said, "we are at least as worried as you are about antisatellite weapons. There isn't much purpose here in debating whose fault this contest is, except to point out that you may also have the capability to blind our satellites and render us impotent and vulnerable and therefore dangerous. We need to know whether you have that capability."

Connaughton said, "I'm frankly not surprised by any of this. If I had guessed about the shopping list on your side it would have been almost exactly what you've outlined. Is that the extent of it?... Not that you haven't asked for about everything that's important."

"I must emphasize the importance of the space systems," she said. "Our people constantly talk about your Star Wars efforts and the threat some major breakthrough might represent. I don't believe we can negotiate any treaty worth anything unless there is some assurance that you do not possess some ability to neutralize our defenses."

"I understand that," he replied. "I ought to, since we've spent the better part of the last year hearing about it from your side here in Geneva, in Moscow, and in Washington." He saw her look at her watch. He paused and looked toward the window, outside of which waited her car and the two men. "What do you need from me today so that Makarov will let me see you again?"

"At the very least I need an assurance that you are prepared to try to provide some of the information I've described."

"I can only do that," Connaughton said, "if I know it's helping get us closer to a treaty. Now I know if we have the kind of information you can get for us from your side, it will increase the chances on the American side for an agreement. What's really holding things back—aside from primitive fear and ideological rigidity—is lack of information. We think we know some of your plans and capabilities. But there's always great dispute about both, and in almost every case, the worst estimate—the estimate of greatest danger—wins. You can call it prudence or conservatism or whatever, but that's the way things work." Connaughton sighed in frustration. "All I'm trying to do is to find out what would happen if both sides had reasonably strong assurance that the other side was *not* seeking superiority, *not* planning some preemptive first strike, *not* going to use its nuclear arsenal to blackmail the other side. We've never really known what life would be like under those conditions, and we've never been able to figure out a system even for finding out if those conditions exist. This may be the road, the only road, to peace and security."

Ekaterina suddenly became animated, almost fierce. "I understand your purpose completely and I believe it is worth the risk . . . for both of us. I see no other way to avoid catastrophe. It is so frustrating to sit in these negotiations day after day sparring around the edges of the problem. Both of us know that we must either agree to limit our nuclear weapons or face the probability of destruction. And like blind giants, we grope in the darkness not sure where the other is or how large or with what weapons. What would happen if the lights were turned on—if we were not blind—if we saw the other side did not have more or larger weapons?"

Connaughton watched her intensely. His instincts about her had been sound. He had believed she would understand his motives and share his sense of desperation, and she did. Now if only she had the courage to follow through. It would not be easy . . . particularly for her. But there seemed to be no other way.

"Say to Makarov that you found me cooperative and willing, for the very *noblest* motives"—he grinned lopsidedly—"to tell you something about our programs, but not to expect that information to be well received by your hardliners. We may be less frightening than some of your generals might wish to believe."

"The generals concern me less, Mr. Connaughton," she said slowly, "than some others in our government."

"For example?" he asked.

"For example, Vladimir Zhdanov."

Connaughton came to full alert. "Ah, yes, the mysterious Comrade Zhdanov." He paused. "We believed he was playing an important role in your nuclear weapons policy."

"An important role is a great understatement. It is safe to say right now he is driving it. Very little happens that he does not have a hand in or manage to know about. He has become a very powerful figure, Mr. Connaughton. You should know that and not underestimate its importance."

"Which undoubtedly means the answers to the questions I put to you will be grim . . . that you are going to have more of everything rather than less. There goes my grand scheme of making a breakthrough on these negotiations."

"Not necessarily, Mr. Connaughton," Ekaterina said. "There is resistance to his proposed buildup and use of force."

"Where from?" Connaughton asked.

"Principally from Defense Minister Kozlovsky and much of the General Staff, curiously enough. That's why I said what I did about generals. I believe some of them think Zhdanov mad."

Connaughton tried desperately not to look as startled as he felt. "And what do you believe? Do you agree with the generals?"

Ekaterina looked at her watch again and got up from the table. "I have spent very little time in Comrade Zhdanov's presence, so most of my information is what you call secondhand. But if he is not mad, then I am, and the whole world is upside down."

She walked to the window and parted the curtain slightly. "And what may I say to Makarov to justify another meeting, besides that you wish to be cooperative?"

"As you know, tomorrow we have agreed to tackle the cruise missile issue in the plenary negotiations. Tell him," Connaughton said moving closer to her, "tell him I will have information on our cruise missile program. And I will need from you," he said very softly, "as much as you can tell me about your future ICBM program. That is very important to us right now."

"And how shall we meet, presuming Ambassador Makarov will let me?" Connaughton felt the nervousness returning that he had seen in the department store.

"Today is Wednesday," he said, consulting a pocket calendar. "Can you meet me a week from this Friday, the fifth of February, in the Cathédrale de Saint-Pierre about twelve-thirty? I'll have a car and we'll go for a drive and perhaps have lunch again."

She smiled again. "You have a certain proclivity for churches, Mr. Connaughton. I had no idea you were so devout. Or are you mocking our state atheism?"

He smiled in response. "It's very practical, Miss Davydova. They usually have a number of entrances and exits. Difficult to cover for the security people. Besides, they customarily have represented sanctuary."

"I see," she said. "I will do my best to arrange this meeting. But it must be Saturday. Friday I must work at translating and correcting the transcript of the negotiations for the previous week. Is that agreeable to you?"

"Perfectly," he said. "How will I know if you'll be there?"

She stepped quickly toward the door. "I will let you know Tuesday at our plenary session." She nodded. "You will know." She hesitated before opening the door, her mask slipping to expose the fear beneath. "Oh, Mr. Connaughton, this is so desperate and so dangerous, what we are doing. I...I hope that it is the right thing. You see, I am not very courageous."

"Miss Davydova, believe me it's the right thing. You and I both know there is practically no choice given the circumstances." His voice sounded surprisingly tender even to him.

"And for whatever it's worth, I think you're very courageous."

With an effort she composed herself, then said quietly, "Wait until I have been gone for several minutes before you leave."

32

AFTER LUNCH MEMBERS OF the United States delegation gathered in the bubble to compare notes on the day's negotiations. Very little of consequence had occurred in the full session or any of the working groups, but each participant reported nevertheless, noting nuances and minor asides. Sid Murray said that Sergei Metrinko, the KGB man, had asked an inordinate number of questions about testing of antisatellite weapons. Murray wondered aloud what might have produced that kind of concern and suggested he would pass it through the intelligence community to see if anyone had any idea. Connaughton perked up briefly from his abstract doodling at that. He would love to know what Sid found out. He could hardly remember once in the past year when the word "Cyclops" had been used in the bubble. Walt Quainton reported that old General Polyakov, keeping to the old Party line, had said too much was being made of disagreements over the number of weapons on each side, and that he couldn't foresee a time when the Soviet Union might lay out its arsenal for the world to see.

Arkwright concluded that Makarov seemed more upbeat than at any time since the current round of negotiations began, and that he had been peculiarly chummy—even conspiratorial—as some in the delegation might have noticed. The interpreter, Wilson Douglas, the delegation wit, said, "Yes, Barrett, we thought it was going to take surgery to separate the two of you at the door."

Arkwright led the laughter as the meeting broke up, and as he had occasionally before he motioned Connaughton to join him in his office.

"Frank, what can you tell me about your lunch?"

Connaughton slumped in his chair, not sure how far to go. "It went pretty much as I expected. She's willing to be helpful to us. Her motives are honorable—if you can use that word under these circumstances—and she's not looking for any kind of payoff or reward from us. I believe she has, or can get, a lot of valuable information for us."

"You don't seem very excited by this potential espionage bonanza," Arkwright observed softly.

"It's not my line of work, Barrett." Connaughton was direct in the way one is with a friend, not a superior.

"Frank, I'm not too sure how to handle this," Arkwright said. "Standard procedure requires that I turn you over to the Agency spooks for handling. But somehow I don't think that's the way to deal with this situation. I put in a call to Emerson late yesterday to talk to him about your situation and he's due to call me back on the secure line tomorrow morning. I intend to tell him that you've turned up a fairly high level source in or close to the Soviet delegation, that I will not identify this individual except to him in person, that only you and I know about this contact, and that I do not intend to alert the intelligence community yet unless instructed otherwise." Arkwright leaned across his desk and spoke quietly. "If your information about Cyclops is correct, there are some key people in our government who are counting on these negotiations failing. If your source comes through, it could help turn the talks around. Needless to say, those key people are not going to be pleased by this development. It could get very hot."

"Barrett, the longer we can keep this between us, and just the Secretary in Washington, the happier I'll be," Connaughton said. "If this turns into a full-blown spy deal with the Agency and the White House and God knows who else involved, it'll be a catastrophe." His voice also was barely audible. "Besides, it could jeopardize our source. If she thinks I'm working for the Agency, she'll take off like some rare bird."

"All right, Frank, I'll keep my end of the bargain and I promise Emerson will too. He'll have to find a way to turn whatever information you get over to the broader national-security community in Washington, but we'll let him worry about that." Arkwright paused. "I just have two questions. Why is she doing it, and how does she get away to make contact with you?"

Connaughton looked out the window. "She's scared. She wants these talks to succeed. She cares about her sons and her country. She's gotten to be terrified of nuclear war. It's that simple." Connaughton took a deep breath. He had anticipated this question. "The contact is simple too," he lied to his friend. "Makarov gives her pretty free rein to move around. She either is or was his girlfriend."

33

THIS WOULD NOT be an ordinary meeting of the Soviet General Staff. That was apparent from the moment Defense Minister Georgi Kozlovsky strode into the formal conference room like a fast-moving thundercloud. And it was apparent from the single item on the agenda—Operation Red Star.

From the beginning Red Star had been controversial within the Soviet military establishment. It was always planned as a grander operation than the periodic Warsaw Pact exercises. It always received extraordinary attention from the politicians in the Kremlin. And it was the first such exercise designed to link conventional and strategic forces. Any one of these factors was sufficient to make the military leaders especially alert. All three together electrified the assembled brass. A web of tensions and ambitions entangled all those in the room.

The fifteen senior generals and admirals representing the inner circle of the General Staff took their seats at the giant oval table, as their support staff composed of slightly less beribboned officers arranged themselves in personally marked chairs along the walls. Kozlovsky rapped a fat pen against a pewter tea mug to get attention. It was unnecessary. The room was already silent.

"Gentlemen, we are here today to complete plans for Operation Red Star. This exercise is scheduled for the period from April fifteenth to April thirtieth. It will involve all the operational forces, as well as some reserve units, of the combined Soviet military forces and elements of Warsaw Pact allied forces. In the past such exercises have been extremely useful in demonstrating our defensive power and purpose to friend and foe alike, and also in revealing shortcomings and weak links to those of us entrusted with the defense of the Soviet Union." Kozlovsky thrust his broad peasant face forward and his bushy eyebrows lowered, almost covering narrowed eyes. The commanders in the room virtually to a man respected and admired him, knowing him to be a hard-driving but fair leader. "If any service, or even any unit down to the platoon, is not ready to go on April fifteenth, there will be hell to pay. So let's find out. General Rusakov, you begin."

The Deputy Minister of Defense and Chief of the General Staff, Viktor Rusakov, seated just to Kozlovsky's right, stubbed out a Western cigarette, hacked a cough from his lungs, and put on reading glasses. He had earned fame as a division commander at Stalingrad and his ribbons and medals covered half his uniform coat. "Minister Kozlovsky, all plans are proceeding but are not fully completed. We are conducting a series of meetings among the Army, Navy, and Air Force, and the Rocket Forces. Our greatest challenge is timing of the activities of all these elements. The unique aspect of involving the Rocket Forces requires weeks of coördination efforts. Because it has never been done before, we must write the book as we go along. The second greatest challenge is fleet readiness. The ocean elements of Red Star are also unique—more comprehensive than anything else we've ever done. We will put to sea four fleets simultaneously, with four to five hundred ships involved, depending on whether coastal patrol ships are counted. It is a massive undertaking to say the least. But Admiral Gorshkov will address that. We are encountering the usual incompetence with our Warsaw Pact friends. I can tell you—and you can tell the Kremlin—right now, there will be major problems with morale and readiness in the Eastern Eu-

ropean forces. With very few exceptions the problems are
the same in every country... equipment is not being maintained, the officer corps is not disciplined and therefore is
not disciplining the troops, tools and parts are disappearing at an all-time high, and drug use and AWOLs continue
to increase." He sighed heavily. "Otherwise everything is
fine." There was a knowing chuckle around the table—a
familiar report. "Comrade Minister, I believe we are prepared to carry out Red Star successfully, even considering
the enormous challenges the scope of this operation im-
poses."

Kozlovsky nodded his thanks and turned to Admiral
Gorshkov, the next senior commander, seated on his left.
Gorshkov had been passed over twice for Rusakov's position as Chief and was now years past retirement age. He re-
tained his active-duty status because of his phenomenal
achievement in converting a third-rate navy into one of the
two most powerful oceangoing forces on earth. "Comrade
Minister, General Rusakov has stated our challenge well. We
must put four fleets to sea simultaneously—the Northern,
the Baltic, the Black Sea, and the Pacific fleets. We have
never undertaken this before and, save for Red Star, would
not do so short of preparation for war. I am the first to admit deployment problems." Gorshkov, Kozlovsky thought,
never ceased to earn his reputation for candor, which ac-
counted for his notable lack of success at Kremlin politics.
"Our ships do not train as much as the American Navy. Our
ships are in port too much, usually for repairs. Many of our
new sailors are well trained and highly motivated. But we are
still drafting too many ignoramuses, drunks, and ne'er-do-
wells. We finally have the number and types of ships we
need to be a first-class power. But the sophistication of nuclear power plants, radars, and new missiles requires an
ever-increasing level of training and retraining of our career personnel. These shortcomings will be revealed by Red
Star, I can warn you. But we will get our fleets to sea."

The one thing in the whole damn operation he was sure of, thought Kozlovsky, was that Gorshkov would have the fleets to sea. "General Ogarkov?"

"The Red Army is ready," boomed the bass voice of its commander. Ogarkov had fought a dozen major artillery battles with the Nazis and sacrificed much of his hearing for his rank and honors. "Thirty-seven Soviet infantry and artillery divisions will participate in Red Star, supplemented by fifteen divisions from Warsaw Pact countries. Too bad the bastards are totally incompetent." Kozlovsky and the others smiled. "We'll have to lead them back and forth from their trucks to the latrines, but we'll get it done. The highlight of the Army's participation in this exercise will be the maneuver of our armored divisions and light infantry. As you know, we have worked for over a decade to incorporate principles of rapid movement into the Red Army's official doctrine. And, by God, I believe we've done it. It took some time and patience with us old farts, but the younger officers have taken to the new doctrines and tactics like fish to water. We are going to show some lightning maneuvers and rapid movements that will make Hitler's panzers look like they were sitting still. Tell our bosses downtown in the Kremlin to come up and watch us work. They'll be impressed and, besides, we'll get our budget for next year." Even Gorshkov laughed along with the others at that. Ogarkov's brow furrowed. "The only thing is, I hope some West German or American one-star on the Central Front doesn't get nervous and fire a couple of tactical nukes over the wall."

Kozlovsky said, "In accordance with established practice, we will notify the NATO representatives in Belgium of our intended exercises. We will not, of course, go into great detail. But they will be expecting some major military activities on land and sea. If they get nervous, it will only be because of our superior capabilities." Kozlovsky hoped the others believed that line more than he did. "General Antonovich?"

The senior Air Force commander looked like a movie character playing his role. He was tall, trim, and had full gray hair. He spoke several languages fluently, including English, was the best educated of the General Staff, and smoked his English cigarettes in a holder. "Thank you, Minister Kozlovsky. We are well prepared for Red Star, if I may say so. These exercises will enable us to unveil our new generation of fighters, Sukarov MiG-29s, and the all-weather long-range bombers, the Breakthrough 2000s. The bombers particularly will confound the West, if they are able to detect them at all. As you know, we have been in competition with the United States to develop the so-called stealth technology that hides planes from radar, and they have assumed we were five to ten years behind. Well, I am pleased to tell you this technology has been incorporated into the Breakthrough."

There were eyebrows raised and murmurs around the table from the other services. This was a surprise to all but Kozlovsky. Antonovich loved the dramatic and had saved this revelation for the appropriate time to impress his peers. "We are working closely with the staffs of Admiral Gorshkov and General Ogarkov to coordinate air exercises with land and sea deployments and movements. Air exercises, like the others, will simulate as nearly as possible actual combat conditions. We are withholding the details of the timing of the operation to better test our rapid-response capability. Finally, we are putting great emphasis on the readiness of support and ground units to operate and maintain our planes in a simulated combat environment." Antonovich looked pleased with himself. He was not especially well liked in the General Staff, but his political and social credentials maintained him high on the military ladder.

"Our final report will come from General Palzin," Kozlovsky said.

"Comrade Minister," Palzin began very slowly, "the Strategic Rocket Forces were honored to be included in these Warsaw Pact exercises for the first time and, as my colleagues on the General Staff can tell you, we have worked very closely together to ensure proper coordination of conventional and strategic forces under Operation Red Star." Palzin seemed to hesitate. He was widely respected for his command of the nuclear strike forces and his comments carried weight. "I will be honest with you, Georgi, and with my other respected colleagues here. I am deeply concerned about the involvement of the Strategic Rocket Forces in Red Star. We have never done this before. To bring our nuclear weapons systems to a higher degree of readiness while we conduct major maneuvers of our land, sea, and air forces will be a very provocative business to the Western powers. There is little problem in carrying out the operation as designed. Believe me, I am not trying to exclude the Rocket Forces from the discipline of the exercise. We are ready and willing to fulfill whatever role the Kremlin wishes for us. It is the timing and scope of the operation I must question. Let me put it this way. If I were in the Pentagon, and I saw this massive exercise under way, and I also saw the nuclear forces involved and called to a higher state of alert, I would be irritated and nervous at the very least, and angry and belligerent at the worst." Palzin hesitated again. "Unless the Kremlin intends purposely to intimidate the Americans and the West, I can see little reason for joint conventional-nuclear exercises."

Kozlovsky was not surprised by Palzin's statement. Palzin had come to him with the same concern a week before and it clearly had been on his mind since Red Star was proposed by the Kremlin six months previously. But Kozlovsky carefully watched other faces in the conference room as Palzin spoke. Most seemed surprised. Antonovich looked slightly disdainful. Gorshkov nodded slight agreement and approval.

Kozlovsky said, "General, I appreciate your candor and forthrightness. You have raised legitimate concerns in your usual thoughtful manner. But these are political considerations—not military ones. Therefore the best I can do is communicate them, on your behalf, to the Politburo. We are meeting this afternoon. It is the reason I wanted to review Red Star with the General Staff this morning. I am expected to report on its status to the Politburo. Unless you object, I will relay your concern at our afternoon meeting."

"Please do so, Comrade Minister, if you would," Palzin said. "Feel free to identify me personally as the source of the concern."

"Thank you, General, I will," Kozlovsky responded. "Our regular General Staff meeting will occur next week at this same time. Each week from now until April fifteenth, I will want a complete status report of the progress toward Operation Red Star. I want particular attention paid to the inadequacies in our Warsaw Pact units and I want the full weight of the General Staff put into whipping them into shape. I also want an all-out effort made to get the fleets prepared. We are asking for an extraordinary performance from the Navy and it deserves our total support."

Kozlovsky stood to adjourn the conference and turned to Gorshkov on his left. "Admiral, will you join me in my office for a few minutes, if you please?" The old admiral was fifteen years his senior, and Kozlovsky always treated him with respect. Gorshkov nodded and followed the Defense Minister out into the wide corridor of the ministry, down the familiar hall, and through two outer offices populated by busy, efficient, and relatively attractive secretaries. Gorshkov waved his several bemedaled aides into chairs in the anteroom and closed the doors to the Defense Minister's cavernous corner office behind him and Kozlovsky.

Kozlovsky gestured to two easy chairs next to a small low table in the far corner away from his desk, where he usually conducted informal talks. He went through the motions of offering the weathered admiral a good Cuban cigar, which he knew would be turned down in favor of an equally weathered pipe. He poured hot tea for them both and said, "You don't like Red Star do you, Nikolai?"

"No, I don't," the older man declared. "If you don't mind my saying so, some idiot in the Politburo—probably Zhdanov—has sold the leadership a bill of goods." The leadership, Kozlovsky knew, included everyone from General Secretary Kamenev to the Defense Minister himself. "The Politburo in its wisdom," Gorshkov said sarcastically, "has clearly decided to use our annual exercises not only for a grand show of force but also for some misdirected effort to confront the United States and NATO. I don't like it and I think it is dangerous politics."

"I could tell you agreed with Palzin." Kozlovsky sipped his tea. "Do you fully share his worries about the involvement of the Strategic Rocket Forces?"

Gorshkov said, "I don't know about 'fully' but I do think getting the nuclear forces into Red Star is a big mistake. Even if we get away with it this time, without some blow-up with the West, it sets a dangerous precedent. Then every time we have a routine military exercise of any kind, some ambitious or dangerous Kremlin politician is going to insist we do it just like Red Star. So nuclear alerts will become part of the operation routinely and the chances will increase that the command, control, and communication systems will fail and some commander in Minsk will get the wrong signal and fire off his missiles. It's madness, Georgi. Do what you can to stop it."

"I intend to, Nikolai," Kozlovsky said, but without conviction. "I already have tried. Just between us, I've opposed the size and scope of Red Star, as well as the involvement of the nuclear forces, within the Politburo. But you're right, Zhdanov is driving the whole thing. He got me aside during the holidays and pushed for a full-scale confrontation with the United States. For some reason—maybe his own age—he thinks the time has come for some final resolution of the cold war. You know how he is with his doctrine . . . struggle between good and evil, death to capitalism, workers unite against imperialism . . . all that stuff. Détente is the dirtiest word he knows and he thinks I'm the worst détentist."

Gorshkov puffed his pipe furiously. "Can't you go to Kamenev? You're his protégé. I can't believe he's letting Zhdanov run the government on a matter of this consequence."

Kozlovsky thought in silence, then finally said, "I've thought of that, Nikolai, but I've resisted getting him in the middle of a tug of war between me and Zhdanov. I despise that kind of infighting in the first place, and the General Secretary is showing his age besides. He resists these power struggles and confrontations more and more. I'm afraid he's pursuing the easiest course and right now that's with Zhdanov." After a pause, Kozlovsky continued, "This is really a job for Zoshchenko. He's in line to succeed Kamenev—I'm not. If he's serious about leading, now is the time to do it. Frankly, I think he's afraid of getting on Zhdanov's bad side. He figures that in the Politburo, having such an enemy would seriously hurt his chances."

"What would also hurt his chances," Gorshkov growled, "is to have the General Staff against him. What would you say if Palzin and I paid him a visit and told him just what we think? I've known Pyotr Zoshchenko for a long time. He's a very ambitious man and he knows Palzin and I have considerable weight in military circles."

Kozlovsky nodded. "It wouldn't hurt. But make sure he knows I didn't send you. He knows my opposition to Red Star. And I don't want him to get the idea I'm lobbying outside the Politburo."

"Done," said the old admiral as he eased himself from the chair to his incredibly erect bearing.

Kozlovsky checked the time, then buzzed for his car to take him to the Politburo meeting. He wondered whether there still might be a chance to stop or at least scale back Red Star and block Zhdanov's mad plans.

THE MEETING OF the most powerful men in the USSR proceeded with only one stir—when Kozlovsky reported on the progress of Red Star. He assured his Politburo colleagues that plans continued apace and that the General Staff was harassing corps and division commanders to make every preparation. Almost as an afterthought, Kozlovsky delicately mentioned concern within some high-level military circles about the political dangers of Red Star and the need for certainty that the Politburo had carefully calculated the implications of provoking the West. Kozlovsky shrugged and said that he had done his best to reassure the General Staff, but that he was committed to bring the matter once again before the Politburo.

General Secretary Kamenev grimaced at the notion of reopening the Red Star debate. The generals should trust the Politburo to have thought of questions such as that and not concern themselves with political matters. He complained that generals were always doing that, not content simply to command troops. Kamenev turned to the Foreign Minister and said, "Comrade Zoshchenko, you may wish to speak to our generals and assure them we know what we are doing and not to fear."

"Revered Comrade General Secretary, it occurred to me I should do exactly that. And with the cooperation of my good friend the Defense Minister, I shall do so."

The meeting soon adjourned and Kozlovsky escorted Foreign Minister Zoshchenko to his car.

"Could this be what Admiral Gorshkov's call was about? He tried to reach me before the Politburo meeting," Zoshchenko said.

"Could be," Kozlovsky replied. "But I must tell you, it isn't just Gorshkov. It's also Palzin."

Kozlovsky slyly watched his rival's eyebrows raise, and he enjoyed it. Gorshkov was a problem. But Palzin was an even bigger problem. If the Strategic Rocket Forces balked at Red Star, some serious diplomacy would be required and, given Kamenév's infirmity, the job was Zoshchenko's. The Foreign Minister would have to do what he most hated: take a stand against powerful opposition.

They arrived at Zoshchenko's limousine, with Kozlovsky's just behind it, as the late-afternoon snow began to fall. The Foreign Minister put on his elegant sable hat and turned to his stocky colleague. "Goddammit, Georgi, how did we let Zhdanov talk us into entering this maze? He set it up so that the General Secretary bought it and then everyone else looked weak if they didn't go along." Kozlovsky nodded his agreement, as if sympathetic to a plight that had now become peculiar to Zoshchenko personally. "To tell you God's truth," Zoshchenko muttered so that his driver couldn't hear, "I've never liked this operation from the beginning. But there didn't seem any way out." He waited for Kozlovsky to suggest a solution.

"Ah, Pyotr, it is a puzzle. But what if Gorshkov and Palzin are right?" Kozlovsky said quietly. "Perhaps the Politburo was too hasty. Maybe the military people are telling us to think about this again. You should listen to what Gorshkov has to say. You could be the key person in determining our nation's future."

34

WHILE EVERYONE ELSE was watching the two ambassadors, she had nodded. Connaughton took that as a signal, her agreement to meet him at the cathedral. On Saturday morning he borrowed Charlie Curtis's well-traveled European Ford and parked it on the narrow Rue Chausse-Coq just four blocks from the cathedral. The dominant architectural feature and symbol of Geneva as the hub of reformation, a refuge for dissenters and victims of persecution, the cathedral dominated the city's horizon.

Connaughton arrived just after noon and, following a small tourist group of elderly Italians, he completed the rounds of the main sanctuary looking unsuccessfully for anyone who might be connected with some intelligence service. The winter rains had returned again to Geneva and he wore a raincoat of the same vintage as Charlie's car and carried a broad-brimmed hat. He positioned himself to the left of the main entrance to the sanctuary through which all visitors initially passed, and just beyond a small kiosk dispensing postcards and mementos of the cathedral. He waited and watched only a few minutes when the now-familiar tall figure appeared. She wore a winter coat as dark as her hair and she shook an umbrella that she had just furled. Like Connaughton, she had entered with a tourist group to make it more difficult for anyone trying to single her out. She paused to let her eyes adjust to the semidarkness of the sanctuary. She started walking in a counterclockwise direction down the far-right aisle away from

Connaughton and he let her go so that he might observe anyone following her. She walked alone, and as she slowly circled the sanctuary no one seemed to take notice of her. Presently she came toward the corner where Connaughton stood and, finally seeing him, came forward and extended her hand.

"Good afternoon," she said. "I see you are still conducting your survey of local churches. Now you come to the largest and most impressive. Are you in search of something and, if so, have you yet found it?"

"We're all in search of something," Connaughton responded. "For some it's money, for some success, for some love, but for all it's happiness. My search goes on. And you?"

"I visit churches when someone interesting invites me. And I search for the same things as everyone else." She smiled.

"And do I qualify as 'interesting'?" Connaughton asked, also smiling.

"Oh, you most certainly do," she said. "Otherwise, why would I be here?"

"Perhaps to join me for lunch in Courmayeur." He gestured toward the exit under the north tower of the cathedral. She followed him toward the front of the sanctuary skirting tour groups and strolling individuals. Once outside he took her umbrella and unfurled it against the steady drizzle. He held the umbrella above her with one hand and took her arm with the other to guide her the few blocks to the car.

Once inside, he guided the nondescript vehicle down the winding side street to the Rue Charles-Galland, down the wide Boulevard des Tranchées a few blocks, then right onto the Route de Malagnou. At the southeastern edge of Geneva the street became the A-40 highway, which crossed the border just south of the French village of Annemasse, then followed the Arve River fifty miles to the village of Chamonix and the entrance to the Mont Blanc Tunnel.

As they slowed for the Swiss-French border posts, Connaughton suddenly said, "I had completely forgotten you can't travel into France."

"That's true," Ekaterina explained, "but if I encounter any trouble Makarov will protect me." The French border guard saw the Swiss plates on the car and the familiar sticker identifying its owner with the U.S. government and waved the car through. As they set out down the superhighway she said, "I have always wanted to make this trip but have never had the opportunity. I hope it does not take too long . . . I must be back at the mission late this afternoon."

"Don't worry," Connaughton said, "we'll have lunch in Courmayeur and be back by four-thirty or five o'clock. Will that cause you any trouble?"

She said, "I suppose to be honest it depends upon what I have to report. I think Ambassador Makarov expects certain 'results' soon in exchange for special liberties such as this and our lunch earlier."

Connaughton kept the car near the 120 kilometer limit as they sped southeastward through the upper Arve Valley. He stopped to pay a toll, then accelerated as they passed through the farmland and snow-spotted rolling hills of eastern France and just south of Bonneville.

"Let's discuss the 'results' as you call them over lunch. I think I can give you enough to justify these contacts for Makarov," Connaughton said to the rain-spattered windshield. He looked across at her. "In the meantime, tell me what he thinks about this arrangement. How have you handled it with him?"

"I've handled it," she replied, looking at the passing countryside, "by telling the Ambassador that you want the negotiations to succeed . . . that you are not a traitor or candidate for defection by any means . . . but that you think the only way to achieve results is to show us some areas where

American nuclear weapons programs are not as threatening as we might fear. I told him you were willing to make information available to us which would enable us to reach more reasonable estimates of your plans and programs and help those in our government who genuinely believe there is room for negotiated limits."

"How does he respond to that?" Connaughton asked.

"The proof is in the pudding, I believe you say. He has no way of testing your faith, or the value of your information, until he sees some results, as I mentioned." She paused to look at the city of Cluses off to the left and Connaughton slowed again to pay a toll.

"What instructions has he given for handling me?" Connaughton asked.

Ekaterina said, "About as you expect under the circumstances. Listen carefully. Take notes if you permit. Try to ask intelligent follow-up questions regarding the subjects you talk about. I suspect I'll get some coaching on that as soon as it becomes clearer what you have for them." Connaughton noticed she said "them," not "us." "The time will come, I am sure, when they will want official documents, perhaps even pictures and blueprints, if that becomes important to verify the authenticity of your information." She seemed in that strange remote mood that Connaughton had noted, to his puzzlement, before.

The car turned east again to pass just north of the village of St. Gervais. They paused for the third toll where the highway narrowed to the normal two lanes as it headed toward the ski center of Chamonix at the northern entrance to the tunnel. Connaughton glanced at her and asked, "Has Makarov brought in the KGB yet? Or is he going to handle this himself? It's important for me to know whether he intends to keep my information within the Foreign Ministry channels or whether he thinks he has to get the spy types involved."

She shook her head. "So far, I report to him only. He said we will keep it that way for a while. But surely at some point what you tell me and I tell him will have to be made available to key people in Moscow at least. I cannot tell you who that might be or how many."

Connaughton fixed his gaze on her until she returned it. "Why does he think I am talking to you and not someone else?"

He thought he saw a small blush spot on her pale cheek as she unnecessarily arranged her hair. "He has not yet speculated. He takes it for granted right now. At some point if the KGB gets involved I am sure motives will become more important."

Mont Blanc now loomed massively above, with the Aiguilles Rouges range to the left behind Chamonix and the Aiguilles de Chamonix standing like sentinels across the Arve Valley to their right. Beyond these pinnacles sprawled the Mer de Glace, a monumental sea of ice.

Connaughton guided the car up the winding road to the tunnel entrance well above the valley floor. He didn't take his eyes from his course when he asked, "Why do you think I wanted to talk to you and not someone else?"

She answered, as they entered the long tunnel, "I don't know, Mr. Connaughton. I choose not to think about it beyond what we discussed in the Russian Church . . . our children, our concern for their future, the fear and frustration wrapped up in these negotiations . . . and all the rest."

They drove in silence the eleven kilometers of the great tunnel. As they emerged into bright sunlight and the Italian border crossing, they could see the lovely village of Courmayeur just below. The guard looked at Connaughton's American passport and Ekaterina's identification card and waved them through.

She had slipped on dark glasses against the sudden brightness. Connaughton could not see her eyes. She asked,

"Was there some other reason—besides pure accident and circumstance—for seeking to involve me in this?"

"None that I'm aware of," Connaughton lied. It was the second time in three days he had done that and both involved her.

"Well," she said as they descended into the village, "at some point, it is safe to say, Ambassador Makarov will assume there is some personal involvement between us."

"Why are you so sure of that?" Connaughton asked.

"Because that is the way his mind works."

Connaughton was silent as he maneuvered the car into the parking area across the road from an Italian restaurant in a Swiss chalet of white stucco with a wood beam roof. He opened her door and escorted her across the highway, past a few hardy souls having steaming drinks on the sunlit patio, and into the cozy dining room with its blazing fire. The lunchtime crowd had thinned and the maître d' awarded them the isolated corner table Connaughton requested in his broken Italian. Connaughton delivered their coats to the hovering waiter and ordered a carafe of Chianti.

Almost literally above them, and dramatically visible out the north window, rose the stark-white jagged spires of the Mont Blanc complex. Their brilliance in the sunlight was almost blinding. Ekaterina kept her dark glasses on, whether to protect against the sunlight or against recognition Connaughton was not sure.

"Miss Davydova," Connaughton began after their lunch had been ordered and served, "the Soviet government has been concerned with our cruise missile program as much as with anything else, except for Star Wars. We have made little progress in negotiating limits on cruise missiles because you don't know how many cruise missiles we intend to deploy and because you have insisted—unsuccessfully so far—on some system for counting production rates of cruise missiles in the future. In short, you want to know how many of these missiles we intend to put in carriers or bombers and how many we intend to put on surface ships and submarines. And you want to know that those limits are not being secretly exceeded by a massive production effort to stockpile extra cruise missiles."

Ekaterina said, "I believe that is correct, insofar as I understand the issue." A casual observer would have thought them an attractive couple discussing some romantic plan or intimacy. They sat close together facing the picturesque scenery framed by the window with their heads conspiratorially close together.

"In exchange for demonstrable assurances of the number of heavy ICBMs you will deploy in the future, I believe we would make available to you total planned production rates of air- and sea-launched cruise missiles for the next five years. And I think we might include where and how those missiles are to be deployed—by bomber or carrier type and by type of ship. You already know the maximum ranges of these missiles." Connaughton took a deep breath.

"You mentioned the problem of verification... of counting future production rates," she said.

"That's right. Somebody on your side is surely going to say, 'What's to prevent the Americans from a breakout— from stockpiling a supply of cruise missiles and suddenly doubling or tripling the number deployed?' Well, there are two solutions to that. First, deployment levels depend on the number of carriers—planes and ships—we have available. And you can count those as they're being outfitted, using your surveillance satellites, just as you can count the number of land-based cruise missile units in Europe. Second, we have a new way for you to check production rates, by uncovering the shipping end of the factories. In other words, our side would let you observe the outlet end of our cruise missile plants so that you could count the missiles coming off the assembly lines."

Ekaterina nodded slowly as if committing his words to memory. "May I ask you some questions, so that I clearly understand? On the first point, you have already argued in the negotiations that the number of cruise missile carriers is itself a limit on the number of these missiles. What is new about this?''

"Simply this," he said. "We'll open up the facilities which produce these carriers so that you can guarantee for yourself that we're not outfitting extra bombers or ships to carry cruise missiles. In other words, you would be able, under this plan, to definitely know the number of air and sea launchers for cruise missiles. You don't have that assurance now.''

She nodded again, absorbing his proposal as accurately as she could. "The second part of this approach is clearly new, even for someone with my limited understanding. But why have you not proposed this new surveillance approach in the negotiations? Why put it forward like this . . . behind the scenes?''

Connaughton liked the diplomatic politeness of her phrase. "This approach—uncovering production facilities—is being resisted by some on our side. They think it's dangerous and unnecessary. To overcome that resistance, we need some concession on your part. I'm giving you this so that your government will come forward with some bargaining position—say on large ICBMs—that we can consider a fair trade. I believe that we would consider a whole fresh verification scheme for limits, maybe even a freeze, on cruise missiles in exchange for a reduction in the number of your heavy land-based missiles. I know a reduction of twenty or twenty-five percent would be very attractive to my side.''

As before, Ekaterina merely picked at the lunch before her. An otherwise bored waiter hovered, offended that such delicious food might actually be rejected. Connaughton waved him away. "That may well be true," she said, privacy restored. "Clearly I did not come prepared to offer such a reduction or even promise some new bargaining position on our side.

"I do think, however," she continued, "I can tell you something on the issue of large land-based missiles which might be significant. During the holiday break in negotiations there were several important discussions involving our negotiating team and their principals in Moscow. Although I did not attend all those meetings—I was in Leningrad—I did attend several. And the subject always was the ICBMs, the heavy missiles. There is still strong feeling in the highest circles that these missiles are the mainstay of our nuclear forces and that we should refuse any reduction in numbers or effort to limit our plans to modernize them in the future."

She waited while a small group of schoolchildren chattered their way to the window to view the giant mountain, then retreated from the restaurant.

"But there is increasing interest within the Foreign Ministry in changing our position on heavy missiles—in putting them on the bargaining table. And, curiously, there is not as much resistance to that notion from the General Staff as might be expected. Many of the younger, post-World War II generals want to shift our deterrent strategy away from land-based missiles because of their vulnerability and toward more submarine-based missiles and cruise missiles such as you have. Defense Minister Kozlovsky seems to support this and even General Rusakov presented the younger officers' views on this. The real resistance came from the Central Committee, and of course from Zhdanov."

"How was the debate resolved?" Connaughton interjected tersely.

"It was not resolved, so far as I could tell. But it was quite bitter at times." She paused, thinking. "Zoshchenko seemed to be the key. They all made their arguments to him and I sensed both sides felt if they persuaded the Foreign Minister they would also have convinced Secretary Kamenev."

The waiter returned, cleared away the largely untouched food, and shortly returned with the espresso they had ordered. Ekaterina excused herself and Connaughton used the interruption to look for surveillance. He had checked repeatedly on the drive down from Geneva and concluded that, if they were being followed, it was by a relay team of real professionals. No one in the restaurant had stayed throughout their lunch and now the only suspicious sign was a dark blue Fiat with a Hertz sticker in the window and three men in business attire located near the car across the highway in the parking area. They were facing the restaurant and seemed in no hurry to be on their way. Ekaterina returned and once seated followed his gaze from behind her dark glasses. She looked a long time and said nothing.

"Do you know them?" Connaughton asked.

"I cannot tell exactly," Ekaterina said. "They may be security from our mission. That is not one of our cars, but they behave the way our people usually do...not very subtle." She hesitated. "Besides, Ambassador Makarov knows we are meeting today—although not where. I can't think why he would want us followed."

Connaughton speculated, "What if it's not Makarov? What if someone else in your mission—the KGB, Metrinko for example—wanted to know what you were up to? What if they found out on their own we were meeting...for some purpose?"

Ekaterina looked genuinely concerned, as if the thought had never before occurred to her. "It is not out of the question. There is one way, of course, to find out. Let's go."

She sipped the espresso and then suddenly rose. Connaughton stood to join her and the waiter scurried up with the check and their coats. Connaughton placed some lire on the table, more than enough for the lunch, and they emerged quickly into the bright sun. He escorted her across the highway and into the Ford, taking care to seem relaxed and ignore the nearby Fiat.

He started the car and drove into the town of Courmayeur. At the main intersection he turned left and made two more left turns in succession. He waited for a moment just short of the stop sign, saw nothing ahead or in his mirror, and turned right onto the highway heading back to the Mont Blanc Tunnel. As they passed the restaurant they saw the blue Fiat had left. They made the short climb to the tunnel entrance and transited the tunnel in silence again, as if their voices might be more easily heard in the dark closeness. On the other side they descended into the Arve Valley in France again. Checking his watch, Connaughton saw it was only 3:45. Once at the main highway he turned right toward Chamonix. He drove into the ski resort area. It reminded him of a brief ski trip he had made to Vail. Most of the hotels were modern-chalet and most of the shops for the tourist trade. He made some elaborate turns and twists through the village, then returned to the highway and turned north and west for Geneva. Initially confused, Ekaterina soon understood the purpose of his maneuvers without asking.

To ease her tension and escape the gloom of nuclear weapons, Connaughton told stories about Montana during most of the drive back to Geneva. The broad valleys, clumps of trees, and snow-patched uplands fled by as he talked about his father and old Grandfather John, the original pioneer Connaughton. He talked about his love of his homestead...the cattle, the rocky ridges that surrounded his ranch, the trees, the wildlife, the streams. His voice was different, she thought. He didn't sound the way he did when he was talking about weapons. His expression was lighter, his eyes shone, and he laughed occasionally at the antics of an ancestor or eccentric neighbor. The miles and time passed as rapidly as the peaceful countryside and they were soon at the Swiss border outside Geneva. They were passed through and Ekaterina asked to be taken to the Hotel Richemond.

Connaughton asked with concern, "Will it be all right? Have you stayed away too long?"

She smiled and said that she thought his information about cruise missiles would make Makarov very happy and keep his mind off the length of time she had been gone. As they approached the hotel, she turned to him. "It was lovely hearing about your home and, in spite of the seriousness of the luncheon conversation, it was a very enjoyable afternoon. Shall I see you again?"

"Certainly." Handing her a small piece of paper he added, "This is the phone number at my apartment. Call me next week if you can get to a phone outside the mission and we'll arrange another meeting. Let's see what results we may get from this one first." Then, "Thank you." She smiled again and was gone, walking to the nearby taxi stand. He turned the car left onto the Quai du Mont-Blanc and toward the U.S. Mission. As he swung left onto the Quai du Président Wilson, he saw, two cars back, a dark blue Fiat. But it contained only two men.

35

"THE VOTE ON BLUE THUNDER was four to one," Secretary of Defense Sternberg notified the members of the National Security Council. "The lone holdout is still Bigby, but the Joint Chiefs operate by consensus, so he's obliged to cooperate fully in the operation."

"May we assume the others are enthusiastic?" asked Secretary Norton.

Sternberg reacted predictably to the perceived sarcasm in Norton's question. "Damn right," he almost shouted. "They believe a demonstration of our strength is just what our allies and even our own troops need right now. A real morale booster, and a real shot in the arm for democracy."

"Mr. President." Norton turned to the head of the table. It was unusual for President Lawkard to attend National Security Council meetings. He was there because his staff felt he had to reverse an increasing public impression that he was inactive and uninvolved in important deliberations. He also wanted to find out more about this infernal Blue Thunder that was kicking up so much disturbance in his administration. "Undersecretary Bilburger has just returned from a tour of NATO capitals and has visited with virtually all our allied foreign ministers," Norton continued. "He reports a total lack of enthusiasm right now for major military exercises this spring. There is an almost unanimous feeling among our NATO allies that the timing could not be worse—with a new round of arms control negotiations under way and with the political violence recently in their countries over the nuclear issue. Whatever the merits of a major NATO exercise later on, I strongly believe it is unwise to go forward with this Blue Thunder in April.''

Sternberg said, ''Emerson, the politicians in those countries are out of touch with the people. The military leaders we've talked to believe just as strongly that an impressive, coordinated show of strength in a couple of months will silence the protesters and give the Russians a real reason to negotiate seriously.''

Vice-President Burgoon jumped in. ''Mr. President, it gets down to this: You have agreed with the recommendation of the National Security Council that this operation be planned and, barring some unforeseen circumstances, undertaken this spring. We have engaged our allies in this operation and their military forces are prepared to go forward regardless of minor resistance from their bureaucracies. Most importantly, the press is aware these exercises have been planned, and any postponement would cause all sorts of speculation and charges of indecisiveness. It seems to me we're committed.''

Burgoon always played the ''indecisiveness'' card when the stakes were high. He knew it to be the charge that stung Lawkard the worst. He had gotten the President to make two or three major decisions against his own judgment on the simple ground that to do otherwise would look weak and bumbling.

''General Proctor,'' Lawkard said, turning to the Chairman of the Joint Chiefs, ''what is Admiral Bigby's concern . . . why doesn't he agree with the program?''

Proctor cleared his throat and sat forward. ''Mr. President, Admiral Bigby argues that the timing is bad. He points out the fact that the Russians are preparing major exercises at the same time in mid-April and that you will, therefore, have the two superpowers and their allies deployed against each other for the first time since the end of

World War II. I don't agree with his concern, but, in a word, that's it."

"Well, I must say"—Lawkard scratched his head ruefully—"I don't recall paying as much attention to that fact as I probably should have when I approved this operation."

Arnold Danzig held his breath. He had superficially briefed the President, as his principal national security adviser, on Blue Thunder as part of crowded agendas. But, at the insistence of Burgoon and Sternberg, he had never presented a decision memorandum to the President for signature. They had merely been using the President's acquiescence in the briefings as authorization. As time went on Lawkard, typically, simply assumed he had approved Operation Blue Thunder sometime before.

"Mr. President," Danzig said hesitantly, "that's probably my fault. I remember mentioning"—here he consulted his heavily annotated daily log—"in my briefing to you on November twenty-first and again on December ninth that the Warsaw Pact forces would, according to our best intelligence, probably be carrying out military exercises sometime this spring also. But there has been a lot going on in the past few months, and I may not have emphasized that fact as much as I should have."

The Secretary of State spoke up. "Mr. President, I strongly agree with Admiral Bigby. Except in the rare cases of a Berlin blockade or Cuban missile crisis, we have purposely avoided using military force to provoke the Kremlin. That has been a hallmark of our foreign policy and one with which I very much agree. We should pay attention to Admiral Bigby's very reasonable concern."

Sternberg interjected, "Emerson, Jim Proctor has said the other Chiefs disagree. We can't make national policy because of one officer."

"Unless he's right," Norton shot back.

Lawkard's brow was furrowed. He strongly disliked controversy, especially among his senior advisers. He addressed Philip Warrenton. "What can you tell me about the Warsaw Pact exercises, Phil? What will happen if we're both out there charging around at the same time?"

Warrenton stirred himself from a momentary daydream of sailing his boat to the Caribbean and never hearing Sternberg and Norton quarrel again. "As far as the intelligence community can tell, Mr. President, the Soviets and their allies are preparing for annual exercises this spring, probably about the time of Blue Thunder. We should not emphasize Warsaw Pact involvement too much because, as we know, they play a minor role in these things. The Soviets mostly use these exercises to keep their allies in line and intimidate the Western Europeans through their show of strength. This operation may be larger than usual, however, in that every five years or so they put on a real show—bring their ships out and put their planes in the air and move their mobile rockets around—just to impress everyone. And it's about time for another one of those gala productions."

"Well, what will happen," Lawkard asked, still puzzled, "if we're both out there charging around at the same time?"

"You should probably ask Jim Proctor that question, Mr. President," Warrenton replied. "But at the very least we could see some Soviet and American ships getting pretty close to each other in the Greenland-Iceland-UK gap, the Eastern Med, and maybe the Baltic—the so-called choke points. Our radar will show a lot of Soviet planes in the air at once—and vice versa. And tanks and troops will be kicking up a lot of dust in Central Europe."

"That's pretty much it, Mr. President," Proctor said in response to Lawkard's quizzical gaze. "On the up side, it will give us a chance to see how we look faced off against each other. And we may not like some of what we see. On the down side, it does offer the opportunity for some trigger-happy commander to get nervous and start something."

Norton sensed for the first time a slowing of the Blue Thunder momentum and decided to gamble. "General, I assume if both sides go through with these exercises simultaneously that our ability to monitor what the Soviets are doing will be crucial."

"Absolutely," Proctor barked.

"What would happen if some of our satellite capability failed during these exercises . . . say, if our high-orbit satellites that monitor their strategic forces failed or were interfered with?"

"By God, I for one wouldn't be pleased, I'll tell you that," Proctor blared. "We would be in one tough spot. The Soviets would have all the potential for a preemptive strike or at least blackmail, without our ability of seeing the hole card. I wouldn't like that situation one bit." He paused, then said more softly, "But if the Russians knock out our satellites, we ought to assume we're on the edge of war right then anyway."

Norton turned to Warrenton.

"Do the Soviets have the capability to do that?" From the corner of his eye, Norton could see Lawkard watching this exchange like a Ping-Pong match.

Warrenton hesitated. "We don't know exactly. They've had an antisatellite testing program for over ten years. For a while it was pretty primitive. But recently we believe they've begun to experiment with some pretty sophisticated stuff—heat-seeking projectiles launched from space, ground-based lasers, and so forth. It's probably safe to assume they could do some damage to our most important satellites right now."

There was an uneasy silence in the National Security Council conference room. Sternberg looked angry, and Harold Burgoon looked uncomfortable. Then the President said, "Yes, but if they did that to us, we'd hit them back.

We're not helpless. We've got our own antisatellite program, don't we? Isn't that the Cyclone . . . or Cylcops . . . or whatever it is, Harold?''

"That's right, Mr. President," Burgoon said quietly and patiently. "You'll recall we discussed the need to have our own antisatellite program as a deterrent to the Soviets—so they wouldn't start anything in this area."

"Right," mumbled the President, still obviously confused by the drift in the conversation.

Norton seized his opportunity. "Mr. President, could we find out from Phil and the intelligence community what the effect would be if we were to preemptively destroy Soviet strategic surveillance satellites?"

"Sure, Em, that's a logical question," Lawkard said. "What about it, Phil?"

Warrenton managed to look smug, detached, and amused all at once. "Mr. President, it is safe to assume Soviet reaction would be exactly the same as ours. They would be, if you pardon the expression, pissed."

Lawkard chuckled at Warrenton's uncharacteristic vernacular and said, "Right. Well, who wouldn't be?" as he looked around the room. Only Proctor looked at him directly, but the President didn't seem to notice.

Presently Lawkard turned to Norton. "Em, come around as soon as you can to fill me in on the latest in the Philippines and give me a little more detail on Bilburger's visit with the NATO foreign ministers. If we're going to do this Blue Thunder thing, we better know what we're doing and what the consequences are. I don't want to cause some political flap with our allies or get the goddam demonstrators back in the streets. But in the meantime, Joe," he said to Sternberg, "you and Jim Proctor go forward with preparations for this exercise full speed while we try to sort out the politics of it. Harold, you continue to be my liaison on Blue Thunder as before and make sure you and Arnie keep me abreast of all developments. I guess this is a bigger deal than I thought and so I better pay more attention to it.''

The President stood up to end the meeting and the others quickly followed. Lawkard signaled Norton to follow him and they exited to Burgoon's furious glare.

As they rode the elevator to the main floor of the White House, Lawkard said, ''Em, come around in the next day or two. I'll clear an hour. I want to talk about this damn operation and I also want you to bring me up to date on the Geneva negotiations. All right?'' Norton nodded as the President bustled down the back hall with his Secret Service escorts to the Oval Office.

36

FRANK CONNAUGHTON AWOKE in his small apartment on the Grand' Rue in Geneva with a start. His dream—nightmare, more precisely—was of pursuit once again. Each time he had the dream the pursuers became more vivid. What had jolted him awake this time was the sense that one of the pursuers was a tall, dark-haired woman. It was 5 A.M. and pitch-black inside and outside. He snapped on a reading light knowing full well his sleep was murdered. He made notes in a frayed journal about his meeting with Ekaterina a few days before, mostly impressions and all in complex code. He found himself spending an increasing amount of time analyzing the details of the information she gave, and the subtleties of her moods, and possible motives for her actions. He found a calendar on his desk and began to consider the pressure of time. Depending on whether progress was being made in the talks, there was the possibility of a two-week break in the negotiations for a brief return to Washington and Moscow. If they were making real progress, that might be reduced to a few days. Connaughton, backed up by the impressions of more seasoned negotiators, sensed that the next four weeks—roughly until early March were crucial. If his exchanges with Ekaterina Davydova were going to lead to any movement, it would be seen during that period.

He rousted himself out of bed, put on the old robe, and started the coffee. It would be at least two hours before Arkwright's car came around to take him to the Ambassador's home for breakfast. He used the time to think about what he would say. Even as he was sitting in the warm backseat of the long car driving to the exclusive residential area of Cologny overlooking Lake Geneva at dawn, he still wasn't sure.

Ambassador Arkwright had arranged to meet with Connaughton for an hour and then have Charlie Curtis join them for coffee and strategy. Arkwright chose to have breakfast served in his library and they got right to business upon Connaughton's arrival.

"Well, what did she have to say, Frank?" Arkwright asked directly.

"If she's to be believed, Barrett, they're ready to come off their traditional position on heavy ICBMs." Arkwright's eyebrows lifted and he whistled. He began to make notes. "Zoshchenko is apparently the key to a major change of policy on their part. Kozlovsky and the General Staff apparently are ready to reshape their strategic forces along the lines of ours, with more emphasis on subs and cruises, but the resistance is coming from the Central Committee types who are stuck with the old doctrine."

"God," Arkwright muttered, "are you sure she knows what she's talking about?"

"They had a series of heavy meetings over the holiday break and, except for a couple she missed while visiting her family, she attended them all. I think the answer is yes. I believe she's telling the truth and we now have a reliable ear inside their highest strategic deliberations."

Arkwright said, "What is it going to take to move Zoshchenko and the Foreign Ministry into line with the Defense Ministry and away from the Central Committee?"

"Some real guts, which he is apparently not known for, and his sense that he can deliver Kamenev on this. What he cannot do, for his own political purposes, is come down on the wrong side of an issue this big. It could ruin his chances to become General Secretary."

"What an opportunity." Arkwright seemed to be thinking aloud. Then to Connaughton, "What do we have to do—sit and wait?"

"I don't think we can afford to, Barrett. I think we could tip the balance. I think you and Secretary Norton ought to convince the President to authorize us to make an offer on cruise missiles—one tied to reductions in Soviet ICBMs—that's so attractive it pulls Zoshchenko our way."

"God, Frank." Arkwright took a deep breath. "That's bold stuff. We'd have some selling to do on our own side. I can see Joe Sternberg and probably Omar King going right into orbit."

"That's why I said go to the President." Connaughton was talking fast and hard. "Outflank the opposition. Get Lawkard on our side first and get the initiative away from the other side for a change." Arkwright was writing furiously. "I thought about this a lot since I saw Ekat...Miss Davydova. And here's the way I think it could be done. Have Norton go to the President—this week—tomorrow. Propose the offer to the Soviets on the ground that, what have we lost if they turn us down?"

"What we've lost, Frank, is diplomatic initiative if they turn us down. Remember how long it took for the Russians to dump on the Carter-Vance proposal in 1977? About an hour. And the Secretary of State had to come home from Moscow hat in hand."

"I haven't finished, Barrett," Connaughton said impatiently. "Don't go public with this proposal. That's what sunk the '77 initiative. Try a two-track approach, both behind the scenes. You take Makarov off in the woods somewhere—like Nitze did with Kvitsinsky in 1982—and lay out the deal. Simultaneously have Norton contact Zoshchenko through Ambassador Dubinin in Washington with the same proposal. No press. No publicity."

Arkwright's eyebrows were up again and he continued to write cryptic notes to himself. "That's fine, but what's the deal?"

Connaughton went over the cruise-ICBM trade-off he'd discussed with Ekaterina.

Arkwright was silent for several minutes as he wrote. He drank his coffee slowly. He finally asked several technical questions, then said, "Are you sure this woman knows what she's talking about? Because if she doesn't, none of this makes any sense." He paused. "On the other hand, if she's telling the truth, this is an extraordinary deal you've put together based on the premise she gave you."

Connaughton hesitated, savoring the irony of what he was about to say. "I'd bet my life on it, Barrett. I've never been surer of anything."

Arkwright walked to the back window of his long library to see the sun coming over the mountains to the east of Mont Blanc. "I intend to spend the rest of the morning going over this proposal looking for flaws. I'll ask a few random questions of Murray and Quainton to see if you're missing something, without letting them know what I'm up to. If this thing still makes sense by noon, I'm going to send an 'eyes only' cable to Em explaining the idea in outline and then whip back to the States over the weekend to talk to him personally about it."

It was now Connaughton's turn to raise his eyebrows. Those two lonely hours earlier in his kitchen might turn out to have been more worthwhile than he could have imagined. "What about the press?" he asked.

"That's easy." Arkwright grinned as he came back to Connaughton's chair. "Our son, John, is playing varsity basketball for Dartmouth against Harvard this weekend and I've never seen him play. Even the most hardhearted reporter will buy that." He rubbed his hands together. He was clearly enjoying the cloak-and-dagger side of Connaughton's proposal, as well as the chance for a major breakthrough after months of fruitless, frustrating negotiations.

Connaughton said, "Barrett, I know this is a long shot and the chances of success aren't very great, given the politics on both sides. But I want you to know how glad I am you're at least giving this long shot your personal support. It means a lot to me."

"Forget it, Frank," Arkwright replied. "I'm not getting behind this as a reward for you. I think it makes damn good sense, at least initially, and it's worth a roll of the dice."

Connaughton eased himself from the leather chair, suddenly feeling great fatigue, and paced the room for a moment. "One thing we haven't got straight yet, Barrett, is how we deal with Miss Davydova...I mean within our own channels. We've been after reductions in Soviet ICBMs for years. So no one on their side will be surprised by that aspect of this approach. But if word starts spreading within our own government, even at very high levels, that we have a source inside their delegation, God knows what could happen. If they've penetrated any of our agencies, word will be in Moscow in hours and she'll be dead or headed for Siberia." He came close to Arkwright and looked him in the eye. "We can't let that happen. I will not let it happen."

Arkwright had known Frank Connaughton for almost twelve years and he both was and was not surprised by his younger friend's intensity. But it did occur to him for the first time that his odd clandestine relationship with the Russian woman had become more than just that. "I promise you, Frank, it will go no further...with one important exception. I must tell Em where the idea started. He's not going to take seriously a negotiating package he thinks you and I cooked up on some lonely winter evening by the fire. The only thing that gives this whole thing credibility is the reported shift in policy under way in some circles in Moscow, and Zoshchenko's possible role as the hinge in the whole business. That's news and it's important. It changes the entire picture and gives us a window we haven't had before. I must tell Em where this came from." Arkwright took Connaughton's arm in an awkward gesture of friendship. "But believe me, it will go no further. I've known Emerson Norton for thirty-one years and there's no one I trust more. In fact, he's named executor in my will. That's our relationship."

"What about the President?" Connaughton asked.

Arkwright gazed toward the ceiling as if to summon guidance. "Our President has never been a man for details, to say the least. Em may mention a new high-level source in the Soviet government. But I would be surprised if he got any questions beyond that. Further, it's rumored in Washington drawing rooms that the President's memory—never too good to begin with—is slipping somewhat. Trust me—I'll tell Em he has to protect us on this. In fact, the arrangement will be that only you, I, and the Secretary of State will know the identity of this source."

Out the front window of the library to the west, Connaughton saw the dark clouds beginning to form on the French horizon. There would be more snow by nightfall. At least it was better than the cold winter rain. He thought briefly of Francesca, hoping she was well and meaning to call her that day, then of Ekaterina's two sons whom he had never seen and probably never would, then of Ekaterina herself, wondering what her life inside that cloistered mission was like. He thought how enjoyable it would be to call her up and ask her to dinner and to hear the visiting London Symphony that evening. He thought of her aged father whom she loved, and his music, so linked with the tragedy of a world at war. Finally, as he saw Charlie Curtis pull into the drive in the weathered Ford he and Ekaterina had used just days before, he thought of the three and then the two men in the dark blue Fiat. He decided for the moment to keep that to himself. If he believed after any future meetings the two of them to be under surveillance, he would have no choice but to bring the matter up with Barrett and seek whatever counsel he might have. Something told him there was very little the American Ambassador could do about the matter, regardless of where the shadows came from.

37

EKATERINA HAD NEVER particularly trusted Makarov. It was not that he was inherently evil. It was more that he had the capacity for vindictiveness. His ego did not tolerate rebuffs lightly and she had found it necessary to rebuff him on several occasions in the past. It was a practice she had developed almost into an art form, and he had finally given up. But, she believed, he remembered and was capable of getting even.

In the case of the contacts with Connaughton, however, she had little choice but to confide in him and therefore to trust him. She had few, if any, alternatives. Metrinko, whom she rather liked personally, was too loyal to the KGB and would have had no choice but to make the Connaughton matter a new—and major—espionage file. Vronsky was, she thought, simply a lecherous fool. Polyakov was too old and too anti-American. The others in the delegation simply didn't have the rank to handle the matter or couldn't be trusted. She had fairly high level professional and social contacts with the Foreign Ministry in Moscow, but they were far away and difficult to communicate with. Makarov was there in Geneva, was her superior, and had to be dealt with. It came down to that.

She had decided after the exchange with Connaughton in the department store, and his invitation to meet in the Russian Church, to take the matter directly to Makarov and recruit him into the enterprise. Her tactic would be to appeal to his weakness—his ego. She first downplayed the contact, saying it probably would lead to nothing and might possibly be no more than a mild, and ill-advised, flirtation. But, on the other hand, if it turned out that the American wanted, for whatever reason, to be helpful, think what a coup that could turn out to be, if properly handled, for Makarov himself. Think how happy and impressed the Foreign Minister himself, indeed the entire Politburo, would be if Mikhail Makarov turned up a source inside the American delegation. The risks of pursuing the contact at least a step at a time were minimal and the potential rewards for the Soviet Union—and Mikhail Makarov—were enormous.

Since she did not know where this trail might lead, the two of them agreed—Makarov thinking the notion to be his idea—to keep the contact just between them. He could justify keeping Metrinko and the security people in the dark for the time being on the grounds that this might be a false alarm and there was no need for everyone to get excited. Makarov personally authorized her to go to the Russian Church. Then that Sunday, immediately following her meeting with Connaughton, Ekaterina reported to Makarov that she believed the American wanted to help the negotiations along by providing some insights into strategy and plans on the American side, perhaps even some specifics on deployment proposals. She apologized to Makarov for perhaps being too bold but explained how she had arranged another meeting, a lunch in Chambesy, on the contingency that Ambassador Makarov approved. She said she felt Connaughton had to be encouraged and not permitted to think too much about what he was proposing to do. That was why she had taken the initiative to suggest another discussion. She also had wanted it to be as comfortable and as social as possible to further put Connaughton at his ease. Makarov's eyes had narrowed as she talked and his mouth twisted into a clever smile. He reached over to the obviously nervous interpreter and patted her tightly laced hands, congratulating her on her quick thinking and absolutely perfect judgment.

After the lunch in Chambesy she reported again to Makarov, saying that Connaughton was prepared to discuss cruise missiles, space systems, deployment plans, and overall negotiating strategies, and in fact he had proposed yet another meeting the following week at the Cathédrale de Saint-Pierre to discuss these matters. At this point the usually poised Ekaterina Davydova seemed to become stressed and distracted, saying that this was not a game she felt prepared to play and why didn't the Ambassador turn this matter over to a more skilled operative in the field of international intrigue and espionage? Makarov seemed to enjoy once more consoling and comforting her and expressed his great confidence in her abilities to handle the situation. He pointed out that she was involved in something much more important to their efforts in Geneva and to her country than interpreting itself, and that she was uniquely positioned to take advantage of this extraordinary opportunity. He smiled shrewdly again and said that Connaughton would undoubtedly feel uncomfortable talking to someone else in the Soviet delegation, that he clearly felt some empathy and rapport with her that could not automatically be transferred to someone else. No, he said, she had no choice in the interest of international peace but to carry through with this contact.

There followed days later the meeting at the cathedral and the drive to Mont Blanc and lunch at Courmayeur. Once again, Ekaterina arranged to meet with Makarov immediately and report on the information Connaughton had provided about cruise missiles and the possibility for a breakthrough on verifiable limits on these new weapons of such concern to the Soviets. Makarov listened intently, took elaborate notes, asked detailed questions—then urged Ekaterina not to discuss any of this information or even the fact of her meetings with Connaughton with any other member of the delegation or employee of the mission. She asked him, almost as a co-conspirator, how he proposed to handle all this. He said it was of such importance that he intended to bypass all bureaucratic channels and deal directly with the Foreign Minister himself.

Ekaterina said, "I am, of course, no expert on these matters. What can the Foreign Minister do with this information?"

Makarov assumed the role of docent. "It gives him a new perspective on thinking in the U.S. government. Clearly there are those who wish to use the cruise missile program as bargaining leverage for our large land-based missiles. This we have expected before, Katya, but your information from Connaughton confirms that the reverse is now true—that we can use our ICBMs to limit numbers of cruise missiles. Plus he is suggesting a novel way of verifying numerical limits. This could be vitally important—a whole new basis for an agreement. Is this something of his own, do you think, or is he reflecting a broader point of view in his government?"

"I am unable to tell, Ambassador," she said. "My strong impression is that he has discussed this at considerable length with experts and policy makers. I gather he is suggesting an approach that has a broader base of support on his side." She was uncomfortable in Makarov's private quarters, particularly on a Saturday evening when many mission employees would be leaving in groups for a film or restaurant dinner. She had spent little time there since the early days in Geneva when the negotiations began over a year before and Makarov had invited her around for cocktails, ostensibly for discussion of her role as principal interpreter, but actually for his unsubtle efforts at seduction. Mrs. Makarov was occasionally in residence. But the portly matron hated Geneva winters, preferring Moscow snow to Swiss rain, and she was presently back in the Soviet Union. Ekaterina assumed Makarov's office to be bugged by the

KGB but she was less sure of his private quarters. He leaned close to her when they talked, but she couldn't be sure that was not simply crude intimacy. He also kept his tape recorder at moderately high volume, which both complicated electronic eavesdropping and aided his own failing hearing.

"I intend to get this information off to Foreign Minister Zoshchenko tonight," Makarov breathed, "and explain as delicately as I can in a highly confidential cable the nature of our source and your role in this. I will be careful to protect you as much as I can and to stress my own strong belief that other elements of our government should not be involved at the present time."

"Other elements of our government" she knew to be a euphemism for the KGB. "How shall I handle this matter from this point on?" she asked.

Makarov became avuncular. "We assume our American friend has other business on his mind...that he will wish to talk with you again, perhaps soon." He lit a black cigarette. "You should go. You should meet with him and hear what he has to say. How was it left, this matter? How is he to contact you?"

"He gave me his telephone number...at his apartment," she said. "He asked me to call him from outside the mission when I am able to get free again. I assume he would like to meet regularly."

Makarov leaned forward. "Then by all means do so. Sometime next week get in touch with him and arrange to meet again. Draw him out. Ask questions, particularly about their future deployment plans, and find out anything you can about disagreements or conflicts within their own government about arms control policy." He wagged a sausagelike finger. "Do not seem too eager. But use whatever skills you have to very subtly bring him out. Make him feel comfortable. Let him feel you are a true confidante."

"Ambassador," she said with genuine concern, "what about others in our delegation, others in our government?

May they not soon become suspicious? How can I protect myself against . . . criticism, if this is found out?''

"Your protection, Comrade Katya," Makarov said expansively, "is with me and with the Foreign Minister. I am sure when he sees what we are discovering here, he will authorize me to do all in my power to protect you and protect our source." He thought for a moment. "Of course, the Foreign Minister will have to make this information available to others highly placed in our government, perhaps to the complete Politburo. But I know him well. And if I tell him we risk the bird flying the nest if we watch it laying its eggs too closely, I know he will understand. He will protect you, be sure of that. And for your heroic efforts and personal sacrifice, needless to say, rewards—great rewards—lie ahead. Your extraordinary role in developing and bringing along this valuable source will be known and remembered by very highly placed people, people who can be extremely helpful to you in the future."

She thought, as Makarov spoke in his hushed but glowing tones, What a pompous hypocrite he is. He is thinking of the promotion this will mean for him and the favor he will curry in the ministry and the Politburo if this truly turns out to be a coup. And he had nothing to do with it. He didn't find or motivate Connaughton—and couldn't in a hundred lifetimes. He's just a messenger, a messenger between me and Moscow. But he was also her buffer and her protection, at least for the time being. She had received what she wanted most, and that was authority to continue to see Connaughton. She was surprised as she saw the darkness envelop Makarov's tasteless sitting room how important that chance was becoming to her. This whole business had happened so fast—all in a matter of days. But a dependency was developing—one that she wasn't familiar or comfortable with, but a dependency nonetheless.

She wondered what made men like Makarov and Connaughton so different. It certainly wasn't nationality. Some of the American men were as tedious and hollow as Makarov. And she had met one or two Russian men who came close to Connaughton's strength and intensity. It was something else—some magic quality. Sadly, too rare, she thought. Perhaps it was places like Montana, places where spirits grow and soar. Her revery was invaded by Makarov's unctuous invitation to stay for dinner, to continue their discussion over a drink or two and perhaps something special from his cook.

She looked at her watch and started to her feet. She unfortunately could not, she pleaded truthfully. He had promised to go to the cinema and dinner with several others from the mission staff and their party was leaving in a few moments. He walked her to the door of his private quarters, taking her elbow to slow her escape. "Remember," he said, "maintain the contact, show genuine interest, ask questions...and most of all don't worry about what you are doing. You are protected. I will protect you. I promise you the Foreign Minister will protect you."

She thanked him elaborately for being so kind and understanding and escaped down the hallway to her room as quickly as she could.

Once inside her room on the other side of the mission she closed and locked her door. Makarov was on his way to becoming drunk and wouldn't bother to check her story about going out for the evening. But he was certainly sober enough to know what she was talking about. In fact, that very moment she was sure he was drafting a highly confidential cable to Zoshchenko laying out the situation with the American. What she didn't know was what the cable would say about her and her role in the whole affair. She felt a desperate need for caution, understanding how easily she could become the victim if the gears of Kremlin politics shifted against her. But the circumstances did not permit caution. She and Connaughton would go on meeting—how many times she had no idea. And each meeting was an occasion for detection by someone. She had been frightened that Makarov might suggest she use his apartment for the purpose of her calls to Connaughton. But even he must know his calls were monitored by the KGB. She felt she must exchange whatever information there was to exchange with Connaughton as quickly as possible and have it done with. Time became a factor. The longer this went on, the more terrible the risk. It was better to take chances now and get the affair over with than be cautious and protract it. That was the only thing she was sure of—time was of the essence. This unbelievable gamble she and Connaughton were taking had to pay off soon, or it had to end. Because if Makarov or anyone found out it was a two-way street, that she was giving as well as getting, then it was over for her. Her parents would not live long enough to see Ivan and little Anton to maturity. Their father was a terrible influence with that horrible second wife. The boys would be the real victims if she was caught. Yet they were also the reason she had to go on.

Later, she tried to sleep, with little success. When she was able to doze her sleep was troubled by visions of exile, torture, and execution.

38

ANDREA CASS WAS PLEASED with herself. She had been very busy and she had that peculiar glow, that combined sense of satisfaction and excitement, the hunter gets upon sighting the quarry. She was on to something, and that thought excited her enormously.

She had been in Geneva now for more than three weeks—not long to cover a story of many dimensions and great breadth, but long enough for frustration to grow. She had felt about this story—the arms control negotiations—the way a miner of valuable minerals must feel. She paced the mountain knowing in her bones and guts there was gold beneath the rocks and crevices but not knowing exactly where to sink the shaft. So she panned. She spent her time patiently sifting through the silt and gravel, looking, always looking for the glint, the speck, the glittering grain of dust that said "gold."

Then came the Connaughton piece. She was sitting in her small rented office on the Place Grenus trying to put the story together. She had interviewed Connaughton for more than two hours over dinner the previous evening. She had talked to Ambassador Arkwright about him and had quotes from other members of the American delegation. She even had a laudatory comment from Ambassador Makarov about what a serious contributor to the negotiating process Mr. Connaughton was. And she was piecing all this together to try to create a mosaic that would be of some interest to the casual reader. The piece had possibilities. It was a different, more personal insight into the arcane world of arms control and international diplomacy. And Connaughton himself was something of an anomaly—Western man with an Eastern education, cowboy with an interest in nuclear weapons, and all the rest. Her editors had even suggested the possibility of lengthening the piece into something for the Sunday *Times Magazine*.

Cass went back over the *New York Times* file on Connaughton. It showed that he had a wife and daughter. He had talked with pride of his daughter, Francesca, during the dinner interview, but asked that references to his family be left out of the profile. Research done by reporters in her Washington bureau had turned up his wife's location and condition, and Cass had already concluded that information was irrelevant to her story. She had some sympathy for Connaughton—he seemed a fairly lonely fellow. Then, on her third reading of the short file she noticed that Connaughton had been a neighbor and boyhood friend of Harry Rafferty in Montana. That was odd. Rafferty had been in the news lately, with his peculiar accident and the antisatellite fuss in the Senate.

She picked up the telephone, referred to her desk-top Rolodex, and dialed the number of the United States Mission. They put her through to Connaughton's office and he happened to be in.

"Mr. Connaughton, this is Andrea Cass. Thank you for joining me for dinner last night. It was very enjoyable and you were kind to give me much of the evening. I did notice one thing in our background file that I neglected to ask you about last night. I see that you grew up more or less with Senator Rafferty in Montana. Is that correct?"

Connaughton said, "Yes, we lived on neighboring properties near Great Falls. Actually, our grandfathers homesteaded that land together about the same time and so our families have known each other for quite some time."

"Did you and Senator Rafferty go to school together and so forth?" she asked.

"Yes," he replied, "we went to the same schools through high school and went out on dates together and played sports...that sort of thing. Harry...Senator Rafferty then went off to Harvard, but we managed to stay in touch and we still see each other in Washington and occasionally when we're both back in Montana."

"Mr. Connaughton, as an old friend, you must have been very concerned about Senator Rafferty's accident in January. Were you there at the time?"

Connaughton began to feel inexplicably uneasy. "Yes, I was in Washington when that happened. It gave us quite a scare until we found out he was all right. Bonnie, Mrs. Rafferty, was very worried of course, but also very strong about it. But Harry was lucky and I understand he's fine now."

"Mr. Connaughton, do you think he was run over on purpose?"

Connaughton held his breath a moment. "Miss Cass, I can't possibly see what that has to do with a profile on me and I have no idea why you would think such a thing might happen."

She said, "It does not have to do with the story on you and I don't intend to use it that way. Why some people think it might have happened is because your friend Senator Rafferty has been kicking up some dust around Washington about antisatellite weapons and has apparently got some people in high places worried and unhappy."

"So far as I know," Connaughton shot back, "that has never been a reason to run over someone, let alone a United States senator, with a truck."

"How do you know it was a truck?" she countered quickly. "That wasn't in the accident report."

"I don't know it was a truck and I have no idea what was in the accident report," Connaughton said with the edge of a tone of exasperation. He was suddenly in an area that made him very uncomfortable and he was beginning to suspect Cass's motives. "Senator Rafferty probably mentioned that he thought it could have been a truck. But I frankly don't see what that has to do with anything."

Cass said, "It probably doesn't. It was just curious that you had that detail. Did you see him that night?"

"Yes, I did," Connaughton said. "I got word that Harry had been hurt and so I went directly to the hospital to see what I could do."

"Did he speculate or suggest to you why he might have been hit?" she asked.

"No, he did not," Connaughton lied. "As far as I know he—and everyone else—assumes it was simply an accident."

"As I'm sure you know," she said, "the vehicle—truck or whatever—has never been located. It's still under investigation as a hit-and-run."

"That so?" Connaughton replied as nonchalantly as he could.

"Indeed," she said. "Meantime, I'm told, Senator Rafferty is not only back on his feet, but he's resumed kicking up dust."

Connaughton laughed for the first time. "That's what we Montanans do, Miss Cass. Kick up dust. Or kick something else."

Cass smiled to herself, knowing what it was of hers Connaughton wanted to kick at the moment. "Yes," she said casually, "he's back on the trail . . . the trail of Cyclops."

There was a very long silence. Connaughton finally said, "Miss Cass, that is not a subject to discuss on the telephone, or for that matter anywhere else. I suspect, if you don't mind, I better get back to work. Thank you very much for dinner. The press officer here will answer any other questions you have for your profile. Good-bye."

Cass looked at the buzzing phone for a moment, then put it back in its cradle. My, my, my, she thought. That little shot in the dark certainly struck a nerve. But which one? His friendship with Rafferty, Rafferty's "accident," or Cyclops? Or all three? What if they were related? That finely tuned, highly instinctive reporter's mind began to work out connections. Rafferty and Connaughton were friends. Rafferty was a senator interested in arms control and Connaughton was on the arms control delegation. She had gotten a tip about the Cyclops project from some still-mysterious, but knowledgeable, source. Why couldn't one— or even both—of them have gotten the same tip from the same source? What if someone high up in the administration was doing something funny with the nation's newest and possibly most dangerous antisatellite weapon? What if the something funny went beyond the bounds of what they could trust even a United States senator to know? Particularly a senator who they knew would be unhappy and inclined to raise hell.

She smiled to herself as she threw her pencil onto the desk. Senator Rafferty, let's put you on the hot seat, she thought. But somehow she couldn't get Frank Connaughton out of her mind.

39

BARRETT ARKWRIGHT'S TWA flight landed at Dulles on time. His eyes were red and he was tired. Worse, he would have to turn right around and do the same thing Sunday night, in just thirty-six hours. He ruefully acknowledged that age was the factor. There had been a time a few years ago when he could—and often did—make such flights and barely notice it, healing the wounds with adrenaline and caffeine. But no longer. This hurt.

The State Department car took him directly to the Hay-Adams Hotel across Lafayette Park from the White House. He knew Emerson Norton would insist that he stay with them that night. But right now he needed a place to shower and shave and get his thoughts together for his discussion with the Secretary of State later that afternoon. He wanted to go over the notes he had made from his breakfast with Connaughton. He wanted to be able to make the case to Norton as cogently as Connaughton had made it to him.

Less than an hour later, he was stepping off the Secretary's private elevator on the seventh floor of the department and walking the short, familiar distance into Norton's small, private office overlooking the Lincoln Memorial in Foggy Bottom.

Norton greeted him with a warmth befitting a thirty-year friendship, touching Arkwright's relatively flat waistline admiringly and inquiring about the squash courts in Geneva.

"Not much time for squash, I'm afraid," Arkwright said. "Particularly this round. Things are really hopping."

"So I gathered from your cable and surprise visit," Norton said. "I thought you had gotten beyond these weekend transatlantic round trips."

Arkwright used the settling-in period to size up his old friend. Norton was Lincolnesque in proportions, standing a somewhat stooped six feet four inches, with large hands and feet attached to overly long arms and legs. His roots were in Pennsylvania, where his father had been Governor in the 1930s. Norton had spent a lifetime in foreign affairs, both teaching and in a variety of special diplomatic assignments under several administrations before reaching the top assignment in the first months of the Lawkard administration. Although it was not publicly known, Norton's doctor had recently warned him about impending heart complications, and Arkwright noticed with concern his old friend had resumed smoking cigarettes. Norton had just lit his second as he slumped in his favorite easy chair.

He waved Arkwright's cable. "I've just reread this idea of yours. It's interesting . . . to say the least."

"Actually, Em," Arkwright said, gratefully sipping his hot coffee, "it's more the idea of Frank Connaughton, who's the Arms Control and Disarmament Agency representative on the delegation."

"Well, Barrett, with all due respect to you and Connaughton, the idea of swapping our cruise missiles for Soviet ICBMs isn't exactly new. Some of us have been advocating something like that since SALT II days. Now, Connaughton seems to have done a little new work on the verification problem and I found that interesting. But beyond that, I don't know where it gets us. The Soviets have shown some interest in a trade of this sort, but always balked when it came time to deal. Phil Warrenton says their best information at the Agency is that the hard-line land-based-missile advocates in the Kremlin just won't let go."

Arkwright inadvertently scanned the small room. By prior arrangement Norton had excused his senior staff people, including his special assistant for arms control, from this meeting. He knew Arkwright had not made this weekend round trip just to discuss this bargaining proposal. There was something else not contained in the cable.

"What's different, Em, are attitudes in the Kremlin. There seems to have been a shift—possibly as recently as the holiday break—and now Zoshchenko represents the balance of power in a crucial change of policy. The military people have lined up fairly solidly behind a shift in emphasis and structure of their strategic forces away from the big ICBMs, more toward a land-sea-air triad like ours. The old Central Committee types are still hanging on to the present force structure and the Foreign Ministry is wavering. In other words, I came all the way over here to tell you that I'm convinced the time is ripe for me to move quietly, outside the conference room, with Makarov—to float this idea with him informally—and for you to contact Zoshchenko through Ambassador Dubinin here, equally quietly, with the same notion. No press, no fanfare, no one gets hurt if it doesn't fly. But I now think it will."

Norton listened intently, his eyes never leaving Arkwright's animated face. "Why are you so sure, Barrett?"

"Because we have a source, a new one. It's a source inside the Soviet delegation. This person has had access to virtually everything short of Kamenev's office." His voice low, Arkwright sat forward in his chair.

Norton lit another cigarette. "Who talks to the source, and how did it happen?"

"Connaughton. He developed the contact. And as I understand it, it happened pretty much by accident. Like a lot of these things, it started out socially and one thing led to another. It's happened since the holidays—since we came back in January. The motive seems to be desperation. Frustration with the failure of the talks so far and a sense of catastrophe if something doesn't happen soon. Although Connaughton's no professional in these matters by any means, he's quick and he's smart and he's convinced this is genuine stuff."

"I don't know Connaughton well." Norton looked off through brocade drapes to Lincoln's marble monument.

Arkwright said, "I've known him and worked with him more than a decade. I've checked his security file within the last week. I trust him—totally. The question is his source. But as Frank points out, what if this person is wrong or is misleading us? The worst that could happen is for the Soviets to say no. If the whole thing is carried out as I've suggested—as Connaughton has suggested—what do we have to lose? I'm no professional spook either, Em, but it sounds like the real thing to me."

"Should I know who this Soviet fellow is?" Norton asked. "If we pursue this, sooner or later someone on our side is going to want to know."

"Obviously, I intend to tell you that, Em, under conditions I've agreed to with Frank Connaughton. But first let me ask you how you intend to pursue this, if you do." Arkwright still sat forward in his chair, conditioned to believe all rooms were bugged.

"Well we've got complications on our side as well—as you know." Norton sighed the sigh of a long-frustrated man. "We pretty much had a line drawn in the sand at the last security council meeting. Burgoon and Sternberg on one side—me on the other. Lawkard was there, which, frankly, is a good sign. He's starting to wake up and get involved. Up to now he's given Burgoon a free hand to set policy as he will. But I think the President is beginning to believe Harold's going too far and I know he was shaken by the demonstrations here and abroad over the holidays." Norton unfolded his long frame and paced the small sitting room. "I've got to get some more people on my side. I've tried Warrenton, but he's gotten to be such a cynical chess player.

He was brought in early to the Burgoon-Sternberg cabal. But he feels as uncomfortable as hell with it. He could be helpful to us. Admiral Bigby is the only holdout among the Joint Chiefs. He's concerned—and rightly so—with the clash that could occur between this Blue Thunder operation and the Warsaw Pact exercises in April. But the other chiefs just sail right along with Sternberg's program."

Arkwright asked, "What about Lawkard? Can he be brought over to our side?"

Norton, still pacing, waved Arkwright's earlier cable. "This could be it, Barrett. If I can get the President to approve this approach and this offer, we've gone a long way to getting him into the game with a stake in seeing it succeed." He grinned for the first time. "Of course, if we do, Burgoon will go berserk—even more than he already is." Norton chuckled to himself at the thought.

Arkwright said, "The only other element is time. The reason I'm pressing so hard on this is because our source indicated things are unusually fluid in the Kremlin right now and time is of the essence. Also if we get to April and we're still stalemated, and the military exercises begin, who knows what will happen. In my judgment it will surely kill the negotiations."

"Oh, I agree with that totally, Barrett," Norton replied. "I've felt all along, as you know, that we had a window between February and April to get something done or we were out of business." He put on reading glasses and looked at the calendar on his small writing table. "It's now February thirteenth. I obviously won't be able to get together with Dubinin until sometime next week. You can't look too frantic with these people or they get suspicious. Besides, I have to get the President's approval first and that will take forty-eight to seventy-two hours. He's asked me to come by and talk to him next week on this issue of Blue Thunder. So the timing couldn't be better. I'll use the occasion to put this proposal before him and try to get his approval to go forward with Zoshchenko. You and I have to coordinate. I assume you want to talk to Makarov about the same time I meet with Dubinin.''

''That's right,'' Arkwright agreed. ''It all has to happen at once for them to think we're serious.''

Norton put the earpiece of his glasses in his mouth and turned back to the south window. He thought for a moment, then said, ''Then there's this goddam Cyclops business. What are we going to do about that?''

Arkwright started. He wondered if his old friend was psychic. ''That's the other reason I wanted to see you, Em. There's something funny going on there too.''

''What do you mean 'funny'?'' Norton queried.

''Curiously enough, it gets back to our friend Frank Connaughton. He came to see me after we got back to Geneva last month. He was all worked up. Seems some mysterious person got hold of him here in Washington and told him an incredible story....''

''Namely?''

''Namely that Cyclops has already been launched—put into orbit—ready for operation. Theoretically, on command the damn thing could knock out most, if not all, of the Soviet surveillance satellites. Now if you believe in conspiracies, you can imagine where a confrontation could occur and our side could find it necessary to preemptively blind the Soviets.''

Norton sighed again, as if weary of the world he had to deal with. ''This is all damned strange, Barrett. Late yesterday Senator Harry Rafferty came to see me. Seems he received the same kind of tip as Connaughton—maybe even the same source—and last week went in search of the truth. Among other things he turned up was that there is a Cyclops the contractor can't account for. Then he went up to Vandenberg and the commanding officer refused to tell him whether a Cyclops payload had in fact been launched.''

''What can we do, Em?''

"We can play poker just like the others," Norton said. "When I see the President in the next couple of days, I intend to say this: Here's a serious arms control proposal which now has a chance of success if we move soon. Based on what you and Rafferty have told me, I'm going to tell him I know about this crack-brained scheme that put Cyclops in orbit. I'll give him a choice. I want his support to offer the proposal to the Soviets—as you have suggested—both in Geneva and directly to Zoshchenko through their ambassador here. That support includes his commitment to neutralize Sternberg and the Joint Chiefs. They have to agree to the terms of the offer—or at least not to torpedo it in the press. If they don't agree or if they go public with their opposition, then the deal is off."

"If they fight it, then what happens?" Arkwright asked.

Norton sat down heavily and lit another cigarette. "Then I resign," he said. "And I threaten to expose Cyclops."

Arkwright whistled. "Would you actually do that—disclose Cyclops?"

Norton winked. "That's the joker. They wouldn't know, would they?" He smiled grimly. "Besides, the bastards froze me out on a major policy decision directly affecting our relations with the Soviet Union, so why not? They're not the only ones who can play rough." Norton looked at Arkwright. "The White House has to be worried about that Cyclops business getting out. It makes the President look either manipulated by his Secretary of Defense or provocative to the Soviets. He loses either way. I know the press is snooping around. *The New York Times* is calling my office for information on antisatellite weapons. So they must be all over the White House and Defense Department. I suspect the mysterious informant is still at work. Clearly someone close to that program is upset as hell by what's going on."

"What can I do?" Arkwright asked.

Norton said, "Use this office this afternoon and write out this cruise-ICBM proposal in detail for my presentation to the President this coming week. If you're free, let's have dinner at my house tonight and go over it in detail. Then if any changes or edits need to be made, you can take care of those tomorrow before you have to go back. How does that sound?''

"Sounds fine," Arkwright said. They stood and shook hands. Arkwright started taking off his coat and loosening his tie.

Norton started for the door to his formal office for meetings he still had that Saturday afternoon. He stopped before opening the door and said, "By the way, in case the President asks, who's the fellow we've turned up in their delegation?"

Arkwright paused, thinking of his promise to Connaughton. "It's not a fellow."

Norton's eyebrows came up in a rare indication of surprise. "That narrows it down, doesn't it? Do I get to know?"

"I agreed with Connaughton to tell you on the condition it goes no further. He feels strongly about it." Norton nodded in a commitment Arkwright knew to be as good as a notarized affidavit. "It's their chief interpreter. A woman called Davydova. Believe me, she has access and has every reason to know what she's talking about."

"Do we know her motives?" Norton asked with elaborate casualness as if asking about a new tennis partner.

"I suspect we never will." Arkwright smiled wryly. "But Connaughton says they're honorable. And that's good enough for me."

40

THE FOLLOWING TUESDAY, after Barrett Arkwright had returned to Geneva, Secretary of State Norton had lunch with the President. But before he did, he called Philip Warrenton and asked if he would mind sending around the agency files on the Soviet arms control delegation. Warrenton seemed surprised, but knew better than question Norton as to the reason for his curiosity. Warrenton did confess the request was unusual and asked whether Norton would mind, under these extraordinary circumstances, if the Director of the CIA came around with the files to answer any questions. Norton had no choice but to accept the condition.

Monday afternoon Warrenton showed up at Secretary Norton's office with his liaison officer for the State Department and the requested files. Norton assured Warrenton he needn't have taken the trouble of coming around himself with the personnel files of the Soviet diplomats.

"But Em," Warrenton said, "it's not every day the Secretary of State takes the trouble of looking over some of our personnel files—even of Soviet personnel. What's up?"

Clearly he's intrigued, Norton thought as he served his guest a very dry vodka martini. It was after five o'clock. "Nothing special, Phil. I was just trying to get a better fix on the opposition. Your people do such a good job on personalities—especially the psychological profiles you do. Actually they're fascinating. It's like reading a really good novel." He smiled at Warrenton. "Do you think I'm becoming kind of a psychological Peeping Tom in my waning years?''

To occupy Warrenton, Norton showed him a copy of the memo he would give the President the following noon. He knew there was a good chance Warrenton would share it with Sternberg or even Burgoon. But it was not designed to remain secret from other key policy makers in the administration and he might just lure Warrenton to this point of view by making him feel like an insider. In any case it kept the CIA Director busy while he looked at Ekaterina Davydova's file.

Norton made a show of going over Makarov's file and Metrinko's, but then slipped out the slim folder on Davydova. There was little there—the short paragraph released by the Soviet Mission when the talks began and bits and pieces gleaned by members of the American delegation during their professional and occasional social contacts with her. Norton wondered idly what she looked like. The blurred photo with the file, cropped from some larger group picture, revealed little. He wondered further about Frank Connaughton's relationship to her.

After a second martini, Norton asked Warrenton what he thought of the arms control proposal. To his surprise Warrenton was excited by it and genuinely grateful at being taken into the Secretary of State's confidence on a matter of that magnitude. He was intensely interested in how Arkwright and Norton had found out about the possible shift in attitude within the Politburo and shrewdly guessed that it somehow related to Norton's sudden interest in the profiles of the Soviet delegation. Cautiously Norton confirmed that, without revealing the specific source, in keeping with his commitment to Arkwright and Connaughton. But it was then Warrenton's turn to surprise Norton yet again.

The Secretary of State joined the President for lunch the following day, with his strategy carefully prepared. After summarizing the situation in Geneva and the reasons for the yearlong and increasingly dangerous stalemate, he presented the proposal outlined by Arkwright based upon Connaughton's suggestion—a straight trade-off of cruise missiles in exchange for Soviet large intercontinental ballistic missiles.

"Explain to me again, Em," Lawkard said, "what makes you think this proposal will fly now . . . what has changed."

"It's a gamble, Mr. President. Very recent intelligence suggests there's a struggle going on in the Kremlin over the future shape of Soviet strategic forces and that Foreign Minister Zoshchenko represents the balance of power in the struggle. This proposal of ours, offered quietly in Geneva and from me to him, is designed to bring him toward us and his own military. We believe he can also persuade Secretary Kamenev. If that were to happen, we may finally be in business in Geneva. Other elements of an agreement could begin to fall together."

Lawkard said, "Yes, Em, but what about our own military? Sternberg and the Chiefs don't want limits on cruise missiles—never have. They'll fight this. And then I've got an ambitious vice-President who's trying to succeed me and he's already running on a 'get tough' platform."

"Yes, Mr. President, but you also have a country and a Western alliance demanding some progress on nuclear arms limitations, and that alliance could blow up if we let a chance like this go by. You also have a Secretary of State who's getting fed up with arms control policy being dictated by the Vice-President and Secretary of Defense."

"What is that supposed to mean?" Lawkard snapped, sensing a threat.

Norton said calmly, "Simply this, Mr. President: I want your authorization to present this proposal to Zoshchenko this week. I have every confidence you'll find the proper way to convince Harold Burgoon and Joe Sternberg this is in the best interest of our country." Norton then played the hole card. "If you need any ammunition, just tell them someone connected with the Cyclops program has been whispering. Tell them that at least two people—Senator Harry Rafferty and the Secretary of State—believe a Cyclops satellite has been made operational under very suspicious circumstances, to say the least. And tell them that if a sound bargaining proposal such as this is blocked, one or the other of us will find a way to prevent them from using Cyclops and the Blue Thunder exercises to start World War III.''

Norton sat back in his chair and tapped his napkin to his lips. ''That should sober them up.''

Lawkard's voice rang with fury. ''By God, Em, I'll not be blackmailed!''

''With all respect,'' Norton replied, ''I think you already have been, Mr. President. But by the wrong side. I've just decided to play by their rules.''

Lawkard glared. ''What makes you so all-fired sure the Russians are now keen for a bargain like this?''

''In the past several weeks, since the talks resumed in January, we've developed a source within their delegation,'' Norton responded. ''We believe the source is both knowledgeable and reliable. I have given a blood oath not to reveal the source's identity. But you might want to call Phil Warrenton for confirmation on my judgment. He's in his office awaiting your call.''

Within ten minutes Secretary of State Norton was on his way from the White House to the State Department with his arms control proposal in his briefcase. The President's initials were on it.

41

"GOOD EVENING, Comrade Defense Minister," said the distinguished, elderly doorkeeper as he opened Kozlovsky's limousine door at the canopied corner entrance of the Council of Ministers Building in the Kremlin. He had seen all the top government officials come and go, all the way back to the prewar days of Stalin, but he particularly liked Georgi Kozlovsky. The Defense Minister discreetly slipped him a good Cuban cigar as his burly form hurtled up the eight stone steps and through the highly polished double wooden doors to the principal building housing the Soviet government. Over his shoulder he heard the clear old voice say, "The Comrade General Secretary is awaiting your visit."

A bright sunset lit the three-story triangular edifice, its dun-yellow exterior walls glowing as the last flash of sunlight brushed them before yielding to the cold February night. Inside the long hallways gave off to a series of simple, often spartan, offices for the senior officials of the Soviet government. Kamenev had two offices, one formal and the other almost an apartment.

It was to this informal living area that Kozlovsky came. He was always welcome here. Kamenev, who had been widowed without children, had found Kozlovsky in the third level of the Kiev City Party Committee almost twenty years before and had seen the bureaucracy did not hamper the promotions Kozlovsky earned and deserved over the years. Kozlovsky turned out to have a genius for motivation and a talent in the field of defense planning. Having Kamenev as a mentor had certainly not hurt, but Kozlovsky had made his way up the Defense Ministry ladder mostly through his own energy and determination. Kamenev had been more his father confessor and seasoned adviser. Their relationship had become like a piece of solid oak furniture, stronger and richer as years passed by.

"Nikolai Timofeyevich," Kozlovsky said, as the two men embraced at the door of Kamenev's comfortable, old-fashioned quarters. The older man had soft slippers on to aid his increasingly shuffling gate. Kozlovsky thought that he seemed to age noticeably now with every visit. They exchanged warm words, the General Secretary asking after Kozlovsky's wife and children, to each of whom he gave gifts every New Year's. Realizing the decreasing length of his senior's attention span, Kozlovsky got down to business quickly.

"Nikolai, I trouble you only for this, because it is important to our country. And I don't want us to make a deeply regrettable mistake that could torment us for a long time. This Red Star business—these military exercises we have been planning—I have come to believe even more strongly are dangerous for us. I know the Politburo has approved this and I know how strongly Comrade Zhdanov and others in the Central Committee feel on the other side. But this must not be a test of wills either within the Politburo or between us and the Americans. We should only go forward with this if it makes sense and if the risks are acceptable. Now, not only I but several members of the General Staff agree that the risks are too great."

The General Secretary sat in his favorite chair with its stiff frame and worn leather upholstery, feet up, looking into the middle distance as the younger man spoke. Occasionally he twisted to relieve an arthritis-plagued joint. "My good friend, you do not trouble me—at least any more than I am already. This is my job. I fought like hell for thirty years to get it. I'm not in a position now to complain about troubles. Since getting this damn job I've only learned one thing…it's nothing but trouble. One of these days I'm going to get all these people who want this job—and it will be a goddam big roomful of them, let me tell you—and I'm going to tell them a secret: It's nothing but trouble!"

He waved his hand, signaling Kozlovsky to continue. "Well, Nikolai, this is big trouble, at least now that the senior generals are involved." He got up from his chair near the old man and began to pace restlessly.

"Admiral Gorshkov says that putting all four major fleets to sea at once is bound to seem provocative, given everything else that will be going on. And General Palzin says bringing the Rocket Forces to a higher stage of alert will certainly be read by the Pentagon as a highly aggressive act, especially during major military exercises in Eastern Europe. Yet here we are," Kozlovsky fumed, "committed to this craziness to please Zhdanov, who thinks we've all gone soft and lost sight of the revolution and wants to stir up a fight with the West. It's a hell of a mess as far as I'm concerned," he stormed, "but I don't know what to do about it."

"Well, as Stalin used to say during the war"—Kamenev smiled wanly—"this is the week we earn our paycheck." He shifted again painfully in his chair and sipped from a dark steaming glass that had more than tea in it. "I can't even remember why I agreed to go along with Zhdanov on this plan. He came to me months ago with the argument that the exercises…what do you call it? Red something…were routinely held, that we had to make them bigger this year to impress the Americans and NATO, and for that matter some of our own friends in Eastern Europe who are always acting up. I remember now he had some argument about getting ready for a show of strength when the negotiations in Geneva fell apart—as, he said, they inevitably would. But he also swore that the General Staff was totally on board this operation."

Kozlovsky stopped the pacing and sat down heavily next to his old friend. "That's true—up to a point. But when we originally planned the exercises, we didn't know they would fall at a crucial point in the negotiations. And the Defense Ministry didn't know Zhdanov would get the Politburo to insist that Red Star be expanded to include full deployment of the fleet and alerting of the nuclear forces." He pulled his chair closer to Kamenev. "Look, Nikolai, we have one last chance to see if we can get a reasonable agreement with the United States. If it fails, then we'll have plenty of time to flex our muscles and scare the hell out of everyone. You and I both know that Zhdanov and others in the Party have been looking for confrontation with the West since the beginning of détente. He thinks this is his chance—maybe his last one—and he is playing all his cards."

"Goddammit, Georgi," the old man growled painfully, "I can barely get through the day, let alone fight another one of these Kremlin cat fights. You and I know that. Thank God, very few others do. But they soon will, and when they decide I'm down they'll be all over my carcass like a pack of wolves. What am I supposed to do? You come here for my advice, and I'm the one who needs the advice. What am I supposed to do?"

"Nikolai, my dear old friend, I have thought much about this and, frankly, in the past few days I have come up with a plan. Let's do it this way. There is a Politburo meeting later this week. Say that I have come to you with concern from elements of the General Staff about Red Star. Admiral Gorshkov is going to Pyotr Zoshchenko on the side with the same argument, and I will, of course, verify what you say. Propose that we give our negotiators until April first to have an agreement in principle with the United States on a comprehensive treaty. If we have an agreement by then, Red

Star will be called off as a gesture of goodwill. If the agreement fails, we will still have time to mount the operation."

Kamenev shook his massive head topped with its short iron-gray hair. "Zhdanov will go through the roof and Ulyanov with him. What will Rusakov do?"

"General Rusakov will buy the agreement if you propose it as your idea, but only if you also promise the exercises can go forward if the treaty fails."

Kamenev said, "Georgi, I'm not going to try this unless I can win. If I propose this and lose, there will be a goddam palace coup the likes of which we haven't seen since Khrushchev and I'll be sitting out in the snow on my bare ass."

"Pyotr Zoshchenko is the key," Kozlovsky said tapping the old man's arm. "He wants to succeed you, Nikolai."

Kamenev growled, "Georgi, you're wasting my time telling me things I already know." Both men laughed together. "What else is new?"

"The way an old fox catches a younger fox is to put out bait," Kozlovsky said as he rose and started pacing again. "Promise him your job if he supports you on this."

The old man sipped the loaded tea, groaned once, and scratched his head. "Goddam." Then he gulped the tea again. "Georgi, you're the fox. I can't guarantee him my job. He has to win the votes in the Politburo himself when the time comes."

Kozlovsky came over and placed an affectionate hand on the General Secretary's shoulder, then grinned mischievously. "You had to find that out the hard way, Nikolai. Let's let Pyotr find it out the same way." They both laughed again.

PYOTR ZOSHCHENKO SAT AT THE imposing desk in his massive office in the Foreign Ministry. He was rereading, with amazement, the highly confidential cable from Mikhail Makarov in Geneva. The cable detailed Ekaterina Davydova's report to Makarov following her meetings with Frank Connaughton. It focused particularly on Connaughton's suggestions during the lunch in Courmayeur that forces were at work within the United States government to press for a trade-off between cruise missiles and ICBMs. Zoshchenko could not decide whether he was more amazed at turning up a valuable—perhaps invaluable—source inside the U.S. arms control delegation at this crucial point or at the fortuity of his proposal.

Zoshchenko immediately and instinctively suspected Connaughton. It was, in fact, the timing of the whole thing that led him to conclude Connaughton had to be planted on them. It was simply too fortuitous. On the other hand, Makarov was no dummy. He had been around long enough to smell a plant as quickly as anyone in the Foreign Service. And Makarov clearly believed this to be the genuine article. Zoshchenko also remembered Comrade Davydova very well—well enough to cause him to smile to himself. He had had his eye on that elegant lady for some time. And he had been attracted not only because of her obvious unique beauty, but also because she was surrounded by a powerful aura of sophistication and ambition. She was notorious throughout the Foreign Service for being personally unapproachable by even the highest-ranking officials. Zoshchenko had been deterred from making his move by his low rejection threshold. She was not a woman easily taken in.

He was faced with a gamble. He could ask the KGB to give him an analysis of Connaughton as a recruitment prospect. But that would then trigger an interest on their part that Makarov strongly urged against. The cable said, keep this close. Only Davydova, the Ambassador, and the Foreign Minister. Zoshchenko knew the reason instinctively. Not only would KGB clumsiness frighten Connaughton off. But this card, if played right, could bring a much coveted Lenin medal to his lapel and might even make him General Secretary. Besides, if Connaughton turned out to be a false agent, only the other two would know. And he had enough on Makarov's personal financial dealings in the black market to keep him quiet for life, and he could always ship Davydova off to the most obscure outpost.

The greatest gamble was jumping sides in the Kremlin dispute. If he abandoned Zhdanov and his dangerous policy of confrontation through Red Star, and joined Kozlovsky and the dissident generals, he would incur the wrath of the hard-liners in the Central Committee, especially Zhdanov's crowd, and possibly lose what chance he had to succeed Kamenev as General Secretary. On the other hand, if he could get the old General Secretary to join him in one last effort to negotiate a settlement with the United States, and if that effort succeeded, he would have the gratitude of many of the Defense Ministry for preventing a revelation of many of their own inadequacies and he would have helped Kamenev earn a final star in his crown before retirement.

Why agonize? he thought. Kamenev was clearly the key. If he could be persuaded to postpone Red Star, or at least hold it in abeyance until the bargaining proposal had a chance, then it was a safe argument to take to the Politburo. In fact, Kamenev himself ought to present the proposal to the Politburo. He, Zoshchenko, would back up the idea based upon Makarov's cable. That was the perfect solution—some risks to his future involved, but Kamenev would be his shield. And, if he had to, he could always trot out Gorshkov. Lord knows, the old admiral hadn't let up on him about Red Star for the past five days.

As Zoshchenko reached for his telephone to arrange an early meeting with the General Secretary, his longtime chief of staff knocked and entered his office with the message that Kamenev had just requested an urgent meeting with him first thing in the morning.

42

ZHDANOV LOOKED LIKE a violent thunderstorm about to break. He was ominously quiet, but his intense eyes flared. Malenkov, hastily summoned to the high priest's office in the Kremlin, immediately knew better than to try the off-handed tack he had used at his dacha. The KGB man took the chair offered by Zhdanov's commanding gesture and waited until the spectral figure—resembling an El Greco painting of the wrath of God—composed himself. Malenkov hoped that he was not the object of the old man's anger.

"I have just returned from a meeting of the Politburo," Zhdanov said in his low, hollow tones. "There is mischief afoot, Malenkov, goddam mischief. The General Secretary has been gulled by that spineless fool Zoshchenko into selling us out. It is a disaster for the Soviet Union!"

Malenkov still waited, not knowing enough even to sympathize.

Zhdanov stood looking out his tall window, back to Malenkov. "Red Star—and all that it represents—is in serious jeopardy. I have just witnessed years of work on my part—years, Malenkov!—go down the drain. We had come this close"—and he wheeled to show a long thin forefinger and thumb less than an inch apart—"this close to ending two decades of détente idiocy and doing what we should have done all along—forcing the United States to back down. And what has happened? We are—once again—

backing down. Goddammit!" he stormed as he turned back to the window.

"And do you know what excuse they used, Malenkov? This is the worst," he grated, his voice full of bitterness. "The military is afraid of provocation. They are not ready to fight a land war in Europe. They are afraid the Warsaw Pact nations will not back us up—that the long-feared uprisings in Poland or Czechoslovakia might occur. They are afraid the whole thing would 'go nuclear' very quickly. They are afraid they might all lose their fancy homes out in the woods." Zhdanov's long finger pointed at Malenkov, who shrank imperceptibly in his chair. He thought he might witness the old zealot actually weep from anger and frustration and Malenkov would be killed for simply being there when it happened.

"Well, by God, if they think I am giving up, they have made a very big mistake," he hissed like a great serpent. "We are going to the very bottom of this, Malenkov, you and me, the very roots. We are going to find out who is behind this and we are going to do it fast. I told you three weeks ago to get busy in Geneva and you've given me nothing. Now I want results!" The hiss grew fainter but more chilling. "I want to know what's going on down there and I want to know soon."

Malenkov finally saw his opening. "What do any events in Geneva have to do with your meeting today? What is the connection? The last I heard from Metrinko there were absolutely no results at the bargaining table. And I had a cable from him yesterday."

"Well, young Metrinko may not be up to the task then. Certainly he does not meet the standard of my dear old friend, his departed uncle. Because otherwise he would have known subversion is going on in Geneva ... subversion of someone by someone. And you, Malenkov, are going to tell me who. If you have to go down there yourself to find out,"

Zhdanov said, poking his finger into the chest of the second most powerful man in the KGB.

"How does all this trace to Geneva, Vladimir?" Malenkov seemed now almost to plead.

"Because, you great fool, Zoshchenko said so! He stood right there before the Politburo and changed Soviet policy and perhaps Soviet history by claiming he had information from the goddam Americans that they were ready to trade off some measly cruise missiles if we were to drastically reduce our most important defenses, our ICBM force, our SS-18s and SS-19s!"

Malenkov was now genuinely shocked. "How could we have a source inside the American government with that kind of information that I . . . *we* do not know about?"

"Because, as I've told you for years, Malenkov, you have idiots, only idiots, in the KGB. You might as well put uniforms on them and put them out in the snow as traffic cops. Do you understand? Idiots!" Zhdanov stood motionless, breathing deeply, clearly trying to control his rage. Finally, he said, "I am going to present this case to you on a platter, Malenkov. Even your protégé Metrinko might be able to handle this. I am sure the key among our people was handed to us by Zoshchenko himself, totally inadvertently. In presenting the authentication for Kamenev's proposal to trade ICBMs for cruise missiles, he revealed that a source—a knowledgeable American source—had come forward. But come forward to whom he did not say, nor was he pressed by anyone but me. Kamenev backed him up when he said no purpose would be served at the present time in disclosing either the American or the person in our mission dealing with him."

Malenkov leaned forward in his chair, eager for any clue however slight.

"But Zoshchenko, at one point, in reference to a question about the American's motives, said she did not know. *She*, Malenkov, *she*. Do you understand? Who else but that woman interpreter?"

43

THE EVENING WAS unseasonably warm, presaging another bout of rain and cold weather already on its way, and the two ambassadors strolled through the tall glass doors of the dining room into the elegant formal gardens surrounding three sides of the three-century-old estate set on a secluded private road off the Chemin de la Montagne in the Cologny section overlooking Lake Geneva.

They pulled on their coats, paused to light their cigars, then Barrett Arkwright gestured for his Russian guest to join him for a stroll along the intricate gravel paths through the garden. They exchanged idle remarks about their careers and agreed that the diplomatic life was increasingly one for younger men. Shortly they came to the end of the mazelike garden walkways, and the gravel path led into the wooded areas that characterized the Cologny hills. Heads down, the two men continued to stroll wherever the path might lead. Well into the evening the woods were dark, except for the ghostly illumination of the unobscured full moon.

After a moment of silence punctuated only by the sound of leather soles on gravel, Arkwright spoke. "Mikhail, you and I have been over here negotiating for a year. I think we both realize if this is going to work, we'll have to do something different. Basically, we've both been shadowboxing and testing each other on the edges of a real arms control agreement. But during the past few weeks there have been efforts within my own government to approach this stalemate differently—to see if there are breakthrough proposals or sweeping trade-offs that might give us a chance to seriously reduce nuclear weapons."

The Russian was silent, so he continued. "Some of us believe there might be such proposals. In fact, we believe if we both can show a willingness to be bold and break with the past in one major area, some other areas of disagreement might disappear rather quickly. Now, I've been at this long enough not to be naïve or have illusions. But I also have concluded that traditional approaches just aren't working."

Makarov finally spoke. "Well, Barrett, I have to agree with that. Bureaucracies on both sides make bold initiatives almost impossible. So much has to be considered by so many offices and bureaus in each government that creative thinking is usually stifled."

"God knows that's the truth," Arkwright agreed, then took a deep breath. "For example, you've repeatedly criticized our cruise missile program and argued that we had to limit the number of nuclear-armed cruise missiles at sea and in the air. On the other hand we've focused much of our attention on the continued expansion of your large land-based missiles. Now we would be interested in knowing what the response of your government might be if we were to suggest overall limits on cruise missiles carrying nuclear warheads—say roughly at current levels of deployment—in exchange for substantial reductions in your ICBMs, especially SS-18s and 19s."

Arkwright thought for the moment Makarov seemed taken aback, and he was not particularly surprised. No serious effort had been made, to date, in linking cruise missiles to American insistence on reduction of Soviet large ICBMs. Arkwright realized he was at some disadvantage in that he could not see the expression on Makarov's face. But of course that worked both ways.

The two men walked silently for a moment along the moonlight-speckled path. Makarov then said carefully, "If your government were to propose a formula trading cruise missiles for ICBMs, in my judgment it would be given very serious consideration by my government. I cannot, of course, predict the outcome of those deliberations. But I can promise you it would not be rejected out of hand—that is, unless you presented the proposal in a way that made it seem merely a propaganda effort on your part."

"I can assure you," Arkwright said quietly but urgently, "it would be proposed through normal diplomatic channels at a very high level—with no publicity. We would not wish to have such an offer rejected publicly either."

Makarov said, "Of course not." And that part of the arrangement seemed firm.

Makarov mastered his excitement and took the next step. "Do you have specific numbers in mind?"

"If such an offer were made," Arkwright said, "it would be to freeze deployment of all cruise missiles at current levels, with limits on production of spares, in exchange for a twenty-five percent reduction in warheads on heavy ICBMs."

Makarov was extremely pleased Arkwright couldn't see his face as he smiled to himself. Davydova had been right on target.

"The other thing, Mikhail," Arkwright said, "is that if this proposal were to be offered by my government we would want a definitive, high-level response quickly. No stalling, no prolonged deliberations. The terms, if offered, would be simple and straightforward."

"But if your government were to make such an offer," Makarov continued, using the curious contingency form of discussion introduced by Arkwright so that they could deny later that a concrete offer had been made if necessary, "there would have to be some negotiation over verification, counting rules, and so forth."

"Of course," Arkwright agreed. "That's what we're here for in Geneva. Details would be discussed in the bargaining process here." They walked on silently again, each man considering his words with painful intensity to make sure exact meanings were exchanged. They both clearly understood the momentous implications of this discussion. "If we were to reach agreement on a matter of this consequence, my government would hope that other major areas of agreement might be explored with equal urgency."

Makarov said, "I guarantee I will pass that expectation along to my government as well."

They were professionals walking a tightrope of words. Arkwright realized Makarov had avoided taking any position on the notion itself—except for saying it would be given serious consideration. That was all he had hoped to hear.

Later that night, after the Makarovs were safely on their way back to the Soviet Mission, Barrett Arkwright sat up late composing a long cable to Secretary Emerson Norton who, by prearrangement, awaited a detailed report on his Ambassador's extraordinary "walk in the woods" with his Soviet counterpart. The key phrase in the cable, again by prearrangement, was "the door is open." That signaled Arkwright's conclusion that the Soviet hierarchy would at least treat the cruise-ICBM trade-off seriously and, depending on internal Kremlin politics, not reject it out of hand.

With apologies to his long-suffering wife, Arkwright returned to the United States Mission just before midnight to transmit the cable personally and reduce the number of staff personnel who would know about the back-door negotiations. As his car took him across a dark and sleeping Geneva, Arkwright reconsidered Makarov's behavior minutely and concluded again that his old adversary would have let him know one way or another if the idea of pursuing this high-risk negotiating strategy were out of the question. There was hope, real hope.

UPON RECEIPT of Arkwright's cable, Norton's operation shifted into high gear. His chief of staff notified the Soviet Embassy in Washington that the Secretary of State would like to see the Soviet Ambassador urgently. It was then 6:50 P.M. and arrangements were made for an early breakfast for the two men in the Secretary's private dining room on the eighth floor of the department. Norton spent the evening poring over the details of the proposal and jotting notes on specific phrases to be used to make his intentions explicit in some areas and cloudy in others.

At 7 A.M. Ambassador Anatoly Dubinin's car entered the basement of the State Department, and after winding around the posts and pillars of the vast garage arrived at the small private elevator leading directly to the Secretary's suite of offices. The uncustomary early hour for the meeting took the normal foreign policy press corps staking out the department by surprise, and Dubinin arrived completely undetected.

Over melon, bacon, and eggs, largely untouched by the two men, Norton presented the idea of a freeze on deployment of all cruise missiles by the United States in exchange for a 25 percent reduction in Soviet SS-18 and SS-19 heavy ICBMs. The proposal was essentially the same as that presented by Arkwright to Makarov some thirteen hours earlier. But it was more explicit in terms of verification of compliance on both sides, including the details Connaughton had presented to Ekaterina Davydova over lunch in Courmayeur ten days earlier.

Norton talked in precise, measured tones for more than twenty minutes. Dubinin did not interrupt, except to raise an eyebrow occasionally in genuine surprise at what he heard. He wrote furiously on a notepad to ensure the accuracy of the conversation he would shortly be expected to transmit in explicit detail to Moscow. The Ambassador had a reputation for an amazing memory of diplomatic exchanges and conversations. But a matter of this consequence could not afford even the slightest error.

When it was clear Norton was finished, Dubinin had only one question: whether this was an official bargaining position of the United States government. Norton answered yes and they stood and shook hands.

By 8 A.M. Dubinin was at his desk in the Soviet Embassy composing his long cable to the Foreign Ministry in Moscow. Within an hour it was completed, reviewed for accuracy, and transmitted "eyes only" to Foreign Minister Pyotr Zoshchenko, who had already been alerted to anticipate an urgent communication from his ambassador in Washington.

THAT EVENING Pyotr Zoshchenko paced his deliberately chilly office atop the vast rambling building housing the foreign policy bureaucracy of the Soviet government. He stopped and stared across the snow-topped spires and still-white streets of Moscow. He could clearly see the lights of the Kremlin and knew instinctively who sat warmed by an excess of good scotch and who was watchful and working. Makarov, the old fox, had been right on target for a change, he thought. They had a source in the U.S. delegation and he knew what he was talking about. Just in time to save Zoshchenko's skin as well. Had he not been alerted by Makarov that an offer of this sort might be under consideration by the Americans, he might have gotten stuck with Zhdanov's hard-liners and missed the chance to seize the moment.

The timing had been perfect—almost eerie. Clearly Kamenev had been listening to Kozlovsky and was getting cold feet about Red Star and looking for some way out at the bargaining table. And here it was. Zoshchenko, smiling to himself, shook his head. Sometimes he marveled at his own incredible luck. It had been the hallmark of his entire career and constantly drove his enemies and detractors, of whom the numbers were considerable, to total distraction.

He remembered his stern dictatorial grandmother telling him as a young boy how cats always landed on their feet. After his severe punishment for testing the theory from heights too great for any mortal cat, he learned soon enough the meaning of metaphor. He was the cat. And he always landed on his feet.

He mentally thanked his ancient grandmother once again as he ordered his secretary to request a meeting the next day with General Secretary Kamenev.

"COMRADE GENERAL SECRETARY," Zoshchenko began, "I know of your concern for the possible dangers in conducting the Red Star exercises without fully pursuing all diplomatic remedies." He was fresh and energized by this high political drama in which he might play the leading and possibly decisive role. But the old man looks awful, he thought. It wouldn't be long. "Dubinin was called in by Emerson Norton yesterday and presented a dramatic arms control proposal which apparently has President Lawkard's blessing. I think it's safe to say it's a blockbuster."

He sat across the desk from the white-haired leader of the Soviet Union, who seemed alternatively fierce and sleepy. Must be the damned medicine, Zoshchenko thought, and he hoped Kamenev was alert enough to track the conversation as he laid out the details of the American proposal.

He needn't have worried about the old man. When he was finished Kamenev looked at him a long time without blinking. Suddenly he dropped his great fist on the desk and asked, "Zoshchenko, do you want this job?"

The smooth and loquacious Foreign Minister was dumbfounded. "Sir?" he finally got out.

"Of course you do. Don't beat around the bush with me. I don't have time for it," Kamenev rumbled. And Zoshchenko knew he was serious. "Well, I'll tell you this. The Americans have dropped a 'blockbuster,' as you say. Get back to Norton and say we're interested. Then pursue it as far and as fast as you can. By God, I think we've got one chance to get a nuclear agreement and if we don't there'll be all hell to pay. Give it a try. But Pyotr''—he shook a stubby finger at the younger man—''keep your hand on your wallet. If you give away the store, Zhdanov and that gang will hang you from the Kremlin clock.''

''What about the Politburo, Comrade General Secretary?'' Zoshchenko asked deferentially.

''That's my responsibility,'' the old man growled. ''I've been sitting on my butt in there too long, or worse yet letting some pissant doctor poke needles in me while you people have been taking this country all over the place. I'm done with that. If I'm going out''—and he smiled for the first time Zoshchenko could remember—''I'm going out with a bang—and a hell of a fight.''

TWO DAYS LATER, immediately after the Politburo meeting in which General Secretary Kamenev asked Zoshchenko to lay out the American negotiating proposal and then lead a majority of the Politburo in voting to instruct the Foreign Minister to pursue it personally with the American Secretary of State, Zoshchenko received a call. It was Vladimir Zhdanov.

''I trust you know what fools the Americans take us for,'' the distinctive hollow voice hissed. ''And if we fall into this trap, you will be the biggest fool of all, my good friend Pyotr. Listen very carefully to me. There is a plot afoot here. There is great chicanery somewhere in Geneva and I will find it out. You may be sure I will find it out, if I have to do so all by myself. I do not intend to see us humiliated once again by this détentist poison the Americans hand out. We are being duped, my friend Pyotr. And if I am right once again about what goes on here, not only will this childish and asinine diplomatic farce prove false, but we will be looking for a successor to our dear General Secretary.'' The voice paused for a lifetime. "And, my very dear friend Pyotr, I assure you with all my being we will not be looking in that grand office atop the cesspool you call the Foreign Ministry."

44

CONNAUGHTON MARVELED at how easy it had become to arrange to see Ekaterina. He maneuvered Charlie Curtis's European Ford up the N5 highway along the southern edge of Lake Geneva past the dormant Parc des Eaux-Vives, La Roseraie which in a matter of weeks would be a carpet of blooming roses, the Geneva Yacht Club, the Villa Diodati where Byron once lived, off to the left toward the still water the magnificent Château de Bellerive occupied by the brother of the Aga Khan, and within a few minutes through the quiet village of Corsier just before the French border.

After being waved routinely through the border barriers, Connaughton looked across at Ekaterina. Her face in profile, softly lit by the setting sun, seemed to glow from an inner light. His breath momentarily was taken away. She seemed almost beatific, as if serenely aware of fulfilling some destiny.

"What are you thinking?" he asked hesitantly, afraid to break the spell.

"I spoke with my children last night," she said. "They are well and they wished me well." She paused. "It was uncanny to me . . . it was almost as if they knew I was involved in some desperate mission. Young children have that sense about them, you know. They were so sweet and brave. They can tell just by hearing my voice so far away that I am under great stress and they wanted me to know of their love."

She shifted toward Connaughton in the confines of the small car. "I have always had a tremendous foreboding about what we are doing. I have always thought it would lead to our destruction. It only concerns me for my children. My father and mother are old. My former husband is no good. If something were to happen to me, the boys would fall into the hands of strangers. You and I . . . we are playing a game on a field too big for us. We will be ground up in the giant machinery of politics. The stakes are too high. Too many important, powerful people have too much riding on the outcome of these talks. We cannot keep doing what we are doing without getting caught and punished by someone. However this turns out, even for the good, we will be sacrificed to those who are defeated." Her words rushed forth like water through a breached dam, as Connaughton drove on through the small villages of Douvaine and Sciez.

"But for the first time last night, I knew I was doing the right thing. I knew I had a duty to my children greater than just being their mother. I knew I had to try to prevent the disaster which was coming. I knew I had no choice but to follow the course we are following." She smiled at him, a rare thing. "So, you see, I feel at peace with myself. I am prepared for what comes."

Connaughton smiled back, suddenly feeling awkward and, strangely, wishing he were less ordinary looking. Sensations clashed. He felt a chill at the phrase "prepared for what comes," because he shared her instinctive sense of a judgment to come for them both. But, at the same time, he was overwhelmed by her radiance and the sudden beauty it brought. The power of his rush of affection for her surprised him. He had not experienced that sensation for a long time. He felt as if she had suddenly been picked up and was being carried forward by forces over which he had no control. He found himself on such unfamiliar emotional ground that he might say or do something he would soon profoundly regret.

His first thought, even as he watched the road ahead, was to ward off the immediate instinct to show affection, or warmth, or understanding. Never particularly good at words in intimate circumstances, he hoped they would not betray him now. "Ekaterina, I hope you understand I have not involved you in this . . . this venture casually. There is a great risk, and I know how you feel about your sons, even though we have not been . . . ah, friends, for very long. We're both in over our heads. But we've created a situation few other people could have—and it could turn out to make an enormous difference in how all the arms control negotiations turn out.

"I have to be honest with you," he continued after a time. "Things could go very badly for us, depending on who wins and who loses. We don't know that yet. We do know this, though. If we—you and I—don't try to make the most of the chance we have, then everyone—including our children—will lose." Miles were flying by. They were approaching the town of Thonon-les-Bains by the lake. "We've gotten ourselves into a trap, I guess you could say. But it's not a trap I'm ready to get out of . . . at least yet."

"Even though Ambassador Arkwright knows we are meeting," she said, "what are the prospects that we are being followed by the CIA? Who else in your government knows of these meetings?"

He noticed the single line of concern had returned between her dark eyebrows. "There is always the possibility. It isn't so much a matter of whether, as when. Sooner or later some highly placed people in the White House or Defense Department or CIA are going to demand to know the source of information coming out of the Soviet government and how it's being channeled. If they don't get a satisfactory answer from Secretary Norton or Ambassador Arkwright, they'll undertake their own investigation . . . which means surveillance." He switched on the car headlights as darkness deepened, and automatically looked in the rear-view mirror. He could see a dark car a quarter of a mile behind, running without its lights. "For all I know, it could already be under way." He studied her face, again in profile. "What about your side? Won't Makarov have you followed just as a matter of course, just for his own safety?"

They drove through Thonon-les-Bains and she tied a dark scarf over her head as if to ward off the suddenly bright streetlights. Connaughton noticed the car behind had illuminated its headlights and drawn closer, but not close enough to identify its occupants. "It could well be," she said as they reached the town's outskirts and increased speed to cover the remaining few miles to Évian. "He would not want to frighten you away. He believes the information we are receiving to be extremely valuable—not just for our government, but for his career as well. But he is not the problem. There are those in Moscow, with agents in Geneva, who do not wish these negotiations well. If they conclude—and they must, perhaps already have—that our meetings will facilitate agreement and frustrate their agenda, they will follow us . . . at the very least."

Connaughton's grip on the wheel tightened and he increased speed almost inadvertently. "What do you mean 'at the very least'?"

"You are a sophisticated man, Frank." (He now insisted that she use his first name and considered it quaint that it sounded more like "Frahnk.") "The KGB has never been known for the delicacy of its operations—although they can probably mount a surveillance undetected. If we are followed and you are identified, they will do everything they can to collect information about you. You should assume they will listen to telephone calls from your home and try to place microphones in your home. They will certainly follow you at all times. Most important, they will not be working for those who wish us well."

"What about you?" he asked.

"Their job with me is easier," she said quietly. "If they follow you, they pick up me when we are together. That is evidence enough. When I am working, it is even easier. I am either at the mission in negotiations or in my quarters.''

Connaughton slowed the car as they reached the perimeter of Évian. The lovely lakeside resort town was largely vacant of tourists in the winter months, but the Swiss often crossed the waters of the lake on the small steamers to sample its casinos year-round. He continued through the main area of town, consulted a small piece of paper, then slowed to make a right turn leading up a steep and winding street. He carefully checked the rear-view mirror and, before making another right turn, saw the dark sedan behind slow slightly, then continue on the lake highway. These basic facts of life cast silence on the couple as they drove the remaining half mile to the deluxe hotel called La Verniez.

"Madame, monsieur, bon soir." The elegantly tailored maître d' bowed them to the corner table Connaughton had requested earlier from the pay telephone at the Hotel Beau Rivage in Geneva. The candlelit dining room was only half-filled, mostly with wealthy tourists or locally successful business people. The only notice they drew came from appreciative male eyes following Ekaterina's tall figure. Connaughton ordered a good Bordeaux to accompany the menus.

After a glass of wine, they ordered a fresh lake fish recommended by the waiter and Connaughton said, "I think we must move fast."

"I agree," she said. "The talks must find a way to break the verification barrier and prohibit testing of new weapons. The talk in our delegation, as well as in the Foreign Ministry, among those who want arms control is that testing must be limited or halted. It will be difficult. There are many who don't want to stop development of new weapons. But"—she leaned forward—"I know there is growing support in the Defense Ministry for some kind of test ban. There are budgetary reasons, and anyway no important tests are planned for two years. The question is how a ban can be monitored.''

"That's an easier problem for you than for us," Connaughton replied. "We can verify weapons tests down to the twenty- to thirty-kiloton range from outside the Soviet Union. But too many of your tests are below that range and our scientists say we have to have some kind of on-site electronic inspection—'black boxes'—on Soviet territory. Your government hasn't been willing to let us do that."

She touched his hand lightly. "They may," she said in a whisper. Connaughton's eyebrows raised involuntarily. "The key may be whether you are willing to share your seismic technology with us. I attended a meeting of our delegation during the holiday break where three members of our National Science Academy conducted a briefing of our experts on verification. They said you had much more sophisticated equipment in this area than we do.... I remember they quoted some figures from the *Aviation Week* magazine published in the U.S. They said we had nothing even half as good. I can't remember all the details . . . it was very complex. They said we have no ability to detect underground explosions below the fifty-kilotons from outside the United States."

Connaughton got out a piece of paper and pen and, after gesturing to ask her permission, began to make notes.

"So you think," he murmured with intensity, "that your side might agree to stop testing if we did the same and gave you the ability to verify that agreement?"

Her nod was confident. "And we would consider, I believe, a limited number of black boxes on Soviet soil so that you could be absolutely sure we are not carrying out small tests."

"Your generals aren't going to like that," Connaughton said, sipping the wine.

"No, you have it wrong. Basically, the Defense Ministry believes the time has come to stop testing, if the Americans will. The real opposition comes from the Party theoreticians and KGB,'' she said.

As the waiter served their dinner, Connaughton made hasty notes on the possible trade. They attacked the food in silence, and in Ekaterina's case with relish, Connaughton was happy to note. It was the first time she had seemed relaxed enough to enjoy good food. She seemed particularly to appreciate the wine and he refilled her glass. Down the length of the dining room, he noticed two men entering the elegant sitting room–cocktail area. Though some distance away, he thought their dark suits to be Soviet bloc–baggy. They occupied a dimly lit table against the back wall of the bar. They were situated not only to watch people arriving at and departing the dining room but also, through the nearby window, cars entering and leaving the parking area. He did his best to watch them over Ekaterina's shoulder without alerting her to their presence.

Shortly, their plates were removed and thick coffee served. Ekaterina asked, ''Frank, have you thought of death?''

Connaughton's eyebrows notched up. ''That's a very Russian question. Of course not. We Americans don't believe in death. We assume one of these days someone's going to invent a way to stop aging...at about thirty-one. You forget, I come from a land of grandmothers on skateboards and eighty-five-year-olds remarrying for the fourth time.'' She smiled and lowered her eyes, but he could tell she meant the question seriously. ''Obviously *you* have thought about it—why else ask?''

''I am religious, Frank. I suppose a surprising number of Russians—at least surprising to you—are. I believe in existence after death...some continued consciousness of my soul—my personality—after I die. I believe in God. It is a very peasant trait among the Russian people. It was, after all, about all most Russian people had to sustain them in the miserable centuries when they were treated like draft horses.

The court and the nobility preserved the forms of worship. But the peasants gave it meaning. They kept the light of faith alive in the Russian soul for many centuries."

Connaughton said, "You clearly come down on Alyosha's side against Ivan in the old bread-versus-freedom debate, I take it?"

She had come to believe he masked his feelings behind an ironic tone and treated the question accordingly. "It isn't quite that simple. Seventy years ago the Russian peasant had neither. Now, at least, he has bread. But I would have thought your own life and country would be proof that one can have both. If Dostoevski were to write today, his half-mad genius would be torn by an even greater dilemma . . . how one reconciles loyalty to one's country with the nuclear age."

"What do you mean?" Connaughton asked as he leaned forward.

"Simply that. What happens when you discover the leadership of your country may be preparing to take unacceptable risks with the lives of its own citizens?"

"That's easy. Vote the bastards out of office." He smiled warmly. "You should try it sometime."

"Is that your answer, Frank? Is that what you are doing here?"

The question entered Connaughton like a small dagger just below the heart. He drank more wine. "It just so happens that our next election doesn't occur in time to save these negotiations. My options are limited."

"Indeed. So are those of the human race." She put her hand on his. He was suddenly aware of the warmth of her touch. "Most people on earth don't get to vote in your election."

The dagger turned slightly. "They have a better chance of that than they do of participating in your Politburo." He squeezed her hand, emotions and political arguments colliding painfully in his mind. "Is that why you are here . . . because you can't vote in the Politburo?"

"Yes. But even if I could vote in the Politburo and it voted wrong on risking nuclear war, I would probably be here anyway."

"Do you think individuals have the right to defy the leaders of their countries?" Connaughton asked. He noticed her cheeks were flushed as he refilled her wineglass for the third time.

"I think it depends on what you mean by 'defy,'" she responded. "I am defying some leaders, certainly. If they found out even the fact that I was meeting with you, it would be very difficult for me, to say the least. But there are others in our government—including Ambassador Makarov and probably the Foreign Minister—who seem to support these contacts. So one cannot say I am exactly defying them."

"I know the risks you're taking. I've been painfully aware of that all along," Connaughton said. "But we both know you're doing more than simply carrying information— valuable information—back to those 'others' in your government. You are also providing information—valuable information—to me and to my government. Whatever you call it, it's pretty serious stuff."

He saw her eyes glisten in the candlelight. "Yes, we have a word for it—*izmena*. It's called treason. If you are caught doing that in the Soviet Union and convicted—and the trial is usually very brief—the sentence is executed very quickly." She looked at him intently for a long time. "It seems to me you are guilty of the same thing, Frank. And quite possibly with the same consequences."

"I know that," he said. "And I'm willing to take the chance . . . for myself." He hesitated. "But I'm not sure I'm willing to take the risk for you."

She gave a fleeting smile, her lips trembling slightly. "You do not make that decision. I do. And besides, I don't know what else to do."

Over her shoulder, Connaughton caught a glimpse of the two men leaving the lounge and heading for the parking area. He said, "Whatever we do further has to be done fast. If both sides undertake their massive military exercises this spring, the negotiations are dead and there will be real confrontation. And the more you and I continue these negotiations of our own, the greater the chance one or both of us is going to get caught. So whatever happens has to be fast."

Connaughton laid out payment for the dinner and the maître d' started across the dining room with their coats. He said, "I'll have Arkwright forward this notion of a test ban verified by on-site inspection to Norton. The way things happened last time, we should see some action quickly—one way or the other. Meanwhile, you see what good you can do with the notion on your side."

Ekaterina shivered slightly as she was helped with her coat. The thought of another intimate session with Makarov repulsed her. But she had little choice.

Connaughton noticed her preoccupation as they stood near the drive awaiting their car. Impulsively he placed his arm around her. She stiffened, then relaxed in the warmth of the embrace and briefly rested her head on his shoulder. It seemed natural for both of them, one more leap of faith among the other chances they'd already taken together. The car arrived and they made their way down the winding streets from the stylish villa to the lakeshore drive. As Connaughton turned left onto the main highway leading back to Geneva, he instinctively looked in the rear-view mirror. Several hundred yards back a sedan turned on its lights and pulled onto the highway from a lakeside overlook. He immediately assumed it to be the same car that had followed them from Geneva earlier, most likely occupied by the men in the restaurant.

He said nothing but took her hand, and she placed her other hand on his, gripping him tightly. They drove silently back to the city and, at her request, he left her at the taxi stand outside the Hotel Richemond. Before she opened the door, Connaughton leaned across and kissed her on the cheek. Then she fled.

45

"YOU HAVE TO SAY this for him. He knows how to pick good restaurants." Malenkov looked up from the papers on his desk in the spare office maintained in the Soviet Mission in Geneva for visiting VIPs from Moscow. Across the desk young Metrinko, his protégé, smiled with self-assurance. What a difference, Malenkov thought. He had known Metrinko's uncle, the notorious Cyril Metrinko, recently deceased head of KGB counterintelligence, very well. He had been a close ally of Vladimir Zhdanov with equal measures of ruthlessness, orthodoxy, and vindictiveness. The nephew was something else. Westernized, smooth, and suave—but equally ambitious.

"Too bad we couldn't try the food," Metrinko said. "The guys had to hide out in the lounge drinking beer while they sampled the haute cuisine. I couldn't trust those demented thugs you sent here to work for me with anything stronger than beer. Otherwise, they would have started a brawl and wrecked the place. But don't worry, I was careful not to be seen. I stayed in the car."

Malenkov resented Metrinko's cheekiness but, as usual, didn't call him down because of the younger man's social and political connections in Moscow. "They're not thugs, my friend." He smiled thinly. "They are two of the best surveillance people we have in the organization."

"Yes, and that's what is wrong with the 'organization.'" Metrinko beamed back. Then his face became cold. "They looked very friendly with each other. He made some notes during the dinner. It must have had something to do with things she was saying." He leaned forward almost rising over the desk. "I think we should pick her up and end this nonsense. It's getting dangerous—for everyone."

"We'll see," Malenkov said. "Right now it's helpful to know he's the one she's getting her information from. The question is, what else is going on there?" The stubby man got up from the desk and walked to the window. "Do you suppose they are lovers?" He smiled at Metrinko, who could not decide whether the smile was more malevolent or lascivious. Malenkov knew Metrinko had lusted after Ekaterina Davydova during their entire year together in Geneva.

"I have no way of knowing," the younger man replied. "We've dropped a couple of microphones in his apartment here—and I looked around a little at the time—but we haven't picked anything up."

Malenkov said, "Well, I want you and your helpers to press harder. I've got to go back to Moscow next week, and I better have something to tell Comrade Zhdanov. Otherwise, he will be very displeased . . . to say the least." He looked at Metrinko again. "What is her 'arrangement' with Makarov?"

Metrinko knew what he meant. "No 'arrangement.' At least so far as I know." Metrinko was offended, offended that Malenkov thought a woman of sufficient stature to interest—and rebuff—him might take up with a lout like Makarov. "I'm sure the good Ambassador has done his best. In fact, after his usual several scotches at more than a few dinners, he's made his interest pretty obvious. But she won't have anything to do with him." His own reputation required Metrinko to defend Ekaterina against the likes of Makarov.

"That's all well and good, my friend. But how does she get to roam about at all hours with this Connaughton? She must have some influence on our chief negotiator."

"He's using her," Metrinko said with considerable exasperation. "That's obvious to anyone. She meets with the American. She gets valuable information. She passes the information on to Makarov. He sends it to Zoshchenko. Zoshchenko uses it to convince General Secretary Kamenev that the Americans are ready to do business on nuclear weapons." Metrinko sounded like an arrogant tutor as he summed it up for his superior. "And Makarov is a hero. And Zhdanov goes berserk and sends you here to kick me in the ass."

The color rose in Malenkov's already florid face. "Look, my *young* friend. There is more to it than that. You better get off your high horse and find out what it is or I *may* kick you in the ass." He leaned across the desk to recapture his role as an intimidator. "How is it the American is giving all this valuable information away? How is it within days of his meetings with Davydova that major nuclear initiatives are put forward here and in Washington? How is it that the policy in the Kremlin suddenly begins to shift toward conciliation and détente? If you think this is as simple as you've described it, you're even more stupid than I thought!" Malenkov was fairly shouting. Footsteps just previously sounding outside the door had halted.

"Let me tell you something, you little popinjay," Malenkov continued through his teeth. "I want you all over that woman, night and day, and not the way you want to be. You let me know every time she blinks. You let me know every bite she eats. I want to know who she sleeps with, and if she doesn't sleep with anyone, why not. And let me tell you something else," Malenkov hissed, "no fingerprints. None of that dummy stuff like the other night following her into restaurants. Even if she's not smart enough to pick you up, the American will. So start getting clever. If we—if *you* let this woman upset Zhdanov's plans, believe me they will not have those fancy cigarettes and fancy clothes where you're going."

46

CONNAUGHTON WAS HALFWAY up the stone steps to his third-floor apartment on the Grand' Rue when the odd thought hit him. Something familiar about the slightly built man in the wide-brimmed felt hat looking in the window of the antique shop across the cobblestone street from Connaughton's building. What was it? Connaughton slowed his steps as he tried to catch the fleeting idea. Even a passing glimpse had told him the slightly worn navy overcoat was well made, stylish. That and the hat were all that he had seen. But there was an impression of something...or someone. It was that eerie sense you had about some people.

Then he knew, or thought he knew. And he dashed up the remaining steps and down the hallway to his front door, slapped the key into the lock, and ran to the window. The man was gone. Connaughton looked as far up and down the Grand' Rue as the window frame permitted. He looked at the shop door a few minutes, glanced at his watch, then realized the shops were closed for the evening.

It was the Russian Church. Three weeks before, when he had met Ekaterina there and introduced his wild proposition, he had let her leave first, then had followed shortly thereafter just as the priest prepared to close the doors. As he had crossed the Rue Toepffer, on the corner formed by the intersection with the Rue Lefort, there was a man sitting on the folding canvas camp chair at an easel carefully painting a watercolor of the church. This had seemed at the time to be both romantic and improbable to Connaughton. And he had been struck by the clean, precise lines of the man and the evident quality of his clothes. He had blond hair and pale blue eyes that seemed to take notice of nothing but his painting. Connaughton had passed close enough to see that the painting was carefully and beautifully done. Colors and brushes were held in an aged hardwood paint box. What Connaughton now remembered best was the dark blue overcoat hanging from the street sign next to the man's outdoor studio. And the wide-brimmed, gray felt hat on top of it.

Connaughton put his briefcase down and considered the possibilities. He assumed by now that he and probably Ekaterina were under some kind of surveillance. But by whom and for whom? Surely Makarov would have her followed to verify it was in fact Connaughton she was meeting at the times and in the places she reported. Makarov would need that for his own protection in case the scheme blew up later. Plus he might have genuine concern about her well-being, although that was undoubtedly secondary. In his own case, Connaughton thought, some very high level people in Washington were not anxious to see progress in the arms control negotiations at the expense of the Blue Thunder exercises that spring. If his meetings with Ekaterina were breaking the diplomatic logjam, those very same people would begin to take an intense interest in his activities and the source of his information.

If he was being watched, it would be by the CIA. It wouldn't be a Sid Murray operation. He was a nuclear weapons expert, not a spook. No, they would send some hotshots out from Washington. Some people Connaughton had never seen. They would also bug his apartment and tap his phone. Of course, the Soviets would try to do that too. At the very least, the Agency shadows would finger Ekaterina as his Soviet source. At the worst they would do all they could to discredit him and provide their Washington principals the ammunition to torpedo the talks.

What about the man in the felt hat from the Russian Church? There were several possibilities, Connaughton thought. The man across the street might not have been the same man. No chance. Connaughton would have sworn the coat and hat were the same. It was a coincidence—being outside the church and outside Connaughton's apartment. Some coincidence. He was working for the Soviets. Couldn't be. He was dressed too well. And they never contracted out their surveillance. He was a far cry from the men in the lounge at Évian two nights ago. Maybe he was working for a third party. Couldn't be. No other country would know about or be particularly interested in his meetings with Ekaterina. That left only the Agency. The big guys in Washington had sent him, and probably some others, out to get what they could on Connaughton and prevent him from mucking up the Blue Thunder scheme. Whoever would gamble on launching Cyclops wouldn't hesitate a minute to get anything they could on him.

Connaughton walked quickly out of his apartment, double-locking the door behind him. After a couple of steps he stopped and went back. He tore a tiny sliver of paper from his address book and balanced it behind the door hinge. He then made his way out onto the narrow street in front of his building. There were a few strollers in the chill night. Otherwise the old street was empty. There was no dapper artist in a felt hat...at least that he could see. He took a few steps to his left, looked up the short Rue du Cheval-Blanc, and saw no one. He walked a few steps farther up the hill and looked to his left down the Rue de la Pelisserie. Again no one. But to be sure, he would have to look in dozens of doorways where someone could stand undetected.

Agitated enough that he could not return to his apartment, Connaughton set off on a tour of the old city. He walked toward the cathedral and made his way quickly through the winding streets. The dinner hour and chill of the evening had driven most people inside. He saw only taxis with parties for dinner headed for restaurants in the area. He walked briskly down to the central shopping area and passed mostly clerks and shopkeepers heading home after closing hour. There was no felt-hatted artist.

Connaughton was briefly tempted to stop in a restaurant, but given his heightened paranoia and general dislike of dining out alone he abandoned the notion and started back to his apartment. As he entered the Place du Bourg-de-Four, he glanced to his left and thought he saw a figure standing in the dim entryway to the Palais de Justice. He stopped, looked, and started to cross the street. He halted for a passing tour bus on its way down the hill and then entered the courtyard of the imposing three-story stone building. No one was there. He looked up and down the exterior walkways leading to various police offices and still saw no one. Whomever he had seen was now gone. But he had, in silhouette, been wearing a long dark coat and broad hat.

Back in his apartment, while soup was warming, Connaughton undertook a mission he regretted not doing earlier. He inspected his own apartment. He interrupted his efforts briefly to eat, then resumed his work. After almost two hours he found a tiny metal capsule, slightly larger than an aspirin, behind some books on a shelf by his bed. He then carefully dismantled his Swiss telephone and next to the transmitter-amplifier found a slightly larger device of a different make lodged in the telephone works. He put the telephone back together, brewed some tea, and thought for some time. He decided to leave both bugs in place—at least for the time being. He wanted to call Ekaterina and warn her. But he could not have done so even if he had not found the intercept device. Besides, she was smart enough to be careful.

What concerned him even more was his discovery two hours before when he had returned to his apartment. The tiny scrap of paper had slipped down the door frame and was on the floor lodged between the base of the door and the frame. And the papers in his leather briefcase had been moved a fraction of an inch from the way he had left them.

47

THERE WAS SO MUCH she wanted to tell him, Ekaterina
thought. Particularly the most important thing. But she
knew she never would be able to. She pulled her coat more
tightly around her as she walked that night around the
grounds of the sealed Soviet complex. Patrols routinely po-
liced the walls and she suspected she was being watched by
others as well. She knew Metrinko would be under great
pressure to find out whether she, or anyone else in the delegation, was playing some role in the sudden forward
movement in the negotiations. The KGB kept such close
account of all movement that they must know about her recent extraordinary behavior. Would they confront Makarov and inform him, or seek an explanation? He might
already have told them not to be concerned, that he had authorized her to move about on her own contrary to regula-
tions.

She had outlined Connaughton's statements about some
linkage between a test ban and on-site inspection yesterday
morning after her dinner with the American's the night before. Makarov had drunk himself to sleep by the time she
came in, and she defied his instruction to report to him that
night because she knew he would be more inclined to make
an advance in his apartment at night after drinking. But in
his office yesterday morning he had reacted excitedly to the
American's notion of exchanging verification technology.
He had questioned her in detail, looking for every nuance.
She knew he had filed his cable to Zoshchenko immedi-

ately and she would not be surprised if he was invited to Ambassador Arkwright's house for dinner by the weekend. A pattern was forming, she thought to herself with a slight smile.

She returned to her corner room. Once inside and warm, she locked her door and began to prepare for sleep. Before retiring she opened her wardrobe drawer to get the diary she kept for her children. Instead of immediately locating it beneath the lingerie in the corner of the drawer, she found it slightly farther back in the drawer. She shut the drawer and closed the wardrobe with a shiver. Someone had been in her room and had gone through her personal things—probably as recently as a few minutes ago when she was walking around the grounds of the complex.

48

THE SAND WAS RUNNING to the bottom of the hourglass ever more quickly.

Now back in Washington, with her editors' permission and encouragement, Andrea Cass pulled out all the stops in an effort to penetrate the mystery of Blue Thunder and Cyclops.

Before leaving Geneva she had perceived subtle tones of conciliation in the negotiations, but she had no concrete evidence. Just a sense of things. How could it be, she pondered, that the negotiators seemed to be making progress while all the visible evidence revealed the superpowers marching toward a confrontation—and doomsday? She felt much like an observer on a distant hill watching two trains bearing down on each other at top speed while tiny switchmen raced to throw the switches necessary to avert the catastrophe.

She had this situation very much in mind when she entered Harry Rafferty's office in the Dirksen Senate Office Building. After Rafferty's secretary served them coffee, she began:

"Senator, you've become much more involved in the arms control issue in recent weeks. How do you think things are going at the talks?"

"Not very well. In fact, I've been pretty pessimistic for some time."

"What happens if this round of talks fails?"

He hesitated. "I want to be careful here and not over-state the case." Then he said, "It could get very rough, particularly this spring. As you know, both sides have planned military exercises. In our case at least, they're quite extensive ... hell, they're massive. For all we know, the Soviets are planning the same thing. Now what happens if we're unsuccessful at negotiating an agreement and the talks break off totally in acrimony and then we both put on these gigantic military shows? Among other things, we'll scare the bejesus out of the Europeans and a lot of others. We'll probably end up scaring ourselves. And that's not a healthy thing. Now, when we get scared or the Russians get scared, bad things can happen. Then, every move is seen as a threat—every action is ominous—and, most of all, people with their fingers on the trigger get nervous. A nervous person with a nuclear trigger is a dangerous thing. That's why we need an agreement—to make both sides feel more secure."

As he drank his coffee, she said, "But, Senator, with all due respect, a lot of people in this country don't trust the Russians."

"Miss Cass, if we trusted the Russians we wouldn't have to negotiate with them. We're not negotiating with the British or French or Italians. Hell, we're not even negotiating arms control agreements with the Chinese. I don't trust the Russians any more than the professional paranoids in this administration do—strike 'professional paranoids'—and that's why we have to negotiate behavior between us. It's people getting a divorce—not getting married—who get themselves lawyers."

"Senator Rafferty," Cass asked with her sweetest smile, "are there people in this administration who want confrontation with the Soviet Union?"

"You bet your sweet ..." He smiled back. "Yes. There are."

"Why?"

"You'd have to ask them that, Miss Cass."

"How would the confrontation come about?"

"Maybe in the military exercises after the talks collapse."

"What about Cyclops?"

"What about it? It's a top-secret project you're not even supposed to know about."

"What do you know about it, Senator?"

"Whatever I know about it, I'm not going to talk about."

"Might Cyclops be used to start World War III, Senator Rafferty?"

"That dog won't hunt, Miss Cass." He stood. "I expect this interview's about over."

She scribbled a note, then started for the door. "Have you gotten any information recently on Cyclops you weren't supposed to have?"

"No comment," he said.

She started through the door, then stopped to look back. "Have they found out who hit you at Montrose Park, Senator?"

"No comment. Good-bye, Miss Cass."

Back at her office as she typed up her notes, Cass tried Arnold Danzig. He wasn't available. The *Times* military reporter had heard from a contact in the Navy Command Staff that the Chief of Naval Operations, Admiral Bigby, was a dissenter on Blue Thunder. She placed a call to his office. The CNO was at Pacific headquarters in Hawaii. Usually reliable contacts at the CIA and State Department wouldn't return her calls. Apparently everyone in town knew the story she was working on and wouldn't talk. Too dangerous.

She thought. She had bluffed Danzig too many times to try again. But there were some others who didn't know that game. She checked the phone book, then called the Washington-based Datasync vice-president for governmental affairs—the giant contractor's chief lobbyist. When his secretary said *The New York Times* was on the line, he took the call. When Cass said she wanted to talk about a highly classified Datasync project, he agreed to have a drink with her at 6 P.M.

"TELL ME ABOUT CYCLOPS, Mr. Tarquin," she said politely after drinks were served at the small back table at Duke Zeibert's.

He managed to smile tightly and frown at the same time. "I'm afraid I can't do that, Miss . . . ah . . ."

"Cass. You ought to, Mr. Tarquin. Everyone else is. There's someone—in the administration, or maybe even in your company—who's talking a great deal. You ought to get your side of the story out."

"We have no 'side of the story,' Miss, ah, Cass. We don't talk about classified projects we undertake for the government. That's why we're able to do a great deal of work of that sort."

"Let's say a very secret satellite, like Cyclops for example, were launched into orbit. How many people in your company would know about it?"

"Very few," he said with grim wariness.

"How do you suppose Harry Rafferty found out about it?" she asked innocently.

Tarquin's eyes showed anger and surprise. "Let me compliment you on a double trick question. 'It' supposes a launch has taken place. And you also assume Senator Rafferty knows something about a launch that may or may not have taken place."

"No, Mr. Tarquin, I believe a killer satellite, produced by your company, has been launched. And I also believe Senator Rafferty has some inside information about that launch."

"Well, that's very interesting, Miss Cass. Congratulations." Tarquin's sarcasm hid neither his anger nor his surprise. He drained his scotch and water in one swallow. "I didn't know *The New York Times* had a new section on fairy stories.''

She said, "Thank you for your time, Mr. Tarquin. If it is in fact a fairy tale, you should be prepared to issue a denial when the story runs in my paper." She picked up her pad and stood. "That's your position, is it not? You deny Cyclops has been launched?"

She held her pen poised above the pad as Tarquin stalked off.

Back at her office in the *Times* Washington bureau on K Street, Cass wrote and filed her story. It was highly speculative, based on unnamed sources, implication, and surmise. But it would be a bombshell. She reported that both sides in the arms race had been researching killer-satellite technologies and the United States was believed to have contracted with Datasync to produce such a capability. The question in the minds of many, she wrote, was whether this capability might already have been deployed.

If this killer satellite had been placed in orbit and the Soviets were to discover this fact, she reported, it would be considered a serious escalation of hostilities. And it would certainly set the stage for a major confrontation when military exercises involving both NATO and the Warsaw Pact forces took place in the spring. She took a deep breath and wrote that a Datasync spokesman had refused to deny that the antisatellite weapon was already in space. She closed the story by recalling the mysterious accident involving Harry Rafferty in early January and noted his membership on the Senate Intelligence Committee and the possible connection of his hit-and-run with murky committee and arms control activities.

She filed the story and returned to her room at the Georgetown Inn to pack her bags for the return to Geneva. An hour and a half later the desk notified her that her cab for the airport had arrived and her office was also calling. She picked up the phone with some irritation, expecting some petty complaint about expense vouchers, and found Warren Corson, the bureau chief, on the line.

"Andrea, what's wrong with you? Did you seriously believe we were going to get that story past New York? They went crazy. I've spent the past hour listening to them scream while I tried to get some comment or confirmation on your story from the administration. I don't know who was more furious, Abe or Danzig."

"Look, Warren, I don't give a shit what Danzig says. He's paid to get mad—especially at the truth. And as far as Abe goes, tell him it's a solid story."

"Solid!" Corson snorted. "This is the mushiest story I've ever seen. You don't have one named source. You've speculated yourself and the paper right out on a skinny limb. And you call that solid?"

"Warren, I *know* something funny is going on. I *know* somebody is setting us up to punch the Russians in the nose in April and this Cyclops satellite is part of the deal. I *know* it."

"You know it!" Corson yelled. "You know it! *The New York Times* is not in business to tell people what you 'know.' What are you, some kind of psychic? We're not running a fortune-telling business here. Get back to Geneva and stick to writing about what can be proved. This story is spiked— killed—dead." And he hung up.

FOUR DAYS LATER in Geneva, Cass got a totally unrewarding briefing from the Soviet press officer at the Soviet compound. He alleged that both sides were working hard, having meaningful exchanges, dealing frankly and candidly with each other, and seeking areas of mutual understanding to achieve peaceful coexistence. It was a total diplomatic brush-off. Cass was still stung by the rebuke from her Washington boss and New York editors. She had got her fanny spanked good, she thought.

So that night she took a big chance. She followed the Soviet Ambassador. If these talks went anywhere, it would have to be soon. Normal diplomatic channels, namely the stilted, drawn-out negotiation process, couldn't produce results that fast. She guessed that if private meetings were being held at the ambassadorial level in Geneva, they would be at night. And she further guessed Makarov and Arkwright both would feel more comfortable at Arkwright's sumptuous house than in the sterile Soviet Mission compound. So for three nights she cruised the avenue fronting the Soviet Mission. Sometimes she waited at the foot of the hill where the Avenue de la Paix joined the Lausanne highway; Makarov would undoubtedly pass by on his way to the Cologny section on the lake.

On the third night her wait paid off. At ten minutes till eight Makarov's limousine descended the hill followed by a dark sedan carrying three security men. She let two cars pull into traffic, then she fell into the line. As the two cars made their way around the lake and up the other side, she gambled on the destination. She had been to the Arkwrights' house for a number of social events, including a press dinner, and she knew its location well. She took back streets to the long drive leading into the Arkwrights' rented estate and parked her car on a dark side street. Within minutes Makarov's two cars swept by and into the Arkwrights' drive.

She had dinner and was back at her post at ten. Within fifteen minutes Makarov's short caravan departed the premises and was on its way back to the Soviet Mission. She noted the times in her notebook and pondered the event on her way home. It could have been merely social. Small chance. Makarov's wife had not been with him and she knew Mrs. Arkwright to be temporarily back in the United States. Besides, Arkwright didn't particularly enjoy Makarov's company. It had to be business. Messages were being passed.

Cass concluded that there was some dramatic, behind-the-scenes effort to rescue the negotiation effort and produce an agreement—before a dangerous military confrontation and its hair-trigger tension arrived in a few short weeks. She further suspected that, somehow, Frank Connaughton was caught up in that effort. It all related to Cyclops. But she couldn't fit it together—at least yet. If Connaughton was the key, then she had to find some way to get him to open the door.

49

ON THE LAST DAY of February, *The New York Times* carried a long background piece on planned military exercises scheduled for the spring by both Warsaw Pact and NATO forces. By the time she had reached Geneva, Andrea Cass had received a message from bureau chief Corson, who had partially relented (and who was just a shade concerned that Cass's renowned instincts were right again). He wouldn't go with the speculative piece about secret weapons in space. But he had convinced the editors that the collision course between arms control talks and military exercises was obvious, important, and—so far—unreported. She had much of the story already in her head and in her notes. She made a whirlwind thirty-six-hour tour of NATO headquarters in Brussels as well as allied command headquarters in Bonn, London, and Rome, and then she filed her story.

Within twenty-four hours wire services carried the story to foreign capitals and other military and foreign policy journalists filed follow-up stories. The net effect was to inflame smoldering fires of protest throughout the West. The first few days of March saw thousands of demonstrators pouring in the streets of the major capitals of Europe and the campuses and larger cities of the United States. For the first time, demonstrators even appeared in Latin American capitals as well as Japan and Australia. On the second and third days of these demonstrations serious violence broke out again, repeating the worst experiences of December and early January. Clashes with riot police were frequent and injuries were horrifying.

In virtually every NATO nation, foreign and domestic ministers battled with defense ministers over the Blue Thunder exercise. The governments of Belgium and Italy barely survived votes of "no confidence" on the question. Pressure on Washington—the Lawkard administration— grew again. NATO partners privately, and occasionally publicly, pressed the U.S. government to postpone the exercises. Defense Secretary Joe Sternberg let the President know that, if Blue Thunder was postponed, he would resign in protest, and he wouldn't be surprised if one or more of the Joint Chiefs joined him. Vice-President Harold Burgoon backed Sternberg up. In the face of their threats, Lawkard reverted to type and authorized Sternberg to issue a statement saying that annual NATO military exercises had been conducted virtually since the formation of the alliance and that under no conditions—save one—would the exercises be postponed. The one condition was a comprehensive treaty halting the nuclear arms race. And that condition was included only after a bitter argument within the National Security Council in which the Secretary of State threatened *his* resignation if it was not. Sternberg fumed, then finally relented, satisfied he had carried the day.

Immediately after the NSC meeting, Sternberg collected the Joint Chiefs in extraordinary session. He ordered them, coordinating with their NATO counterparts, to begin implementation of the early stages of Blue Thunder. Admiral Bigby was the only one to resist, complaining about the difficulty of moving large fleets without Soviet satellite and "tattletale" ship detection. And Sternberg said, "By God, get those ships to sea. What do we care what the Soviets detect? They're going to detect a whole hell of a lot more ships—and planes, tanks, and troops—in six weeks. So they sure as shit better get used to it. Besides, once they get used to it, maybe they'll get the goddam message."

General Ben Ellison noted his intention to head for Europe immediately to ensure that the commander in chief of NATO and his allied counterparts had the proper timetable for call-up of reserve units in the Netherlands and elsewhere and the insertion of the appropriate Army reserve units into the Central Front in Europe. General Omar King reported that he would start in Omaha and conduct a quick tour of Strategic Air Command bomber bases to carry out an unannounced inspection of emergency readiness, and then head for the intermediate-range bomber bases in England and selected fighter bases on the Continent. He wanted to ensure that the allied air forces were prepared to fulfill their role in simulated air interdiction and close air support missions. Karl Bigby, clearly under pressure from his peers to get in harness, gloomily announced that he would start at the Second Fleet headquarters in Norfolk later that week, then visit the Sixth Fleet in the Mediterranean, stop off at NATO Southern Command in Naples and the carrier task group in the Indian Ocean, and visit CINCPAC in Honolulu and the Third Fleet home port at San Diego, before returning to Washington in ten days to two weeks. Sternberg noted acerbically that Bigby would not be starting his inspection and readiness tour until several days after the others.

Sternberg himself intended to stay in Washington for most of the next six weeks before Blue Thunder got under way to make sure someone was standing watch. In their own individual ways they each knew he was staying put to help Hal Burgoon keep the President on the reservation and prevent the likes of Emerson Norton and the State Department softies from derailing the plans.

As they stood to break up the meeting, Sternberg instructed Bigby to order carrier tasks forces and fleets at sea to remain on station throughout the exercises, and to produce a timetable of deployment of fleets in port over the coming six weeks. Bigby grumbled a response and left. As

Chairman Proctor walked out in conversation with General Ellison, Sternberg motioned for Omar King to stay behind.

"Omar, you've got to kick Jim Proctor in the ass. He's got to keep Bigby in line. I can't do it all. Bigby's responsible to him as Chairman. And Bigby is our big worry here. If he refuses to order the ships out, the exercise collapses. It's that simple."

"I understand, Joe, and I'll do my best," King replied unenthusiastically. "Karl Bigby's never been a team player and he's always been a pain in the ass... and I suppose he always will be. But he's not our biggest problem right now. One of these days we're going to have to load our computers with targeting data for Cyclops. When we do, some additional people are going to know about the bird's capabilities and the fact it's in orbit."

Sternberg pounded the table. "Well, do it anyway! Get it ready. Do whatever has to be done to make the goddam thing fully operational. I don't want Norton or some flunky in the White House getting panicky and deep-sixing this thing before we get it wound up and ready to play." He lit a cigar. "Who else has to know?"

"We'll have to bring someone in from Datasync—probably that woman physicist, what's-her-name. Then we'll need to bring in a couple of computer wienies from the National Security Agency and a couple of 'em from the National Reconnaissance Office," King said.

"Do you trust them?" Sternberg asked sharply.

"Got no choice, Joe," King replied. "They're the ones with the smarts. God knows I don't understand it. Besides, they got every security clearance known to man. So, I'll tell 'em it's life and death—and they're all gonna end up in Point Barrow if this gets out."

"How soon can you do it?"

"I'll get goin' right now, and we should have the key people in here and working within forty-eight to seventy-two hours," King said.

Sternberg said, "Make it twenty-four." And as King started to leave, he added, "And let me know when it's ready to boogie."

50

THREE DAYS LATER Harry Rafferty was in Geneva. He called Connaughton just before getting on the overnight flight. After a plane change in London and a stopover in Frankfurt, Rafferty arrived in midafternoon, checked into the Intercontinental Hotel not far from the U.S. Mission, and took a shower and short nap. Connaughton was in all-day negotiations and had left a message for his friend to meet him at seven at Les Armures on the Rue de Puits-Saint-Pierre in the old city near the cathedral. The restaurant was just a block from Connaughton's apartment; the management knew him well and would seat them well away from the normal dinner crowd.

Connaughton got there a few minutes early and ordered a drink. Presently his old friend's blocky frame filled the doorway to the dining room.

"You sure haven't shrunk any since Christmas," Connaughton said, rising to shake the square paw.

"You need all the strength you can get these days, particularly in my line of work," Rafferty said, threatening the integrity of the old wood chair as he collapsed into it. The nap had helped, but the jet lag was evident in his bloodshot eyes. He was clearly glad to see Connaughton. "Did you make any progress today?"

"Never enough," Connaughton said laconically. "But we do our best and life goes on."

"Don't give me that phony cowboy philosophical horseshit, Frank. We've known each other too long. Tell me what's really going on." He paused to order a double Irish whiskey. "Then I've got some news for you."

Connaughton told him, leaning close, "We've had a breakthrough. A back channel has been opened up involving Arkwright and Makarov here—they've been floating proposals back and forth informally—and Norton and Dubinin in Washington. It looks like we're pretty close to agreement, exchanging limits on cruise missile production and deployment on our side for reduction in the number of ICBM launchers and warheads on their side. The delegations were actually discussing specific numbers today and we're very close together. It's significant—it's the first real achievement in over a year of these talks."

Rafferty expressed surprise and delight. "That's great, Frank. What happened? How did it come about—particularly given the angry state of affairs over the holidays?"

"I can't really say, Harry," Connaughton lied. "Something had to give way at the top, I guess. One day nothing is going on. Then the next day, we've got the beginning of a framework for a treaty on the table and everyone at my level is negotiating like crazy. You never know about these things."

Connaughton had had serious discussions with himself in the few hours since he learned his friend was coming. He desperately wanted to tell Rafferty about Ekaterina and the strange events of the past three weeks. He needed a confessor, a counselor. He especially wanted someone to know about his increasingly complicated implication in high-level intrigue—just in case something strange happened. But his soul was now so entrenched in secrecy that he couldn't break it free. He trusted Rafferty with his life, but he instinctively resisted enmeshing him in a world becoming murkier by the minute.

"What caused you to jump on the plane over here all of a sudden?" Connaughton asked to change the subject.

Rafferty replied, "Because I had a sense something was going on and I wanted to get it from you while the Senate isn't voting for a couple of days. Besides, the State Department said I could sit in on the negotiations if it's OK with Arkwright."

"I'm sure it will be. And I'm glad to see you," Connaughton said. "Is there talk in Washington that there's movement here?"

Rafferty answered, "Not exactly. But I check in with Norton's chief of staff occasionally, and a couple of days ago he sounded real upbeat. So I said, why not?"

Connaughton knew it wasn't that simple. He said, "You told me you've got something for me. What is it?"

"Well, after I talked to State earlier this week, I started sniffing around. You know how I am about that."

"Do I ever," Connaughton said. "One of these days you're going to sniff once too often and somebody's going to end your sniffing days forever. But at least you'll be reincarnated as a hound dog." They laughed, ordered dinner and another round of drinks.

"Anyway," Rafferty continued in as quiet a voice as he could manage, "an old friend of mine out at the Agency took me in the corner. He knows you and I are buddies. And he said, 'Tell your friend over in Geneva to take care of himself.' And I said, 'What do you mean?' And he said, 'Just what I said. Some people are watching him. Don't ask me why, because I don't know. But he must be involved in something.' That's all he would say, but it scared the you-know-what out of me, Frank. What's he talking about?"

Connaughton thought a moment and twirled his whiskey. Then he grinned. "Oh, you know, Harry. The spooks run out of things to do. Then they practice on some of us doing this sensitive negotiation work. Keeps them sharp— gives them something to do when things are slow."

Rafferty studied him for a while. Then he said, "I don't buy it, Frank. Something's up. What is it?"

"Maybe you can help me find out," Connaughton said. They both brought their foreheads almost together across the table. "My place is wired. So's the phone. There may be some human surveillance going on also."

Rafferty brought his glass down with a thud. "The hell you say! Why? Who?"

Connaughton said softly, "Unless it's the Russians, it's got to be our guys—Agency, I guess. Who else? Why? I don't know."

"Come on, Frank," Rafferty growled, "you've got to have some idea."

"All right, Harry, here's my idea. Somebody in the administration—Burgoon, Sternberg, who knows—has decided I've got something to do with the breakthrough in the negotiations. I've never been on their good list anyway. They get hold of Warrenton, tell him they've got some indication I'm a security risk, and ask him to check it out. Simple as that."

"That ain't simple, Frank."

"I have no proof it's our guys. Could be the Russkies," Connaughton said. "But I'd be surprised if they were that stupid." He grinned at Rafferty. "Anyway, it goes with the territory. I'm sure it will go away soon."

"Let me know if it doesn't," Rafferty said. "I'll go over to the Agency and kick Warrenton around. I'm still on the Intelligence Committee and they still have to deal with me on their budget and covert operations. And they know I can be trouble when I'm stirred up."

"Don't worry about it right now," Connaughton said. "Tell me what else you've got on Cyclops."

"Interesting you should ask, Frank. If you want to know the truth, that's really why I came. Day before yesterday, I got another call. You know, like the one I got the night I got hit. And probably from the same person who tipped you off in the cemetery over the holidays."

Connaughton became alert. "And?"

"And," Rafferty said, "the mystery caller—strange familiar voice—said that Sternberg had just ordered the National Reconnaissance Office in the Air Force to program the computers that control Cyclops."

"My God, what's that mean, Harry?"

"What it means, Frank, is that the goddam thing will have its orders by the end of the week and be ready to shoot."

51

WHEN ANDREA CASS monitored Makarov's second evening visit with Barrett Arkwright, it was the occasion for the two ambassadors to discuss the proposal initially conjured up by Connaughton and Ekaterina during their dinner in Évian. As before, the next morning Connaughton had gone into the bubble with Arkwright and told him that Ekaterina believed the Russians were ready to strike a test ban deal. The Soviets would accept a two-year moratorium on all nuclear tests and permit a limited number of test-monitoring black boxes on Soviet soil in exchange for American seismic verification technology.

Arkwright pressed hardest on the politics of the idea. Where had Davydova gotten the notion their leaders were interested? Connaughton said, as before, during holiday conferences in the Foreign Ministry. Some of the Defense Ministry scientists had reported that further tests would not be crucial to the modernization of Soviet nuclear forces for two years at least. It was clear also that the Defense Ministry—Kozlovsky particularly—felt the continued expenditures on nuclear weapons were bleeding funds from his Army and Navy, which were having serious morale problems in the ranks in any case. Davydova also told him she had heard discussed the need for more sophisticated instruments for verifying a test ban, and that several senior officials had openly advocated exchanging black-box rights for the most modern American seismic technology, which the Soviets needed to detect American tests.

Arkwright then zeroed in on Ekaterina Davydova's bona fides. He insisted on knowing every nuance of her behavior, every scintilla of evidence about her motivation. Connaughton repeated his strong belief that she was operating out of genuine conviction, that she desperately wanted to see some results from the negotiations and an end to the arms race. He said he strongly believed she was loyal to her country and not a potential defector—that she had in fact never suggested such a possibility. Connaughton repeated that she was sufficiently highly placed to know what she was talking about and that she had a very strong character and high intelligence.

"She's very attractive too, Frank," Arkwright said. "Or haven't you noticed?"

Connaughton looked at the floor and hoped his face was not reddening. "Now Barrett, if you think she's a KGB setup, forget it. I'm too sophisticated for that, and she is too, frankly. Of course she's pretty. With all due respect, I've caught you looking her way a couple of times. Hell, even Walt Quainton seemed smitten once or twice—and that's a real compliment to her." They both laughed.

Arkwright then said the proposal had a lot of merit and that he would forward it to Norton forthwith and follow the same procedures as before. If Norton bought off on it and could get the President to agree, he would recommend the Secretary of State to call in Ambassador Dubinin and have the proposition sent directly to Zoshchenko. And, if Norton agreed, Arkwright said he would get together with Makarov at his house and sound him out on the package as before.

AT THE SAME TIME Connaughton and Arkwright were meeting in the bubble, Ekaterina Davydova was reporting to her superior in his office in the Soviet compound. She laid out the same set of proposals and exchanges, but with the notion this had come from Connaughton. She said the

American felt the chemistry was right in the U.S. government for a two-year test ban and that the United States would trade detection technology for the right to position that same detection equipment on Soviet soil.

Makarov listened keenly, soberly. He seemed extremely excited by this development, presumably, Ekaterina thought, because it continued to elevate his importance in the Soviet hierarchy and confirmed his first report that the Russians had a real catch on their hands with the American in Geneva. Zoshchenko would be pleased and that pleased Mikhail Makarov.

Displaying no particular emotion, Ekaterina asked the Ambassador whether she should respond to Connaughton if he sought any further meetings with her. Makarov said that for his part he was in favor of further contacts, but that he would check that with the Foreign Minister. Ekaterina replied that she would appreciate that—for her own protection. Makarov understood immediately and told her she was entitled to have official authorization and approval from the Foreign Minister so there would be no "misunderstanding" in the future.

Ekaterina thanked Makarov, and then as she was leaving the office she paused and asked, "Ambassador, would there be any circumstances under which our security people might want to follow me—perhaps having to do with these meetings?"

Makarov at first was affronted, then calmed himself. "No one but myself and the Foreign Minister knows you are carrying out these contacts. He has agreed to protect you. I suppose it will not be news to you to know that—for state security purposes—all members of the delegation are, ahem, scrutinized. But that is also for your protection . . . to make sure no harm comes to you. It is not impossible that the security people may have been carrying out that protective function when you were meeting with the American. If so, they will surely report to me, and I can assure you it will go no further."

Ekaterina thanked him, knowing full well if she was seen with Connaughton it would be back in KGB Central within minutes, and the "scrutiny" would be intensified. If that happened, specific authorization from Zoshchenko would be the only thing to protect her from a terrible retribution. She was thankful the notion of even that thin shield had come to her during the sleepless hours of the night before.

TWO DAYS LATER Makarov gratefully, but without surprise, accepted Arkwright's dinner invitation for the following night. After dinner he listened patiently, taking notes as Arkwright outlined a potential new negotiating proposal. The fine dinner wine encouraged him to smile to himself at the close similarity of Arkwright's proposal to the notion Ekaterina Davydova had outlined. The cold, damp evening prevented the two men from walking through the woods as before. Otherwise, the evening closely paralleled their first informal discussion, which even now was producing vital bargaining results. Makarov thanked his host and excused himself, explaining that he knew his fellow ambassador would understand his eagerness to forward the American idea to the Foreign Minister. He also said he understood the same proposal would be presented by Secretary Norton to the Soviet Ambassador in Washington late that day.

Now the process rolled forward with building, rushing momentum. Both Kamenev and Lawkard signed off on the proposed testing moratorium and verification exchange, and within four more days the delegations in Geneva found themselves seriously working out the details to implement the plan. Harry Rafferty sat in on the negotiations on his second day in Geneva as this second major building block in a prospective treaty began to fall into place. Having observed the lassitude of the process from the States for a full year, he was amazed at what could be done by the negotiating teams when given the green light to reach real agreement. He could hardly wait to get together with Connaughton that night for dinner to find out how it had happened.

But when Frank Connaughton joined Rafferty at eight that evening in the Palais de Justice restaurant on the Place du Bourg-de-Four, he was not a happy man. When the drinks came, Rafferty said, "What's up? I expected you to be on cloud nine."

"Last night, Harry, you asked me why the Agency might want to tail me and I said somebody in Washington might have gotten the notion I had something to do with the sudden takeoff of these negotiations. Well, tonight for the first time since I got my security clearance fifteen years ago I was denied access to classified material. Denied access!"

Rafferty boomed "Why, for God's sake?" loudly enough that a couple across the room looked over.

Connaughton made slight, quick hand gestures to quiet him down. "I don't know. But late this afternoon I went to Sid Murray's office to get a CIA report on Soviet verification capability—that clearly is on the front burner, as you could tell from the discussions today—and he said it wasn't available. He said he had just sent it back by diplomatic courier to Langley. Well, he looked very uncomfortable—he's a terrible liar. I sent my secretary to document control, and she found out a diplomatic courier hasn't gone since we got back from the holidays and no classified documents have gone back to Washington since mid-December."

"That's hardly enough to ruin your evening," Rafferty said with a tentative smile meant to cheer Connaughton up.

Connaughton said grimly, "There's more. About ten days ago Walt Quainton refused to let me see the Joint Chief's assessment of Soviet laser testing. Now that's no big deal, except I later found out everyone else in the delegation had seen it. He told me they weren't circulating it because it was preliminary. Then three days ago there is a discussion in the bubble involving Quainton, Murray, the Defense Department's top satellite guy from Washington, and the delegation security officer. And I went in for the morning briefing and they all suddenly shut up like clams.''

Rafferty said, ''Frank, why don't you just talk to Arkwright? No use to get paranoid . . . even if people really are following you.'' The big man laughed. ''He likes you. This couldn't be going on without him knowing it, and I can't believe he would sanction it.''

''Oh, I will, Harry. But I don't rule out the possibility that Defense, the Agency, even some in the White House have gotten suspicious given the way things have suddenly turned, and they would be looking for a scapegoat, particularly in the delegation and particularly someone from the State Department or ACDA. That narrows things down. And don't forget the bugs and taps in my apartment and odd-looking sorts hanging around outside.''

Rafferty's bonhomie had faded as his friend talked. ''What can you do, Frank? You can't do a job here if the others don't trust you.''

''Clearly, Harry,'' Connaughton replied. ''The key is Barrett. After the experience with Murray this evening, I intend to talk to him. He'll shoot straight with me if something is going on. If he genuinely doesn't know about it, he'll try to find out. But keep in mind the clock is ticking. These talks have just about a month to succeed. If we don't have a treaty all wrapped up by Easter, the tanks start rolling—on both sides—and the genie's out of the bottle.''

The two men talked through their dinners and until the restaurant closed. They agreed it was better not to go back to Connaughton's place for a nightcap given the wires in place. So Connaughton bade Rafferty good-bye as a taxi approached. The Washington flight left the next morning. Rafferty said he would track the progress of the talks through the State Department and would do his best to find out if Connaughton was under any kind of suspicion. But he assured his friend as he shook hands and entered the taxi that it simply could not be.

AWAKE IN HER ROOM across town, Ekaterina Davydova was not nearly so sure about suspicion. Again she had walked the grounds that evening, and again security guards had made themselves more visible than usual. She had burned the slip of paper with Connaughton's phone number on it. But the number was also burned forever in her mind. She longed to walk out the gate, go to a phone, call him and talk to him. Hearing his voice had suddenly become extremely important to her. His flat, ironic, occasionally sad and distant tone was something she had come to miss and need. Even when they talked hurriedly and professionally about sophisticated weapons systems, there was still a closeness and intensity, an identity of purpose, that she had never known but always wanted.

She felt increasingly out of place in the Soviet Mission. It didn't seem like her home away from home anymore. It seemed more and more an alien, threatening environment, one where her presence was not natural or welcome. She had never felt so suffocated, even during the oppressive closing months of her marriage as she waited for the state divorce. She badly needed some document, some evidence from the Foreign Minister that she was authorized to do what she was doing. She knew that Deputy Director Malenkov of the KGB had been in the compound for almost ten days. The place was abuzz. She pretended not to care. But she listened for every word of casual corridor gossip about what might occasion his visit. His presence—especially for that period of time—was extraordinary. He was rarely seen and spent little time with the Ambassador. So he couldn't be there to hold Makarov's hand.

Ekaterina was convinced it had to do with her—and Connaughton. She had not seen the two men in Évian. Nor had Connaughton told her. But she could sense his unease, his checking across the room, his constant glances in the car's mirror. She was being followed all right. And probably even Makarov didn't know it for sure. The KGB wouldn't check with him. If powerful people in Moscow felt threatened, the word would go out quietly and steps would be taken and diplomatic niceties and chains of command would not be observed. Find out. Get information. Do it *now*.

Malenkov sent chills through her. She knew by hearsay that he was close to Vladimir Zhdanov, whose wrath could destroy individuals and entire families with the blink of an evil eye. She believed increasingly with each day that those in Moscow who opposed an arms control treaty would do anything they could to defeat the negotiations and leave open the way for the massive military show of force. A little fish like Davydova—and even that little fish's family— would get ground to dust by that kind of power.

And the fears were not imagined merely because of Malenkov's presence. The attitude of those on the delegation was markedly changing. She was beginning to be a pariah. The lascivious Vronsky no longer flirted—an almost obsessive trait with him. Old General Polyakov was barely polite. Colleagues shunned her in the compound dining rooms. There was some sense that word had gone out she was unclean. Within the space of a month the result of her gamble would be known, and her fate would be determined along with it.

She longed to talk to Connaughton.

part

THREE

52

EKATERINA DAVYDOVA HAD REASON for her fears. "Bring pressure to bear on the woman," the cable from Moscow to Malenkov read. He knew who "the woman" was. Zhdanov was apoplectic with rage. He had just discovered the second major departure toward reconciliation. Kamenev had convinced the same narrow majority on the Politburo that had endorsed the earlier cruise missile-ICBM swap to accept the American offer of a moratorium on nuclear testing coupled with a new verification plan. Zhdanov had argued bitterly and long that it was an American plot—a trap to lull the Soviet government into accepting sensing devices on Russian soil as a first step toward formalizing a sanctioned system of espionage. But Zhdanov and his allies could not overcome the intensive lobbying by the General Secretary and the combined support for the proposal by the Foreign Minister and Minister of Defense.

Zhdanov now clearly saw that a pattern was established. The woman met with the American in Geneva. He planted these ideas in her mind. She forwarded them to that fool Makarov, who was merely a conduit to the ambitious weakling Zoshchenko. Zoshchenko had seduced the aging General Secretary (Zhdanov insisted on thinking of Kamenev as an old man even though the latter was younger than he was by almost two years) into believing a nuclear treaty would be a fitting capstone to his career and permit Kamenev's retirement in favor of Zoshchenko. That was the scheme. And it would go on until a treaty was signed and the Red Star exercise postponed. The thought of another long era of détente seared the old ideologue's soul. The venom in his heart now rose to the back of his tongue.

The woman was the key. Comrade Davydova. Get her and you break the chain, he thought. Prove her faithless, demonstrate her to be twisted, and the neat little scheme collapses, he thought. If there is no Davydova, there will be no one readily available for the American to subvert and use to insinuate his sinister schemes. Destroy her and you destroy the monster that has infiltrated the Soviet government.

The plan he communicated to Malenkov in Geneva was to throw a net around the woman, tighten it as quickly as possible until it became a cage, then use it to squeeze her to death. She should be constantly watched, her possessions should be periodically searched for incriminating evidence such as notes of her meetings or documentation of some personal relationship with the heinous American, and she should be at all times intimidated into forgoing her contacts with Connaughton. All this had to be done with a sufficient degree of subtlety that she would have difficulty proving harassment to Makarov. Zhdanov did not want Makarov complaining to the Foreign Minister that his chief interpreter was being persecuted by the KGB political opponents in Moscow. Davydova must be frightened but given no tangible evidence to substantiate her fears. She must be frightened enough to break the chain from Geneva to Washington to Moscow, back to Geneva.

It certainly wasn't as if Vladimir Zhdanov had no experience in provoking fear. He had a lifetime of such experience. And in the case of strong-willed individuals like Ekaterina Davydova, the most effective fear was not always fear for one's own well-being, but rather fear for loved ones.

ON THE NINTH OF MARCH, Ivan Davydov was pulling his younger brother, Anton, in his sled along the canal near their grandparents' apartment building in Leningrad late in the afternoon after school. They laughed and threw snow, knowing soon their grandmother would send the old door-keeper to summon them for a delicious hot dinner. Tonight they would have borscht, a favorite. Suddenly, two very large men towered over them. "Are you Davydovs?" one asked menacingly. Before they could answer or run, the other said, "You might fall in the icy water, playing so close to the canal like that. You should tell your mother that. She should look after you better."

The boys were old enough to know the men were not there to look after their safety. Ivan took little Anton's hand and, leaving the sled, started running for the house. They were sure they heard heavy running steps behind them and Anton began to cry in fear. They raced into the apartment house entryway, almost knocking down the inebriated elderly doorman. They dashed up the three flights of steps, certain they were being chased in the deepening gloom of the evening into their own quarters. But as they threw open the heavy apartment door, dashed inside, and slammed the door behind them, no one was following. Hearing the racket, and thinking the boys to be playing some noisy game, Mme. Davydova came into the front room to corral the renegades. Instead she immediately saw the boys to be in deadly fear. They told her of their terrifying experience and now fretted that their only sled was lost. It would take until next winter to find one in a store. It had been their mother's New Year's present to them.

The elderly lady, possessing stronger legs and better sight than her husband, pulled her heavy coat from the hall closet and followed the boys outside and around the corner to the wide, frozen canal. There was no sign of the men, except for the evidence of large, male footprints in the fresh snow. But just below the walkway on the rocky edge of the frozen canal was the new sled, bashed to pieces. Even the metal runners had been twisted, as if with savage strength.

The following afternoon, after a regular session with his elderly string-quartet colleagues, Anton and Anna Davydov returned to their apartment to await the arrival of the grandsons from school. It was evident, immediately upon entering the door, that someone had been in their living quarters during their two-hour absence. Chairs were wrongly positioned. Sheet music was on the floor. Drawers at the writing desk were opened. There were even wet shoe prints on the polished wood floors. The place had been thoroughly searched, although not quite ransacked. Whoever had done it had not particularly cared about secrecy. Nothing was missing, but privacy had been invaded and violated. The old doorman had nothing to say; he had seen no one. Either he had been drunkenly asleep, or he'd been paid off.

Ekaterina made her weekly call that night and the boys told her of the scary men and battered sled. Little Anton cried and asked her to come home. Later the old couple told her about the apartment being searched and asked her what it meant. She assured them it meant nothing, that it was either the doorman looking for a drink or perhaps the police poking around in the wrong place. In response to their questions, she told them over and over that it had nothing to do with her work.

In the common room in the Soviet Mission compound, Ekaterina hung the telephone up. She went to the empty women's room so that no one would see her. For the first time in years she began to tremble, shaking visibly. She started to splash cold water on her face and suddenly heard a sharp noise behind her. A startled yell escaped her, surprising the dumpy charwoman who had just brought her cleaning equipment bumping into the room. Ekaterina fled the place, dashing from the building out into the snowy wet night and across the compound to the dormitory building and her corner room. Once inside she closed and locked the door and sat on her bed weeping violently.

It had never seriously occurred to her that anyone in the Soviet government might involve her family in her desperate affairs. But surely that was it. She was being warned. Connaughton had talked to her about the seriousness of their undertaking—that powerful people on both sides would be angered and important plans threatened by their exchanges of information. Now those powerful people were reaching out, not only to intimidate her directly but to jeopardize all she cared for. She thought frantically of someone to help her. But aside from Connaughton, she suddenly realized, she had no one.

ON THE SAME DAY the Davydov children were threatened, Vice-President Harold Burgoon sat in his study in his residence on Observatory Hill in Washington. He was studying a classified field report on the activities of Frank Connaughton based upon personal surveillance and electronic detection. It specifically discussed, in considerable detail, Connaughton's lunch with Ekaterina Davydova on January 27 in Chambesy, Switzerland, his lunch with the same Davydova on February 6 in Courmayeur, Italy, and most recently, their dinner on the night of February 17 in Évian, France.

Certainly gets around, Burgoon thought. Wonder what she looks like. He made a note to himself to get her file from the Agency. On the other hand, he thought, our man there is good enough that he can take the picture himself. Probably already has. I'll check on that and leave Warrenton out of it.

Now he had to piece together this Connaughton's role in the new initiatives in the negotiations. These meetings obviously had something to do with it. But he seriously doubted Norton would tell him if he was confronted directly. How about bringing it up in the Security Council? Burgoon mused. Be hard for Norton to squirm off the hook with the others sitting there watching him. That was probably the best approach.

It just made common sense. These arms control negotiations go on for a year and get nowhere. Then, out of the blue, this guy Connaughton starts wining and dining a Russian interpreter and the whole thing turns around. It's circumstantial evidence, Burgoon thought, but it's damn convincing. Somebody is giving information to somebody else. And that information is being used to alter fundamentally the course of these talks. Worse, Burgoon agonized as he paced around his desk, the possible success of the talks jeopardized Blue Thunder. For Burgoon this was not simply an ideological issue; it represented a threat to his springboard to the presidency. If Burgoon could take credit for successfully carrying out the biggest allied military maneuvers since World War II, he would have a major accomplishment to carry into the fall election and distinguish him from an otherwise colorless administration. It would certainly go a long way to dispel the political rap that he was weak and ineffective.

On the other hand the exercises would certainly be postponed if a major nuclear arms control treaty was signed in the spring, and even if they were later undertaken, the chance of using Blue Thunder as a show of force to intimidate the Soviets into weakening the Warsaw Pact and withdrawing from Cuba and Afghanistan would be virtually eliminated. It seemed somehow, Burgoon pondered, that the success of the treaty negotiations hinged on this man Connaughton. He was the key and he had to be controlled. They had wired his rooms and phone and they had done a good job of surveillance. But more had to be done.

Connaughton had to be made to feel, to *know* that his actions were being scrutinized by powerful elements in his government. He had to be made to understand that circumvention of normal diplomatic channels to speed up negotiations or overcome obstacles to successful negotiations that Burgoon and others had constructed would meet with harsh judgment—even retribution. In short, he had to be made to feel afraid. Neither he nor anyone like him could be permitted to sidetrack the plan Burgoon, Joe Sternberg, Omar King, and Arnold Danzig had worked so hard to create. Too much rested on it.

Burgoon picked up his secure phone and gave the operator a private number. "Intensify the effort on our friend in Geneva," he said. "It's now crystal clear he's our problem. Find out about these meetings. Get everything you can on his friend. We have to find out what her angle is and who she's working for. If possible get incriminating documents or tapes—tangible evidence of disloyalty. As soon as you have anything concrete, let me know immediately, and we'll move. We have to roll him up—fast. We don't have much time." He listened, then said, "That's good. Keep it up. By the way, keep an eye on his highly placed friend here. That's right—the big one. And let me know the minute you get something."

ON SATURDAY, MARCH 12, Ekaterina Davydova organized three other women from the secretarial pool and went to the early film at the ABC Cinéma on the Rue du Rhône. She had worked feverishly translating and correcting the negotiating record from the previous week to keep herself occupied. She had written a long letter to her sons and her parents assuring them that the events of the previous week were an aberration—even though she didn't believe it. But she could not tolerate spending Saturday night alone in her room. The clerical women were flattered to be invited to join her although only she could understand the French in the feature film, *Les Misérables*, one of her favorites.

Throughout the film, she felt a presence—an uneasiness brought on, she assumed, by some lurking KGB agent nearby. For most of the three hours she was able to submerge her fears and become absorbed in the travails of Jean Valjean. But as the story's climax came, she felt a touch on her shoulder in the darkness. She jerked involuntarily and started to twist in her seat. But the hand held her still, as if to reassure. She could not turn, nor would she have been able to see in the darkness if she could. Suddenly she realized that a message was being passed. She reached to her shoulder, touched a rough masculine hand, and felt a slip of paper. She quickly crumpled it in her hand and, when the lights came on and the audience stood to file out, dropped it into her handbag.

After a quick dinner at the Vedia Restaurant near the theater, the four women took a taxi back to the Soviet Mission. She bade her companions good night and hurried to her room. Once there she threw off her coat and dumped the contents of the handbag onto her bed. She took the crumpled paper and spread it out on her bedside table under the single lamp. It read:

Short's Pub
Rue du Cheval-Blanc
8-9 P.M., any night next week
F.C.

53

THE RUE DU CHEVAL-BLANC was a narrow brick street in Geneva's old city no more than seventy-five yards long. It began twenty paces from the front door of Frank Connaughton's apartment building at 15 Grand' Rue and terminated at the Rue des Granges. Along its brief course were a few shops and old apartment houses and one publican's establishment—Short's. The small wooden sign over the door announcing its presence seemed incongruous. Together with the leaded glass windows it seemed to have been lifted from London's Soho and dropped arbitrarily into the Reformation capital of Europe. The explanation for all this, Short himself, had slipped into obscurity—although legends abounded.

Connaughton frequented the place. Not only was it close by, on the frequent evenings when he arrived home late from hours of tedious meetings and complex negotiations in no mood to cook a meal, but he enjoyed the fish-and-chips ambience and felt at home with the regulars having a jar standing up at the bar or seated at small round tables against the red imitation-flocked wallpaper. It had occurred to him more than once in the past month that he would like to take Ekaterina there. Not, heaven knows, because of the cuisine. But because he felt at home there and particularly enjoyed the small outdoor courtyard in the spring and fall.

When he did stalk her to the theater that Saturday night, he had three reasons for proposing a meeting at Short's: A few days of early spring weather made the courtyard a possibility; there were two entrances to the pub; and they would be only a few steps from his apartment, where he wanted to take her now that he'd decided to remove the microphones. Contacting her at all had entailed great risks. First, he'd had to stake out the Soviet Mission much the same way Andrea Cass had days before. But he had become desperately lonely for her and was not content to watch her, and occasionally catch her eye, across the bargaining table twice a week. So, again, he had borrowed Charlie Curtis's old car for a few hours and driven up and down the Avenue de la Paix hoping to see her in the early evening on Saturday. Luckily he had caught a glimpse of several women leaving the compound in the mission sedan and had followed them across town to the theater. The place was not crowded and he had no trouble spotting them, identifying Ekaterina on the end of the row before the lights went down, and then slipping in behind her. Just being that close for three hours made him feel good. It was hell not being able to talk to her when he wanted to. It now surprised him that such a need had developed so quickly.

He could not specify a particular night the following week for a rendezvous, because he didn't know when—if at all— she could get free. He had to depend on her ability to convince Makarov that it was important. She was smart enough to tell Makarov that Connaughton had new, valuable information to share. He was certain Monday night was out, because Ekaterina had once told him the delegation routinely had dinner together that night to discuss the coming week's business. So on Tuesday, the fifteenth, he dropped into Short's just before eight o'clock for a pint and a sandwich. Nine o'clock came and went with no Ekaterina. Wednesday night he was back and stretched two beers out until 9:30. But she still did not come. He walked across the street and up to his apartment lonely and discouraged. The fine hair he had carefully placed against the telephone receiver was gone. His cleaning woman did not come until tomorrow.

Thursday night, the seventeenth of March, he went to Short's just at eight o'clock. It was a slow night and the genial barkeep greeted him warmly without mentioning that he seemed to have become a regular. Connaughton sat at the back corner of the dining area beyond the small dark lounge area and near the door to the courtyard outside. As he sipped the pint he thought about the progress the two negotiating teams had made that week in agreeing on the details of a treaty to ban all nuclear tests for two years, and the even more complex terms for locating seismic detectors on Soviet territory and exchanging equipment. It was entirely possible, if understanding could be reached on the remaining major issue—weapons in space—that a treaty could be signed by Easter or shortly thereafter. He was still amazed at the amount of work that the two sides had done together in the past few weeks. Words had been carefully chosen to express agreed meanings, phrases had been elaborately crafted to ensure common understandings in both languages, and whole paragraphs had been jointly drafted to guarantee future compliance with proscriptions on weapons production and deployment. Just showed what could be done, he mused.

But layered on top of that dimension of goodwill was another level of existence . . . the sense of walls closing in, of a heavy lead ceiling descending to crush him. He was not going to get out of this without paying a price—a heavy price, he was sure. A treaty could be negotiated, but the forces opposed to it would still be there and eager to take revenge on anyone at Connaughton's low level held responsible. And Ekaterina's situation was even worse. Once she was back in the Soviet Union, not even Zoshchenko could protect her. That would be low on his list of priorities as he scrambled further toward the top. Makarov would be put out to pasture and was powerless in any case. If there were those in the Kremlin aggrieved by a treaty with the United States, and if they correctly identified her as an instrument in that achievement, she would be defenseless. She would have no protection. They would destroy her.

There she stood. Connaughton started from his reverie. He jumped to his feet and helped her with her coat. She smiled and touched his arm. He led her out the back door into the unseasonably warm evening in the courtyard. The small area held only four tables, all unoccupied. They took the farthest. She glanced about. They were totally surrounded by the five-story walls of the ancient stone buildings. The immediate courtyard area was surrounded by ivy-covered latticework. Empty windowboxes, soon to be filled with spring flowers, underlined the apartment windows overlooking the secure, enclosed area. Just behind their table, a tree rising almost three stories reached to the limited overhead light for sustenance. There were four black lamp-posts shedding uncertain light in the gathering night. The evening was still warm for March, but in an hour it would cool quickly and Connaughton put Ekaterina's coat over her shoulders.

She smiled again, clearly pleased at the surprising privacy. "How nice to see you again," she said presently.

"It's even nicer to see you. It seems like a very long time."

"Indeed," she replied. "Very long."

"Did you have much trouble? Coming here, I mean." He was genuinely concerned.

"I had the most trouble finding a taxi whose driver knew the street," she said with a small laugh. "They all seem now to be from southern Italy, or Iran. And they do not know this short white horse."

He pressed, more seriously. "What did you say to Makarov? What did you have to do to get out?"

For a moment she seemed her old confident, controlled, slightly detached self. "As I told you, he lets me move about as I wish, so long as I produce the results which have benefited him so much recently." Then she seemed to change, almost to sag. "I just left. I didn't tell him. I didn't tell anyone. I just left."

"You did what?" Connaughton gasped.

"I just walked away. I have tried to get Ambassador Makarov's approval for the past three days. But he is immersed in these intensive negotiations and seems very preoccupied by Moscow politics right now." The wine Connaughton had ordered arrived. "There is a very big KGB man here now—Malenkov." Connaughton's eyebrows shot up. "I thought you would know him. I think he makes Makarov nervous. I know he does me."

"What's he doing here?" Connaughton asked. "And how did you just 'walk away'?"

Ekaterina said, "Honestly, I believe it has to do with me...with us. He is here because some important people in my government, in the Kremlin, are very disturbed by what is happening here. He is here to try to stop the negotiations, to find something that can be used to prevent a successful treaty. He is here, Frank, to defeat us—you and me."

"But how did you get out without Makarov's permission?"

"Tonight, or tomorrow, I will simply tell him that you contacted me and offered more information. And I will say I believed he had already approved any productive contacts we might have. And he knows I have been trying to talk to him for several days. So he will simply have to accept it," she said. "Rather than not see you, I walked to the compound gate tonight, showed my identification, and walked out. A taxi was passing and as I got in, I could see the gate guard on the phone. But they were so surprised, I don't believe they were able to organize any tracking team before the taxi drove away into traffic." She smiled ruefully. "I'm sure a lot of them are scattered about town looking right now."

He smiled back, both at her audacity and his pleasure at her presence. "Ekaterina, I want you to come see my home. It's just around the corner. But just in case it turns out there are too many people in the street to get there without detection, let's talk about one final effort on these negotiations.

The last hurdle is space weapons. To get a treaty, we have to tackle that."

Now she retrieved a pad and pencil from her handbag and began to make rapid, cryptic notes.

"You know the basic problem," he said, "because it has surely been discussed at great length during the last year's negotiations. Your side believes we have a substantial lead in space technology and that we intend to use that superiority to launch Star Wars—to defend our own weapons and people and threaten yours." She nodded. "On the other hand, our side sees yours building huge radars designed for nuclear battle management. And we know you've conducted experiments with ground-based lasers that can knock out our reconnaissance satellites. And finally, you've begun to develop a generation of ground-to-air missiles capable of intercepting incoming nuclear warheads. In other words, most of our leaders believe you're doing the very same thing you've accused us of. So there we are."

Ekaterina said, "Yes, I understand this description. I know we can never have an agreement until this new kind of arms race is dealt with."

"Here's what I think can be done," Connaughton continued. "Tell Makarov to propose to Arkwright—and have Zoshchenko make the same proposal to Ambassador Hartman in Moscow—that the Soviets will suspend deployment of SS-X-12 ballistic defense missiles, terminate antisatellite laser experiments, and close down the Krasnoyarsk radar installation. This would be in exchange for United States agreement to clarify the Anti-Ballistic Missile Treaty to clearly prohibit the kinds of space experiments that your side worries about the most." Ekaterina again was writing hurriedly. "The key is, this has to be done fast. We're running out of time. If the people on your side—and on mine—who don't want this treaty organize a counterattack, they can turn these negotiations around again. The momentum for an agreement can be broken. Reasons can be found, or manufactured, for not achieving a treaty, and we'll be back where we were at the end of the year—with an eyeball-to-eyeball confrontation. Only this time there will be some major military deployments to deal with."

"I understand," Ekaterina said. "I'll pass this on to Ambassador Makarov tonight or tomorrow morning."

Connaughton interjected, "Make sure he understands the initiative on this proposal must come from your side. I'm not sure I can sell one more blockbuster like this to Arkwright, who then has to sell it to Norton, who then has to sell it to Lawkard. It will be much better if the process is reversed and Zoshchenko makes the first move. It will be easier politically if all the proposals don't come from this side."

"How will Foreign Minister Zoshchenko know your side will accept this?" Ekaterina asked.

"Because," Connaughton assured her, "Lawkard has been looking for a way to back off from the Star Wars idea for some time. I know through Barrett Arkwright that he has complained in our cabinet and National Security Council for months that the whole scheme is questionable and could well bankrupt our government. But he can't call a halt to the development of the system while your side continues to build these radars and missiles and conduct your experiments. So he's looking for a way out. And a proposal from your side can give it to him."

Ekaterina nodded her understanding, then continued making Russian shorthand notes.

Connaughton touched her arm. "Let's go to my place. It's just across the street." He stood and helped her up. The night was now cool and she put on the black cloak with its fur collar.

Before stepping back into Short's dining room, she stopped him and asked, "What if there is someone outside? What if I was followed—or what if you were followed here?"

He smiled reassuringly. "We both came in the front door off the Rue du Cheval-Blanc. That's the door they would

watch. But there's another way out. It opens out onto the
Grand' Rue, just across from my apartment building. When
we leave, just follow me. We'll move quickly and be out before anyone knows." He threw down Swiss francs for the
wine and opened the door from the courtyard into the noisy
restaurant.

Once inside, he took her arm and they moved around the
tables in the darkened dining room and out the side door of
Short's. It opened into a winding corridor that passed
through a small arcade of shops. In a moment they came to
the entryway from the street. He held her back in the darkness and looked out onto the Grand' Rue. There were a
normal number of clerks and shopkeepers heading home
from the closing of the stores at 9 P.M. and a few couples
were out strolling in the premature spring weather. But he
saw no one standing guard or seeming to lurk, so he took a
chance. He took Ekaterina's arm and they moved down the
street about ten yards, then across and into the gateway at
15 Grand' Rue. They passed through the ornate late-
seventeenth-century wooden door frame and before the
first-floor Librairie des Amateurs, now closed. The door of
the concierge just beyond the entryway was closed, Connaughton noted. They then entered the second gate and
turned right up the outdoor stone steps to the upper floors.
Rather than wait for the elevator, and risk meeting a ten-
ant, they walked up to the third floor, entered the corridor
door, and walked down the hallway to Connaughton's front
apartment. They had seen no one.

He opened the double locks of the door and waved her in.
He was glad to see the automatic timer he had installed two
weeks before was working. Two small tablelamps were
turned on at eight every evening to give the impression to
anyone watching from outside that someone was home. He
did not turn on any additional lights, but did start a small
fire in the fireplace before taking Ekaterina's coat. He noticed she was shivering.

He started to say "Let me make some tea," when she fell into his arms. Her arms locked around him with surprising strength, her head against his shoulder. He was startled to sense that she was quietly crying. He held her tightly, saying nothing until she became calm, then led her to the small couch before the fire. He pulled her to him and held her silently for a full five minutes. She was so quiet she seemed almost to be asleep. Then she sat up with the hint of a sad smile. "I'm sorry, Frank. I didn't mean to fall apart like that. I'm so afraid... for my family, for my children."

"But Katya," Connaughton said to reassure her, "what you're doing will make it safer for them. You must understand that."

She shook her head. "Right now, Frank. I fear for them right now." She told him of the incidents the previous week involving her children and parents in Leningrad. "There will be more of that. Zhdanov and his followers in Moscow have located me. They know I'm the one involved in this. The KGB must have followed us before and linked our meetings with the change in negotiations. In spite of Makarov's promise of support and protection, the millstone has already begun to grind against me. I really don't know what they will do, Frank. I worry much less about myself than I do my family. If they hurt my old parents or my sons, I couldn't stand it."

He held both her hands in his. They were cold and still trembling. "Oh, Katya, how could I have gotten you involved in all this? It seemed so easy at the time. It seemed as if we could get it done and escape the punishment. I gave no thought to your family—and I should have."

"I am a grown woman. I knew what I was doing," she said. "I calculated the risks. But for myself only. I did not think they would threaten innocent people... children."

Connaughton said, "It isn't too late to quit. Don't pass on this last proposal to Makarov. Tell him you're not going to see me again, that it's all over. Word will get back to the KGB and Zhdanov's crowd and they'll leave you alone."

"I cannot do that, Frank. We are too close. I believe more than ever in what we are doing. It is working. Otherwise there would not be the furious response—the harassment." She shook her head. "The next two weeks are crucial. If we can keep the two sides talking, if we can keep the two ministers communicating and exchanging proposals, we can help produce a treaty. But if the space business does not get solved, the rest will fall apart."

Connaughton pulled her back into his arms to calm her. "Then get some protection from Makarov. Tell him Zoshchenko must intervene to call off the dogs. Those people either want this to work or they don't. If you and I can't talk, I don't know whether we can clear this last hurdle. It won't be long now. They must protect you."

"We will not clear the last hurdle without our contacts," she said. "We both know that. My side will only listen to these ideas—these exchanges—because they think they are getting secret information from the highest levels of your government. And your side thinks the same thing. The notion we are telling each other secrets has not occurred to them yet. When that happens, then it is the end for both of us." She shook violently.

Without thought, he kissed her softly. During an eternity when time seemed suspended, his only realization was how long he had wanted to do this. They clung to each other, fearing even to move, fearing some magic might escape them forever. The fire cracked and blazed as the embrace went on. Neither wanted to separate or break the spell. Then finally they breathed, still holding each other. He touched her cheek, then her hair, marveling at its blackness. Her fingers roamed the rough lines of his face as if to memorize the contours for a long time to come.

Then she said in a whisper, "I want to love you, to make love with you. I want to more than anything . . . right now." She could feel him nod in agreement. "But we cannot, yet, can we?" Again he nodded. It was an immediate understanding that it would happen, but it had to wait. He held her closer.

"Soon," he murmured. She then nodded, still holding him as if he might instantly vanish if she let go.

"Soon," she replied.

They stood and embraced again before the fire. They kissed again, softly at first, then almost violently. He was amazed at the passion in a woman so self-contained, seemingly so remote. Then she broke off and walked quickly to the chair where he had placed her coat. "It is time," she said. "I must go now, quickly."

He helped her with the coat, then walked into the darkened front bedroom. He stepped to the side of the window and carefully parted the edge of the curtain an inch. He could see no one down one side of the street. He repeated the maneuver at the other window and saw only one couple, disappearing around a corner. Then he went back to her, quickly took her arm, and opened the door. He locked it securely behind them and they walked rapidly down the back steps, again avoiding the elevator. Once on the street he looked in both directions again. They then turned right and proceeded at a fast walk down the Grand' Rue. They turned right and almost reached the church at the Place de la Fusterie when a taxi came by. She assured him this was the best way for her to return, then gave his hand a strong squeeze as she entered the car and closed the door.

Although he had seen no one, Connaughton sensed they had been watched entering and leaving his apartment building. He had not seen, in the entryway four doors up the street, the slight man in the dark blue coat and broadbrimmed hat.

54

THREE DAYS AFTER Ekaterina and Connaughton met at Short's Pub, Andrea Cass got a break.

Like their civilian chief, Joe Sternberg, the top U.S. military commanders were not pleased with the direction of the negotiations. And when the Joint Chiefs were not pleased, Walt Quainton was not pleased.

While Quainton was not sophisticated in world-class politics, he knew one trick of the trade—the background, anonymous press leak. He also knew the *New York Times* reporter presently in Geneva, Andrea Cass, was all over the negotiation story, trying desperately to find out what was going on. So Quainton told her.

On "deep background" with total guarantees for protection of his identity, Quainton confirmed much of what Cass suspected. Major agreements were being discussed, and he gave her some of the details. Norton and Zoshchenko were in touch with each other through the ambassadors in each capital and Arkwright and Makarov were backing these contacts up.

Cass, drinking black coffee in Quainton's small living room, asked, "How did all this come about? Did something happen over the holidays in Washington? Because it seemed to me nothing had changed when you all came back here, except that Lawkard tossed Norton a bone: one more final round of talks before the armies marched."

"Well, that's the thing," Quainton said in a voice lowered to confound unseen auditors, "I'm convinced the 'breakthrough' didn't occur in Washington or in Moscow."

"All right then, how could it have happened?"

"For now let's skip *how* it could have happened," Quainton responded softly. "But I think I can tell you *where* it happened. I think it happened here . . . in Geneva."

"What do you mean? What happened here in Geneva," she asked insistently, "and who's involved?"

"It's someone on the inside," Quainton said smugly. "Someone who knows what he's doing."

"'Someone on the inside' has to mean someone in the negotiations—someone in the delegation. Are you saying someone in the U.S. delegation put this whole thing together?"

Quainton smiled.

"Who is it?" Cass demanded. "How could he have turned this process around? Or is it a she?"

Quainton said, "You're going to have to figure out the rest of it for yourself. I wouldn't tell you if I knew, and I'm not even sure I know." But he smiled slightly again. "There is the process of elimination. Some on our side want these talks to succeed more than others."

"Well, that leaves you out as the culprit, Admiral." Cass hoped she didn't sound too sarcastic. "That narrows it down to no more than half a dozen people. Care to give me a hint?"

"No, Miss Cass, I can't do that. Because I don't know for sure. But I have my own suspicion," Quainton added.

"What about how he did it?" she persisted.

Quainton looked surprised. "How else, Miss Cass, but by talking to the other side?"

CASS ALMOST LASHED the taxi driver getting back to her office. If she filed the story by midnight, it might possibly make next day's paper. What a blockbuster! This would knock their socks off in Washington. A high-level back channel, ambassadorial walks in the woods, deep divisions inside the U.S. delegation, and, quite possibly, an inside free agent—even a spy. My God, she thought, this is Pulitzer material!

She phoned her bureau chief in Washington and the editors in New York to hold the paper for a major story on the arms control negotiations and gave them a hint of what she had. She suggested strongly that, when they got the first few paragraphs, the bureau seek a response from both the White House and the State Department. Then she attacked the computer.

Within minutes after the computer in New York printed out her version of Quainton's information, Andrea Cass's office phone began ringing in Geneva. She smiled as she sipped the Dubonnet she had poured to toast herself. She had known the call would come.

"Goddammit, Cass, who is it?" She recognized the cigarette-rasp voice of Abe Rosenwald, her managing editor. "Are you saying we have a double agent—a spy—in the U.S. delegation over there?"

Cass said, "Abe, I don't know who it is. I have my own suspicions. But you don't pass on personal suspicions even to your own editor without proof. Besides, my source claims not to know. But he does believe quite strongly that's the way the whole thing started rolling."

"Who's your source?" Rosenwald demanded.

"Come on, Abe," Cass shot back, "you don't expect me to tell you. If I have to go to jail, I don't expect you to go with me. I'll just say this. He's a member of our delegation. Otherwise I wouldn't have filed the story. He knows what he's talking about."

She could hear a struck match and furious puffing over the transatlantic line. "We can't run the story anyway," he finally said.

"What!" she screamed. "What do you mean we can't run the story? Goddammit, you've already killed one important story of mine, and I'm not going to let you kill this one.

This is important! Can't you people in New York understand anything!"

She expected Rosenwald to fire her. He had several times before. But when he spoke his voice was apologetic. "It's not my call, Andrea. It's Punch's." He could hear his reporter gasp. "He got a call from the White House."

Cass hissed, "That sonofabitch Danzig. You mean he dared call the publisher of my paper and kill a story this important? I'm going to call that bastard and turn him every way but loose."

Rosenwald waited for her to take a breath and said, "It wasn't Danzig, Andrea. It was the President of the United States. Old Willie Lawkard himself." He heard Cass gasp again. "Said it was the first and only time he had done that in almost eight years in the White House. Said he really needed the paper's understanding. Said these were absolutely extraordinary circumstances. Said he worshiped the First Amendment above all else. But then he said the national security was involved and he prayed...that's the word he used...he prayed the paper wouldn't run this story."

"What did Punch say?" Cass asked.

"He told the President he wanted to think about it. He called me and we talked about it. Then he called Lawkard back and said we would hold the story for a few days. But at some point, absent a direct showing of danger to the nation, he would put it in print."

Cass sighed. "How long?"

"I don't know, Andrea," Rosenwald barked. "I don't like it any more than you do. It's no way to run a paper. But what can you do when the President himself calls? Tell him to stuff it?" He took a few deep breaths and started over. "I would guess a few days, at the most. I'll do what I can. But in the meantime see what you can do to follow up with your source. Tell him we can't run the story without more information. Try to get him to finger the culprit...if that's what he is, I'm not sure. And follow up with every other contact you have. The more support we get for this story, the more reason we have to run it."

Cass sighed again. "All right, Abe, I can't quarrel with the boss. But do me a favor. Have Corson get the guys in the bureau to put a full-court press on the State and Defense departments and the White House. If Lawkard and Norton know we have this story, they're going to be very nervous. And sometimes nervous people are more inclined to talk."

After she hung up, Cass poured another Dubonnet. She was deeply disappointed but also exhilarated. Things were really popping now. Something really big was stirring. Quainton wasn't talking simply out of personal pique. The hard-liners were fighting back. They wanted Blue Thunder badly. It went to the heart of their approach to the superpower conflict. And to disrail it was to alter history. The stakes were historic, and a titanic struggle was under way for control of the nation's foreign policy for the next four to eight years, and perhaps its very existence.

But what if Quainton was right? What if someone on a lower level was conducting his own negotiations? Suddenly she jumped from her chair and paced to the window. Outside the weather, so warm the previous week, had turned wet and cold again. But who was doing all this? It was a narrow field. It wasn't Arkwright himself. Too visible. Had to be either Charlie Curtis, Sidney Murray, or maybe Frank Connaughton.

For my money, it's Connaughton, she thought to herself. But if I think it's Connaughton, the others must too.

As she stood before the window she thought, I'll bet they've got that poor bastard under a microscope right now.

55

FORTUNATELY FOR HER, Mikhail Makarov was more excited by the prospect of a Soviet initiative to halt development of space-based weapons than he was by Ekaterina Davydova's two-hour absence the night before. In fact, Makarov, well into his third scotch when notified that Ekaterina had left, had assumed she was off to meet the American to solicit more information. The KGB was concerned. Augmented by off-duty security guards, Metrinko had his men and women all over Geneva looking for her. He feared a defection. That would be embarrassing and he would get the blame. But even worse, if she returned and passed on to Makarov information that led to yet another major achievement in the negotiations, Zhdanov would be beside himself. It would be difficult enough for Metrinko to have to explain her escape to his superior on the scene, Malenkov. It would be impossible to deal with Zhdanov. If Metrinko wasn't able to establish enough evidence to convince the Kremlin that Davydova was a spy very soon—enough evidence to overcome any protection she might receive from the Foreign Minister—then his career was in ruins, and he was good only for a very long assignment in the distant wastelands.

The search efforts were in vain. She arrived in a taxi just about 10 P.M. and walked into the mission compound as if according to established behavior. She notified Makarov's secretary she needed to see the Ambassador for half an hour before the start of negotiations the following day, and then went to her room. Once in Makarov's office the following morning, she outlined the American's proposal, emphasizing his idea that the initiative come from the Soviet side. Ekaterina stressed particularly the willingness of the American government to renegotiate the Anti-Ballistic Missile Treaty. This she knew, and Connaughton had emphasized, was very important to the Soviet government, which had been trying to make the language of the treaty more restrictive since the United States began its Star Wars program. Makarov would get a big plus from Zoshchenko and the Politburo for passing this bit of information along. It would be vital in holding off Zhdanov's anti-treaty forces in their effort to discredit his gamble in Geneva.

Ekaterina had thoughtfully set up her appointment in the Ambassador's least amorous portion of the day and had cleverly scheduled it against the time when the U.S. delegation would arrive for a special session. Makarov explained how deeply thankful he was for this very important achievement on her part and invited her to dine with him during the weekend. She once again begged off on the grounds of an extraordinary workload of translation and transcript correction, and then escaped out the door.

After the negotiating session Makarov spelled out the American proposal on space weapons in a highly classified, "eyes only" cable to the Foreign Minister and waited for his instructions. They came by secure phone call almost immediately. Zoshchenko was highly excited. He told Makarov to make contact with Arkwright forthwith and propose the framework of the space agreement exactly in the form the American had suggested it to Ekaterina. He also said he would call in Ambassador Hartman in Moscow and make the same offer to him. "But," he told Makarov, "make sure Ambassador Arkwright understands time is of the essence. We must have the earliest possible response from the U.S. government on this matter."

Later that day in Moscow, the American Ambassador appeared at the Foreign Ministry as requested. Zoshchenko was at his urbane, charming best. "Ambassador," he began, "my government wishes to propose an approach to the complex dilemma of weapons in space that has caused so much conflict between our two countries. Given the wonderful results of our recent negotiations in Geneva, we now would like to suggest a new solution to this vital matter in order to break the remaining deadlock delaying a comprehensive arms control agreement." The Ambassador sat formally in his chair as he scribbled in his notebook. Zoshchenko continued, "General Secretary Kamenev has personally approved a proposal that requires us to dismantle our new large radar at Krasnoyarsk, freeze the deployment of the new generation of ground-to-air interceptor missiles..."

"The SS-X-12s?" Ambassador Hartman asked incredulously.

"Indeed," Zoshchenko answered evenly. "And, finally, to halt experimentation on lasers...the ones that you have always felt could interfere with your satellites—but of course we deny that." The Foreign Minister smiled blandly.

Hartman asked, "And what would be our contribution to this arrangement?"

"Simply to agree to a clarification of the ABM treaty that would outlaw space-based ballistic missile defenses," Zoshchenko replied.

Hartman's pen wagged furiously, then he looked up inquisitively.

Zoshchenko rose from his desk and said, "That is all, Ambassador. It is really quite simple." He smiled broadly as he walked the American to the door at the other end of his vast office. "One other thing," he said as they shook hands, "we would appreciate your response as quickly as possible. Ambassador Makarov will be discussing this idea more fully with Ambassador Arkwright in Geneva in the next forty-eight hours. And we believe time to be of the essence. Given the momentum of the present negotiations, and realizing this area represents the remaining roadblock to success, we believe we must...how do you say?...strike while the anvil is hot." He bowed Hartman out the door, laughing at his own cleverness as he did.

TWO DAYS LATER, Sunday, March 20, Barrett Arkwright accepted Makarov's offer of a cocktail. His car pulled into the Soviet Mission compound in the late afternoon as he pondered his discussion the day before with Emerson Norton. Hartman had cabled Norton immediately with the Soviet proposal. And Norton had taken it midday Saturday to the White House for the President's reaction. Lawkard had thought about it, waved off Arnold Danzig's caveats like so many obnoxious flies, and said, "Go ahead with it." Norton had told Arkwright to get as many specifics as he could from Makarov and summarize his own recommendations by cable. The two ambassadors met for almost two hours with Makarov answering every question Arkwright could devise. Makarov was clearly pleased to see the American on the receiving end of an initiative for a change and relished his role as initiator. As Arkwright rose to leave, Makarov said, "So, my friend, you know this is a good deal for your country. Just say OK. That's all you have to do. Say to Secretary Norton that if we get over this hurdle we have a treaty. We have turned ashes into life. You and I can retire to a happy life. No more politics. Just a toast to peace every sunset." He laughed. "Let us know as soon as you can. This is a bold but simple proposal. It does both of us good. And it wraps up our work very soon. We are home by April. OK?"

Things are moving awfully fast, Arkwright marveled on his way to the U.S. Mission to file his cable. Faster than at any time in my diplomatic career. The pressure on both sides was clearly coming from the military exercises now only three weeks away, he reflected. And everyone knows if we get a treaty we back away from the brink. If we don't, it's nose to nose at the brink.

BY TUESDAY, MARCH 22, the framework for an agreement on space weapons had been accepted and one set of negotiators immediately set to work drafting language to spell it out, while others continued to hammer out the final terms of the cruise-ICBM limits and the testing moratorium. The negotiating teams, or subsets of them, were now meeting in marathon sessions five days a week and into the evenings. Translators and typists were doggedly working well into the night in shifts to keep up with draft after draft of language forged, modified, shaped, and reshaped. Individual words and phrases took on monumental importance. Meanings attached to them would mold the superpower relationship for years, possibly decades, to come.

But in the superpower capitals there was frantic activity of a different sort. In Washington, Harold Burgoon participated in a late-night session at his home at the Naval Observatory. Present were Arnold Danzig, Joe Sternberg, General Jim Proctor, and General Omar King on his way from one SAC base to another. "I have to know one thing," the Vice-President said. "Do we trust Warrenton enough to put his agents on this guy Connaughton? Or will he warn Norton or even the President that we put him up to it? We're down to that. We must discredit Connaughton. We must prove he's a goddam Commie or we've seen the last of Blue Thunder for a long time."

Danzig said in his thin, accented voice, "You can look at it the other way around, Hal. If Connaughton's credibility is eroded, the whole house of cards falls. You don't have to prove he is a Communist. Just prove he has been dealing out of channels against instructions in a highly unauthorized manner, and the entire thing comes down. We have known for the last ten days he is at the bottom of this thing. Now we have to get him. But we don't have to run him over with a steamroller. Just discredit him."

"Goddammit, Arnold," Sternberg said through his cigar, "the guy is a traitor, a sell-out. How else could he have pulled this off on his own? I wouldn't doubt if the rotten sonofabitch hasn't worked for years to infiltrate the goddam arms control process just to throw a monkey wrench into our plans at the last minute. And I'll bet the clever bastard got a lot of help from the State Department in the process. I say smash him—as a warning to any others like him skulking around!''

"Calm down, Joe," Burgoon said. "I'm as angry as you are, but we've got to think this through. Arnie's right. All we have to do is taint this guy—find something bad enough that Norton and the President can't have anything to do with him. If we get some evidence, we give it to a friendly paper and he's done. One story and everyone in this administration who has gone along with this charade in Geneva will get so far away from it there won't be anyone to pick up the pieces—except perhaps for our good friend Emerson.''

"That's one consolation," Sternberg mused. "If this guy Connaughton comes down, it's pretty clear he brings Norton with him. Good old Em couldn't survive a scandal like that.''

"But how do you destroy Connaughton simply for working a Soviet agent?" Arnold Danzig fretted. "His defense is that he was serving his country...his boss authorized these tête-à-têtes. Why he could come out looking like a hero if this plan works.''

Burgoon's tone was feigned patience masking exasperation. "Arnie, we're not here to presume the guy is innocent. We're here to prove him guilty." He thoughtfully sipped his drink. "The whole thing stinks. He meets with this woman. He comes back with inside information on the secret deliberations of the Kremlin. He finds out who's in favor of what, and how to frame proposals that will sell to the Politburo. Those get passed on to Norton, who uses them to convince the President to put the idea on the table. Then, lo and behold, the Soviets buy it. Goddam! It's just too neat.''

The five men sat drinking silently and morosely. Then Proctor asked, "Who is she? How did she pick Connaughton out? What do we know about her?"

Burgoon replied, "I've been trying to find that out—mostly through Phil Warrenton. He showed me a file on her that seemed pretty straightforward. She comes from a good, old, non-Party family, divorced, two kids, been a top-level interpreter most of her career. Nothing much beyond that." Burgoon reflected. "I somehow got the sense from Phil that the file wasn't complete. He said stuff like 'We're still trying to develop more information,' and so on. He said they had people on her. I don't trust Phil enough to press him on it...although maybe I will if we don't have any other choice. I'll say this for her, from her pictures, she's a looker."

"Well, that's it." Omar King spoke up. "Connaughton's sleeping with a Russian woman. What else do we need? That's enough to can his ass right there."

Sternberg jumped in. "Omar's right! What the hell else do we need? That's grounds right there to hang him...woggling a Russian broad right in the middle of the negotiations."

Burgoon's eyes rolled slightly heavenward. "Joe, we don't know that for sure. So far as we know they've been to two or three public restaurants together. And there is some indication from our people in Geneva that he may have taken her up to his apartment for a few minutes."

"Time enough, Hal," Sternberg shot back. "Are you defending this guy?"

Burgoon, still exasperated, said, "No, I'm just not jumping to conclusions that can't be supported by some evidence. If we're going to leak a story that the Arms Control and Disarmament Agency's representative on the SALT III delegation in Geneva has compromised himself with a Russian woman to the detriment of our national security, we better be able to prove it."

"There is that *New York Times* story that we have on hold," Danzig said. "Andrea Cass clearly has someone over there who is talking." He looked at Proctor and King. "May we presume that was Quainton?"

"No comment," Proctor said.

King grinned. "You know Walt. He's a simple guy. He gets frustrated, he's like all the rest of us. He wants to tell somebody."

"Dammit, Omar," Burgoon snarled. "If anyone is going to talk, I don't want it to be Walt Quainton. Button him up." He thought a moment. "On the other hand, the stage is set. We have a *New York Times* story on hold that won't wait forever. It says some mystery person in Geneva is essentially carrying out his own negotiations. That could bring a ton of pressure on the administration either to deny it or establish that it was authorized. In either case, the Connaughton-Arkwright-Norton link is put under an incredible microscope." He turned to Danzig with his eyebrows raised.

"The President feels strongly about this," Danzig said defensively. "He does not want that story out, and we cannot get it out on our own. This is a deal between the President and the publisher of *The New York Times*." He hesitated. "On the other hand, the *Times* will not hold it forever, even for the President. The deal is short term."

Sternberg asked, "Who do we have watching this guy Connaughton? Are they Warrenton's?"

"Not exactly," Burgoon said. "Used to be. They're mostly free-lance and contract. Just two. Former Agency. I still don't know whether to trust Warrenton. But the people we're using are good. They just can't pin anything on Connaughton—yet. And keep in mind he's working under the approval of his immediate superior—Arkwright—as well as the Secretary of State. It's not as if he's completely out there on his own."

Danzig queried, "So what are our options?"

Burgoon looked at each of them, pondering. "We only have one." He turned to Proctor. "Jim, I want you to lean on Bigby to get his ships out to sea. The President has issued no orders—yet—to stand down on Blue Thunder. Until he does, we are free, in fact we're required, to go forward.''

Proctor said, "I have Bigby's promise—reluctant as it is—to have the Second Fleet carrier task force out of its home port in Norfolk and headed for the North Atlantic within a week. The Third Fleet is already out of San Diego headed for Pearl and units of that fleet will cover the Sea of Japan for the Seventh Fleet, which will deploy north off the Kamchatka Peninsula and Vladivostok, where most of the Soviet Pacific Fleet is in port. Finally, the Sixth Fleet has already been ordered to forgo its scheduled port visit at Naples and will continue on station in the Eastern Med, and the carrier task group in the Indian Ocean will remain there to watch the Strait of Hormuz instead of starting its rotation back to the States.''

Burgoon nodded approvingly as Proctor continued his report. "Omar here has already told you that his Strategic Air Command will assume a higher state of alert beginning in seven to ten days. That not only puts our bases on alert, it also puts more B-52s in the air at any given time. The Minutemen and MX squadrons are also brought up to higher alert at the same time. And Ben Ellison is in Europe coordinating the NATO reserve call-up, which begins one week from tomorrow. All ground and air forces under NATO command go to combat alert in ten to twelve days and that will put a hell of a lot of people in motion all at once.'' He smiled broadly. "Believe me, the Russians are going to notice.''

Burgoon looked at his watch and stood up. "This is the twenty-third. Jim, you and Omar and the others keep maximum pressure on the troops to get Blue Thunder under way...we need to be absolutely as committed to those exercises as we can. Arnie, you wait two days and jog the President on that *Times* story. Frankly, I don't think he'll need to be jogged. Corson or Rosenwald is going to be calling hourly threatening to run it. I'll continue to run our contacts in Geneva to see what can be turned up on Connaughton and that woman. I think we all agree one or both of them will be the key to stopping this treaty.''

56

"WE ALMOST HAD HER," Zhdanov said. "If those idiots you have working for you down there had one ounce of sense, they could have taken her during an unauthorized absence from the mission. Then Makarov would have had the duty to justify her absence and we could have had them both. That would have been the end of it."

He listened on the secure telephone. "It is absolutely inconceivable to me, given all the resources you have, that you do not know where they went. You must have someone on him all the time—every single minute. Every time she gets out she goes to him."

He listened again. "Malenkov," he gasped, "*replace* them. If you couldn't place the devices where he wouldn't find them the first time, then do it now. Clearly he located them and removed them...probably before taking that woman to his apartment. If we only had those tapes, that is all we would need. So you have failed twice—miserably. You didn't catch her outside. And you didn't get tapes of them together at his place. I know that's where they went! My God, you are a hopeless man.

"Listen," Zhdanov said to the KGB Deputy Director, "she must be stopped. If you cannot get evidence, manufacture it." He sounded like a teacher lecturing a very slow pupil. "The point is to discredit her, don't you understand? Let her or Makarov or even Zoshchenko deny that she is a traitor. You provide me enough to implicate her in an espionage scheme with the Americans, and I can turn the Politburo around on these negotiations. Understand?"

Then he spoke very softly and slowly. "But, Malenkov, we don't have much time. It must be done *now*—in the next few days. Otherwise, never mind. Things will have gone too far. The next week is crucial."

57

AFTER LUNCH AT LA PERLE DU LAC near the delegation headquarters at the U.S. Mission and just off the Rue de Lausanne, Arkwright asked Connaughton to walk along the lake with him. The day was crisp and bright, but despite the sun the temperature did not rise at midday above 40. The two men wore their coats as they strolled along the lakeshore walk north past the GATT Building, then back past the restaurant. Arkwright telegraphed his troubled state of mind by remaining silent, except for an occasional expression of pleasure at the progress of the now-frantic negotiations, throughout the lunch. Once outside, however, his concern became apparent.

"Frank," he began, uncharacteristically puffing a cigarette, "your role in this undertaking has always involved a certain calculated risk...you're aware of that."

Connaughton knew he would speak in euphemisms—"this undertaking"—because it was Arkwright's style from a lifetime of diplomacy...and because outdoor conversations could readily be monitored by parabolic microphones in parked or passing vehicles. He only nodded in reply, curious about his mentor's direction.

The elder man continued, "You've been around this business long enough, I suppose, not to be surprised to learn you're under surveillance."

"I assumed that I would be," Connaughton replied ruefully. "What I don't know is who they're working for."

"Some are working for us and, depending on where you've been and who you've seen, I suppose some have been working for them."

"Let's leave 'them' aside for the moment. Who exactly is 'us'?"

Arkwright ground his cigarette out on the walk, looked at Connaughton, then resumed his stroll. "Burgoon and his cabal seem to have two or more people on you. The best that I can tell is that they're contract types, former Agency. I haven't exactly raised the subject directly with Warrenton because I don't totally trust the cable system or even the secure phones on matters such as this. But Em has been in touch with Warrenton, who doesn't seem exactly to have taken sides in the political tug-of-war. At one point he was pretty close to Burgoon and Sternberg and that group. But I gather he has backed off a bit and seems to be taking his cue from the President and watching to see who looks to be coming out on top."

Connaughton walked on silently.

"At any rate, I had Em interrogate him indirectly on this point and he denied having any kind of methodical surveillance under way where you're concerned. But he did say his people had routinely picked up that a couple of alumni were on the job for high officials in Washington." Arkwright smiled slightly. "So, by process of elimination . . ."

"What did he mean, 'no *methodical* surveillance'?" Connaughton asked with an edge to his voice.

Arkwright said, "Phil left himself quite an opening there, didn't he?"

They walked for thirty yards in silence. Then Connaughton said, "Let me see if I have the picture right. The Vice-President, Secretary of Defense, and senior military commanders are having me followed by free-lance spooks. The Director of the CIA may or may not be tracking me, if for no other reason than simple idle curiosity. And surely the Soviets have their gorillas somewhere back there." He looked, with a grim smile, over his shoulder. "Must be getting pretty crowded."

"You're a sophisticated man in a highly unusual situation, Frank, and I assumed you were aware of all these possibilities. But I felt it necessary to...well...warn you, I guess. Things could get very rough for you and for the lady in the next few days. A lot of very important people—on both sides—with very long range agendas have an enormous stake in the outcome of our efforts here. As intelligent as you are, you haven't had the exposure to the kind of viciousness international politics is capable of when so much is riding on the game."

Connaughton's face, Arkwright noticed, suddenly took on an older, tougher cast. Arkwright couldn't know it, but at the moment he looked much like his wiry old frontier grandfather John Connaughton. "I can look after myself, Barrett. And, believe me, when it comes down to it I will. But what about Ekaterina...Miss Davydova? What's going to happen to her?"

They continued south along the lakeshore almost to the Jetée des Pâquis. Arkwright shook his white-thatched head. "Honestly, Frank? I really don't know." He looked at Connaughton, then stopped and lit another cigarette. "If we bring this thing off—and it's by no means a certain thing even at this point—there will be some angry people in the Kremlin also. Warrenton is trying to figure out the politics of the winners and losers right now. But in all human institutions, the ones to suffer retribution from the powerful losers are those least able to protect themselves. And this is your friend."

"Can't Zoshchenko help her?" Connaughton asked, his voice suddenly husky.

"Of course he can. The question is, will he? I would imagine if the treaty prevails and the exercises are sidetracked and we enter a period of relative tranquillity for a while, Zoshchenko will have his hands full with affairs of state. There will be elaborate ceremonies surrounding the treaty signing. That could happen fast and totally preoccupy him. Then there will probably follow in fairly short order some collateral agreements on trade, air traffic landing rights, cultural exchanges, and the like. They've all been backed up awaiting the outcome of the nuclear negotiations. And then of course, this ambitious fox is one of the few in line to succeed Kamenev, who's in failing health.'' Arkwright stopped Connaughton with a fatherly hand on his arm. ''He's going to have a lot more to think about than the welfare of one of the Foreign Ministry's interpreters.''

Connaughton turned to look out across the sunlit lake toward the Mont Blanc peak beyond in France. ''Goddammit, Barrett, we've got that woman out in the cold. She'll get eaten alive. I know it,'' he said with grim intensity, ''and so does she. She's scared to death . . . for herself and for her family. We've got some responsibility here.''

Arkwright stood quietly beside him. Then he said, ''Frank, I understand what you're saying—believe me.'' And, after hesitating, ''But I don't believe there's much we can do. The main thing right now is for both of you to keep your heads up and don't make a mistake. There are people on both sides who want to ruin you . . . who know the only way to win is to destroy you. And, Frank, they'll do it any way they can.''

Connaughton turned away from Arkwright and started walking, alone, to the car.

BEFORE THE TWO MEN arrived back at their desks, the command telephone on the desk of the Minister of Defense in Moscow rang. ''Yes, Admiral,'' Georgi Kozlovsky said with a heavy note of resignation, ''I'm afraid we have no choice. I have studied the satellite data for the past four days. They have four fleets on the move and two remaining on station beyond their tour of duty. It is massive naval movement. As reluctant as I am, under these circumstances we must go forward. Issue the appropriate orders, then give me a full report when action is taken.''

By nightfall, the Soviet Northern Fleet at Archangel and Murmansk and the Baltic Fleet at Leningrad were making steam and calling their shore-based crews to duty stations. The Black Sea Fleet had been given three days' prior alert, due to the threat of being bottled up in the Bosporus, and was making way from its home port at Sevastopol at flank speed for the Mediterranean. The Northern Fleet was also putting out of port at Vladivostok. One battle group was already deployed semipermanently at the vast naval complex abandoned by the Americans at Cam Ranh Bay in Vietnam.

Within seventy-two hours the major battle groups of the two largest navies in the world would be at sea for the first time since 1945. The difference this time was that the Soviets had a surface fleet as large and modern as that of the United States. And it would be augmented by most of the Soviets' three hundred attack submarines—the largest submarine fleet in the world.

Once the Soviet fleets were at sea and beyond the possibility of being bottled up in their coastal waters, the Red Star countdown called for seventy-five Soviet and Warsaw Pact army divisions in Eastern Europe to be placed on battle alert and the beginning of simulated combat maneuvers, including the movement of two dozen armored divisions with panzerlike tank battalions toward the Central European front. To the NATO observers and their monitoring satellites overhead, it would look a great deal like an all-out attack. Those same observers were on notice, as they had been on similar occasions in the past, that these were merely exercises. But there was always an element of doubt.

On the same date these orders were confirmed by the Defense Ministry, the twenty-eighth of March, a top-secret report appeared on Kozlovsky's desk prepared both by the KGB and military intelligence. It confirmed that orders for the call-up of all NATO reserves had been issued by the NATO high command that day. Kozlovsky shook his head in dismay.

By the end of the week, the first of April, all orders for the preparation of the Red Star exercises would be issued. And Kozlovsky knew, from his intelligence reports, that the NATO exercises were on a virtually identical timetable. Beyond that, there would be very little chance of reversing the momentum of a very complex and very high speed train that had left the station and was hurtling down the track. In fact, he reflected, there were two such trains—headed down the same track—toward each other.

Beginning on the third of April, Kozlovsky reflected, he would be called upon to validate the orders to the Soviet Strategic Rocket Forces to bring their ICBMs—the giant SS-18s and SS-19s as well as the new SS-24s and SS-25s, and the intermediate-range missiles aimed at Western Europe, the SS-20s—to a level of readiness just below full combat alert. This would all be noticed by the West's most sophisticated satellites and reported to the National Command Authority in the U.S. It will be interesting to see how they react, Kozlovsky thought ruefully. For all we know, they are planning the same kind of alert in their Blue Thunder exercises. Alone in his office he shook his large, square head in contemplation of how happy all this would make Vladimir Zhdanov.

BUT, AS THE SAND in the military hourglass ran out faster and faster in Moscow, in Washington, and in the European capitals, so was it matched by equally frantic efforts at the bargaining table in Geneva. In fact, there was no longer a single bargaining table—there were several.

Charlie Curtis and his counterpart, the deputy chief of the Soviet delegation, Oleg Yurovov, were meeting daily to conclude a test ban agreement.

Normally, Barrett Arkwright would have assigned Walt Quainton the task of finalizing cruise missile and ICBM limits. But Quainton was increasingly fighting the negotiating process, and his counterpart, General Polyakov, was virtually deaf. So Arkwright, with Makarov's concurrence, assigned Frank Connaughton to the task of tying up the loose ends. As the Curtis-Yurovov task force of staff and interpreters was meeting at the Soviet Mission, Connaughton's group—including his counterpart, Lev Vronsky—met each day at 9 A.M. at the U.S. Mission. In spite of Vronsky's flighty personality he was a professional, and he and Connaughton worked furiously at the tedious task of designing counting rules for cruise missile carriers and new types of ICBMs. By the middle of the week of March 28, they were the closest to completion of the three working task forces. Now they were defining individual words with painstaking precision, using half a dozen or more Russian-English, English-Russian dictionaries.

The third and final group was headed by the ambassadors themselves. Like the other task groups, they met daily and worked into the evening, at the U.S. Mission. Arkwright and Makarov had the most difficult responsibility—translating the Connaughton-instigated "Soviet Proposal" on space weapons into treaty language. The almost violent Soviet opposition to Star Wars nearly caused a breakdown at first. But since the framework for discussion came from the Soviet Foreign Minister himself (with some help from Ekaterina Davydova), Makarov had every incentive to get down to business. Besides, as they all knew from reading the daily cables from their own ministries and the popular press, the massive military machines on both sides were grinding with alarming rumbles into operation.

At ten o'clock on the evening of the thirtieth of March, Connaughton threw down his pencil, leaned back in his chair, and rubbed his eyes reddened by tobacco smoke and tedious concentration. "I've had enough," he said to Vronsky facing him across the table. The two men and their aides, sitting around a conference table littered with overflowing ashtrays, books, documents, and wads of paper, with their ties loosened and hair tousled, looked like gamblers in an all-night poker game. For Connaughton, that was what it seemed. "Let's pick it up first thing in the morning. Is nine all right? OK. Let's get out of here."

As he was arranging his papers for the following morning, Connaughton's secretary entered the conference room to tidy up. She was more than ordinarily frazzled.

Connaughton realized his deputy from the Arms Control and Disarmament Agency was nowhere to be seen, and asked, "What happened to Eileen? She wasn't around this evening, and she seemed under the weather all day."

"Mr. Connaughton," the secretary replied with great concern, "didn't you see the ambulance about five o'clock? That was for Eileen."

Connaughton remembered some brief commotion. But given his preoccupation with Arkwright's warning and wrapping up the negotiations with Vronsky, he had thought little of it. "Eileen Malmstrom? What happened to her?"

"Oh, Mr. Connaughton," the secretary said, "poor Eileen has been taken to the hospital. She's having emergency surgery. They think it's a burst appendix. I just called, and they say she's going to be fine."

Connaughton, his mind quickly wandering again, lamely commiserated and told the secretary to send flowers.

Connaughton stood to escort Vronsky to the elevator. The Russian took him by the elbow and said, "Lets get fresh air, Frahnk."

With aides trailing behind, the two men descended the three floors to the street and the waiting Soviet cars. Vronsky pulled Connaughton off to the side onto a small grassy plot just beginning to show early signs of spring. "Frahnk," Vronsky said, standing with his back to the three Soviet sedans, "I have been asked to give this to you." He pulled a long plain-white envelope from the breast pocket of his rumpled coat. "I know nothing about it. In fact I deny I just gave it to you." Then he smiled and winked as Connaughton slipped the envelope into his own pocket in one swift motion. He became serious very quickly. "Your friend is in trouble. Serious trouble, I think." His voice very low, he

said, "I do this for her because she is a nice person. And for
an American, you are not so bad yourself." Vronsky could
hear, and Connaughton could see, the KGB drivers stamp-
ing their feet impatiently in the background. They would
become more than curious soon. "I take no sides in all
this," Vronsky said. "Big-time politics makes me nervous.
I am what you call, I think, a survivor. I do that by not taking chances—except, maybe, the stupid chance I just did."
He smacked Connaughton on the shoulder with a sweeping
right hand. "So bye-bye. Sleep well." Then as he began to
turn for the cars he added, "Maybe when this is all over,
maybe I come see you in Moan-tahna, huh?" Connaughton's eyes became misty as the Russian headed for the cars,
laughing as he went.

Connaughton bade his colleagues good night with instructions to gather at 7:30 in the morning and be prepared
for another long day, and then waved off his car and driver.
He needed the long walk back to the old city in the clear,
crisp night. Once he had descended the slight hill to the Rue
de Lausanne, he slipped into a dark entryway and opened
the sealed envelope.

It said simply: "I will call you at the public telephone
outside the mission at 12:15 P.M. tomorrow, Thursday. The
number at that phone is 555-1013. I miss you and I need
you. Love, E.D."

In the twenty minutes or so it took to walk home, Connaughton considered his options. No doubt things were
closing in. No doubt he was in trouble—however the negotiations turned out. No doubt Ekaterina was in even more
trouble than he was. The immediate thing was to prevent
their long-term trouble from getting in the way of a treaty.
They were getting so close. It was now a mere matter of
days, perhaps even hours, until a draft treaty was ready.
Then it was a political judgment for both sides whether to
go through with the formal signing. But the political options were limited. The United States government would
bear the brunt of enormous condemnation in world public

opinion if it backed off at the last minute. The protests would be like nothing ever seen. The solid foundation of NATO would be seriously fractured. It would take years to repair. For their part the Soviets were not in much better shape. If they torpedoed the agreement, they would look extremely bellicose and would be held responsible for the military confrontation and increased world insecurity that resulted.

No, Connaughton thought as he approached the Pont des Bergues across the Rhone River, the forces against the treaty on one side or the other would have to prove the process flawed to create grounds for rejection of the results. And the only "flaws" in the process were the meetings between himself and Ekaterina and their relationship. Tomorrow was the last day of March, he reflected. They would know by Monday, the day after Easter, whether they had an agreement. It would only take a few days for the sides to decide on signing. The whole matter might be disposed of within two weeks, or even less. He started up the steep slope at the lower end of the old Grand' Rue and considered both what a short and what a long period of time that could be.

He got to Number 15 and looked about. He saw no one. But he had also been so deep in thought as he walked across Geneva that he had not noticed the sedan that followed at a crawl a block behind. He climbed the two flights of steps and let himself into his apartment. Again the sliver of paper at the hinge had been dislodged. He now assumed his privacy was being violated by one or both sides fairly regularly. He threw off his coat and started water boiling for tea. On second thought, he shut off the burner and poured a shot of Jameson. He sat before the cold fireplace where he and Ekaterina had held each other just a few days before and read the note again. She was clever. She could get to the pay phone in the U.S. Mission where she was interpreting for Makarov at the lunch break and call him at another pay phone at his lunch break. They avoided the tap that was doubtless back in place by now. But there must be some urgency for her even to take that risk. He put the note aside, then went to his desk.

Connaughton liked maps. He enjoyed collecting maps. Now he got them all out. Maps of Geneva. Maps of Switzerland, of southern France, of northern Italy. Dozens of maps poured out of the stuffed cubbyholes in the desk. He sipped the Jameson, then began to spread the maps out. He got a yellow legal pad and two sharp pencils and started to calculate mileage. He knew travel times to most of the major cities in the region from his weekend travels over the previous year. He performed some calculations, then began to look farther away. He was drawn to northern Italy because he had enjoyed traveling there often in the past. Perhaps when the negotiations were over, he could take a leave of absence for a week or two before returning to the States and drive over there. That would be a great escape.

Suddenly he saw Lake Como and the triangular peninsula that created its two legs, and the jewel called Bellagio at its tip. He recalled the conference at Cadenabbia across the lake on its west side that he had attended as a graduate student just before receiving his degree at Princeton. It had been twenty years before—when Katherine was well, he thought. It had been the happiest four days of their lives. The place had always held a unique spot in his memory. And he had always vowed to go back, perhaps to live for a short time. That's where he would go. He folded up the maps that linked Geneva with Bellagio, and put them in his briefcase. His last thought before sleep was of a springtime lunch with Ekaterina on the piazza of the Grand Hotel Villa Serbelloni.

HE HAD A NOTE on his desk to see Barrett Arkwright before starting his negotiations at 9 A.M. with Vronsky. He walked down the hall to Arkwright's corner office and the Ambassador's personal secretary waved him in with a frown. Arkwright said, "Sit down, Frank. Tell me how long you're going to take to wrap up your discussions."

"We'll have it finished today," Connaughton said, somewhat puzzled. "There may be some sweeping up on Friday, but we'll have a finished draft section of the treaty on your desk and on Makarov's no later than five on Friday. Then it's up to the policy makers. Why?"

Arkwright walked to the window and turned his back on Connaughton. "I assume you remember our talk yesterday when I warned you about things getting rough. Well, they are. Apparently as some sort of last-gasp effort to derail this treaty, Burgoon and company have convinced the President that you ought to be "interviewed" by the Agency and some special security types that are coming over from Washington. They'll arrive tonight and want to talk to you as soon as your work's done. It happened before Em could stop it, and Warrenton had no choice but to go along. I don't mean to upset you unnecessarily, but I think you should know the cable I just received alleges that, based on preliminary evidence, you may be accused of subverting the national security interests of the United States."

SHORTLY AFTER NOON, Connaughton broke off his discussions with Vronsky as the staff was delivering sandwiches for a working lunch in the conference room. He didn't bother to put on his coat but simply gave a cursory wave to the Marine guard in the Plexiglas booth at the elevator entrance on the third floor of the mission and descended to the street. He walked fifteen yards to the corner of the building and turned right around the corner to the public phone booth. He pretended to dial a number, but held his hand on the receiver catch. The number on the phone was 555-1013. At 12:17 the telephone rang and Connaughton immediately answered.

"Frank?" the familiar voice said.

"Yes, Ekaterina. How are you?"

"Frank, I must speak quickly. I only have a moment. I took the risk with Vronsky because Ambassador Makarov told me yesterday that I am ordered to accompany Malenkov back to Moscow this weekend as soon as my translation is done. I have been ordered not to speak with anyone—most especially you—about this." Her voice caught. "I have been told they want to discuss all aspects of our discussions...and our friendship. Makarov told me I must tell them absolutely the truth, because they will require lie detector tests and new drugs they now use." Her voice was trembling. "Oh, Frank, what can I do? I am so very much afraid for the first time in my life."

"Ekaterina, listen to me," Connaughton said slowly and firmly. "I'm going to help you. I will not let this happen." Then he thought quickly. He had already made up his mind that morning. "Tomorrow after the negotiations break, leave our mission by the service entrance." He described the route to the exit used by the service staff. "There will be a taxi waiting. I'll order it tomorrow morning. Tell the driver to take you to the Russian Church—where we first met. Bring whatever personal things you can with you. I'll meet you there. We'll be gone for a while."

She was silent for an eternity. Then she said simply, "Yes."

"Ekaterina," Connaughton said, "I love you."

58

THE SOUND OF RUSTLING PAPER awakened Connaughton from a terrible nightmare. It was dark, and groggily he tried to think where he was and why he had paper all around him. Slowly, painfully, he sat up. He was on his own couch and his neck ached from being propped against the arm of the couch for hours. He rubbed his eyes until they focused dimly on his watch. It was not quite 6 A.M. The papers all around him were maps and notes. He had been awake until the early hours of the morning calculating travel times. He blinked in pain as he turned on a lamp. He gathered up the jumble of papers, folding the maps and putting them back into his briefcase with his notes. Though still not awake, he made sure no notes were left on the floor. One sheet containing the final calculations he folded carefully and put in his shirt pocket. Then, shivering in the morning chill, he pulled off yesterday's clothes and turned the shower on full blast. Naked, he went to the kitchen and put water on to boil. Although he had not eaten since the morning before, he wanted only hot coffee. The steamy shower brought him awake and loosened the stiff muscles in his neck and back. Even as the bathroom atmosphere turned into a boiling fog, his mind began to clear. He grimly considered how long it would have to remain completely clear and fully alert.

The car was the problem he had been studying when he had fallen asleep. They would check public transportation and rental car counters first. They would have a fix on Charlie Curtis's car immediately. Description and plates. That wouldn't do.

The car problem was tough, but it had to be solved. They would have to cross several borders. Switzerland to France. France back into Switzerland. Then Switzerland into Italy. That was the one that counted. They had to get across the Italian border before the alarms went off—or at least before the alarms reached that far.

He turned the shower off, dried quickly and roughly to get the blood circulating, and pulled on his tattered robe. He poured the boiling water onto instant coffee—double portion. It tasted like medicine but it woke him up. He had until the afternoon to get ready and to solve the car problem. He made a mental checklist. A few clothes and toiletries. He'd buy a few things for her. She wouldn't be able to bring much, except what she could stuff into a purse. Hit the bank on the way. He had a couple of thousand dollars in his account. Passport. That was about it.

Dammit! Passport. She wouldn't have hers. Soviet security kept it. They could probably clear the French and Swiss borders without it. But she would have to have it at the Italian border. He rubbed his head. Dammit! Taking the steaming coffee he went into his bedroom and started pulling out underwear, shirts, sweaters, and casual trousers. He folded them quickly and placed them in a battered canvas-and-leather duffel bag. Shaving gear and his slim leather briefcase went on top. He zipped it shut as he thought, If I have to I'll steal one. Then he began to think of the women at the delegation who came anywhere close to Ekaterina's description.

Then he got dressed. He put the packed duffel bag under extra blankets stored at the top of his linen closet. Then he quickly jotted some notes on his legal pad representing hasty calculations of distances from Geneva to Lausanne, then to Bern and Basel, north into France toward Strasbourg and west toward Nancy. He hid the pad under the duffel, then looked around carefully and closed the apartment door. He prayed the searchers would not find the bag.

Just as he started down the Grand' Rue to catch a taxi in the lightening dawn, it struck him.

He walked as fast as he could to the bottom of the hill and almost bowled over several storekeepers and clerks on their way to open their businesses, in his effort to grab the first taxi available. During the ten-minute drive, all he could think of was—Eileen Malmstrom has a car. He raced into the mission and burst out of the elevator, waving his identification card as he strode past the startled young Marine at the checkpoint. Luckily, he was the first one in. But others would be arriving soon. He turned on the lights in his own office, hung up his coat, and took a deep breath. He mentally crossed his fingers as he walked three doors down the hall to Malmstrom's dark, empty office. He walked past her secretary's desk and back to her own. He carefully began to open her desk drawers, starting at the top of the standard gray government-issue metal desk. Then, in the bottom drawer on the left, he saw what he wanted. He reached down and carefully removed her purse.

He unzipped the large bag and was dismayed at the clutter. He searched through the rubble to the bottom and located what he wanted. Rather than take the added time of trying to locate the car keys, he removed the entire key ring. Then he quickly replaced the purse and closed the desk drawer as he heard footsteps in the hallway. He was back in his office by the time the Marine guard rounded the corner and put his head in the doorway to see that Connaughton was all right. Connaughton assured him he was simply in a hurry to get prepared for the day and that all was well.

By the time others began to arrive, Connaughton had used the staff directory to locate Malmstrom's apartment in the community of Meyrin near the airport just off the Avenue Louis-Casai. On his way to the conference room to meet Vronsky for the concluding day of negotiations, he passed Arkwright on his way to the U.S. Mission. Arkwright gloomily instructed him to report for his "interview" with the intelligence types at 9 A.M. the following morning in the secure bubble. "If this is Good Friday for the treaty," Arkwright said with a thin smile, "perhaps tomorrow will be Passover Day for you."

Throughout the morning Connaughton had difficulty keeping his mind on the tedious task of word refinement, instead finding himself going over and over the details of what had to be done in the coming hours, and wondering where the night would find them and where they would finally hide in the following days. Shortly after noon he excused himself, saying he had errands to run. Vronsky in turn had to make a trip to the Soviet Mission. And they agreed to resume at 1:30. Once outside, Connaughton walked three blocks from the headquarters, caught a taxi, and gave the address of Eileen Malmstrom's apartment building. It turned out to be a modern four-story building with a parking lot in the rear. He took a turn around the building and quickly located Malmstrom's white Opel. He went into the apartment building, found her apartment number—3D—on the mailbox, and, after trying several keys, let himself in. He was relieved to see she lived alone in the small one-bedroom place. He left his winter gloves on as he looked around the main living-sitting room. He went to her desk and began to open the drawers. He needed only the top one. In the corner was the familiar black diplomatic passport. Eileen Malmstrom was forty-three, as tall as Ekaterina, fair complexion and green eyes, and heavier. She had very blond hair. Connaughton put the passport in his pocket, closed the desk drawer, and left the apartment. He drove the Opel across Geneva and left it on the street in the Place du Bourg-de-Four. He walked to his apartment, took the duffel bag from the closet, but left the pad and misdirections under the blankets, then returned and stowed the bag in the car trunk. He then went to his bank down the hill and withdrew almost all his funds, bought some cosmetics at a nearby pharmacy, then took a taxi back to the headquarters.

The afternoon dragged on. By 4:30 P.M. the Connaughton-Vronsky task force at the delegation headquarters had completed its work. Connaughton's secretary brought a bottle of champagne and plastic cups and they toasted themselves, better understanding, and peace till the bottle ran out. Connaughton shook Vronsky's hand and they slapped each other on the back. Connaughton promised to see him the first of the week to proofread the section of the treaty they had just completed. Before leaving the headquarters Connaughton ordered a taxi to arrive at the service entrance to the U.S. Mission at 5 P.M. He then took a taxi to the old city, picked up Malmstrom's Opel, drove it eight blocks to the Russian Church, and parked behind the church on the Rue Sturm.

At twenty past five a taxi arrived at the church and Ekaterina got out. She had only her coat and a large handbag. Connaughton pulled the car around the corner, after determining that she was not being followed, and opened the passenger door for her. As he maneuvered the car down the hill through the Friday rush-hour traffic to the lakeshore highway, she was still. But her look was one of terror.

Once on the highway out of Geneva he asked, "Did you have any trouble?"

She shook her head silently. Then she asked, "Where are we going?"

Connaughton said, "Away."

"Where?"

"Italy."

"How long will we be there?"

Connaughton drove in silence for a moment, then replied, "Until they find us."

She put her face in her black gloved hands and wept quietly.

After several minutes she wiped her eyes, composed herself, and looked directly ahead. He took her hand in his right hand.

"We had no choice," he said. "Otherwise, tomorrow you would have been on a plane to Moscow, I would have been under the CIA's heat lamp, and I would never have seen you again."

She gasped. "The CIA?"

He told her what Arkwright had told him as they approached the French border. He instructed her to pull her black scarf around her head. The young border guard noted the Swiss plates on the car, looked in briefly, and waved them on. He continued the story as they drove over the same highway they had taken to Évian three weeks before. He kept the Opel as near the 120-kilometer speed limit as he could, but made sure that he never went over.

The farther they drove from Geneva, the more she seemed to collect herself. "Why would the CIA be involved at this point?"

"Same reason the KGB is after you. The people on my side who are against this treaty are playing their last card."

"But surely when we are missing—together—that will be proof enough."

"It's a gamble. But I don't think so." He slowed to pass through Évian, then speeded up on the outskirts. "This treaty is virtually completed. There have been detailed press accounts in the past few days about how close we are to completion. There's building speculation in both capitals and around Europe that there will be a summit ceremony to sign the treaty within the next two weeks. Either the people after you or those after me have to catch one or both of us, extract some kind of confession of treason, and then persuade the ruling circles on one side that we engineered an international agreement by trickery or deceit. Frankly, neither side can afford to say a word to the press until they catch us, and they certainly can't devise an acceptable reason for not signing the treaty without one or the other of us. So you see," he said with a wan smile, "without us the thing has to succeed."

"Then what?"

The smile disappeared. "Then I don't know." They passed through the small village of Meillerie and shortly approached the equally small lakeshore village of St. Gingolph on the way back to Switzerland. Dusk was rapidly advancing into night as the border guard once again checked the Swiss license plates, looked inside, and waved them back into Switzerland. Very soon they were at the east end of Lake Geneva where the highway turned south to follow the Rhone River upstream. Within a few minutes they passed through Monthey and crossed the Rhone to pick up the modern four-lane motorway south, then crossed the Rhone twice more before passing north of the town of Martigny and heading east along the Rhone Valley toward Italy.

Connaughton checked his watch when they turned east at Martigny-Ville. It was almost seven-o'clock and night was settling quickly along the long and broad Rhone Valley. Within two hours they would be nearing the Simplon Pass and Italy just beyond. They would have to start looking for lodging once they made it across the border. If we make it across the border, Connaughton thought to himself. He turned to Ekaterina, silent beside him.

"I brought a few personal things for you," he said, handing her the package from the pharmacy. "I had no idea what you would need. I haven't done this kind of thing before."

She smiled and touched him on the cheek.

"You'll certainly need some more clothes. We'll be in Sion in about twenty minutes," he said. "We can pick up anything else you may need for tonight."

"When will they miss you? When will they know you are gone?"

"Tomorrow morning when I don't show up for my 'interview.' How did you leave things at the mission?"

She sighed heavily, as if reluctant to remember. "We broke up just at five o'clock. The ambassadors agreed to meet further tomorrow to complete their portion of the treaty. The translators and interpreters were to collect again about this hour to finish work on today's drafts. They will miss me now."

"I imagine the KGB will be searching your compound and interviewing your people right now. They won't know I'm gone—yet—so they'll assume you're on your own, probably somewhere in Geneva. I would imagine they'll be desperate enough to notify Swiss—and maybe French—authorities to look for you. Although I don't know what their practice is on things like that. My guess is they won't do that until late tonight at the earliest and probably not until tomorrow sometime. Then, as time goes on, they'll have to broaden the search and probably get other agencies—even Interpol—into it. They won't admit you're a defector—they'll say you've been kidnapped. Saves face."

"Frank, we can't get into Italy," she said urgently.

"Why not?"

"Because I don't have my passport—only an identification card. They keep the passport. Besides, we would not want to show two diplomatic passports—one Soviet, one American. That would awaken even the sleepiest border guard."

He patted her folded hands as they entered Sion. "Don't worry. You are now Eileen Malmstrom, a member of the U.S. Mission in Geneva." And in response to her puzzled look, he added, "She's in the hospital and won't need her passport for a few days. I 'borrowed' it—just for a while." He showed her the picture. "Somehow your hair mysteriously turned black in the past few days. So keep your scarf on."

There were still shops open on Friday night in Sion and he parked near a cluster that included a women's clothes store and a small pharmacy. He handed her a roll of Swiss francs, which she took reluctantly. In a quarter of an hour she returned with two shopping bags and he pulled back onto the highway. It was now so dark they could make out neither the high ridgeline to the north nor the Matterhorn beyond Zermatt to the south.

"What will they do when they find you gone?" she asked.

"Probably they'll think we're together," Connaughton replied grimly. "Arkwright knows about our meetings, of course—at least most of what there is to know. And he'll be bound to cooperate with the CIA types up to a point, even though he's not sympathetic with the purpose behind their effort. But I don't know how long it will take my side to figure out that you're gone too. Certainly our translators are going to miss you tonight and notice all the consternation and scurrying around on your side. And they'll report that. The Agency will be able to put two and two together."

"Then what?"

"Then," he continued, "they'll ransack my place. I left a couple of feeble clues to throw them off. They'll use all the foreign intelligence services, our own stations, and Interpol. And they'll spend the next two or three days checking public transportation, car rentals, and the like, trying to figure out how we're traveling. Eileen will be home from the hospital in about a week and will discover her keys and car missing. It won't take them long to put that together."

They passed through Sierre and the sign on the outskirts pointed them on to Brig. "I still do not understand why Zhdanov, or those on your side opposed to the negotiations, will not use our escape to halt the treaty," Ekaterina said.

"Ekaterina, if they had taken you to Moscow, filled you full of drugs, and put you on a lie detector machine, they would have found out we were sharing information about the internal politics of our own governments and possible bargaining positions and that would have been the end—not only of the treaty, but of you. Likewise, even without drugs, I would undoubtedly have been forced to go through the lie detector business, and the same thing would have come out. Either way we'd lose. At least this way, we may be able to save the treaty."

"But why will they go forward even now?" she asked.

"Because Kamenev wants it and Lawkard wants it, and our absence—by itself—isn't grounds to justify reversing policy," Connaughton explained. "Neither side can say, we have completed negotiations for a sweeping arms control agreement, but at the present time we will not sign it for reasons that we cannot explain. Or worse, we will not sign it until we catch two missing people whose disappearance we deny and whose whereabouts we know nothing about."

She laughed for the first time, like a schoolgirl on an outing. "How long, then, will it take to set up the ceremony for signing?"

He knew she meant, how long must we absolutely remain undiscovered? "You see," he replied, "the heads of state, Norton, Zoshchenko, and all the others who have cast their lot politically with this treaty are going to want the earliest possible signing date. I know Arkwright was in touch with the State Department yesterday discussing dates, locations, protocol, and the like. The White House and State Department were sending an advance team to Geneva to start making arrangements. It's possible it could happen in the next two weeks."

Connaughton held his breath. A Swiss patrol car was less than fifty yards behind them. He checked to make sure he was not speeding. They drove in silence for ten miles, then began to see notices that they were approaching Brig and the turn to the Simplon Pass. Within minutes they entered the small Swiss town of Brig and turned right onto the highway, which very quickly began its winding thirty-mile climb over the southern Alps pass into Italy. Connaughton noted from his watch they had been gone just over three hours. The Swiss police car remained in Brig.

As the small Opel began its climb they noted the wind blowing more vigorously and spurts of snow brush past the windows. Connaughton turned the car heater up to compensate. Ekaterina turned sideways in the seat and placed her head against the headrest. Connaughton had noticed at the previous borders and in Sion that the black scarf completely covered her hair. She seemed exhausted by weeks of long work hours now compounded by the tension of the past few hours. He said nothing but continued to drive into the descending night.

Within an hour they were near the mile-high pass and he saw the Italian border post just ahead. There was little traffic at this hour, so there would be little wait. He aroused Ekaterina to alert her and suggested that she feign sleep, turning her head slightly to face the opposite window. He pulled out both American diplomatic passports as she pulled the black scarf tight around her head and close to her face. Only a profile was visible from the driver's side.

Connaughton eased the Opel into the lane indicated by the guard, heavily cloaked against the early spring snow and cold wind. He rolled his window halfway down and handed out the two passports.

"Buona notte, signore. The purpose of your visit?" the young officer asked politely as he looked at each passport and then inquisitively into the car.

Connaughton leaned slightly forward as if finding it difficult to hear. *"Turismo.* We are heading for south of Italy—beyond Roma—to find someplace warm."

The guard looked across at the sleeping figure and back at the passport. "Anywhere in Italy is warmer than here, *signore.*" He handed the passports back to Connaughton and saluted. *"Buona notte, signore."* Connaughton pulled away as the guard took one last look at the car and headed back to his warm booth. Connaughton could hear Ekaterina sigh with relief. She had not breathed during the exchange.

Connaughton drove on a few miles to the tiny village of Iselle near the entrance to the Simplon rail tunnel. He saw a few lights on, some at a small chaletlike restaurant. He stopped the car in front and left the motor running for the heater. Inside he inquired about lodging and found that the aunt of the proprietor, Signora Massone, did indeed rent guest rooms in her house up the small road behind the restaurant. He also warned Connaughton the restaurant would be closing at ten o'clock—in just fifteen minutes—in case he wished something to eat. Connaughton returned to the car and reported the arrangements to Ekaterina. Like Connaughton, she had not eaten since the day before and they agreed they needed food. Connaughton returned to the restaurant, ordered dinner, and said they would be back shortly. He then drove up the hill and managed to rouse Signora Massone, who was just turning out the lights. She looked them over briefly, then waved them in from the cold, noticing they both seemed to be reasonably well-off Americans. She showed them to the upstairs room and bath, quoted the rate payable in advance, and included breakfast at her nephew's restaurant in the bargain. This would be their refuge for the first night.

In the small restaurant Ekaterina said little and ate even less. The escape had exhausted her and, after two glasses of wine, she seemed on the verge of collapse. Connaughton wolfed the hot spaghetti and meat sauce as if famished and finished off the bottle of wine. The proprietor locked the restaurant behind them, saying that he would be open for breakfast after 7:30 A.M. Connaughton drove the drowsy Ekaterina back up the hill and helped her into the house.

Ekaterina went into the bathroom to put on the inexpensive flannel nightgown she had bought in Sion. When she returned she found the bed turned down and Connaughton curled up with the heavy spare comforter in the soft chair by the bed.

She touched his face and took his hand saying, "Partners in crime must at least sleep together." She led him to the bed as she turned out the light. She curled backward naturally into his protective embrace and they were both instantly asleep.

In what seemed to Connaughton to be only a matter of minutes, he was startled into wakefulness by the blinding light of the new sun through the thin curtains of the bedroom's east window. Ekaterina slept on, still closed in his arms. He moved his left arm slightly and saw that it was almost 7:30 A.M. Reluctantly, gently, he woke Ekaterina. He wanted to avoid, if possible, a daylight confrontation with Signora Massone or her nephew. Ekaterina groaned and started to turn, then awoke with a start. She smiled and they kissed. "It is a shock to wake next to a man," she said.

"Welcome or unwelcome?"

"In this case, very welcome," she said, and kissed him again. She moved quickly out of bed, taking her clothes down the hallway. Connaughton dressed in a sweater, casual slacks from the duffel, and yesterday's sportcoat. When she returned he took over the bathroom, looked in the mirror, and decided he needed the shave.

Minutes later they were in the Opel and on the highway down the mountain pass into Italy. They stopped in Domodossola for espresso and hard breakfast rolls, and then were back on the road descending gradually another twenty miles to Verbania. The pleasant lakeside town was beginning to come alive on Saturday morning as Connaughton pulled off at a tourist center to look at his map and inquire about the ferry across Lake Maggiore. The friendly guide waved them on two miles and they drove past elegantly restored eighteenth-century villas beginning to show evidence of springtime flowers in their elaborate gardens. They arrived at the ferry and saw half a dozen cars waiting for the first departure, in less than thirty minutes. Connaughton bought their tickets and shortly they followed the line on board. After the boat filled up for crossing, the motor churned into action, the horn sounded, and they took outdoor seats on the upper deck. The bright sun was already warming the day and the crossing was beautiful. Large estates and vacation homes dotted the shores on both sides of the blue lake. Sailboats were beginning to appear in the soft spring breeze. Connaughton put his arm around Ekaterina and marveled at how pleasant life might be outside the stress and danger of international diplomacy.

She smiled and said, "It is strange how, at a time when most of the police of the world are looking for both of us, I have never felt freer."

They got back in the car and as they drove off the ferry onto the eastern shore of Lake Maggiore she said, "We are in Italy. Now where are we going?"

Connaughton answered, "We're going to the next lake—Como—and then to a little town I once visited on that lake a long time ago."

"When will we arrive?" she asked.

He looked at his watch. It was almost ten o'clock. The CIA agents would be gathering in the bubble for his "interview." "We'll be in the town of Como in about one hour. Then we'll be where we're going by noon."

"Why don't we just keep going?" she asked.

Connaughton said, "Because the searchers from my side at least will start circulating my description and perhaps even my picture very soon. The more we're seen in public places—hotels and restaurants—or on the highways, the more danger there is."

"Where can we stay?"

"I don't know yet," Connaughton answered. "When we get to Bellagio, I'll look around. We'll try to rent some rooms."

"We should begin to decide who we are going to be, shouldn't we?" It was more a declaration than a question.

Connaughton slowed the car as they passed through the winding streets of Varese and then continued southeastward toward Como. "Who shall we be? You decide."

She brightened, taking to the game. "You are an American professor, from a small but prestigious university in the West. You teach international relations. I, of course, must be your wife—much better than being traveling companion or mistress. Much more proper. My accent comes, like my name, from Scandinavia—probably Norwegian. To account for my dark hair, my grandfather came to Norway from . . . well, I guess, Russia. I also do some translation to help augment your not large university salary."

"Not bad," Connaughton said. "Why are we traveling in Europe?"

"You are on a spring sabbatical from your university. You are doing research on your new book on . . . ?"

". . . the nuclear arms race," he continued. "We've been in Geneva and have come over here for a holiday before going on to interview leaders in other NATO countries." He wondered, "Do we have children?"

"Of course," she said laughing, "we have a teen-age daughter in school in the East and two small sons at home. Their grandparents are looking after them during our trip."

They were now entering the outskirts of Como, located at the southern tip of the lake. "It all fits, doesn't it?" Connaughton said as he maneuvered the Opel through the bustling Saturday morning traffic. He looked for, and finally found, the sign pointing to the road leading up the eastern shore of the lake to Bellagio.

"Yes, it does, Frank," Ekaterina said wistfully. "It fits very well."

After artfully dodging through the chaos of Como city traffic, Connaughton brought the car out of the other side on the narrow, winding lakeside road. They're all over my apartment by now, he thought. I hope they give the nasty old concierge a hard time. Poor Arkwright, how disappointed he'll be.

The lake road was built into the side of the steep cliffs that descended directly into the lake. Every time he encountered a car he had to slow because it was so narrow. He couldn't afford an auto accident at this time and he certainly didn't want to drive the two of them off into the lake. The sun glistened on the clear water of the lake, and the white and dun plaster of the houses on both sides shone brightly. He pulled dark glasses from his pocket.

"Now you do look like a spy." She smiled.

He chuckled. "I must play the role when we arrive at our destination."

She said, "This is the first time I have ever gone where I wanted to go outside the Soviet Union. I have never in my life simply done what I want to do. It is like a freedom."

Yes, he thought, a freedom. We must enjoy it while we can. He shuddered to think what freedom, if any, she might have after they were caught and she was taken back to Russia. For that matter, he wouldn't have much himself.

"Here we are," Connaughton said. "This is Bellagio." They saw early spring flowers beginning to make an appearance along the winding street as they came into the small town. The rolling hills that made up the peninsula were covered with green shrubs and trees, and clustered about were two- and three-story stone houses covered with white, gray, and pinkish-orange stucco, all with wooden shutters and traditional red-orange tile roofs.

They drove through the streets of Bellagio slowly, taking the measure of the place and thinking where within this small community they might unobtrusively stay. Connaughton looked at his watch. It was just noon. Presently he parked the car in the central parking area of the village. Connaughton kept on the dark glasses and watched as Ekaterina went directly to a small shop on the lake-front square where she purchased a wide-brimmed hat that partially obscured her distinctive features.

They strolled through the few commercial blocks of the town noting pharmacies, groceries, clothing stores, and finally what appeared to be a realty business. There were pictures of houses to rent, but all seemed to be large estates or required a three- or four-month rental for the summer. Connaughton observed in each case the extremely high rent.

As they examined the properties in the window display, the proprietor arrived and they quickly moved on. Connaughton wanted as few people as possible in the town to see them, especially together. He left Ekaterina in a dress shop and returned to the real estate office.

"Do you have short-term rentals...perhaps by the week?" he asked in makeshift Italian.

"Little, very little" came back in makeshift English. "What do you look for?" The man looked Connaughton over quizzically.

"My wife and I need an apartment, perhaps for two weeks or slightly more," Connaughton said.

The proprietor replied, "We have very little now. But come back Monday. I will show you what we have. In the meantime, is there a hotel where you can be reached?"

Connaughton thanked him and retreated. He found Ekaterina, who had bought some clothes, and they continued around the village. The afternoon wore on and he noticed the town filling up with tourists arriving for dinner at the various hotels. He wanted to take Ekaterina to the Grand Hotel Villa Serbelloni, where he had been so many years before. But they couldn't risk the exposure. The problem of shelter and refuge was gnawing at them. They took the Opel to a gasoline station on the outskirts of town to fill its empty tank. With Ekaterina's help he managed a mangled conversation with the station operator about small quiet restaurants in the area. In typical fashion the man happened to have a cousin who owned "one of the very finest restaurants in the entire area." He drew on a greasy sales slip with a dull pencil directions to the Bellavista Ristorante on top of a hill overlooking Bellagio in the neighboring village of Visgnola. His cousin's name was Enrico.

The directions turned out to be incomprehensible, but through trial and error they located the restaurant in the early evening. It was still warm and they chose one of several outdoor tables on the graveled patio overlooking the lake and village below. Flowered umbrellas over the table had been furled and they found only two other couples at the tables covered with their yellow-and-white-checked cloths. Enrico greeted them and Connaughton suggested he choose the dinners for them both. He presented a bottle of his best red wine and poured two glasses with a flourish. For the moment the couple could almost believe their recently created fictional lives. Grim pursuers and hidden machinations seemed a million miles away.

After an elaborate dinner, Connaughton asked the effervescent Enrico if he might happen to know any local residence where they might stay for a few days. He gestured grandly in the direction of a house thirty yards away, hidden in the trees from the road.

"Who owns the building?" Connaughton asked.

"All I know, *signore*," said Enrico, "is that a very old man lives there. He is a foreigner. He has lived there many years. Some call him father or sometimes grandfather. They think he was some kind of priest some time ago. Others call him the ghost or the fox... because no one knows much about him."

Connaughton asked, "Does he live alone?"

"It is not clear," Enrico said. "There is some young man, perhaps some relative, who tries to run a competition for me. You will see if you go there. But the old man keeps to himself. A few times he has people stay there"—spreading his hands—"for the money, *signore*."

Connaughton thanked him and gave him American dollars for the bill with apologies for not having changed to lire. Ekaterina smiled beneath her hat and remained silent to conceal her accent.

They left the Opel outside the restaurant and walked up the road to the house. It sat above the road, its elevated yard fronted by a low gray rock wall topped by slender metal rods tapering to spiked points. Incongruously, at the near border of the property was a long wooden sign recently painted to read PIZZERIA (in red) BIRRERIA (in yellow), both words above the more stylized lettering *La Torretta* (in brown). The sign was meant to be visible from the main road to Visgnola, but the intervening trees made that no better than a slim hope. The front yard was overrun with low, unkept shrubs among which were a low stone table, a few stone benches and chairs, and some random rocks and spots of bare earth. Over it all loomed a giant tree, the trunk and branches of which were host to thick layers of heavy ivy vines. Once visible, the house itself was a minor monstrosity. It was two stories in construction with a square turret-like third floor jutting up from one corner. Originally built in the eighteenth-century Palladian style, its turret, a second-story solarium, and various wings and extensions toward the back had badly disfigured whatever symmetry it may have once possessed. Heavy exterior moldings around the first-floor windows were of elaborately handworked plaster. But the arched porch entryway holding a small second-floor balcony was of simpler design. Like others of its type in northern Italy, its stone structure was plaster coated. But its ocher surface was badly worn, leaving streaks and patches of gray to show through like elbows in an old sweater. All the front windows on both floors were either shuttered over or heavily covered from the inside. The house could well have been deserted, except for the fresh sign on the road.

Connaughton thought he felt Ekaterina shudder as he knocked on the front door. The hollow thuds seemed to reverberate throughout the length and breadth of endless rooms and hallway with no apparent results. He knocked again, and yet a third time. Connaughton looked at his watch and took Ekaterina by the arm. Darkness was descending fast and they had to have accommodations very soon—at least for this night. They started to turn when the heavy door cracked open. The light was too dim to see the figure inside, but the thin accented voice said, "Yes?"

They turned back suddenly and Connaughton cleared his throat. "Yes, ah, we were trying to find the owner of this property."

The invisible figure again said, "Yes?"

"Ah, we were told at the nearby restaurant that rooms might be available here," Connaughton went on uncertainly. He felt compelled to explain. "We are touring in the area and were looking for private accommodations. We are sorry if we disturbed you. Perhaps we were misinformed."

"No, you were not misinformed," the voice said. "But it is constantly amazing how word gets around." The door swung slowly inward and the voice said, "You may come in."

Ekaterina clung tightly to his arm as Connaughton entered first. The only visible lights were near the rear of the rambling structure. The heavy door swung shut behind them with the gravity of a bank vault closing and they found themselves in almost total darkness. There was shuffling in the background and suddenly a match flared and just as suddenly an antique brass candelabra rose up, its three candles ablaze.

They discovered themselves to be in a surprisingly elegant living room. All the furnishings were old but of evident and distinctive quality. Thick drapery fell from high ceiling to floor. Heavy old furniture made by skilled artisans filled the room. But most surprising was their host, now holding the glittering candelabra. He was thin in the manner of the aged who have chosen to use up body weight rather than eat. Of medium height, he had wispy white hair and parchmentlike skin paled almost to translucence by the absence of sunlight. He wore a dark brown monkish robe that touched the floor, belted about his frail frame with braided rope material, with a hood lying across the back.

"How do you do?" he said. "Sit down, please, and let us introduce ourselves."

Connaughton thought quickly. "We are Americans. My name is John Frank and this is my wife, Katherine. As I said a moment ago, we are looking for rooms, for a short while . . . in a quiet place."

"This is a quiet place," the wizened old man said. "How long do you intend to stay in Bellagio?"

"Probably no longer than two weeks," Connaughton replied. "But depending on the rental fee, we might stay longer."

The man stood up. "Normally, in the rare instances when I rent rooms, I consider no less than a month. I do not wish to consider transient occupants—if you understand. Please come see the rooms." He started toward the large stairway leading up from the central hallway. "My name is Tolstoi.

Most people in this area simply call me father. They think I am a priest.''

The old man slowly ascended the stairs, stopping at the landing for breath. At the second landing he explained that the rooms in the front were closed. The suite of rooms for rent was in the back. He preceded them, lighting long tapered new candles as he went. They were shown into three large rooms—a living room, a sitting room-study, and a bedroom with bath. All were furnished as below—heavy, elegant, hand-crafted nineteenth-century furnishings. As the old man shuffled about lighting more candles, Ekaterina squeezed Connaughton's arm and smiled. He raised his eyebrows inquiringly and she nodded her approval. Connaughton followed the ancient monk slowly down the stairs, leaving her to acquaint herself with the new surroundings. Downstairs, Connaughton told the old man they would very much like to stay there and readily agreed to the weekly rate in lire. His proposal to pay for two weeks on Monday when he could change his money was accepted. Connaughton went back outside and down the road, picked up the Opel, and drove it behind the house where the old man told him to park. He then carried his duffel bag and Ekaterina's shopping bags up the back stairs to their rooms. As he set them down, she smiled and embraced him, her head on his shoulder. "What a lovely place to hide from the world. You have even managed to find our own Russian priest."

The dinner wine and stress of escape combined, as on the previous night, to exhaust them both. Connaughton closed the door to their suite of rooms and they soon were together in the stately four-posted, canopied bed. This time, however, neither was satisfied with tension-troubled sleep. They embraced and kissed hungrily, as if each wished to be lost in the other. They were awkward, unaccustomed to being with someone else. Soon, Ekaterina let Connaughton know she wanted him completely, a need he shared and longed to fulfill. Their lovemaking was urgent and quick, then, later, longer and with more deliberate passion. Finally, holding each other tightly, they fell into a deep sleep.

Much later Connaughton felt her kiss and her touch and stirred himself awake. He could see her face, but the room was dark. She slipped, naked, from the bed and parted the heavy folds of the drapes. Light beamed into the dark room and he rubbed his eyes. He looked at his watch, realizing it was ten o'clock. She laughed at his confusion and got back in beside him.

"Apparently, you are both confused and... depleted?... from being in bed with a woman," she teased.

Connaughton growled in her ear, "You are not just 'a woman'—and I am not 'depleted.'" She began to say "So I can tell" when they found themselves again in the grasp of desperate passion. Then Connaughton confessed to being depleted.

Later they went into Bellagio and had croissants and coffee at a café. As tourists began to accumulate from the ferryboats busily plying Lake Como in the spring sunlight, they decided to get out of sight. But first Connaughton bought all the available newspapers. The only reports from Geneva featured the rapidly concluding negotiations and a cautious statement from *Pravda* that an early signing of the treaty was desirable if remaining obstacles could be overcome. Similar sentiments emanated from the Lawkard administration in Washington. There was no indication of missing diplomats.

Their landlord had welcomed them to use the kitchen facilities and at Ekaterina's suggestion they brought food back to prepare for their meals. The old ascetic declined to join them at their simple dinner. But afterward he materialized in the dining room without a sound and gratefully accepted their offer of a glass of wine.

In the formal living room he told them of his life. He had traveled to Paris in 1919 with his family, part of a large White Russian community voluntarily exiled during the

Bolshevik Revolution. He had been nearing ordination into the Russian Orthodox priesthood when the revolution interrupted his studies and tore his life asunder. After almost a decade in Paris, his wealthy parents had died and with a considerable inheritance he had migrated with other White Russians to Italy. He had lived in the house where they then were for almost fifty years—an exile, a recluse, a mysterious figure with few friends.

The pizzeria? The notion of his grandnephew—the son of his brother's son. A young man adrift in Europe, he had been rescued from a drug-spiced aimless existence by the old man's offer, with his remaining funds, to start a small restaurant and disco in the basement of the old estate. The young man had gotten as far as erecting the sign, then ridden off on his motorcycle with his friends to southern Italy for the remainder of April before returning to start up his business.

Presently, the old man held up his wineglass and bade them a happy Western Easter. Connaughton, shocked, realized he had forgotten the date, the third of April. He knew sometime in the next few days he would have to make contact with Rafferty to assure him all was well and to ask him to look after Francesca through whatever might come.

Connaughton asked, "Is Tolstoi actually your family name?"

"Indeed," the old man said. "My family is distantly related to the great writer. His later life in part inspired me toward the religious vocation."

Then looking directly at the couple with his pale blue eyes, he asked, "Is Frank your real family name?"

Connaughton started to speak, then hesitated. "No…it's not," he admitted.

"And you, madame"—he looked at Ekaterina—"are not American. You are a compatriot, a fellow Russian. Where, may I ask, are you from?"

"Leningrad," she said.

"You still live there and have your family there," he said. It was more a declaration than a question.

She quietly answered, "Yes."

"I know nothing of politics, nor do I care any longer. But I know you are both running away," he stated with certainty.

Connaughton said, "We'll cause you no trouble, father. Before those seeking us arrive, we'll be gone."

The old man asked, "And how long will that be?"

"I don't know," Connaughton replied. "It won't be long."

"I do not believe you are people who have stolen secrets or betrayed your countries." He smiled benignly. "It must have been difficult for an American and a Russian to offend two political systems at the same time."

"It wasn't hard at all, father," Ekaterina responded. "We tried to stop the nuclear weapons."

Father Tolstoi was silent for a time as the house became dark once again. After several minutes he rose, struck one of his large wooden matches, and began to light the candles to dispel the gloom. The light flickered on the drapery folds, the damask furniture covers, and antique tapestries. "It seems if that is all you have done, then only those who treasure these weapons could be against you."

Connaughton said, "That's the simple explanation. Unfortunately, it's somewhat more complicated."

"What will happen to you if you are caught?" asked the old man. "Will you be shot?"

Ekaterina smiled sadly. "We will be caught sometime... probably soon. We hope not before some good comes of our efforts. Needless to say, the Americans will be kinder than our government."

The elderly man shook his head. "It is not my government, young madame." Then, "Will some good come of your efforts?"

Connaughton said, "If we can remain in hiding long enough, there's a chance our countries may sign an agreement to achieve what we've been seeking—what brought us together.''

Father Tolstoi again was silent for a time. Then with difficulty he got to his feet. "This is Easter Sunday in the West. Would you be offended if I offered a blessing for you both?''

Connaughton took Ekaterina's hand and they stepped forward to face the old man. He placed his left hand on their clasped hands, raised his right arm, and silently beseeched heaven with eyes closed and face lifted. He made the sign of the cross according to the Russian Church as his thin voice intoned, "In the name of the Father, the Son, and the Holy Ghost. Amen." His bony fingers gripped their hands and then he said, "Bless you both. Good night.''

59

THE WORLD OUTSIDE BELLAGIO—the public world that Connaughton and Ekaterina had so recently abandoned—was rushing pell-mell in two different directions. Reserve call-ups continued in NATO while armored battalions rolled westward from the Warsaw Pact nations. Fleets of both sides steamed to battle stations. Strategic submarines, missiles, and bomber squadrons flashed to higher alert status. News media around the world carried increasingly alarmed and alarming stories throughout the Easter weekend about the preparations of Goliath and Colossus for a seemingly inevitable and terrifying confrontation.

Yet on Monday, the fourth of April, *The New York Times* led with a story by Andrea Cass, datelined Geneva, predicting—based on "highly placed, reliable administration sources"—that a far-reaching nuclear arms control treaty had been consummated and would be signed within a matter of days. No sooner reported than done. At noon that day, in joint statements released in Washington and Moscow, the governments of the United States and USSR announced that the basic terms of a treaty had been agreed to and, after completion of minor technical functions, the treaty would be officially signed within days.

Simultaneously, Foreign Minister Pyotr Zoshchenko left Moscow for a direct flight to Washington to confer with Secretary of State Emerson Norton on final arrangements for a summit in Geneva. The lead editorial in *Pravda* released before his landing in the United States made it clear General Secretary Kamenev would attend a ceremonial summit only on the condition agreement had also been reached to stand down the massive military exercises on both sides scheduled for the following week. A helpless world tensely waited to see how the crisis would unfold.

AS DRAMATIC AS EVENTS WERE on the apron of the world's stage, they were even more dramatic behind the curtain. In the preceding seventy-two hours, the security forces of the major powers had swung into frantic activity. The KGB had flooded Europe with agents lashed to a frenzy by their superiors in their search for Ekaterina Davydova. For a short time the previous Friday evening her colleagues translating drafts of documents at the U.S. Mission assumed she had become ill and returned to the Soviet Mission. When, later in the evening, they returned to the compound, they discovered their error. Makarov was notified, then Malenkov and Metrinko, and the KGB began to extend its long powerful arm. Connaughton's apartment building was staked out but no movement was seen. Hotels and restaurants were systematically checked with no results. And, finally, in the early hours of Saturday morning, Soviet agents discreetly notified customs and border officials of neighboring countries to be alert for a missing diplomatic official identified by written description and photograph as Ekaterina Antonovna Davydova.

Saturday morning, after Frank Connaughton failed to appear at the mission for his meeting with the CIA, calls placed to his apartment met with no response. By noon, agents were sifting through the contents of his apartment, where they found assorted maps and, under blankets in his closet, a pad with calculations of travel times and distances into France. Despite Arkwright's assurances that Connaughton would not have taken unauthorized leave of his duties, the Director of the CIA, under pressure from the Vice-President and Secretary of Defense, cabled all stations in Europe to undertake an urgent full-scale search for Frank Connaughton. Interpol and intelligence services of all allied countries were asked for assistance. Connaughton's picture and physical description were circulated throughout the intelligence and security networks.

As members and staff of the arms control delegation were being interviewed in connection with the search on Monday morning, April 4, one of the junior interpreters recalled the curiosity of the missing Soviet interpreter Davydova the previous Friday evening at the U.S. Mission. The head of the CIA detail from Washington repeated that to Arkwright and asked for his thoughts. Arkwright had been on the secure phone to Emerson Norton repeatedly over the weekend, discussing the situation largely in euphemisms. They agreed the Connaughton-Davydova contacts should be minimized. Accordingly Arkwright recalled seeing the two of them talking to each other once or twice during social events and did not rule out the possibility of additional contacts beyond that. But he doubted seriously if Connaughton's disappearance had anything to do with the Russian woman. Certainly it was beyond possibility, he argued with conviction, that anything romantic was involved.

IN MOSCOW, on the night of the fourth, Vladimir Zhdanov finally got the audience with the General Secretary he had been seeking since Saturday. Kamenev could not stall him any longer.

"Comrade General Secretary," Zhdanov said, fixing him with a stare, "no treaty must be signed so long as this woman is not in custody and the possibility of high treason against the state is alive."

Kamenev sighed, then put an edge to his words. "Vladimir, there is no evidence of treason, except your suspicion. Our Foreign Minister does not support your case at all. And the treaty stands or falls on its own merits. It either is or is not in our nation's interest. And what I think matters less than the fact that a majority of the Politburo, our Minister of Defense, and a majority of our General Staff—our most

senior military commanders—think it is in our interest.
Therefore, the woman has nothing to do with it.''

''She has everything to do with it, and everyone in the
Kremlin knows it,'' hissed Zhdanov. ''She sold us out to the
American government.''

The burly Soviet leader heaved himself painfully to his
feet. ''Out of here, Zhdanov!'' he roared. ''That treaty is
going to be signed next Sunday in Geneva—unless you find
that woman and *prove* she's a traitor!''

THE FOLLOWING MORNING in Washington, President Lawkard attended a meeting of his National Security Council.
Emerson Norton reported that Foreign Minister Zoshchenko would be arriving at the State Department that noon
to discuss final arrangements for signing the treaty. He
urged, and the President readily agreed, that the sooner it
was signed the better, and the following Sunday in Geneva
would be the target date. Harold Burgoon heatedly pro-
tested.

''Mr. President,'' he said, ''we have an international
search under way for a key member of our negotiating delegation, who may or may not be with a member of the Soviet delegation, with whom he may or may not have
betrayed his country. I hardly think this is the time for a
summit meeting to sign a treaty that may have been produced by treachery.''

Norton snapped, ''Treachery? What treachery? If Frank
Connaughton is guilty of treachery, then I suppose I am as
well...and for that matter everyone who has negotiated this
agreement. What do you intend to do, Harold, hang us
all?''

Lawkard intervened. ''That's enough, gentlemen. I'm
tired of this bickering between you two. Phil, where is this
Connaughton?''

Warrenton spread his palms. ''Somewhere in Europe. An
hour ago we got a cable from our Rome station. An Italian
border guard remembers seeing someone fitting Con-

naughton's description crossing the border at the Simplon Pass over the weekend, possibly last Friday night. We're spreading people all over Italy and beyond on the chance he was the one."

"Was he traveling alone?" Burgoon sneered.

Warrenton sighed. "This person apparently was not. The guard remembers a woman with him."

Burgoon threw his hands up triumphantly.

"She had an American diplomatic passport," Warrenton added.

"Well there you are," Lawkard said. "He needed some time off after the negotiations and"—winking at the others—"decided to slip off with some embassy sweetie."

"Mr. President, no 'sweeties' are missing," Warrenton reported. "We checked. On the other hand, it could have been an employee from one of our other embassies down for a holiday." He made a note. "We'll check that right away."

Lawkard pounded the table. "Goddammit! What do 'sweeties' have to do with this treaty anyway? I say we are going through with this—unless, Harold, you or somebody else around here can tell me why not. And why not means finding this Connaughton guy and proving he's a traitor. Otherwise, Em, go forward with Zoshchenko and set up the ceremonies for this weekend. I'll leave on Friday for Geneva." And as the meeting broke up, Lawkard said to Norton, "Tell Zoshchenko I agree to Kamenev's condition that we postpone our NATO exercises—presuming he will also postpone his—*if* we sign this treaty."

LATER THAT DAY in Geneva, Eileen Malmstrom had recovered sufficiently from her appendectomy to ask that her friends look after her apartment and car. When the car was discovered to be missing from the parking lot at her apartment building, its theft was reported to Swiss police. Word also circulated throughout the delegation that someone had stolen poor Eileen's car, and it didn't take long for the head of the CIA task force to realize that it was Connaughton's mode of transportation. The car's description and plate numbers were rushed to Swiss, French, and Italian security forces.

AT THE SAME TIME Emerson Norton and Pyotr Zoshchenko were meeting at the State Department in Washington, it was almost 8 P.M. in Bellagio. Connaughton had driven the Opel into the village for food for dinner and his daily collection of newspapers. As he was walking down the narrow, winding street from the grocery store into the square, he saw two *carabinieri* systematically checking the license plates on the double row of cars. He waited until they had walked slowly to the end of the long row of cars, then quickly walked to the Opel parked at the near end, threw in the packages, and drove slowly around the other side of the square and more rapidly up the winding roads to nearby Visgnola. When he arrived at Father Tolstoi's run-down pizzeria and sanctuary, he cautiously drove into the small yard behind and placed the car in such a way that it could not be seen from the road.

Once inside he said nothing to Ekaterina. She began to prepare the food for dinner as he skimmed through several day-old foreign papers. The *International Herald-Tribune* had a front-page story, as did the other papers, that preliminary agreement had been reached on an arms control treaty between the United States and USSR and there was some prospect for an early summit to sign the treaty—perhaps as early as the coming weekend. Ekaterina smiled as Connaughton read her the story. Later she translated similar stories from the Rome papers and the *Zürcher Zeitung*.

After a simple dinner, Father Tolstoi asked them if they cared to join him in the front sitting room. "Do either of you regret your actions?" he asked.

Connaughton looked at Ekaterina seated next to him, then replied, "Given a choice, I don't believe either of us would have fought the wishes of elements of our own governments."

"Did you have, then, no choice?" the old man asked.

"It wasn't that simple," Ekaterina said. "Efforts—strong efforts—were under way both in Russia and America during recent months to sabotage any nuclear weapons treaty and to seek power through confrontation and force. The buildup of nuclear weapons has gone on for almost forty years. There are those on both sides who want immediate resolution—some through treaties and some through what the Americans call a showdown."

Father Tolstoi said, "But those are people in authority—people who have a claim of legitimacy to govern, to rule. It is a long-held principle of the philosophers that man is bound to obey legitimate authority...or in the alternative to remove himself from its claim."

"And that is what you did almost seventy years ago," Ekaterina said. "You removed yourself from Bolshevik authority. But in more recent years not all of us have had that chance. What are we to do if we love our country but cannot accept policies which we feel doom those we love?"

The old man smiled. "Ah, you see," he said, speaking to Connaughton, "scratch a Russian and you find a revolutionary. Underneath, we are all revolutionaries."

"But isn't that what nuclear weapons have done?" Connaughton asked. "If otherwise sane governments persist in practices that are potentially insane, don't they alienate concerned people...don't they make them revolutionaries?"

"Jesus did not come to bring a revolution to political systems," Tolstoi said. "He came to bring a revolution to the human heart. That was the good news. He preached the one profound truth of the ages...change a man's heart and you change his actions. Peace does not lie in perfecting the political system—it lies in changing the attitudes and beliefs of those who live in it."

"It was our own changed attitudes," Connaughton responded, "our love for our children and our genuine love for our countries, that caused us to do what we have done.

If we have defied authority—or at least those authorities who are now looking for us—does that make us disloyal? Does that make us traitors?''

"Loyalty to one's country and its government, obedience to legitimate authority, even the definition of betrayal are political and legal notions," Tolstoi said. "Only the state can decide matters of that sort. But we who are believers know that there is another judge—a higher judge. He is the final judge of right and wrong. He can judge truly because he knows the human heart. He knows why we do what we do. In his judgment our faith must rest." The old man slowly got to his feet and filled their empty wineglasses. "There are some lines of Tennyson's which sustain me:

"Our little systems have their day;
They have their day and cease to be:
They are but broken lights of Thee,
And Thou, O Lord, art more than they."

"BUT, FATHER, you speak of final judgment," Connaughton said. "Soon the two of us will be judged here on earth, and probably pretty harshly. Are there not situations where political authority has power but not legitimacy? Can there not be a situation where the true patriot resists authority which has eroded its own legitimacy? We Americans, like you Russians, are the product of revolution. My country honors those two hundred years ago who defied authority which had become oppressive. Many Americans would welcome a time when Russians and others rose up against their own governments."

The old man smiled again. "It is always easier to preach revolution for someone else—for those in foreign lands—rather than to look at one's own shortcomings."

Ekaterina said, "So you believe we must suffer whatever judgment is rendered against us when they come to take us?

Our own motives are not material . . . the reasons why we cooperated are not important?''

"Of course, they are important," Father Tolstoi replied. "I am sure, even in the Soviet Union, if you were genuinely acting on behalf of the greater good—not just selfish purposes—you will have some political support. Clearly, you could not have brought about the seeming miracle of this treaty if it were not seen by some powerful people on both sides to be in their interests. I can only pray, for your sakes and the sake of the world, that your sacrifice will not be forgotten when judgment is rendered on your actions." In a distant recess of the house, a solemn old clock began to chime. Tolstoi again stood up slowly. "I am afraid given my age and condition, praying is all I can do for you now."

He started down the hallway to his room in the back of the house. "Patriotism means to love and defend one's country. You have both surely done that."

THE FOLLOWING AFTERNOON *carabinieri* from Bellagio routinely checked at the local real estate office in response to a nationwide request sent from state security officers in Rome. Following the automobile alert the previous day, they had been asked to determine whether a couple fitting Connaughton's and Ekaterina's descriptions had sought lodging locally. A check of hotels and tourist rooming houses revealed nothing. But at the real estate office, the proprietor looked at the picture and immediately recalled such a man asking about apartments or houses for rent on a short-term basis. After some thought he placed the contact during the previous weekend—undoubtedly Saturday.

The following morning three CIA agents flew to Milan and were driven to Bellagio. They were joined by two more agents from the Rome station and Italian intelligence officials. By that afternoon they were meeting in the Municipio a few blocks from the village square. The chief of the local *carabinieri* agreed to distribute Connaughton's photograph to all of his officers at the evening and morning musters and, further, to instruct them not to make an arrest without notifying the CIA agents who had taken up residence in their headquarters in the Municipio.

The KGB was not far behind. Connaughton's absence from the concluding negotiations had been noted by the Soviet officials and it required little logic to conclude Ekaterina Davydova was probably with him. Since she was not traveling on her own passport and had probably affected some disguise, the KGB agents' task was more complicated than that of their American counterparts. So, aside from routine kinds of investigative procedures, they did the simplest thing they could think of—they piggybacked. The new CIA types from Washington were easily identified in Geneva by sharp Russian eyes and were visible coming and going from the U.S. Mission and Connaughton's place. Their colleagues in the major stations, including Rome, were also well known. The KGB merely tailed them. And it was easy, for the CIA agents made no attempt to conceal their movements.

Within forty-eight hours of the concentration of the CIA search on the Lake Como area, a team of KGB investigators arrived in Bellagio. Their appetites were whetted by their discovery of a ferryboat operator from Verbania who remembered a striking woman much like Ekaterina Davydova crossing Lake Maggiore on his boat the previous Saturday morning. Inexorably the net drew tighter.

FOR THEIR PART Connaughton and Ekaterina knew the clock was ticking. They limited their outdoor exposure to walks in the countryside around Visgnola in the late afternoon or early evening. Connaughton each day hired a small boy from the house across the road from Father Tolstoi's to ride his bicycle to the local grocery for food supplies. For an additional fee, the boy would also ride into Bellagio and pick up the newspapers each day. On Thursday the papers were full of stories about the impending summit in Geneva the following weekend. President Lawkard was scheduled to arrive on Friday night to take up residence in the elegant Maison de Saussure outside Geneva. And General Secretary Kamenev would follow the next day and locate himself in the Soviet Mission compound. Connaughton and Ekaterina embraced that evening and made another mark on their April calendar.

On Friday, Connaughton knew he had to take one last chance. He negotiated a loan of the bicycle from the boy across the road and late in the afternoon rode down the long hill and around the winding roads and streets to the Villa Serbelloni, the grand hotel on the point of the peninsula at the far edge of Bellagio. Leaving the bicycle on the edge of the great estate grounds, he walked into the hotel lobby, and placed a call with the desk clerk to Harry Rafferty's office in Washington.

After fifteen tense minutes, and several broken conversations with the desk clerk, Connaughton learned that Rafferty had left his office some time before to catch a plane at Dulles Airport for his home in Montana. Connaughton insisted that the harried clerk penetrate the intricacies of the overseas telephone system and have Rafferty paged at Dulles. Another twenty minutes went by while Connaughton sat in a corner of the lobby, his face covered by the raised *International Herald-Tribune*. Triumphantly, the exhausted desk clerk summoned him. "Mr. Frank, your call is complete."

"Harry? It's Frank."

"Frank, where in the hell are you?" Rafferty's booming voice seemed peculiarly thin. "Are you all right?"

"I'm all right, Harry. Listen, I have to talk fast. I want you to do something for me. Call Francesca. Tell her I'm all right and that I'll call her just as soon as I can. Tell her not to worry if she sees my name in the paper. I'm OK and everything will work out fine."

Rafferty shouted into the phone in the private lounge behind the United ticket counter at Dulles, "What the hell is going on, Frank? What have you done?"

"Nothing bad, Harry. What have you heard?"

"Only rumors. My friend out at the Agency told me yesterday that you're in a shitload of trouble and if I had any way of contacting you I ought to tell you to come back. What the hell is he talking about? Why are they after you?"

"Harry, believe me, I haven't done anything wrong. But the Agency and some other security people are after me. I took off from Geneva. Burgoon and the others have convinced the Agency I'm a traitor. They're desperate to stop the treaty."

"Hell, Frank, even I know that. It's all over the papers today that if Lawkard signs the treaty, Burgoon and maybe some others are going to resign. Apparently Burgoon thinks that's the only way he can keep his hand in with the rightwingers for the election next November. But all hell is breaking loose here." The line crackled and faded. Then Connaughton heard, ". . . when they find you? What will they do?"

"They'll get me in front of some cameras as fast as they can and claim I'm a traitor and was instrumental in collaborating with the Russians to rig a treaty against my own country. But we're down to the homestretch. It has to be dramatic. They'll demand that the treaty not be signed, at least until there's some kind of full-scale investigation."

"Oh God, Frank," Rafferty groaned. "Look, I'm going to cancel this flight and go to work on this here. Just stay out of sight until Sunday, and then the whole ballgame changes. Can you do that?"

"I don't know, Harry. I have a feeling they're getting close. Listen, I can take care of myself. But I'm worried about Frankie if this gets in the papers. If you and Bonnie could look after her for the next few days—have her stay with you—it would take a great load off my mind. Can you do that?"

"Of course, Frank, don't worry about it. It's done. But I'm also going to work on your case behind the scenes—

build some political backfires. I think you're going to need them."

The connection faded again and Connaughton was increasingly nervous because of the time he had been in the hotel and the possibility the lines were being checked. He said, "Thanks, Harry, thanks a lot. See you soon. Tell Francesca I love her." Then he hung up. He left the hotel quickly, retrieved the bicycle, and followed the back roads to Visgnola as fast as he could.

Fifteen minutes after Connaughton left the Villa Serbelloni, a plain sedan carrying three CIA agents and two *carabinieri* pulled rapidly into the long winding drive. Within minutes they had all the details of the call from the frightened desk clerk. Now they knew they were closing in on the fugitives.

THE FOLLOWING DAY, Saturday, the ninth of April, two Italian-speaking KGB officers pulled into the Bellavista Ristorante in Visgnola. They were hungry and tired after three days of combing the countryside in ever-expanding concentric circles, showing local people Ekaterina Davydova's picture and asking about her whereabouts. Before reporting in on another unsuccessful day, they ordered a full meal and the local wine. After their pleasant meal in the late-afternoon sun, the proprietor, Enrico, came to claim their money. Almost as an afterthought one of the men pulled out the now-wrinkled photograph. Enrico studied it, then gestured toward the old house up the road with the pizzeria sign in the yard.

By nightfall, a half-dozen KGB men had taken up positions near the house. They would wait for instructions. They would not wait long.

——— 60 ———

"ON A BRILLIANT, SUNLIT AFTERNOON in Geneva, President of the United States William A. Lawkard and Soviet General Secretary Nikolai Kamenev formally signed a far-reaching nuclear arms control treaty described by Mr. Lawkard as 'the most comprehensive effort to control the spread of nuclear weapons since the dawn of the arms race.'" So read the first paragraph of the story filed by Andrea Cass with *The New York Times* on Sunday, April 10, 1988.

Together with a small army of journalists she had just returned to her office having witnessed the elaborate diplomatic ceremony on the lakeside lawn of the Château de Bellerive outside Geneva. The previous two days had been exhausting for her and her fellow journalists. The dramatic conclusion of the treaty, the rapid-fire preparation for the summit, the tremendous upsurge in public acclaim around the world for the successful conclusion of negotiations so recently at the brink of failure, all combined to saturate her sensibilities.

But she did have a nagging sense that all was not as it seemed. There was the still-unprinted story from Quainton that the back-channel negotiations were heavily influenced by unusual and perhaps unauthorized contacts between the delegations. There was Frank Connaughton's absence, noticed by no one but her in the chaos of occurrences. But she attributed it to a decision by the Secretary of State to remove the possibly controversial character from the scene. Connaughton had most probably been ordered home. She would pursue that as a possible sidebar story in the next week or two when the diplomatic dust settled.

In her second paragraph she wrote: "Among other notable achievements represented by the new treaty was a personal agreement between the heads of the two superpowers to postpone indefinitely the long-scheduled military exercises planned for the remainder of April. Had the treaty not been signed, plans called for massive displays of hardware and force projection both by NATO nations as well as the Warsaw Pact. Knowledgeable observers believed these exercises, involving strategic as well as conventional forces, could have led to a serious confrontation in Europe and perhaps at sea. Forces deployed and orders issued in connection with the competing exercises have been withdrawn in acknowledgment of the new government and a renewed spirit of East-West cooperation."

Cass's story led the *Times* on Monday and accompanying coverage of the events in Geneva dominated the news in the United States and elsewhere. The *Times* did carry a long piece about the impact of the treaty on American politics and the national election in the fall. The story began by emphasizing the conflict on arms control with the Lawkard administration, and particularly the opposition of Vice-President Burgoon to the negotiation of the treaty and the strong identification he had developed with the Blue Thunder military maneuvers now shelved. The effect of the story was to question Burgoon's chances to achieve the nomination of his party in light of this serious breach with his own president.

THE FOLLOWING WEDNESDAY, April 13, Vice-President Harold Burgoon called a press conference and announced his resignation. He heavily criticized the treaty, saying that it was not in the best interests of the United States and that he felt obligated to campaign strongly against its ratification by the United States Senate later in the spring. He was joined by Secretary of Defense Joseph Sternberg, who stated flatly that cancellation of the Blue Thunder exercises jeopardized American security. Sternberg announced that he would serve full-time as the chairman of the newly formed Burgoon for President Committee. In response, the White House press secretary strongly questioned Harold Burgoon's commitment to peace and emphasized the President's renewed belief that the military confrontation favored by the dissident hawks could lead to war and devastation.

ACROSS THE WORLD, Nikolai Kamenev called his old friend and protégé Georgi Kozlovsky to his suite of rooms in the Kremlin. He said that, though the world would never know it, Kozlovsky was the true hero of the Red Star affair and that his resistance to the military confrontation had been instrumental in changing the chemistry of the Politburo and enabling Kamenev to support a protreaty policy. He then said he would soon announce his retirement, to take effect following the Party congress in the spring. He asked Kozlovsky's help in organizing support for Pyotr Zoshchenko to succeed him. "It's not the best we can do, Georgi," the old man rumbled, "but it's the price we had to pay to get this treaty and prevent Zhdanov and his crowd from getting us into war."

VLADIMIR ZHDANOV HIMSELF was far from defeated. Within a week of the signing of the treaty he was meeting at Lev Malenkov's dacha outside Gorki with Malenkov and Vladimir Ulyanov. They discussed possible candidates for Kamenev's job when he stepped down and agreed on the need to head off Zoshchenko's candidacy by all possible means. Zhdanov's mood was curiously restrained given the virulence of his opposition to the treaty and frantic efforts to promote the Red Star exercises. As the discussion broke up late in the evening, Malenkov, the host, escorted the most senior guest to the door after the others had left. "Tell me,

Vlad, why are you so calm after the terrible setback we have just endured?'' The eyes set deep in the long narrow skull stared back with a fire close to hatred and the ominous hollow voice intoned, "I am not through. I do not give up. I will not rest. Even if that fool Zoshchenko succeeds Kamenev, there will be a day. The Communist revolution burns on in the hearts of a few of us. Our day will come...soon...and when it does, these craven hedonists and détente worshipers will be the first to be dealt with.'' He turned and started for the door. In the threshold he said, "Let me talk to her.'' And then he was on his way slowly through the thawing snow to his car.

61

THE DAY OF THE TREATY-SIGNING ceremonies in Geneva, Connaughton and Ekaterina had climbed to the third-floor tower of Father Tolstoi's sanctuary. He showed them the stairway, saying that it had been months since his grand-nephew had gone up there and years since he himself had used the room. That Sunday morning the sun had climbed well into the sky and shone brightly off the lake spread out to their right and their left. There was a fine morning mist clinging to the far shores of the lake, hiding the villas and houses that dotted the shoreline as far as they could see. Out of the haze climbed the craggy hills, creviced and eroded, that bordered the bright blue water. Immediately below them they saw the village of Bellagio slowly coming awake in the spring daylight. The giant tree in the yard before them obscured certain parts of the view but also framed a variety of gorgeous scenes spread out in all directions.

Connaughton wished they could walk out of their prison, almost tangibly becoming the center of a giant search even as they stood there. With his arm around Ekaterina's waist, he talked about strolling through the village again, lunching at the grand hotel, taking the afternoon ferry back and forth across the gleaming lake and sipping wine. She closed her eyes and leaned her head against his shoulder as he talked, imagining the scenes.

Then she asked, "When will they find us, Frank?"

He kissed her hair and said, "Tomorrow, or soon there-after."

"What will they do to you?" she murmured. She had asked the question repeatedly in the past few days, usually as they lay in bed at night.

"Don't worry about it," he said again. "I'll be all right. I'll be raising so much of a fuss at the State Department to insist on fair treatment for you that they'll want to get me out of their hair, instead of the other way around."

"When will you see Francesca?" she asked.

"Soon," he said. "As soon as I get back. And when will you see your sons?"

"I don't know. I really don't know how I will be treated. Throughout the past few days they will have had my family under house arrest. They will be concerned about me. If those who supported this treaty solidify their positions in the Politburo—and if I am not totally forgotten—someone will see that the treatment is not too severe."

Connaughton said by way of reassurance, "Of course they won't forget you. There wouldn't have been a treaty without you. The government signed the treaty. There's no way they would permit the others to do anything to you." He seriously doubted that his words were true. His darkest fears were that she would be forgotten by the winners and severely punished by the losers. Or the winners would give her to the losers as a sacrificial lamb. Who would care about her in the high-level politics that followed? She would be fair game for those bent on revenge. They would start with her and work upward. Connaughton was deeply concerned.

"Ekaterina, I can assure you your name will be brought up daily in communications between my government and yours. I'll insist that Ambassador Arkwright and Secretary Norton demand a constant report on your situation. Believe me, Zoshchenko is going to get tired of hearing from the United States government about you." What concerned him most was the first few days. If the KGB found them first, it would have total control of her from Bellagio to Geneva and back to Moscow. And no telling how long he would be sitting under CIA and FBI interrogation before he could even talk to Arkwright or Norton. But all he could do under the present circumstances was seek to bolster her spirits.

He kissed her again and said, "I'm going to rent the bicycle again and go pick up the papers. They must have signed the treaty today. There should be something out about it by now. I'll only be gone about thirty minutes. When I get back, we'll go for a long walk in the hills...away from the people."

She knew it would probably be their last time together, the last opportunity to feel the breeze, to hear the music of the outdoors, the last night to sleep together. She turned and held him as tightly as she could, trembling and trying not to cry. "Oh, Frank, do hurry back—and be careful." As he started to walk down the steps she kissed him. "I have two things to tell you," she said. "One I will tell you now—and the other I will tell you when we walk outdoors. It will take longer."

He raised an eyebrow. "What do you have to tell me now?"

"I love you."

On the edge of Bellagio was a small shop with souvenirs and items of clothing. The previous Sunday Connaughton had bought newspapers there. He took the bicycle down the hill to the shop and purchased four papers. He paused outside in the warm sun to read the headlines. They all featured the ceremonial summit in Geneva that day to mark the signing of the treaty. Connaughton smiled to himself. Ekaterina would be happy. He had to get back to tell her.

"Frank Connaughton?"

He turned, dreading what he knew he would find. There were two of them, Americans, in suits and ties.

"I will be glad to show you identification if you wish. I'm Wallace Moore with the Agency and this is Tom Mancuso of our Rome station. We've been looking for you."

Connaughton looked up and far away. He drew a deep breath and thought about running. Then he knew it was useless. Better our guys got to us first, he thought. They'll treat her better on our way back to Geneva than the other side would have. As they walked to the waiting car, he saw a large graceful bird soaring higher and higher in the clear skies over the lake.

They put the bicycle in the trunk and Connaughton got into the backseat with one of the agents. He showed them the way up through the low hills to Visgnola.

When they reached the corner where the Bellavista Ristorante sat, they turned onto the road up to Father Tolstoi's house. Out of the drive of the house came three cars, one of them of foreign make. The cars approached the three Americans at increasing speed and raced past them onto the street leading toward the road away from Bellagio and southward toward Milan.

Connaughton tore at the locked car door and yelled *"Noooooo!"* in a wrenching wail. Struggling in the backseat of the second car in an effort to reach him was a desperate Ekaterina Davydova.

epilogue

JULY 4, 1988
INDEPENDENCE DAY

THE SMALL FIGURE on the horizon gradually gained stature and definition even against the grandeur of the landscape. The rider was a half mile or more away, but given the direction of approach and the increasing size of the figure it could only be one person.

Connaughton sat his tall chestnut horse and waited, right leg thrown around the pommel and arms crossed on his knee. Rafferty was now at a full gallop, but it would still take him a couple of minutes to get there. Connaughton took his stetson off and waved it in welcome, glad to feel the hot July midday sun on his face after more than a year in close diplomatic quarters in faraway Europe.

He was finally home. How often during those endless weeks and months—and, yes, even years—he had thought of the mountains, had actually felt part of his soul to be far away under the big sky. Now he was back, immutably, for good.

The big black horse was lathered from the run, and Rafferty let him canter the last quarter mile. After a moment Connaughton's old friend pulled alongside and reined up, sitting head to hindquarters the way they had done countless times since they were young boys on their first ponies.

"Frankie said you'd gone for a ride," the big man said, huffing harder than his horse, "and I figured you'd come out this way. It's where you always came."

"How's it goin'," Connaughton said flatly by way of greeting.

Rafferty laughed. "Well, you know, more horseshit on the Potomac. Couldn't wait to get outa the place. Don't know how much longer I can stand it, actually."

Then Connaughton laughed. "Horseshit, yourself! They're gonna have to drag you outa that place. And you know it!"

Rafferty tapped his horse with a heel and Connaughton reined the chestnut around to parallel him as they headed for the willow grove on the river. They walked their horses for a hundred yards and Rafferty said, "I really came out here to give you some news. Just before I got on the plane last night to come home, the Senate agreed to vote on treaty ratification later this week."

Connaughton said nothing, but Rafferty saw his mouth tighten slightly as if he had tasted something bitter.

Rafferty continued, "The White House head count shows we now have the votes to ratify with two or three to spare. All the hearings and stalling and delay and debates this spring gave them time to break some arms and make some deals." Rafferty's laugh had a harsh edge. "In the end it wasn't Burgoon's arguments we had to overcome—it was just old-fashioned political pork barrel. Lawkard had to promise a dam, a new airport, and some fund-raising dinners this fall to get the last few votes. Ha!" It was like an expletive.

"That so," Connaughton replied. It was a comment instead of a question.

They rode down toward the riverbank where they had settled many a score wrestling in the mud and conducted an endless competition for trout throughout their boyhood. They dismounted and let the horses graze freely as they stretched their legs out and leaned into well-worn boles of the giant willows. The water rushed and rustled busily by endlessly ignoring human care.

Rafferty continued on with his report, ignoring his friend's silence, knowing he was interested in spite of his seeming unconcern. "Gonna be a hell of an election thi fall. Burgoon's crowd is goin' all out against the treaty and the President. If Burgoon gets his party's nomination next month at the convention, he'll be dangerous. He's a demagogue and a fool, but he can't be taken lightly. There's still this right-wing fanaticism around the country and he'll play to it right down to the wire. Against my better judgment I'm goin' to our convention in San Francisco in a couple of weeks and work for Arthur Milbank's nomination. I don't like the bastard, but he'll stand the best chance of beating Burgoon."

"Yup," Connaughton said, "'spect you're right."

Rafferty continued on. "Lawkard cleaned out the Joint Chiefs. Made Bigby the Chairman and told him to reform and reorganize the whole setup. Bigby, you know, was the only one who dragged his feet on Blue Thunder. Basically, a decent guy." Rafferty let out a nasty chuckle. "That Lawkard's really gotten to be quite a card in his closing days. When he announced Bigby at the press conference he said, 'I'm reminded of what Voltaire said about the British—they hang an admiral occasionally to encourage the others. Admiral, in your case I hope it's just the opposite.'"

Connaughton lowered his hat over his eyes and chuckled at that himself.

Rafferty said, "I got this interesting note in the mail the other day...marked 'Personal and Confidential.' Guess who it was from. It was from a woman named Arlette Gwynn. She's a hotshot physicist who helped design a system called Cyclops for Datasync. You remember Cyclops, don't you, Frank?"

Connaughton pushed his hat back off his eyes and looked at Rafferty slightly sideways.

"Well, it seems Miss Gwynn was our Deep Throat." Connaughton sat up slightly. "She went up to Vandenberg for the secret launching and was smart enough to figure out something funny was going on. She had seen your name in the paper as the Arms Control and Disarmament Agency representative on the delegation and tracked you down over the holidays to tip you off. She knew I was strongly for negotiations and called me also. She was the strange voice on the phone—she was the person you met in the cemetery. She just quit Datasync and has gone into teaching at some small university. Didn't tell me where."

Connaughton asked, "Did she tell you who hit you?"

"She didn't know any more than I did. I guess we'll never know whether it was on purpose or an accident. But I'll tell you this," Rafferty said as he pitched a small stone into the river, "I wouldn't put it past Burgoon's crowd to have done it. Those guys were prepared to go all the way. It was a close thing."

A slight breeze came up and the two men slowly got to their feet, stretched, and walked toward the grazing horses.

Rafferty said, "I've got a little bad news for you."

Connaughton commented laconically, "You're just a walkin' newspaper."

Rafferty went on, "Got a call this morning from William Henry Morrison, that old gasbag president up at the State University. He said he was deeply regretful, but they couldn't use you on the faculty this fall. Of course, I raised hell and swore a little and finally he came clean. Seems that right-wing defender of the faith and perennial flag-waver the Reverend Jimmy Mooney, chairman of the board of trustees, blackballed your application. He's on Burgoon's campaign committee. And he told that stalwart protector of academic freedom Morrison that you were a pinko and he would raise nine kinds of hell if they put you on the faculty."

Connaughton kicked a year-old cow chip absentmindedly. "Can't say as I'm particularly surprised. I don't think I would have liked it up there anyway. Teaching has got to be as competitive and bureaucratic as the government or Wall Street."

"What are you gonna do?" Rafferty asked with evident concern.

They mounted up, facing each other.

"I'm in no hurry," Connaughton said. "Frankie and I are goin' into town tonight for the Fourth of July fireworks. You and Bonnie and the kids wanta come along? That's about as far ahead as I can see right now." He looked toward the skyline, then added, "I'll get Frankie back in school this fall, then I'll think about the future. There's a good bit of work to be done around here for the next few months."

They reined around again and started back toward Connaughton's place.

Rafferty took the chestnut's reins and held it up. "Frank, I got somethin' else to tell you. What I really came out here to say."

Connaughton nodded, not knowing what to expect.

"It's about her," Rafferty said. He cleared his throat. "It seems she was one of ours all along."

"What!" Connaughton said. "What!"

"Yeah. Warrenton called me out to the Agency yesterday. He told me this story. Three years ago she was in Paris at a conference, interpreting for Zoshchenko. She made contact with one of Warrenton's people and said she wanted to help. They didn't know what to do with her or how to use her. They tried a couple of contacts in Moscow and that didn't work. They tried to establish contact all last year and couldn't get it done...at least on any continuing basis. Then this crisis occurred at the end of last year, it looked like we were headed for World War III, and she just took things into her own hands. She picked you."

Connaughton was numb. He was silent now because he couldn't sort out the thousand questions instantly in his mind.

"You both took a hell of a chance, Frank. It was really dumb—and it only worked because Lawkard got suspicious of Burgoon and his cabal of true believers and finally woke up to what was going on. Norton knew how to capitalize on that. And Warrenton thinks it only worked on their side because Kozlovsky called on a lifetime of goodwill with Kamenev and helped turn him around. Apparently there has been a hell of a power struggle in the Kremlin. And between them, Kozlovsky and Kamenev conspired to get Zoshchenko on their side in exchange for making him the next big shot over there.''

Connaughton's thoughts were racing from his ten-thousandth recollection of the desperately struggling Ekaterina in the Soviet car in Geneva to their first real conversation at Arkwright's house after New Year's. He barely heard what Rafferty was saying.

"What triggered things on both sides was your proposal to Arkwright that she represented a window into Kremlin politics and her statements to Makarov that you represented the same thing to them. Each side thought they were getting something for free that they couldn't pass up. And it came at a time when things were coming to a head on these military exercises. Sober minds began to realize what real confrontation might lead to."

Connaughton remained silent as Rafferty concluded. "What it amounts to is that we got lucky."

After a long moment Connaughton asked, "Why didn't she tell me? It would have made things a lot easier."

"I don't know all the answers to that. My guess is," Rafferty said, "that she didn't know whether to trust you with her life at first. And then as things got more involved and you both got into danger, she probably thought she was protecting you. If her side pulled you in, she didn't want you to know—for your own safety—that you were involved with someone who was really working for us. On the other hand, if you got brought back over here, she didn't know who in our government was on whose side. Hell, I haven't quite figured it out yet myself. You might have said something to the wrong person, and you'd both be in the soup."

They started to walk their horses slowly as Rafferty continued. "It took the President of the United States and the Secretary of State to keep you from the wolves. You came up clean with the Agency. Warrenton sent the word down, at the insistence of the White House, to write your escapade off as a romantic interlude that had nothing to do with the treaty. Of course, Warrenton figured out pretty quickly, from Norton's sudden interest in the woman, what was going on. He told Norton, and Norton told the President right from the start that she was one of ours and that she was using you to send her information up the line and into the back door of the White House. Nobody involved—including Zoshchenko—wants her story out. It's one thing to have a back channel that's diplomatic. It's another thing to have a back channel involving an agent. Your case was closed and you were hustled out of Washington not so much to protect you as to protect her."

Connaughton swallowed hard and blinked back the sudden wetness in his eyes as he looked beyond the horizon. "I don't see that we protected her all that much. Life can't be very pleasant for her these days." He stopped for a moment. "If she's alive at all." Then he turned on Rafferty, his eyes blazing. "Why didn't we just get her out of there—save her—get her out of Geneva?"

Rafferty said, "You know the answer to that, Frank. She couldn't leave so long as the treaty was in doubt. If she had skipped any earlier, the KGB types would have figured it out pretty quickly, the Politburo would have turned around overnight, and that would have been the end of the treaty. She took off with you because she wanted to save the treaty—even though she knew they would catch her eventually. And, old hoss, she was in love with you."

Connaughton said bitterly, "And I guess Norton and Lawkard and all the politicians have given up on her too . . . especially now that I'm safely out of town and not about to harass them about it anymore."

"Not quite, Frank." Rafferty turned his horse to look at Connaughton head on. "In fact, they've kept after it with Kamenev and Zoshchenko pretty steadily for the past three months. They've made her their number one human-rights

case and they've banged on the Soviet Ambassador about
it every day. Hell, Lawkard even warmed up the hot line on
her account the other day." He paused. "And guess what,
Frank?"

"What?" Connaughton said.

"They're going to let her go. They're going to let her and
her boys emigrate. Maybe even eventually her parents. She's
coming over here, Frank. She's coming to America. She'll
be here sometime next month."

Rafferty reached over and shook his friend's hand. "I
thought you'd want to know." The big man started to ride
off, saying over his shoulder, "We'll be by this evening to
take you to the fireworks. See you later." And then the black
horse took off at a full gallop, and as it drove full speed for
the horizon Connaughton heard a distant whoop echo off
the mountain walls.

Connaughton sat on the tall chestnut for a long time.
Toward the mountains a solitary eagle circled higher and
higher until it disappeared from sight.

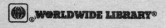